A BROKEN *hallelujah*

A NOVEL

JUDITH FORGOSTON

ATLANTA

This is a work of fiction. While some illustrations in this book are composites of real situations, all names, events, and dates have been altered and woven in to a fictional account.
The Road Not Taken by Robert Frost: public domain.
The Merchant of Venice by William Shakespeare: public domain.

Dans Nos Obscurités: copyright © *Ateliers et Presses de Taizé*, 71250 Taizé, France.

Scripture quotations are taken with permission.
John 14:12, Ps 147:4, Rom 15:20 are taken from the *Holy Bible*, New Living Translation, copyright © 1996, 2004, 2015 by Tyndale House Foundation. Used by permission of Tyndale House Publishers, Inc., Carol Stream, Illinois 60188. All rights reserved.
Isa 53:5, Ps 118:17 are taken from the King James Version and are public domain.

Paperback ISBN: 978-1-7372457-0-4
Hardcover ISBN: 978-1-7372457-1-1

Cover Design by Fresh Design
Printed in the USA

T

With whom goin
became

Your love taught me
join the C

Two roads diverged in a wood, and I—
I took the one less traveled by,
And that has made all the difference.

Robert Frost, *The Road Not Taken*

PART I

Summer 2015

Atlanta, Georgia
Zürich, Switzerland

Chapter One

Justin Friedman pulled out of his neighborhood early Saturday morning, rolled the window down, and turned the music up. His black Jeep wound its way through the backstreets of his Atlanta suburb as the wind played with his dark brown curls. The Wrangler, with its thirty-three-inch all-terrain tires and suspension lift, matched his adventurous spirit. He lit a cigarette, relaxed, and allowed a little smile to play on his face. It was going to be a good trip. Exciting, lucrative, and a little dangerous. Just the way he liked it.

He pulled into Cora's neighborhood, and her apartment door opened only moments after he had parked in front of the complex. His brunette girlfriend walked out with her signature ready-for-anything smile.

"Hey, handsome!" she said as she swung herself into Justin's Jeep.

"Ready for an adventure?" Justin kissed her and they settled in for the long drive. They let hip hop music compete with the noise of the wind in the open Jeep as they headed north. Justin wasn't sure why Cora was taking such a risk by accompanying him today. Maybe it was the extra cash she would make. Maybe she too just needed to push the boundaries. He didn't need to know her reasons, he just knew her company was advantageous for him in many ways. For one, having a girl with him made things look less suspicious. For another, he could trust her, which was of most importance for a trip like this.

They had been in what he called a relaxed relationship for a couple of years now. She immediately caught his attention when he first met her at a gym. Gorgeous, smart, and several years older than him, she had seemed unattainable for a college freshman like himself and was therefore exactly the challenge Justin was looking for.

It wasn't only his brown curls and winning hazel eyes that helped Justin, but more so his indestructible self-confidence. When Justin Friedman really wanted something, he was going to get it. With Cora, it had taken him several months and a few setbacks, but as his nineteenth birthday rolled around, they had attained the kind of relationship Justin liked: fun, romantic—but without a serious commitment.

They headed north to Charlotte, then into Virginia, and finally took I-81 all the way to New York. The fifteen-hour drive ahead of them would have been pleasant under other circumstances—a beautiful drive through an ever-changing scenery up the East Coast. As it was, Justin and Cora were quite distracted. The bag with $45,000 in the back of the Jeep kept their nerves on edge.

"Let's stop for gas and something to eat soon. I know you want to keep going, but I'll need a break every once in a while," Cora suggested around eleven a.m. when they had just passed Charlotte.

They stopped at a run-down gas station to use the restrooms. After filling up the tank and getting some sandwiches, they kept driving north. They spoke little and let the music distract them from any worrisome thoughts. The risk they took was calculated, Justin told himself, as he had told Cora, and the whole trip was worth it.

Cora seemed to think about the same thing. "What are we

doing again?" she asked playfully, an adventurous spark in her eyes.

"Nothing much, really." Justin played along. "Just hoppin' to Syracuse to buy fifteen pounds of high-grade Canadian weed for forty-five thousand dollars. No big deal."

She smiled at him. "You're pretty crazy, Justin Friedman, do you know that? Crazy and awesome."

The whole trip to Syracuse and then back to Atlanta would take them about thirty-six hours, and the $45,000 was going to turn into $75,000 within the next weeks if all went according to plan. The double life Justin had been leading for the past several years was working wonderfully. A charming personality since childhood, he had always known how to be liked by teachers and friends alike. His mom would often comment on how other parents loved to have Justin over and swooned over him being the most respectful and polite young man.

But his peaceful personality was only one side of him. The other was a young man searching for a thrill and looking for a way out of what he considered a dull life. With Cora behind the wheel now, Justin relaxed and let his memories go back to that September morning the previous year when he had landed his first big deal. A satisfied smile crept on his face, and Cora noticed it.

"You know, I really wish you'd let me peek into that beautiful head of yours, Justin. What were you just thinking about?"

Although he usually followed the rule to talk as little as possible about his drug deals, he also liked sharing his successes with others—especially if they were attractive and impressed by his stories, as he knew Cora would be. He decided this was a good time to give her some more details into what she had signed up for when she became his girl.

"I was just thinking about my first deal with Exit Ten." When Cora didn't react, he explained, "During high school I worked part-time at a shoe store. The manager and I often smoked pot together during our breaks, and his stash was amazing. After a while, I asked him to buy extra for me and started reselling it in quarter ounces to my friends. By the end of high school I had saved up enough to buy a quarter pound at a time, which my manager sold me for twelve hundred dollars." He looked over to see if she was following him. "By the middle of my freshman year in college, I'd saved enough money to buy a whole pound for four thousand dollars. It was the wholesale price that made this whole thing irresistible to me. Finally, I earned enough trust with my manager to give me a chance to meet his source personally."

Cora's face betrayed her fascination.

"I met the source at an apartment complex off Exit 10 of GA 400, which is why he's known just as Exit Ten. I traded a serious amount of cash for a pound of some of the highest-grade pot you can find in Atlanta. From then on, it was easy: my supply increased, the demand followed, and so did my cash flow. The pound turned into two, and then four, and my income grew steadily over time."

Justin leaned back and let the wind play in his hair. In actuality, the money was only one thing. Knowing he was his own master was an even greater motivator. His business had given him power and a constant rush of adrenaline, both of which he had gotten quite addicted to. Girls were attracted to him, and more friends wanted to hang out with him than ever before. And having hundreds or sometimes thousands of dollars in his pockets gave him an additional buzz.

"What happened after that?" Cora pulled him out of his thoughts.

"Well, Exit Ten must've been impressed with my turnaround, because he eventually connected me with his own supplier in upstate New York."

Which is why I'm here today, driving to the Canadian border to make the biggest drug deal of my life. He had found his own way of defeating frustration, disillusionment, and boredom.

He was still reveling in the memories of his accomplishments when he heard the police car with flashing sirens appear behind them.

Chapter Two

From her cozy apartment in Scherz, a village surrounded by rolling hills and a farming community only half an hour from Zürich, Switzerland, Sophie Schmid set out for her daily walk. She cherished her early morning strolls that led her around the village, past small ponds, and through patches of woods.

Most villagers were still asleep, but the woods already bustled with life at this hour. The bright voices of the birds competed with the chirps of the squirrels, who jumped between massive oaks and slender birches. On lucky days, she would spot an occasional doe and her young dashing through the undergrowth. Being out here in the early morning always gave her a sense of peace.

After returning from her walk, she had a light breakfast before first taking the bus to Brugg and then a busy local train to the College of Wettingen, where she had started her dream job only one semester ago.

Nestled into a bend of the Limmat River, Wettingen was considered one of the most beautiful college campuses in Switzerland. It was breathtaking and full of history and charm. A former monastery for Cistercian monks, the college grounds came complete with a chapel famous for its thirteenth-century stained-glass windows. There was a cloister where the monks of old used to stroll and meditate, as well as libraries, small cubicles now used as study rooms, hidden little attics, charming gardens, and a pond. Even a small vineyard and herb garden with heirloom plants, grown like in medieval times, were part of the grounds.

The aura of a long, rich history, mixed with modern renovations to house a state-of-the-art college, made this one of the most sought-after places to work and study. Having been a student at Wettingen herself, there was no other place for Sophie to return as a teacher than here. It had an inexplicable feeling of home, not only to her but to most who spent a part of their education there.

She arrived early and got ready for her first class, German literature. The stimulating conversations and discussions in her literature classes were her favorite part of each day. Her Swiss college students—independent and intellectually precise—voiced strong opinions that gave grounds for daily debates, sometimes heated, often followed by laughter, but never boring. Sophie was well liked, mostly because she taught out of a personal passion.

Ever since learning how to read, she had found no greater pleasure than that of a book in her hand and a cozy place to curl up to read it—delving into a world outside her own yet feeling completely part of it. The students could see this and responded with a rather un-college-like enthusiasm to her classes.

On the way home that evening, Sophie sat across from a young, beautiful couple holding hands and lightheartedly teasing each other. Something about the easy air of intimacy between them pierced her. Sophie urged down the wave of sadness rising insider her. The woman was not only beautiful but was dressed fashionably and carried herself with confidence as she leaned into her handsome man. *It makes sense that she's not alone.*

Unconsciously, Sophie glanced down at herself. Her unflattering clothes were an expression of a broader insecurity about her looks and herself in general that had followed her all her life and dampened the otherwise positive outlook Sophie had in life. When she had to change trains, she chose an empty compartment so she could call Laura. Her best friend always brightened her mood.

"Hey, good to hear you! How's your day been?" Laura's voice was cheerful as usual.

"Let's see. I discussed Goethe's *The Sorrows of Young Werther* with my students, gave a lecture on the great authors and poets of medieval Britain, and graded the poems of twenty-one literary hopefuls. I think I'm going straight to bed!"

In reality it was the kind of day Sophie absolutely loved—stimulating and intellectually satisfying.

"But . . .?" Laura apparently wasn't fooled.

"Well, it's one of those days when I just feel like something about me, or maybe even I myself, must be out of place. I mean, why do I see so many beautiful, self-confident women around me, all of them with dashing men at their side, and I feel like I'm from a different planet?"

"First of all, forget the I-see-all-these-beautiful-women part. You're very attractive, Sophie. The problem is just that you don't believe that about yourself. Do you know what I would do to have your long blonde hair trailing over those bronze shoulders . . . don't even get me started!" She was interrupted by Sophie's laughter, but then continued, "When it comes to feeling like you don't belong, rest assured, you're not the only one. In fact, if you've turned twenty-five and have never felt that way, something's seriously wrong with you!"

Sophie appreciated Laura's attempt at lightening her mood. Yet, the fact remained that she often felt overwhelmed in the real world of witty jokes and ever-changing fashion and cultural norms—and despite her life being filled with meaningful conversations, wonderful books, and philosophical ideas, something was missing.

"You know, sometimes I think about all the wonderful things in my life, and then I think, what good is it all? I can't share it with him. And I might just have given up hope that anybody else will ever fill the void."

"I'm sorry, Sophie. I know the days when you're reminded of him are hard. But giving up hope? Let me just say I know for a fact that you've not gone unnoticed by the men in your life. Want me to give you some examples?"

Sophie smiled sadly. "That's kind of you, and I guess you're right. But as my therapist points out, even though my ability to go deep in a conversation often strikes a chord in men who are looking for an actual connection rather than just entertainment, there's also my insecurity. And that fosters co-dependence, which is why my experience with men has mainly been long talks and romantic dreams, followed by the guy fleeing out of my life. 'Your tendency to cling to someone scares them more than your qualities attract them.'" Sophie imitated the therapist's voice and in turn made Laura laugh. They chatted lightheartedly about the hardships of single Swiss twentysomethings for the rest of the conversation.

When Sophie hung up a while later, she felt a lot better. Laura had a way to encourage her without trying to always fix the problem, and since Sophie knew there was no quick solution to her problems, she appreciated her friend's gentle approach.

She spent the rest of her train ride with Steinbeck's *Sweet Thursday*. Sophie had always found solace in her books. And yet, eventually, that *something* inside of her would rise again, and she would feel the effects of a loneliness that not even John Steinbeck's novels could ease.

Thirty minutes later, Brahms's Piano Concerto No.1 wafted peacefully through Sophie's tastefully furnished loft. Classical music was one of the few precious gifts her parents had given her as a child. As a little girl, she would sit in her favorite spot tucked under the Steinway grand piano and listen to her mother, a piano teacher, play melancholic concertos that snuck under the little girl's skin. Her dad, a stoic academic of few words, would put on Beethoven or Strauss and conduct with closed eyes while sitting on the couch. Sophie never saw her parents more rapt than while engaged with music, and it instilled her with a love for it that remained into adulthood.

As she sat on her couch with closed eyes like her dad, her thoughts wandered back, as they did so often, to the one man in her life who hadn't been concerned by her neediness. The one who had been free to be vulnerable in front of her and receive her own vulnerability as a gift. The only man she had ever truly loved.

Chapter Three

Panic gripped Justin when he heard the sound of the sirens wailing behind them.

"What the hell! I wasn't speeding!" Cora's face had drained of all color, and she clutched the steering wheel so tight her knuckles turned white.

Justin's heart raced, and his old companions—fear and adrenaline—kicked in. Just then, the police car sped past them and toward a red Mustang weaving in and out of traffic ahead of them. His relief was so great that Justin was shaking.

"That was close." Cora let out her breath slowly. For minutes afterwards, both of them stayed silent, imagining what it would look like if they'd been the ones getting stopped.

"Man, I hate cops!" Justin cussed under his breath. "Have I ever told you how much headache these guys have given me in my life?"

Cora looked over at him. "No, but it sounds like an entertaining story."

"Yeah right. It's entertaining only on the other side of it."

"Well, are you gonna tell me or not? I want to know how my boyfriend turned into the star of every party we ever go to!"

"Well, the police have nothing to do with that for sure." He smiled and winked at her. "But anyway. My first friendly encounter was when I was in high school. We'd been smoking pot behind the neighborhood pool house and had to dash through the undergrowth of the backwoods while a police officer chased us. Lucky for us, we knew the neighborhood better than the cop."

Cora laughed. She seemed to enjoy Justin's crazy stories.

"There have been other close encounters of course. Nowadays you can't even smoke pot in the woods outside the mall or during lunch at the edge of the school parking lot without being on constant alert. My high school friends have actually commented on my ability to sense the cops before anyone can see them. But it's like second nature for me to scan parking lots or malls. I even do it with all six lanes of the interstate while I'm driving."

"Actually, I have noticed that!" Cora exclaimed and looked over at him. "I've been wondering on several occasions how you could spot a police car sitting at the other end of a parking lot!"

It's because you're not living the kind of life I live.

"It's just intuition, I guess," he said with a shrug and looked back out the window. The flashing lights earlier had brought up a memory Justin couldn't seem to shake. Although his careful and smart decisions had kept him safe most of his life, it hadn't helped him that spring night three years ago. Justin's mind wandered back, and it felt as if it had happened yesterday.

"Hurry up! Open the window and throw it out!" Stan had shouted as the police closed in on them.

Justin hurriedly opened the passenger window while his teenage friend steered the car within a few feet of some roadside bushes. A second later, the sack disappeared in the undergrowth. Knowing he couldn't outrun the police car, Stan slowed and let the car roll a few yards farther before stopping.

"Look, he won't find it, okay?" Stan said. "And if he does, we'll say it was never in our possession. Just play it cool!"

The fear behind Stan's reassuring words matched Justin's own. Cold sweat dripped down his spine as he sat up straight in an effort to look inconspicuous. The flashing blue lights behind them only increased his panic.

"I can't believe it. Why did you bring that stuff into the park? We're screwed now!" Justin's words were a mixture of anger and despair.

Stan was about to respond when the officer appeared at their window.

"Step out of the vehicle, one at a time. You first." He pointed to Stan. His voice was cold. "I saw suspicious activity at the park before you got into your car. Now lean against the car and do not move."

The officer searched them and the car thoroughly. Justin allowed himself a small glimmer of hope. He had just started breathing a little bit lighter when the cop took his flashlight and shone it back up the sidewalk. Within a couple of minutes, he returned, holding the sack containing a dozen small, neatly packaged plastic bags of marijuana, ready to sell.

"Whose is this?" The officer's voice had a threatening edge as he sat the sack on the hood of his car.

Neither of them said a word. A minute later both of them were handcuffed.

"As of right now, you're both under arrest. You better tell me which one of you was in possession of this stuff, or both of you are going to jail." The man looked Justin in the eye. "And I'm not talking about juvey. Since you're both seventeen, you will be charged as adults, and that means Atlanta City Detention Center."

Justin held the man's gaze. His stomach turned.

"Alright. Get in the backseat while we wait for the police van."

Half an hour later, Justin and Stan were on their way downtown to the jail on Garnett Street. The van made several stops to pick up other troublemakers who'd been arrested in the last hour. The long ride gave Justin plenty of time to worry.

At midnight, the hungry and frightened teenagers sat in a crowded holding cell they shared with at least fifty scary-looking men. Since the marijuana found with them weighed more than an ounce and was bagged for sale, they were charged with a felony for possession with intent to distribute. The felony charge required they remain in custody until they could appear before a judge. There was nothing their parents could do to get them out. They were going to spend the night.

Justin's back hurt from sitting on the metal bench for hours. The scent of body odor and sweat hung in the air, and the clanking bars and harsh voices only reinforced his panic. Justin's mind, exhausted from the sensory overload, was playing tricks on him. Was that huge man across the way staring at him? The guards patrolling outside the holding cell seemed distracted with other things.

Unexpectedly, the man walked over and sat down next to Justin. His movements were almost snakelike, despite his size. Something in his eyes made Justin's insides turn. The man leaned his massive frame toward the teenager and revealed a razor blade he had hidden inside a pocket in his sleeve. Apparently, Justin's terror gave him a buzz.

Justin panicked. His eyes darted wildly between the man and the hallway. Where are the guards? His heart sank when he saw that they were busy with a drunk man trying to start a fight with another prisoner.

Justin almost squealed with fear and pain as the man's left hand dug into his shoulder. His right hand revealed the blade as it moved toward the teenager. His breath smelled of liquor. He got closer, his eyes bulging, and whispered, "I could kill you with this."

"Justin? Are you ok? You look pale."

Cora's voice brought Justin back to reality. He shook his head as if to rid himself of the memory that had haunted him many a night for the past three years.

Had one of the guards not eventually noticed the big man leaning over Justin and told him to leave the boy alone, Justin could only imagine what might have happened. But the memory of the sounds and smells of that cell, even the feeling of utter vulnerability, was nothing compared to remembering the absolute terror on his parents' faces when they had finally been allowed to bail him out. He also still remembered the warnings of the judge at court.

"The only reason I'm letting you get away with ninety hours of community service and your record expunged," the judge had said with a serious voice, "is because your friend has admitted to ownership of the bag of pot." Justin later learned that Stan had made a deal with the court, and so Justin escaped without serious consequences.

His parents, struggling to cope with the secrets revealed about their son, had followed up with some serious talks in the coming weeks. Justin assured them that this experience had forever taken away his desire to be involved with this type of lifestyle. And although deeply troubled by the incident and more suspicious than before, his parents had chosen to believe him and never investigated his social life. He kept being the successful student and likable young man, and so his double life stayed intact.

"Yeah, I'm fine," he finally managed to reply to Cora. He'd always been able to fool her when it came to what was really going on inside of him. Maybe it was his convincing personality. Maybe she didn't even want to know the whole truth.

The arrest had shaken him up alright, but not in the way his parents thought. The actual resolve the incident produced in Justin was to push the boundaries further. He was not going to let anyone, drug dealer or police, put him into a situation of such vulnerability again. He looked at the arrest as a round lost but a lesson learned in how to better play the game.

And this time, he wasn't some careless teenager anymore. He was twenty, and he knew exactly what he wanted and how to get it.

Four hours after their last stop in Charlotte, they reached Richmond, VA, and finally allowed themselves a proper break. Cora was exhausted, and Justin welcomed a break as well. Nevertheless, only half an hour later, the cautious part of him urged them to keep going. The meeting with the contact was set up for midnight at a hotel in Syracuse, and they were still at least seven hours away from their destination. Cursing under her breath, Cora got back in the passenger seat while Justin drove them further north.

They arrived at the Holiday Inn on the north end of Syracuse shortly after eleven p.m. Justin had gotten increasingly nervous and excited the last hours of the drive, and after checking into their room, he texted the supplier, Bill, to let him know they were here.

The knock on the door came about twenty minutes later, and a familiar tension gripped Justin's body. He walked to the door, waited for a second to calm his nerves, and asked, "Who is it?"

Chapter Four

Sophie had finished listening to the piano concerto and curled up on her oversized couch with a glass of wine. Like they did so often when her mood turned melancholic, her thoughts wandered back to Nathan.

They had met in a book club for French literature, and she still remembered their first conversation like it was yesterday. Both had been part of the book club for a while but had never really talked to each other. Then, on that particularly warm late-summer day with smells of fall in the air, Nathan and she had somehow ended up at the same spot outside the library after book club was over. They each noticed the other's preoccupation with the discussion still lingering in their minds. It was Nathan who made the first move.

"Well, that was a memorable morning! I don't agree at all with Julie, which you might have guessed by my comments. But I feel like you didn't either, am I right?" He looked at her with a twinkle in his eyes.

"Oh, I didn't know I was being so blunt," Sophie replied, surprised that he had noticed the subtle remarks she'd made earlier. "It's just that it bothers me when people try to reduce this fabulous work to a simple love story." When Nathan raised his eyebrows slightly, the blood rushed to Sophie's cheeks, and she defended herself: "There's nothing wrong with love stories, but *Les Misérables* is so much more than that. It's like calling *Le Petit Prince* just a cute children's book."

This time Nathan laughed out loud. His voice was strong but somehow gentle at the same time, and Sophie suddenly wondered why she hadn't noticed his green eyes or his confident posture before.

Or his absolutely stunning smile.

"Well, I certainly agree. I have been fascinated with the history of Paris for quite a while and have yet to find a more detailed and personal description of that city. But something tells me that's not what makes this book special to you either," he said.

The blush came again, and there was nothing she could do about it. She had not revealed many of her thoughts in the group and had mostly listened instead. Yet this guy she had known only from a book discussion must have picked up on the occasional comment she had made and not only understood what she was saying but what she had omitted as well.

"I tell you what," he said while Sophie was still thinking of a response to his last words, "how about some coffee and croissants at Lauber's so I have a chance to continue my interrogation?"

"I definitely need some coffee before I reveal my deepest thoughts about one of my all-time favorite books," she said with a smile. Although she was something of an introvert, talking to this stranger with beautiful green eyes seemed the easiest thing in the world.

She put the glass back into the sink. Allowing herself to get engulfed in those memories would only hinder her healing process, she knew, but sometimes she didn't care. She was willing to pay the price just to be with Nathan, if in no other way than in her memories. Deep down she convinced herself there was no healing from this pain. It was part of her. And every time February came around with its bitter frosts and icy snow flurries, she was right back there, convinced there would never be a winter where she would not be reminded of Nathan.

Their breakfast had turned out to be the first of many to come. Soon, book club to Sophie was more about the time after than the actual meeting. All throughout the fall, they would spend Saturdays together, often going for bike rides after the club let out, visiting parks, or going to the movies. Two months after their first conversation, Sophie walked into Lauber's to meet him for breakfast, only to find a bouquet of roses at their usual table. She sat down to wait for him. *First roses ever,* she mused, but excitement won out.

"They are no match for your beauty, but they were the prettiest I could find," Nathan whispered in her ear as he walked up behind her. Sophie got up and melted into his outstretched arms. And she knew something was happening to her that she'd been dreaming of for a long, long time. She was truly in love.

A mutual love for literature contributed to the powerful bond between them, as well as a strong physical attraction. But it went further than that. Sophie's heart was at home with Nathan. He made her smile, he seemed to read her thoughts, and talking to him felt like writing in her diary, which had been her only confidant thus far. Plus, he didn't react like other men who backed away when things got too intense.

Sophie's trust in him grew steadily. She told Nathan everything, and she went about it like peeling an onion—the outer, easier layers first, and when she didn't get hurt, the deeper layers as well. She told him about her childhood with a father unable to show or receive emotions, as well as the pain from her insecurity that resulted in a social awkwardness and earned her many lonely weekends as a teenager. Nathan not only understood her but responded with a gentleness and fierce protectiveness that touched her. Their willingness to be vulnerable in front of each other produced trust and resulted in a passionate and beautiful love neither of them had known before.

They were inseparable. Although Sophie was the needier of the two of them, Nathan never pulled away from her. He understood her insecurity and loved what he saw underneath it. He lived in a village only ten minutes from hers and would drive his Yamaha up to her apartment almost every day after work. They would sometimes talk all night long, exploring each other's souls and getting to know the fabric of their everyday lives. Nathan couldn't seem to get enough. Like a connoisseur savoring a precious wine, he wanted to experience and understand her more.

They faced their own relationship challenges. For one, their lives were very different. A few years her senior, Nathan worked as a software programmer in a small company in Zürich while Sophie was finishing her teaching degree. It sometimes took them a while to get back into a place of feeling unified after being occupied all day long with such different topics. But they made it a point to experience whatever they did outside of work together, creating more and more bonds between them.

That fall and winter they spent as much time together as they could, often curled up with a book on the couch in Sophie's apartment. They experienced the intimacy of being together in silence. It was in these nights when they were so close together, yet also part of something much bigger than themselves, that Sophie first experienced actual peace. And she knew she never wanted to live without it again.

As she turned off the lights to go to bed, her eyes fell on a pile of ungraded papers strewn across her desk. It was getting increasingly harder to keep up with her work as a teacher while trying to keep that dark monster inside of her at bay. The monster grew day by day, and there was no telling how much longer Sophie could control it enough to get out of bed in the morning.

Chapter Five

"Let me help you, Ronnie, please! Let me talk to the guards!" James McLeod urged his brother for the umpteenth time. Whenever he visited Long State Prison to see his younger brother, his hands became clammy. And when he heard the way the other inmates treated him, chills ran down his spine. Ronnie didn't belong here.

"No, James. You have no idea what happens to me in here if the others find out you ratted on them to the guards. I'm better off without your help." Ronnie's face darkened, and life seemed to drain from his eyes. "Besides, it doesn't matter anyway. My life basically ended six years ago. But thanks for coming, bro." With that, he signaled the guard he was ready to be brought back to his cell.

James buried his head in his arms in the visitation room, and his thoughts wandered back to that fateful October morning six years ago. Two foolish teenage brothers on a chase for some thrill. Lafayette's, a French fine dining restaurant, had a valet service and some well-to-do customers, and the boys had come up with a brilliant plan. They knew where the keys were stored, how to distract the valet boy, and how to exit the parking lot on the far end of the restaurant so the missing car wouldn't even be noticed. They took some rich person's sportscar for a little joyride and planned on returning it within the hour, well before anyone got suspicious.

Driving a new Corvette around town gave them quite a buzz. That was, until their inexperience driving such a powerful car caused them to swerve out of control and hit a telephone pole. The driver's side was smashed, and Ronnie's leg was broken.

"Run, man!" Ronnie shouted frantically when the first shock had passed. "There's no need for both of us to get in trouble. They'll send the ambulance soon. Get the hell out of here!"

Ronnie wouldn't take no for an answer, and so by the time help arrived, James had disappeared. Ronnie was charged with grand theft auto and was sentenced to one year in prison by a harsh judge who believed that the harder the sentence, the more fear would be instilled in young people and the less trouble they would get into.

James tried everything he could to fight the sentence. Since the judge wouldn't let James talk to his brother, he instead sought out the police officers who had found Ronnie that night. He pleaded that Ronnie was still a kid, and that he knew his brother would never do such a thing again. He begged for a second chance for Ronnie.

The officer looked at him with hard eyes. "See, that's where you are wrong. All this talk of reformation is a bunch of crap. Do you want to know what I really think?" He lowered his voice, and his words were like piercing darts finding their way to James's heart. "I think that there are two kinds of people: good ones and bad ones. And your brother has just shown which side he belongs to. That's why I arrested him instead of giving him a so-called second chance. Because deep down"—his cold eyes locked with James's—"deep down, bad people never change."

When realizing he couldn't influence the sentence, James tried to ease Ronnie's life in prison. He kept in touch constantly, visiting him and bringing whatever practical gifts he could think of that would help him get through this year. But Ronnie did not adjust to life behind bars. Before long, the influence of the people around him got him involved in drugs and acts of violence that prolonged his sentence to what was now his sixth year.

Leaving the visitation room and stepping back outside the prison located in southeast Georgia, James brushed his arm across his face wearily. Even the beautiful spring weather could not chase away his chills. His brother's tales of violence, fear, and hatred were an ever-painful reminder of the mercilessness of the American justice system. Ronnie had insisted during the trial that he had been in the car alone, never giving up his brother. It drove James mad that he could do nothing in turn to help.

During the drive back to Atlanta, the words of that police officer replayed in James's head. *That's why I didn't give him a second chance. Because bad people never change.* A thought that had brewed in James for a long time now suddenly rose to the surface with clarity. Yes, there was nothing he could do to help his brother.

But there was something he could do for people like him.

It was a year ago that James had received his police badge and started working as a field officer.

Chapter Six

"Hey man, it's Bill."

The voice outside the hotel room sounded surprisingly nonchalant. Justin relaxed. Maybe it would all work out effortlessly. He was surprised when he opened the door and saw an average-looking thirty-year-old man wearing blue jeans and a polo shirt and carrying a large hockey bag.

"What's up?" Justin said. He ushered Bill inside, introduced him to Cora, and locked the door behind them.

"Had a nice drive? How's Exit Ten?"

"He's good. The drive was fine, no hiccups. But I admit we were a bit nervous."

"Oh yeah, I bet you were. And it will be worse on the way back! But you'll get used to it," he added lightly. "Well then, let's get to it. As agreed, I've got fifteen pounds for you, straight from the Native American reservation on the other side of the border."

The tall man spoke with ease, which intrigued Justin. He wondered how much or how little he should talk, as he certainly didn't want to risk messing up this connection. But his curiosity won over his caution. "How did you get the stuff from the reservation?" The man looked so ordinary. Justin could not imagine him smuggling pot out of an Indian reservation and across an international border.

"Hells Angels." A smirk crossed Bill's face. "Don't look shocked! They're actually very friendly people if you don't mess with them. And they're some of the few people Natives will work with."

Bill opened his hockey bag and displayed, under a sports towel, fifteen vacuum-sealed, odor-proof plastic bags filled with the pale green flowers of *cannabis sativa*. It was more pot in one place than Justin had ever seen in his life. Adrenaline surged through him and he grinned. This was what he was made for! He pulled out a gallon-sized Ziploc bag from his backpack, which contained a mixture of twenty, fifty, and one-hundred dollar bills, all neatly banded together in bundles of $1,000. Bill sat down on the bed, took out the money, and started to meticulously count it while Justin continued to marvel at the enormous hockey bag full of pot. Neither was overly worried about the other one cheating, because they were both interested in repeating this deal—possibly as frequently as once a month, depending on the quantity and speed Justin could move the pot in Atlanta.

Canadian pot was very well liked because of its potency and flavor. Bill was asking $3000 per pound, but Justin, using other small-time sellers, could easily get $5000. After giving Cora her $2000, it would leave Justin with around $28,000 profit. If he kept his partying at a reasonable amount, he'd have saved up enough by the next trip to buy at least twenty pounds. Not bad at all, Justin thought, especially if he considered his working hours. Those consisted mainly of late evenings inviting customers, sometimes several back-to-back, to his apartment where the deals would take place. After finishing, they would relax and smoke together. It was a rather pleasant way to work, if you could even call it that.

Justin forced his thoughts back to the deal. He quickly counted the bags and proceeded to weigh them with a small scale he had brought with him. Bill was still counting the money, but they both knew that everything would be right. Afterwards, they repacked everything neatly and finally relaxed for a cigarette on the balcony. Justin was exhausted after the long drive, but he forced himself to start a conversation with Bill. If he wanted to continue working with him in the future, it was wise to have Bill as a friend.

"So what else have you got going on besides this?"

"Well, I have a wife and a three-year-old boy. Don't look at me like that," he said as he saw Justin's face. "It's a good life. I can offer my wife most things she wants, and I'm not a slave to the man, working nine-to-five so that some guys at the top can get rich. We live in the suburbs, my wife takes night school classes finishing her degree, and I make good money doing this. It's all about calculated risk, man. Here's a piece of advice I can give you, though. Stick with pot, because once you start selling hard stuff, you will enter the other side. People don't kill for pot, even in larger quantities than this, but . . ."

Bill's voice wandered off. He now had the undivided attention of both Justin and Cora. When he continued, his voice was hoarse.

"A good friend of mine decided last year to start selling something 'more lucrative,' to use his own words. He was engaged, and his fiancé was planning their wedding when he was killed. It was only his third coke deal, but it's an entirely different crowd when you mess around with blow, and he didn't know what he was doing. So, I'm telling you, when it comes to selling, don't get greedy. You seem like a sharp guy; I'm sure you'll be fine."

Justin nodded. What Bill said resonated with him. Since he was a little boy, he'd always felt a voice inside of him that warned him of any kind of real danger. Listening to this voice had kept him away from harm before and was going to keep him from hard drugs as well—of this he was sure.

It was now way past midnight, and Justin's body was shutting down. After Bill left, Justin double-locked the hotel room door and fell onto their bed. His last thoughts before sinking into a deep, dreamless sleep were that he had done it once again. He had defeated mediocrity and was about to head home with not only enough pot to make a lot of money, but also a way to escape the life most of his peers were doomed to live. Justin had found a way to be completely independent. And independence was something he had strived for all his teenage years—with an intensity that bordered on obsession.

Chapter Seven

"Believe me, it's the adventure of a lifetime. You will want to return to the Wadden Sea for the rest of your life."

Sophie hung on the words of her old school friend Seraina as she listened to the young woman's stories about her recent sailing trip. They sat next to each other at Sophie's elementary school reunion, and Sophie had expected little of the evening other than everybody inwardly comparing themselves with each other and hoping they'd come out on top. It had been almost a year since that conversation with Laura on the train, but Sophie's insecurities were often still getting the better of her.

But not so on that night. She found herself effortlessly connecting with Seraina, who'd become a passionate traveler. This was right up Sophie's alley and, ignoring everybody else at the reunion, she wanted to know everything there was to know about her friend's adventures.

"The Wadden Sea is a unique marine ecosystem north of the Netherlands. It's an intertidal zone, which means that depending on the tide, it is either covered by water, or it is dry land," Seraina explained.

"And that's where you went sailing?" Sophie raised an eyebrow.

"Yes. It enables a yacht to dock on dry land during low tide. You can then exit the yacht and walk through the temporarily dry seabed and discover all kinds of little creatures." Seraina's eyes had a distant look. "After dusk, we sometimes saw fluorescent algae floating in the water, as if someone had set the ocean on a cold, otherworldly fire."

Please don't stop talking. Seraina's words reached a place inside of Sophie that stirred a longing she had forgotten was there.

"But the best part . . . the *very* best part are the sunsets over the water when you set anchor to wait for the tide to move out. I have never seen the sun set like it does over the Wadden Sea." Seraina looked at Sophie. "But I'm doing a bad job describing it. I'd much rather show you in person!"

Sophie needed no time to decide: her lifelong love for the sea and anything related to it had been rekindled. They started making plans for a summer trip to the Netherlands before the reunion had even ended.

The next day, Sophie delved into her new project. She prepared for her adventure by reading books about sailing and about the Netherlands, about marine life and everything else she could get her hands on. Enthusiasm filled her days and was joined by joyful anticipation. Her parents and friends noticed the change, as her demeanor now was very much unlike the Sophie she had become in the past years.

After Nathan's death almost three years ago, Sophie had spiraled into a depression. She had been pursuing her teaching degree and was holding up on the outside, but a part of her on the inside kept getting darker. Every year winter would come around, the icy rains would pour down, and she would fall apart.

For it was on one of those February mornings that he'd

gotten stuck in a downpour, and what had started as a harmless ride had turned out to be a treacherous situation for motorcyclists. They supposed hydroplaning had caused him to lose control of the heavy Yamaha.

She'd gotten the call from Nathan's mother from the hospital in Zürich. He'd died while still in the ambulance. And Sophie thought that surely the whole world must stand still and mourn with her as she realized she had lost the only man she had ever loved. Her friends had tried to help her climb out of the depression and sadness that had become her closest companions, but it had gotten hard to motivate herself to get out of bed.

Until the reunion.

During her preparations for her trip, Sophie's spirits came back to life. The lines of sorrow drawn on her face by Nathan's death began to recede ever so slightly, and she slowly emerged from the darkness.

The last day before summer break, only three days before her trip started, she called Seraina and nearly shouted into the phone, "I'm ready! I graded every paper and did all the prep for the first week of next semester. We're heading to sea!"

Seraina celebrated with her over the phone. The two had become close during the past months, sharing anticipation, excitement, and practical preparations. They were looking forward to sunsets, bike rides through small windswept Dutch islands, and to days and days at sea with nothing but the horizon to distract them.

Little did Sophie know what else was awaiting her in this charming gem of a country.

They took the night train from Zürich to Amsterdam and a bus from there to Harlingen, a small port on the northwestern coast of the Netherlands. They would set sail there the next morning. Their boat was a hundred-year-old tjalk, a wooden sailing vessel with side panels characteristic for use in the stretch of sea between the Dutch coast and a line of five small islands about a hundred miles off the coast. Those islands shielded this particular part of the Wadden Sea from the rough weather of the Atlantic Ocean. The ship was large enough to hold twenty people and had a large wooden mast to hold up the sails.

Seraina had brought together a colorful group of people to join her on this trip. They were mostly her friends and coworkers, but also some people from the church she attended. Sophie didn't know anyone, but she didn't mind. She hadn't come for company but for the experience of wind and sea and open sky.

On the night before the start of their adventure, everybody met at a charming port café for dinner and a group introduction. Sophie was confident that she'd get along with this vibrant mix of people that shared a love for the ocean. She enjoyed several conversations and listened to Seraina introduce Peer, the skipper. It was on his ship, the *Noordfries*, that they would spend the next two weeks. Peer was a weathered and likable man, and the knowledge he had of the region and of sailing fascinated Sophie as much as the stories he told them that night.

When Peer made the first of his many jokes to come, Sophie noticed an older man in her group awarding the joke with a deep belly laugh. His laughter was warm, and his eyes sparkled as he addressed the skipper.

"Well, Peer, it's good to see we didn't completely scare you away from your job the last time we sailed with you. Thinking of how some of us folded those sails and tied those knots, I'm really impressed you're willing to take us on for another round!"

Peer broke into a wide grin. "I meet a lot of folks in this job, but I gotta say, this group is one of my favorites. At least, most of you guys are." He winked at the older man. "Thomas here, I don't know about him. He gave me a hard time last year, and if any one of you has figured him out, let me know about it!" He gave the old man a friendly hug.

"I'm quite sure I haven't figured myself out yet, Peer! But seriously, we are so excited to have you as our skipper again. This group has some new people as well, and I for one can't wait to meet everybody. But for now, who's excited to set sail tomorrow?"

Sophie raised her glass with the group to toast to their upcoming adventure.

They spent the night at a B&B next to the port from which they would sail the next day. When morning came, Sophie woke up well before her alarm clock and was dressed and ready to go in less than ten minutes. They ate a small breakfast and then headed to the port to examine the ship. Smaller than Sophie had imagined, the ship had a cozy, romantic feeling. Cabins and jobs were assigned for the day, and soon after, Peer steered the *Noordfries* into open waters.

Exhilaration filled Sophie when the sails were set for the first time. The wind, the salt in the air, the seagulls inspecting their ship from above, and the endless stretch of water ahead of them made her feel free and alive beyond words. With Peer's permission, she and Seraina climbed over the bow, and holding on to the bowsprit, they climbed into the strong safety net attached to the spar in front of the boat. It was the most adventurous place to be on the yacht—literally ahead of the ship in a net held only by the wooden beam extending like a spear into the air. Laying there, they were only feet from the water, very likely to get soaking wet and seeing only endless ocean stretching out in front of them. Sophie fell in love with that spot instantly and decided to get down there whenever she could.

The extremely shallow Wadden Sea, sometimes no deeper than five meters, made Peer's job dangerous and one that only experienced skippers took on. The crew's job was much easier, consisting mainly of setting and bringing in the sails, kitchen and cleaning duty, or helping with various small jobs when docking in a harbor. Sophie spent a lot of time sunbathing on deck with a good book or losing herself in thought in her favorite spot in front of the ship. The nights spent in harbor, she fell asleep in her cabin to the ship's soft rocking motion.

In the mornings, Sophie got up early and sat on deck to watch the sunrise, observe the harbor stir to life, and see people emerging from their cabins below the ships. Peacefulness permeated not only her but everybody on board. Breakfasts were happy occasions, with thick slices of white toast buttered and then sprinkled with the famous hagelslaag. Sophie had never before thought of putting chocolate sprinkles on her breakfast toast at home. But as it often was with foods enjoyed in special places, she would for years to come associate chocolate sprinkles with the *Noordfries*.

The third day was their first island exploration day. They docked on the small island of Vlieland and rented Dutch bikes. Because of the flat landscape, these bikes came without gears and still allowed the group to pedal effortlessly on small paths through beautiful, windswept dunes, little patches of pines, and past small farmhouses. There was something simple, rough, and beautiful that made Sophie fall deeply in love with this region. They ate sandwiches on the beach and drank coffee in a charming coffee house. The day was over way too fast, and Sophie couldn't wait to explore the other four islands in the days to come.

That night, the whole group went out to dinner on the island. Sophie found herself seated across from Thomas. She was looking forward to getting to know him better, but she also felt awkward starting a conversation and instead concentrated on a story the woman on her left told about her recent sailing adventures. Although the topic was of great interest to Sophie, she couldn't help but simultaneously follow the conversation Thomas was having with the man sitting next to him. Something about Thomas's demeanor, the way he talked and how he looked at the person he talked to, drew Sophie toward him.

"I'm so sorry to hear what you're going through, Tim.

Believe me, I know how it feels and how much it hurts. I have experienced a similar loss many years ago." He leaned closer to Tim, and now Sophie definitely felt guilty for eavesdropping. The last thing she heard before turning her head was Thomas asking Tim in a gentle voice, "Would you allow me to be your friend through this?"

For the rest of the meal, she stayed quiet and pretended to be busy eating, but her attention kept returning to Thomas. His compassionate and caring words reminded her soul of something missing in her life that, until now, she'd been able to keep below the rim of consciousness. But it wasn't just the kind words. His very presence produced in her a desperate longing. She was aware that being drawn like that to someone she didn't know at all was ridiculous. It wasn't a romantic attraction, either, as she guessed he was in his early sixties. It was different—as if his gentle voice and compassionate eyes let her longings out of their cave, and she had no idea where that would lead.

When dessert was served, she excused herself and told Seraina she would go for a walk along the small pier outside the restaurant. While the salty sea breeze touched her face, Sophie tried to calm down. Instead, tears welled up. She probably had daddy issues, as her psychology professor liked to call it. But still. *What adult bursts into tears at the sight of a friendly old man across the table?*

Just then she felt a gentle touch on her shoulder. She spun around and looked into the eyes of the very man who had caused all the conflicting feelings inside her.

Chapter Eight

Justin was sitting in his favorite spot in the main cafeteria of Georgia Tech with some friends when he got the call.

He had been sipping on his second cup of coffee, feeling very pleased with himself. At the age of twenty-one, when most young men his age were either struggling to find a job or piling up huge student debt in college, he had transferred to one of Georgia's best universities to finish his degree—but not because of career dreams. It was more to satisfy Cora, who had gotten increasingly worried about his lifestyle and insisted he needed to finish his business degree. Attending Tech got her off his back while providing him with quite an enjoyable life. There were plenty of potheads here whom he liked hanging out with, and since he didn't have to worry about tuition and classes remained fairly easy for him, his life was a pleasant blur of being drunk or stoned all evening, only to wake up the next morning to coffee and Adderall to get him through his classes for another day.

He had been right about Bill, the contact in Syracuse. The connection had turned into a steady business, and over the past year, Justin had taken the trip to New York with Cora every other month without any problems. He was smart enough not to live too extravagantly. Staying under the radar of police and any other officials, not to mention his parents, was a skill he learned long ago. People always came to his apartment at different times. Nobody came to a deal drunk, and he never allowed anyone to talk about it over the phone or by text. All these precautions had ensured that since his arrest four years ago, he hadn't had a police run-in. And wouldn't in the future either, he convinced himself.

His phone rang, and he answered with a bored "Yup?" A moment later, all the blood drained from his face. "They're WHERE?" Justin let the phone drop to the ground. His head spun, and the ground seemed to shift underneath him, causing his world to slowly fall apart. His first thought was what a cruel irony it was. It was his best friend who was ending Justin's dreams, his future, and even his life—or what he thought made life worth living.

One of his friends noticed the change in Justin's expression and knew something serious had happened. "What's going on, man?"

Justin's response came slowly. He felt like he was in a dream, incredulous and like a child overwhelmed with a situation completely out of his control. "That was the manager at my apartment complex . . . there was a break-in. A neighbor saw it and called the police." Justin's fists clenched, and his breathing became erratic. His mind was spinning when he shouted out the next words. "They are at the apartment. Do you understand? The police are at my apartment!" The words came out in sheer desperation. *By now, they'll have discovered everything. The cash, the drugs, the gun.* Justin began to add up the number of years those felonies together would put him in prison for.

But he didn't need an exact number to know that his life was over.

When Justin pulled up to his apartment, it was after what seemed like the longest half an hour of his life. After scrambling off campus and getting in his car, he found himself actually slowing down the closer he got to Roswell. After all, these were going to be his last minutes as a free man. He might as well stretch it for a little longer than the simple drive from midtown Atlanta to the northern suburb where he lived. The thought of fleeing the state had occurred to him, but he had dismissed it right away. He imagined being on the run from the law, living in fear and hiding for the rest of his life. He knew he didn't have that in him. He was still calculating risks, and it seemed easier to face prison—although he knew that *easy* was not the word to describe what his next years would look like.

As he drove toward his apartment, he experienced, for the first time, something he had heard about before: his life flashing before his eyes. Wild arrays of images shot in and out of his brain, with no way to control or process—memories of his older sister chasing him around the house, playing catch with his dad, and fishing with his grandpa at the small lake where he grew up.

All of it came rushing at him with a force he didn't expect. Tears burned in his eyes, something that hadn't happened since he'd been an adult. There was no way he could fight these emotions as he realized, for the first time ever, how valuable his life was. He knew that the people in his life mattered and that freedom was a priceless gift he had carelessly taken for granted. The vulnerability was overwhelming.

Sure, it had been a wild ride during the past couple of years. He had made more money than he ever thought he could, partied more, and won the respect of his peers. But now, in one moment's turn of events, he felt utterly alone and started crying silently as the realization settled in that he had risked everything and had lost it all.

The first thing Justin noticed when he got out of his car was several neighbors out on the street, shamelessly enjoying the excitement of what promised to be the talk of the day. The sensation of shame, mixed with the intense fear that had by now settled like a massive knot in his stomach, gave Justin the feeling of a small child; he wanted to crawl under a chair to hide from the world. Having tried to pull himself together during the end of the drive, he now feared losing it again at the sight of this public humiliation. He silently vowed to never stop and watch any kind of police-involved incident again.

As soon as he got out of the car, his apartment door opened, and a tall young man walked out. His movements were calm, his face serious, and he walked toward Justin with a certain urgency.

"My name is Sergeant McLeod. We got a call from your neighbor at around nine thirty a.m. He was witnessing a break-in at your apartment. I was at the gas station around the corner and therefore arrived at the scene just when the suspect was walking out the front door with a cash box under his arm, which, as it turned out, had around thirty thousand dollars in it."

The officer watched Justin intently as he continued. "The suspect, Stan Meyer, who you apparently know well, was arrested on site and is currently being transported to the Fulton County Detention Center."

He paused and waited until Justin looked at him. Then he said, "We had a little talk before he was taken away."

Justin's stomach tightened. Indignation battled with fear as he tried to comprehend that the same friend who, years ago, he had been willing to go to prison for, had turned around and betrayed him. But fear soon won over every other emotion, as he knew that this time, there was no chance for him to get out of this without spending several years in prison. And he knew more than he wanted to know about the Atlanta prison system. Panic rose inside of him. The situation was out of his hand,

and it was the first time since being an adult that Justin Friedman had completely lost control over his life.

The police officer was still looking at him. The man seemed to be searching for something in his face. *What does he want?* Justin thought while his mind was reeling. Was the man trying to get a confession? Clearly it was too late for this. All the evidence was there, and confessing to the cop couldn't possibly do much good at this point.

Help, please help! He didn't say it out loud, and he didn't address any particular entity. It was a plea coming from the depth of his soul. Justin closed his eyes, and to his own surprise, an inexplicable sense of peace swept over him. It was subtle but strong enough that Justin's panic subsided.

"As I said, I had a little talk with your friend who broke into your apartment," the cop repeated and raised his eyebrows. "He told me you were a drug dealer and that I would find not only drugs and cash in your house, but an unregistered Berretta 9mm as well." He paused and looked at Justin once more. The peace Justin had just felt threatened to leave, and his heart sank.

"That's some friend you've got there. Didn't only try to rob his friend but then thought he'd help himself by ratting on you as well. Things like that don't sit too well with me. But back to you, young man. I found the pistol under your bed, the box of cash, and the big jar of pot in your dresser. I know what you are and what you do. Looks like things didn't go your way today."

Justin hung his head but was still listening intently. The officer's voice was as professional and cold as could be expected in this situation. But Justin noticed something else in it that puzzled him. There was an urge and a concern in the man's voice that he certainly didn't expect—as if he was personally interested in this case.

Confused, Justin closed his eyes. The mix of terror and anxiety he had experienced in the past hour produced an emotional exhaustion in him. On top of that, there was the knowledge of having been betrayed by his friend, as well as the strange behavior of the police officer. He wanted to crawl under the covers like he used to as a little boy, shutting out the world and feeling safe in the dark.

Officer McLeod gathered some papers and ushered Justin toward the police car. As he did so, Justin's brain worked slowly, and everything seemed to happen through a fog. He wondered why he hadn't been handcuffed yet, and he also realized that the officer seemed to have touched neither the gun nor the drugs. Was a special unit going to collect the evidence later? But then why had he not called anybody in yet? Justin became more and more puzzled by the man's behavior.

When they got to the car, the officer opened the driver's door. Instead of handcuffing him and putting him in the backseat, McLeod just turned around and looked at him intensely.

"Justin." It seemed like he chose his words slowly and carefully. "Do you go to church?"

Justin was completely taken aback. Did he go to church? He felt so overwhelmed by the events of this day, he could think of nothing but the truth. "No. I've never been to church before. I didn't grow up Christian," he said simply.

The man looked at him for a long time without saying a word. But Justin would never forget those eyes—this urge and this care that he couldn't understand. He would also never forget what the man said next.

"This is your chance to turn your life around."

The officer got in his car, closed the door, and drove away.

Chapter Nine

"Thomas. I—I didn't know you were here!"

Sophie tried to collect herself. When he had touched her shoulder a moment earlier, a shiver had swept through her whole body, and she had blushed.

"My apologies for startling you, Sophie," he said and looked at her for a moment with a compassionate expression. "I'll leave you alone if that's what you wish."

Sophie looked at him, knowing he could tell she'd been crying. "Please don't," she said after a moment, and then added, "I feel so stupid. I have no idea why I'm crying in the middle of a beautiful sailing vacation."

"Emotions have a way of appearing in their own time." He smiled. "And more often than not, they are stirred up by something beautiful we experience. I wouldn't worry about it at all."

Sophie gave him a small smile. "You are right. There certainly was a lot of beauty around us in the last couple of days."

"You want to walk a bit?" he suggested. They slowly walked along the now-deserted dock, while the warm summer breeze caressed their skin. "I noticed your interest in my conversation with Tim earlier," he said lightly. Although he seemed to be able to read her easily, she wasn't threatened.

Thomas's voice was gentle. "I like Tim a lot. He is going through a tough time right now, but he has an admirable attitude about it. I was encouraging him to stay on the path and not lose faith in God and in people. We all need to be reminded of that from time to time."

He looked at her while talking. He seemed genuinely interested in her response, not just looking for a chance to keep talking. But his comment about faith in God threw her off. She tried to hide her irritation and wished he'd change the subject. But his eyes held hers, and she knew he wasn't letting her get away that easily.

"Is it the faith in God part or the faith in people part that makes you feel uneasy?" he asked, his voice as gentle as before.

She decided to be straightforward. "It's both." Turning her head and looking over the dark water across the pier, she let the memories of Nathan surface like the tiny bubbles on the waves beside her. Why did the only man she had ever truly loved have to die? And why did a complete stranger bring up her longing for a caring father in a way that made her lose control and embarrass herself? But most of all, why did she feel like she wanted nothing more than to tell all of this to a man she didn't know but felt like she trusted already?

She looked over to him. It surprised her that he didn't deem it necessary to comment on her confession of struggling with God. He was apparently a religious person, and in her experience, those people normally couldn't wait to lecture you about why it was wrong to doubt God. Thomas, on the other hand, seemed completely at ease with the ongoing silence, as if he knew Sophie had to work through the decision of what to do next.

She didn't want to talk about religion, of that she was sure. However, the yearning this man produced in her was undeniable. Her own father was a distant man, an academic who lived in his own world and had never been able to connect to

Sophie emotionally. With her strong, independent spirit, she had learned early on to push aside the need for a father's embrace or approval as soon as such a longing would make itself known. She was ok on her own, she told herself and others, and soon believed it deeply.

But this gentle stranger, in whose eyes she could see such fatherly love, had already started to crack her shell. She sat down on a small dune overlooking the ocean and gestured for him to join her. He sat down next to her, his eyes closed, and Sophie thought this must be what people talked about who had experienced the presence of a sage.

Over the course of the next hour, she told him about Nathan, about her depression, about the walls she knew she had built and about how they seemed to have just come down for the first time. Thomas listened intently, his eyes resting on her with a gentleness that warmed her. When she told him about the day Nathan died, she could see in his face that he knew the pain she was describing. When she confessed about the days she didn't want to get out of bed, she saw compassion in his eyes. And when she finally admitted that all of this had led to her being somewhat allergic to the topic of religion, he just nodded in agreement.

When she was done, they sat in silence for a long time. Then Thomas slowly got up. Sophie, unsure of what to do, followed suit.

What happened next burned itself into Sophie's memory. Thomas gently turned her around so she faced him, and then he embraced her. But unlike an empathetic hug or a friendly squeeze, he held her firmly and wouldn't let go.

Overcome by unknown emotions, Sophie realized she just wanted to stay in his embrace forever. At the same time, being so needy felt embarrassing, and she tried to let go. But Thomas's embrace stayed firm. The unconditional love she received from him threatened to unravel the independence, self-sufficiency, and control she had built around herself so carefully and over such a long time. Staying in this embrace might result in letting another person—and maybe life itself—touch her again. And although that was what she desired more than anything, it was also what she feared more than anything.

Apparently, Thomas knew well what was going on inside her. She heard his gentle words in her ear. "It's ok. Just let it go." At those words, her resistance melted as she finally leaned fully into his embrace and allowed herself to be vulnerable for the first time in years.

Chapter Ten

The shaking wouldn't stop. Justin gripped his coffee mug until his knuckles turned white and his muscles ached. He had to get control of his body, but the shock of this morning was too vivid for him to shake off. He now regretted coming to Waffle House, but it was the only place he could think of going. It was a place of familiarity that gave him some much-needed comfort.

After the police officer had driven away only two hours earlier, Justin had at first stood there outside his apartment, dumbfounded, for what seemed like an eternity. He didn't notice the neighbors still standing in their doorways; he didn't think of how vulnerable he was making himself while all the evidence was still in the apartment.

He didn't think of anything other than the absolute impossibility of what had just happened. Nobody he had heard of had ever gotten away in a situation like this, certainly not with evidence as strong as what was in his apartment. It overwhelmed him and scared him more than he liked to admit. His strength and confidence had always come from being in control of things or finding a way to dodge the consequences if he lost control. This, however, was different, something he couldn't wrap his mind around.

Suddenly, a memory stirred in Justin from long ago, an almost forgotten incident that forced itself back into his consciousness as if it had happened yesterday. He had been maybe ten years old, and his dad had taken him on a canoeing trip on the Etowah River. Buddy trips with his dad were always a highlight for Justin. Growing up in a family where strife between his parents and with his older sister was a common companion, he cherished the peacefulness when being alone with his dad.

That weekend, they had ventured out to a specific part of the river that his dad had not been on before. After riding the river for a couple of miles and enjoying the beautiful wilderness of that part of Georgia, the river suddenly disappeared in front of them into a tunnel. There was time to disembark and walk the canoe around the hill. But they could smell the adventure. Having been out in the woods, they felt brave and invincible, as men often do when in the wilderness among themselves. Justin and his dad looked at each other, smiled, and steered the canoe into the tunnel.

It was only after about thirty seconds of cheering and hollering, and after the first adrenaline kick had worn off, that they realized the stupidity of their decision and the danger of their situation. The tunnel was pitch black, and they had no idea about the condition of the river or the length of the tunnel. Capsizing on a rock now could be life threatening. A cold fear suddenly gripped little Justin's heart, and he clung to his dad's waist in the canoe as the boat silently glided through complete darkness.

Several minutes later, they heard the sound of falling water. *A waterfall!* Justin thought and panicked. They would come out of the darkness only to see their canoe tip over and rush down a waterfall, where it would crash on the rocks far below. Jumping out of the canoe in the darkness was just as impossible as staying inside, not knowing what was ahead. Hearing the sound of the waterfall ahead, Justin was now convinced he was going to die.

In that moment, a strange sensation rushed over him that he'd never felt before or after. Something inside of him transcended the panic and reached out to a power he could not comprehend. His heart—or his intuition, whatever it was—responded to the situation and did the only smart thing to do: it asked for help. It was a wordless, shapeless, and impersonal prayer that Justin felt inside of him. And yet, his panic slowly subsided. It was a most astonishing experience. He still couldn't see a thing, and he still was convinced he was going to die in the waterfall that came closer and closer. But for some reason, in that brief moment, it seemed bearable. He became quiet and waited for the end of the tunnel, which he now could see dimly ahead.

The air seemed blurry at the tunnel exit, and the noise grew louder and was now clearly that of water falling over rocks. Justin and his dad clung to each other, confused and afraid, as they came closer to the exit.

"It's a wall of water right in front of us! Hold on!" Justin's dad shouted as the canoe was pulled into a stream of water. It hit them hard and drenched them, and their boat started filling with water. But then it stopped as quickly as it had started, and sunlight blinded their eyes.

Still in shock, they turned to see that they had just come out of the tunnel through what was the *bottom* of a waterfall. The river streamed peacefully ahead of them. The relief palpable, they clung to each other for over a minute without saying a word, silently letting the fear subside.

Only after this solemn minute did they come back to reality, shouting and crying and giving high-fives and eventually deciding that this had been the craziest, stupidest, and most awesome thing they'd ever done. So great was the adventure story he later told everybody, that Justin soon forgot the part about that inexplicable peace he had felt in the moment of his great fear and how he had somehow asked for help and had somehow been helped.

This story came back to Justin as he sat at Waffle House, trying to make sense of it all. Like in that tunnel long ago, he had felt completely powerless in front of the cop. And like in the tunnel, he had found himself silently asking for help once more. And for that short moment where his life had hung in the balance, a peace he couldn't understand had rendered the prospect of prison just a tiny bit more bearable.

He sat in his booth bewildered, clasping his cup like a drowning man grabs a life ring. Even though the peace he'd experienced had felt wonderful, it had also exposed him as needy. And needy people were vulnerable. He didn't like being vulnerable. As far as he had observed in his young life, those in power did not show vulnerability. They took the reins and controlled the vulnerable.

It was no question he would have to stop dealing drugs. It was way too risky to keep selling, as the chances of police watching him now were high. At least he'd made plenty of money, and he'd be able to keep up partying and using drugs himself. But he was not going to let anyone decide his fate anymore.

Rushing back to his apartment, he called a friend to come pick up all the evidence in case the police came back. During the drive he thought about the question the police officer had asked in the end and the look of care and concern written on his face. Clearly he had been hoping Justin would do something wise with the freedom he had just been handed.

A tinge of guilt came over him. But he had decided as an eleven-year-old who was growing up in a tight-knit but dysfunctional home that his goal in life was to be free from the influence and control of others.

And not even a man who gave him his freedom was going to stop him from doing what he wanted.

Chapter Eleven

When Thomas slowly released his arms, his eyes were moist. "Thank you," he said quietly as they started walking slowly across the dunes.

Sophie knew those words were not a pleasantry. What had just happened in their embrace had connected them on a level of healthy intimacy that happened between loving fathers and their daughters. How astonishing that this man, who for some reason cared so much and seemed to understand so easily, had appeared out of nowhere to help her discover in herself the little girl who wanted more than anything a daddy to hold and love her.

They walked quietly for a while. The fact that Thomas hadn't commented on her previous critical remark now made her want to bring the topic up herself. "The whole God thing —I'm not sure I buy any of it, you know? I mean, I've always felt like believing in God was just being intellectually dishonest. There's so much contradiction in the Bible and so little relevance for the things that concern people today." She shrugged and only briefly glanced in his direction.

Thomas didn't seem fazed. "That makes total sense. And

you're not the only one struggling with these topics. But that's not actually your biggest problem, am I right?"

Sophie looked up, and a memory came to mind. It was the night she had gotten the call from Nathan's mother. The night she realized every dream she had for her future was destroyed. Her first reaction had been an instinctive, desperate prayer for help. Sinking to her knees for the first time in her life, she had tried to bargain with a God she didn't even believe in. Later, sitting stupefied in front of her phone, she had clung to an irrational hope that they would call back and tell her they'd been wrong, that it hadn't been too late to save him. She had waited for a miracle, even though she was the first to tell people that only irrational minds believe in miracles. When she fell asleep from exhaustion in the early morning, her last thoughts had been those of despair. But just under the surface of that despair was something she right now saw clearly for what it was: anger—and an accusation against a God who didn't care enough, who didn't answer prayers, and who did not work miracles.

"If God exists at all, I guess the fact that He didn't do anything to keep Nathan from dying doesn't exactly help my view of Him," she offered finally after a long pause.

Thomas's expression became compassionate. He nodded and silently waited for her to continue. She noticed that he had done this before in their conversation—holding off on answering a question that was in the air, one to which he'd surely have some sort of answer; instead, he gave her more space to express what she was thinking.

"I feel like the only God I could believe in would have to be powerful enough to keep major tragedies in the world from happening. And if He is powerful enough and still won't do it, then He's not good enough for me to trust in Him. So I guess I decided to leave it all alone and instead focus on being the best person I can be."

"And has this view of life turned out helpful?"

Sophie could tell it was an honest question, and she appreciated it. "It seems more satisfying, intellectually. But on some other level, it feels like there's something missing. It can also be pretty lonely at times."

Thomas was quiet for a long time, long enough for Sophie to notice the intermittent cries of the seagulls above their heads and the loud noise of the waves breaking on the shore. The wind had picked up. She pulled her sweater tightly around her. Just as she was about to suggest they head back to the restaurant, Thomas finally broke the silence.

"The Theodicy Question."

"The what?" Sophie asked, sitting back down.

"The big question theologians and Christians all over the world have wrestled with for thousands of years. If God is good, then why do bad things happen? And if He's the Almighty Father, why doesn't He protect His children?"

"Sounds like a good question to me," Sophie responded dryly. She waited for him to continue, but he stayed silent. She was surprised that Thomas wasn't trying to explain this but rather expanded the question further. Even though she wasn't offered an answer, the fact that he understood her question and the despair behind it helped her feel connected to him and, in a strange way, made her feel less alone.

"I have a feeling you're not going to answer this thousand-year-old question for me tonight, am I right?" Sophie finally broke the silence. Instead of being disappointed, the heaviness that had come over her while thinking about Nathan's death lifted just a tiny bit. She had met somebody who understood.

"You're right—I won't be able to answer this question for you. In fact, if you get an answer from above"—he winked and raised his eyes to the sky—"would you kindly pass it on to me? I've been interested in that answer for a rather long time.

"But on a more serious note . . .have you noticed that you don't fully understand even the best of your friends? When's the last time you told someone, 'Well, once you've explained everything about yourself to me and I've had every one of my questions answered to my satisfaction, we can be friends?'

Don't we rather become friends, then get to know each other better, and after some time get answers to some questions and then realize that other questions about this person will possibly never be answered?"

Sophie realized how immature her earlier statements must have sounded. "I guess you're right—I might have judged God without knowing the full story," she admitted. But she couldn't keep an edge of defiance out of her voice when she continued. "Yet I can't really see God as anybody worthy of love. To me, if He exists, He's more like a rather cruel deity that seems to enjoy the suffering of humans. Not really somebody I'd like to be friends with." Surprised by the words that had found their way from her heart onto her lips, she looked over at Thomas. How would he take that statement?

Thomas was smiling.

"You look like you're excited about what I just said," she remarked with confusion.

"I actually am," he answered with a chuckle. "Believe me, it takes a lot more to ruffle my feathers." Growing serious, he said, "Your statement is actually evidence of your desire for God."

"What do you mean?"

"I understand your disappointment and anger at what life tends to throw at us better than you think. And when we're honest, in the end it's not *life* we're angry with, but God. God can't be controlled, and sometimes we just really would like to control Him as we like controlling other people. If we can't, we get mad. It's a normal part of any close relationship. But as we get over it, we continue the relationship and hopefully have learned something about ourselves."

"I like how you talk about us and God in relationship terms, even though it's not like that for me. But it's a more inviting view of religion than what I've heard in the past. And I must say," she added with a thankful glance over to him, "you really find positive words for people who are desperate and completely confused."

"It's what friendship is all about, Sophie. It's the best thing there is on this earth. And my, I believe there's one starting between the two of us right now."

Sophie smiled happily and got ready to get up again, but this time he was faster and was already holding his hand out to her. Together they started back toward the restaurant. With a little dance of her heart, Sophie realized that although she had even more questions now, she still felt less stuck than before the conversation.

Feeling the need to let out the built-up emotions of the past hours, Sophie broke out into a run on their way back through the dunes. Thomas protested how running in the sand was hard on an old man but followed her nonetheless, a boy-like grin on his face that made him look a lot younger. When they got to the water, Sophie, flipping her sandals off, ran into it and splashed around like a little girl. Thomas stayed on the shore, watching her with a chuckle.

It was past midnight when they finally got back to the restaurant. The others had left long ago. Sophie found out that Thomas had paid for her dinner before he went looking for her. They strolled toward their ship and hugged goodnight before going to their respective cabins. When falling asleep that night, Sophie felt something she had stopped feeling a long time ago: cherished. And loved.

Chapter Twelve

The voice of the dispatcher at the Roswell Police Station shook as he confirmed the location of the accident and dispatched an ambulance together with the police car to the scene. He was used to hearing about freak accidents, but every once in a while, his emotions still got the better of him.

All he had gotten out of the upset woman on the phone was that she had watched the truck in front of her suddenly swerve to the left, causing the car in the other lane to lose control in a curve and smash full speed into a tree next to the road. The dispatcher sighed and muttered a short prayer that they wouldn't have to raise the number of road deaths again by the end of today.

Sandy and Adam had had a good night. Any party their friend Justin attended was a good one. It was a bummer that he left early those days because of his overly worried girlfriend. And since everybody knew the party was going to fizzle out after Justin left, they decided to call it a night as well and started the short drive back to their apartment.

They were driving down a dimly lit side street close to home when Sandy suddenly yelled, "STOP!" and Adam hit the brakes so hard they squealed.

"What the . . .!" he shouted, but Sandy had already dashed out of the car and was running down a little embankment off the side of the road. Now Adam saw it too. A black Jeep Wrangler with a Georgia Tech sticker was planted right into a maple tree down the hill from where they had stopped. It took Adam a second to register whose car it was. Now he shot out of the car too. "Justin!" he yelled as he caught up with Sandy.

"Oh my God, Justin! Can you hear me?" Sandy screamed after she had peered through the smashed window of the driver seat. "Justin, are you ok? Are you hurt?"

Justin's head slowly turned to her. His face showed confusion and fear. "What happened?" he finally managed to say.

Sandy could tell he was too shaken up to realize where he was or what he had just survived. But for some inexplicable strand of luck, he seemed to have gotten out of this without any apparent injuries. She and Adam got Justin out of the car and examined him closer. There was not a scratch on him. He was slowly coming to.

As Sandy's voice slowly reached through the fog in his brain, Justin forced himself out of his comfortable haze of drunkenness. He looked around and bit by bit pieced together what must have happened. Then he remembered.

"Whoa! That was insane. Some guy in a souped-up Civic was taunting me at the traffic light, so we started racing . . ." He only now noticed his car. "Of course, I didn't stand a chance in my Jeep, but I went for it anyway. The road was winding, and he slowed down at the curve, but I thought I could make it and just kept my foot all the way down." He looked at his friends as if asking for help with his explanation.

"I came up on two wheels, and when they hit the ground again, I completely lost control."

Even in his state, he realized he had to come up with a plan, since another car was bound to be driving by any minute and calling the police. A DUI-related speeding accident would get Justin in a lot of trouble. He quickly processed through the situation and his options.

"Sandy, Adam, listen carefully! We need to come up with a story so the police won't think I'm drunk and give me a breathalyzer! We're gonna pretend we don't know each other and that you guys witnessed the accident."

"One thing's for sure," Sandy said with a raised eyebrow, "it's amazing how well your mind works considering the alcohol and the shock you've just had! Tell us what to do because I sure don't have any idea!"

"Call 911, but you need to sound frantic! Say you just saw a large pickup truck swerve into the other lane where there was a Jeep. Tell them the Jeep lost control when trying to avoid getting hit by the truck and ran into a tree. Then say . . . say the truck drove off, and you couldn't see the license plate, and that the young man in the Jeep seems to be ok."

Justin was experienced enough to act sober when he needed to. This was the moment to use this skill. They rehearsed their story while Justin put on cologne from his glovebox and ate mints to cover up the smell of alcohol on him.

The police got there before the ambulance. A very worried officer rushed down the embankment and stopped in surprise when he found three unharmed people outside a severely damaged car. Sandy relayed the story and faked an excellent witness. Justin kept his eyes down most of the time, shaking his head as if still in disbelief of the other driver's actions and his own luck. The latter he didn't have to make up. It was now slowly sinking in that he very well might have died tonight.

The officer seemed to buy it. He was, in the absence of finding injuries, more fascinated than concerned. He sent word for the approaching ambulance to turn around. Then he inspected the car closer and finally turned back to Justin.

"Well, you are one lucky guy. Look at your car!" He shook his head again. "The chances of walking away from an accident like this without so much as a scratch . . . This might very well have ended deadly. I must say, I have never seen anything like it before." He proceeded with some instructions about calling the tow truck and how Justin was going to get home. Sandy, who still had to pretend she had never seen Justin before, talked about having been in a similar situation herself one time. She made a point of knowing how Justin must feel and suggested she and Adam stay with Justin until the tow truck came, and then they would bring him home afterwards. She had already noticed the officer glancing at his watch with the familiar body language of a man who wanted to get going. Justin's amazing ability to fake sobriety even spared him the breathalyzer, and their gamble worked out. Since they had no license plate number, it was not possible to file a complaint against the reckless driver, and after reassuring himself that Justin was unharmed, the officer walked back to his car and drove off.

The three friends sat in silence for a while. Justin didn't know which part of this night was the craziest. The fact that he avoided an arrest again, or the fact that he easily could have been killed—and what about the coincidence of his friends driving on the same road after him and finding him before anybody else? It was spooky.

After Justin's car had been towed, Sandy drove him home. During the ride, Justin was very quiet. Something unfamiliar and powerful had pushed itself into his conscience. It was guilt on one side and relief on the other. But there was now also fear. Twice he had been spared from arrest in a situation he had never heard of anybody else getting out of. Tonight's experience would have been an amazing story had it happened to someone else. But experiencing it himself gave him a serious fright. There was something at work in his life. The two instances where he was in danger and had asked for help now seemed like accusing fingers pointed at him. Had he ever acknowledged anything or anybody for sparing his life and his freedom? He remembered the urge to thank somebody, but not knowing whom to address, he had eventually let it go.

After Sandy dropped him off, Justin sat down on his couch, unable to move. He experienced what many people encounter right after escaping injury or death. Strangely disconnected from his surroundings and even from his life, he felt at the same time a heightened sense of reality. It was like being extraordinarily alive.

And in this focused state, where the distractions of life were momentarily drowned out, he could no longer deny it. There was something influencing and changing the trajectory of his life. But it was more than that. Justin realized that he knew, and had always known, that it was not just *something*.

It was *someone*.

Chapter Thirteen

The next couple of days of their vacation in the Netherlands, Sophie found herself seeking Thomas's presence more and more. He was making friends with a lot of the crew but seemed to always like hanging out with her as well. His ability to listen and his wise, loving words made him an attractive partner for conversation. Besides spending time together on the ship, they took bike rides, went for walks along the dunes and, toward the end of their trip, were preparing for the anticipated highlight of their vacation.

It was the second to last day on the *Noordfries*. They had enjoyed the day on Schiermonnikoog, the easternmost of the Dutch Frisian Islands and a feat for any non-Dutch to pronounce. The island was beautiful and even had its own national park with bike paths. But instead of settling into the harbor toward the evening as they usually did, they headed back out to sea after dinner.

Sailing into sunset, Sophie thought no movie she'd ever seen had gotten it right. The beauty of the Wadden Sea was breathtaking. Before night fell, the captain dropped anchor far out in the water, which was still only a few yards deep in certain places. Everyone went to sleep early, giddy like children.

At three a.m. they were woken, got dressed, and came on deck. As part of the intertidal zone of the North Sea, large parts of the Wadden Sea became dry land during low tide. For a couple of hours, the seabed was exposed, the ship actually stranded on dry land, and those on the ship, equipped with mud boots, flashlights, and buckets, would exit the ship over a ladder and walk on the seabed.

Sophie and Thomas set off together. The thought of walking where mere hours from now would be an ocean again was at the same time exciting and a bit frightening. They collected shells and mussels, Thomas holding the flashlight and Sophie looking for the bubbles that indicated where the animals had buried themselves. Then they chased each other over the rippled seabed, their laughter carrying far over the deserted flatlands. The magic of the moment would stay with Sophie for years to come.

After about an hour they walked back toward the ship to avoid getting surprised by the returning tide. From the safety of their vessel and with steaming cups of hot chocolate, they watched the water return slowly until, when dawn had come, the ship was floating again and they set sail to continue their journey. It was right in time for Sophie to return to her cabin and take a long morning nap. The skipper had chosen well to reserve this treat for the end of their trip. The feeling of otherworldliness, together with the poetic beauty of the sea in early morning, was a worthy finale.

The next evening, their last on the *Noordfries*, a torrent of conflicting feelings rushed over Sophie. This had been the best vacation of her life, and she was happier than she'd been in years. But, as a result of this, she was dreading their departure almost physically. How was she going to capture all of this for her friends back home, none of whom had any particular interest in sailing? Whom would she be able to share beauty and conversations and adventures with now? Of course, she had daydreamed about a future friendship with Thomas. But what would a friendship with a man forty years her senior look like in the reality of everyday life? Would they lose the magic of what they had shared over the past days?

Thomas found her staring out over the ocean after dinner in a melancholy mood. "Thinking about going home? Isn't it fascinating how an event far away can change the way we perceive life at home? It takes an effort not to feel disappointed by the everyday things we appreciated before."

Sophie gave him a small smile. Not to her surprise, he had hit the nail on the head again. "You're right. I should be thankful." She sighed. "And of course there will always be a next year on the *Noordfries*. For you, too, I hope?" she added rather shyly.

Thomas broke out into another one of his contagious grins. "My dear Sophie, you *are* a silly person! Do you think I would let you disappear from my life until next year? Not a chance. In fact, I have already planned to invite you for a visit to come and meet a few of my friends about two weeks after we get home. I hope you will say yes? If nothing else, it makes for a nice visit to our nation's beautiful capital, which happens to be my hometown."

Sophie was elated. "Oh, I would love to meet your friends. And to see you again . . ." she broke off, embarrassed by the enthusiasm she had displayed. What if he thought she had romantic feelings for him?

And what if she did?

Thomas held her gaze. He seemed to be able to detect the slight change in her demeanor. He gently touched her arm with his hand and spoke with unconcealed affection. "Sophie, you have become like a daughter to me in the short time we've known each other. I care deeply for you, and our friendship means more to me than you might understand. And I hope our friendship will grow so strong and deep that one day, I will sit close to the front row when you walk down the aisle on your wedding day. Will you give me the honor of becoming such a friend in your life, Sophie?"

A smile appeared on the weathered face of Peer, the skipper, as he saw Sophie receive a fatherly hug from Thomas on the deck behind him. Their friendship had not escaped his attention, and being a father himself, it warmed his heart to see what a safe place this man provided for the pretty young lady he had come to appreciate himself.

"Here we go again," he muttered amusedly to himself. "I told the management we should charge extra for every friendship forged on this ship."

Chapter Fourteen

Justin sat on his couch, his head buried in his hands. The quietness of his apartment was becoming unbearable.

Cora had broken it off with him the day after his accident, exactly two weeks ago. He thought she'd be back after a week or so. Instead, she called him yesterday, saying she should have split up with him long ago, and that there was only so much crazy behavior a girl could put up with. She told him to get help, go to AA, and not call her anymore.

Although Justin had always liked the casual relationship they'd had, he nonetheless had always assumed that when it was time to end it, it would be him to make the call. He was not the kind of person who got dumped. And for Cora to suggest he needed help was an insult that stung deep. It also underscored the loneliness and identity crisis he had been experiencing more and more since he had to stop selling pot. His position among his friends had changed, and besides, it was unwise to be seen with them any longer. But other than them, he didn't really have anybody. This realization clutched itself like an icy hand around his heart.

His best friend had broken into his apartment.

His girlfriend had left him.

His drug business was over.

He was a failure.

Utter desperation overcame him. Had he been of a different inner disposition, he might have tried to harm himself. As it was, his desperation and disappointment drove him in a different direction. Justin went to his well-hidden stash of drugs. Maybe it was the perfect time now.

Shortly before the break-in, one of his patrons had given him a small packet of white powder after a deal. "Just in case you ever need a real trip," he had said with a mysterious smile. Justin knew what it was and didn't want to accept it.

"Come on." His friend waved him off. "It won't hurt to have it just in case you ever want to try. I know people tell all kinds of scary stories about it. But hey, you haven't been alive if you haven't smoked it at least one time!"

Justin had shrugged but slid the little bag in his pocket anyway. At home, he wanted to throw it away but then couldn't get himself to do it. A fascination gripped his heart whenever he thought about it in the months that followed, especially when Cora and he would fight.

He got the small packet out and sniffed it. Yes, if ever there was a time when he needed a place to escape, it was now. And what did he have to lose, anyway? All the important things in his life were gone. He got some weed and a paper ready. Then he carefully sprinkled a small amount of the heroin powder into the weed before rolling the joint. His friend had told him that just the smallest amount would be enough to start out. Taking a deep breath, he lit the joint.

It started burning and, after a few seconds, died, leaving behind a thin trail of smoke.

At this moment of reckoning, Justin couldn't get himself to take the first draw. It was as if something held him back. He closed his eyes, trying to muster up the courage to light it again and this time breathe in the smoke and forget everything else. Instead, as his eyes were closed, pictures flashed in his mind.

Family vacations when his parents were still together. Soccer games with his best childhood friends. Sitting at a campfire with his dad and carving animals out of wood during one of their men weekends in the mountains. Without warning, a tear slowly made its way down his cheek. He sat still, joint in his trembling hand and heart racing wildly.

He didn't want to die. And no matter what his friend said, and no matter how small the initial amount was, he knew that one draw of this drug could easily be the start of the end of his life.

He didn't know how long he sat on the couch with the cold joint in his hand, but he knew he wanted to live, and he could no longer live the life he had been living.

As in the moment before his almost arrest, he now again felt himself uttering a silent plea for help, this time coupled with a determination to take seriously any answer he might get. He sat on the couch silent and motionless. His focus was turned completely inward, as if exploring a world he had not previously known existed.

What he found in the depths of his heart was that he had always known there was more to this life than what he could see and that he was held up by a power beyond himself. And however vague and unrelated it had appeared while he was a teenager, he had never let go of it completely. He could tell it was time to get to know that power.

Justin left his eyes closed. Although he was under no influence of drugs, he felt strangely disconnected from his physical surroundings. Gradually, he became aware of something. He could *feel* a presence in the room, which startled and fascinated him at the same time. He didn't dare open his eyes, but he suddenly knew with absolute certainty that he was not alone. He wouldn't be able to see anybody, even if his eyes were open, but he could just tell someone was there with him. To his own surprise, it wasn't scary, but almost comforting—a bit like coming home after a long, frightening journey.

Sitting there on the couch, Justin felt the parts of his life shift, like puzzle pieces moving together. The disconnectedness he had felt all his life was lifting. He was a spectator watching an inner transformation as an overwhelming joy and peace washed over him. He was still clueless about what was happening to him but was ready to accept it all.

"Tell me who you are," he whispered into the room.

The answer to this question came back as a whisper, but with a power that would change his life forever.

The whisper came in the form of a memory of something that had happened right after his reckless canoeing trip with his dad through the tunnel on the Etowah River. They had disembarked shortly after coming out of the tunnel and had sat down in the sun to dry off. Justin's dad became very quiet. Justin was only a boy, but he already understood the feeling of guilt and self-accusation his dad must be feeling. Even though he would push this conversation aside later on, in that moment Justin was alert and more serious than usual.

"Dad, do you know something? When we were in the tunnel, something weird happened. I was somehow asking for help, although I don't know who I was asking. But do you know what? I felt so much better afterwards, as if somebody heard me!"

When Justin said this, his dad's face changed. The guilt slowly left and his expression softened, revealing a joy that made him look younger. He answered only after a long time of reflection. "That's because there *is* someone who loves you, Justin." His dad's voice was tender. "And it is his wish to protect you from harm. His name is Jesus."

Justin was confused. Jesus was the guy that the Christians in his school believed in. But Justin grew up in a secular Jewish home and had never heard anyone in his family mention this name in a positive context, especially not his dad. Why would he now say that Jesus loved him?

"I have never told this to anyone, Justin. You know, I have searched for truth all my life. Before you were born, I traveled the world and backpacked through many countries in search of peace and truth. I studied with gurus in India and with other mystics in many countries. You don't understand all of this yet, but you will in your time. What I found through all my searching was a person. Not a religion or a philosophy, but a real person, someone who loves me and takes interest in me. I have given him my life, and I pray that one day you will too."

Justin gasped at the force with which this memory came back to him. How was it possible that he had forgotten this? He remembered his dad making him promise to not talk about this among his family and relatives because of the deep offense it would mean to them. He needn't have bothered, anyway—Justin was ten years old and more interested in telling everybody about his adventurous canoeing trip than about some Jesus he didn't understand. He had left it at that and hadn't brought it up again. But now it was the only thought that had any room in his heart. And with a certainty that astounded him, he knew that Jesus was the presence he had experienced and the person who had just answered his question. So many things that had been blurry and confusing suddenly became focused. Jesus had been there all his life, keeping him from harm and protecting him from himself. He had also been the one tugging ever so gently at Justin's heart all the way to this moment.

Joy and gratitude washed over Justin as he was trying to contain a heart so full he thought it would explode. The longing he would feel when looking up on a starry night, wondering about the vastness of the universe and knowing somewhere deep down that this universe was not the product of a random event; the yearning for something beyond the natural, which eventually led him to experiment with drugs; the beauty he experienced when hiking with his dad in the wilderness of the north Georgia mountains—it all came together like turning a carpet over to the right side for the first time to reveal the true picture, the real beauty.

Awe overcame him about this reality that had been around him all his life and the ripples of which he had felt, though subconsciously, since childhood. Justin fell to his knees and surrendered his life to the person he now felt he had known for so long, and who he knew had known him all his life.

Chapter Fifteen

"I'm over here, Sophie!"

Thomas grinned from ear to ear as he spotted her getting off the train in Bern, his home city and capital of Switzerland. It had been three weeks since their sailing trip, and although they hadn't been able to meet so far, they'd been on the phone often since then.

Coming home from the Netherlands, she'd felt the common sensation of people who get fully immersed in an experience, a place or a group of people, only to return to find that they can't share this with anyone who hadn't been there. Sophie tried to describe the sunset over the Wadden Sea to her best friend, Laura. She received a polite "that's nice, I'm glad you enjoyed it" from Laura and soon changed the subject. Talking to her friends about Thomas had proved even more difficult. How could she describe how this man, who could be her dad, had become so important to her? Would they be disconcerted or even tease her about whether she had fallen in love with a guy more than twice her age? Although Laura was usually a good listener, she was, as many Swiss were, also quite quick to judge. Sophie did not feel safe to share a friendship so precious and somewhat complicated as hers and Thomas's with anyone else yet.

Their phone calls had become an important part of Sophie's life. Sharing adventures, as well as much of her heart with him on the ship, she now wanted to talk about everything else with him as well—her dreams, but also her day-to-day thoughts. And now, Thomas had invited her into his life one step further. She was going to meet his friends, as he had invited her to do on their last day on the ship. But it wasn't going to be at a party or in a restaurant. They were going to a study group Thomas was leading. He called it a community group, but when she asked he confirmed that they often talked about God in this group, and some people even brought Bibles with them.

It's going to be a Bible study, Sophie thought to herself a bit defiantly. She was more than a little uncomfortable at the thought of it and was glad he suggested coffee at one of the lovely street cafés before going to the meeting. They walked off the platform and into a café where Sophie ordered her usual latte and nervously played with the cup once it came.

Thomas tried to set her mind at ease. "I know this is out of your comfort zone. But please trust me that these people are loving and nonjudgmental folks. You will feel right at home with them."

It was more his reassuring voice than the words that helped Sophie calm down. What was she going to say in a room full of religious people, when she knew nothing about the Bible, God, or anything else related to that topic? Nobody but Thomas could have gotten her to come, and she knew in her heart that it was his company, not the conversations, she was looking for. Growing up Catholic, Sophie had associated most things about God with boring litanies from an outdated book, delivered by conservative, old people. It all was too backward to be of any interest to her, and she had soon dismissed everything about faith as irrelevant.

Except for one thing.

As a child, riding her bike to a friend's house would lead her past the village church, and sometimes she would sneak in there by herself. She loved the church when nobody else was in it. There was solemnity and a sense of reverence in the place. Sitting in the silence and smelling the frankincense, she would tell God that one day, once she was old and somber like the people she saw on Sunday morning, she would become a believer. But she intended to live a fun and adventurous life in the many years before that, without being slowed down by religion.

Sitting across from Thomas now and sipping her latte, she smiled at those memories. Sure, Thomas wasn't young anymore, but he was anything but boring and somber. How much fun he was, and how much life and energy he had in him! When he raised his eyebrows amusedly, she just remarked with a mocking voice, "I just remembered my earlier experiences of church and religion. It's mostly memories of boring old people . . . don't know exactly where you fit in there."

Thomas replied with a teasing smile. "You might be in for a surprise, Sophie . . . that is, if you're adventurous enough to go through with it!"

"Is that a dare? Well, I'm ready for your group, Bible and incense and all!"

Sophie instantly loved Thomas's home, which was nestled in one of the older neighborhoods of Bern. It wasn't big, but it had character. It was a place that, in her opinion, fit Thomas's personality perfectly.

In spite of Thomas's reassurance, Sophie could feel her prejudice when the guests started arriving. It took her a while to realize that these people were quite different from the church goers of her childhood memories. For one thing, most of them were around her age, with a few of them Thomas's age and a young man who looked like he was still in school. She also noticed that some of them dressed very trendy, while others were more laid back. All of them seemed to feel very much at ease with each other.

"I'm so glad to finally meet you, Sophie!" a tall, middle-aged man said as he held out his hand to her. "I've heard quite a lot about you from my friend here. My name is Daniel. Welcome to this crazy bunch!"

Sophie smiled as her tension eased. Daniel introduced her to the rest of the group, and after singing a few songs accompanied on the piano by the college-aged-looking guy, they sat down in Thomas's comfortable living room. A few took out their Bibles, but most of them just leaned back in their chairs.

A young lady who introduced herself as Sandra seemed to be the leader that night. She welcomed Sophie and invited her to just listen or join the conversation and then addressed the group. "In the last couple of weeks, we've been talking about some of the fascinating aspects that characterize our faith. We talked about trust, forgiveness, and love. Before I tell you what today's topic will be, I'd like to tell you a story set during the French Revolution, following a man who spent half his life in prison for trying to save another person's life."

Sophie perked up.

"After nineteen years on a galley, he finds that as a former convict, nobody is willing to help him start a new life even after serving his sentence. He tries to find shelter but is turned down again and again until, freezing and desperate, he knocks on one more door. This time he is invited in and shown hospitality by the owner, a bishop."

By now, Sophie knew that the group was talking about her favorite novel. It was the last thing she would have expected.

"After his first satisfying meal in almost two decades, the man is offered a room to spend the night. But sleep doesn't come easy for someone who has suffered so greatly for so long. The reflexes of survival take over, and he robs the house, knocking the bishop over the head during his escape."

Sophie's eyes were closed as she listened to the story she already knew by heart.

"The man, whose name is Valjean, doesn't get far with the silver. He is spotted and returned to the bishop by the police the next morning. 'This thief told us that you'd given him the silverware as a gift,' one of the constables tells the bishop, 'but of course we knew he had stolen it and we will be happy to send him back to the galley where he belongs!'"

Sandra looked around the room to see if she had everybody's attention. "This is where this story intersects with the story of why we're all here today." She found Sophie's eyes and held her gaze. "Because no one would suspect what the bishop did next.

"'Of course I gave the cutlery to him! But tell me, young man, why didn't you take the candlesticks I gave you also?' He grabs the candleholders and stuffs them in the bag with the silver. After sending the dumbfounded police away, he locks eyes with Valjean. 'You are no longer a convict, my son. With these candlesticks, I have bought your soul for God!' And with these words, the bishop sends him away.

"Perhaps you can imagine the impact this has on a man who has never received anything but hardship in his life. In one moment, through one act of grace, Valjean's life is forever changed. He devotes the remainder of it to help, to save, and to extend grace to anyone he meets, even the people who persecute him. The author Victor Hugo illustrates what the characters in the Bible experienced so many centuries ago and what writers throughout history proclaimed: *Mercy triumphs over justice.* And grace thrones over them all."

For a while, the room was silent. Sandra's words had a profound impact on Sophie. She had known and loved this book for years. She had cherished the historical, the social, and the political depth of it, along with the great love story and beautiful language. And yes, she had always felt a strange sensation when she read the passage Sandra referred to, sensing the concepts of grace and forgiveness but never connecting them with God. Had she really missed it all this time?

She looked up and saw Thomas's eyes resting on her. For one moment she almost doubted Thomas's truthfulness, wondering if he had set this up. But then it dawned on her that they had never even talked about this book before. It had to have been a coincidence.

Sandra's voice interrupted her thoughts. "Let's think now for a moment about an instance in your life where you have experienced grace—an unmerited, undeserved favor."

That sounded like a hard task to Sophie. Surely, not many people had experienced such a thing before. And after several people in the room had given examples, Sophie got somewhat defensive. She knew people interpreted things they experienced based on what they believed, and it was very obvious in this group. What Thomas's friends called *grace,* she called luck. Or fate. Or, on days when she felt confident enough, she called it skill or intelligence. Hearing these people recounting similar experiences and calling it an undeserved favor from God annoyed her. Weren't they just turning life's ups and downs into religious ideas that fit their preconceived ideas? She tried to brush it aside as that, but as the stories continued, she had to admit that the authenticity and vulnerability displayed by those talking made a deep impression on her. A couple of times, she found herself wondering if maybe she had to rethink the origins of certain events in her own life.

After the meeting, Sophie chitchatted with several of the people who hung around for a while. She had to admit that the group was exceptional company. Most of them were well read, and she was positively surprised that they read not only authors known inside the Christian community, but their reading spanned various interest groups and included some of Sophie's favorite authors like Goethe, Shakespeare, Dostoevsky, and Tolkien. For a lover of literature like Sophie, nothing could have opened her heart more easily to these people than for them to share an appreciation for this form of art. This community group was for sure different than what she had expected, and she was grateful she had experienced it.

When, quite a while later, the door closed on the last of Thomas's guests, she expressed her surprise. "I really, really liked those people. They're actually very smart and modern in their views!" Only when she saw Thomas raising his eyebrow did she realize what she had just implied and her face blushed.

"Yes, isn't it amazing how people change once you get to know them?" Thomas said with a friendly banter. Turning more serious, he added, "You know, I'm really glad that you like my friends. We always want those dear to us to like each other, and I consider it a privilege to have shared part of my everyday world with you. And I'd love to have you come back and join us again. But before you do that, I want you to take me to meet *your* friends soon. Deal?"

As they took the bus back to the train station after the meeting, Sophie thought about his last statement. *We always want those dear to us to like each other*. She realized that her different sets of friends hardly knew each other. She had some friends at the college. She had friends at her volleyball team, some in the book club, and even some way back from Girl Scout times. But her friends didn't connect with each other. Most years, as was common in Switzerland, she would put together a little birthday party for herself and invite friends from these different sections of her life. But during those events she was the only link that held the party together, since her guests hardly mingled past their own circle.

Thomas's group, on the other hand, included people he had met in various places and stages of his life, but he had managed to bring them together into a strong community where people really connected. To think that she was invited to be part of it was a wonderful thought. At the same time, it made her more aware of what was missing in her own life. Looking at the brightly lit Capitol building as they drove by, she told Thomas about her thoughts.

"It's a common disease of our individualistic society," he said after some thought. "We don't think of a person as this incredible being waiting to be known. We think of him as a companion for our lunch break. Or a good choice for our tennis team. Or perhaps just the least nuisance when trying to cover our loneliness. But real relationship only happens when I see a person for who they are, or, even better, who they might be in the future—regardless of the connection I have with them right now or the benefit we can bring each other. It is incredibly freeing to interact with people like this, because I don't have to worry if there's enough common ground or if we will agree on important issues.

"Instead, I see an opportunity for myself to grow, because I get to experience a person that is very different from me. And aren't these often the most interesting encounters we have? Our Swiss culture—and many other Western cultures as well—are unfortunately prone to create many separate circles of people. Each circle has specific interests, viewpoints or activities, but we do not see the need to connect those circles or the people in them."

Sophie nodded empathetically.

Seeing her interest, Thomas continued. "So people are busy and their lives are filled with interesting activities. But they also feel like their lives are compartmentalized." He looked at her. "It's stressful to keep up with the different parts because life can't flow between them. It's like a mom watching several children, each playing in an individual room, and her running between rooms constantly to keep an eye on everyone. Although she likes the fact that she has each child under control individually, she's also extremely stressed. Of course, you could have all the kids play in one room. But that might get noisy and chaotic, and you might not be in control all the time anymore."

"But you'd feel like you're exactly where you're supposed to be!" Sophie interrupted suddenly as she got the implication of his story. "Although I'm often in wonderful places and with wonderful people, I mostly feel like I never arrive but keep running from one place to another, from one group to the next. It's really exhausting."

"You feel like this because life is not meant to be lived that way." It wasn't hard to tell that Thomas was talking out of personal experience. "God longs for you to find a place of real peace inside of you. Such a peace comes from an understanding of where you belong. You belong to Him. He is your home, your purpose, and your best friend. When that sinks in really deep, you naturally find yourself treating other people like *they belong* too. And those compartmentalized parts of your life start to merge and turn into this free, fun, and wholesome person that I can already see in you. It's a miracle, I'm telling you!"

Sophie marveled at how important she apparently was to this wise man who had so many friends and needed neither her company nor advice. For her, it was hard to imagine not needing people and seeing relationships just as a gift rather than a need. She still thought about this long after Thomas's outline faded in the distance and the train carried her toward her cozy but lonely home.

Chapter Sixteen

James McLeod sat at his desk and cursed under his breath. His week had been uneventful, and there was no apparent reason to be in a bad mood. Except for what he had learned a week ago.

Looking over his idling computer, he spotted his friend Eli, who worked at a bank nearby and occasionally dropped into the precinct during his lunch break to say hi and catch any interesting news going on at the station. Eli had always had a good listening ear and sound advice, both of which James needed right now. He pulled him into his office.

"Hey, Eli, I'm so glad you came by today. I've been brewing over something and have got to tell somebody about it."

Eli sat down and put his feet on the desk. "Go for it. I've got another thirty minutes before I need to get back.

James shut his office door. "Something's really been bothering me these past few days. Remember how my colleague Matt described this accident about two weeks ago where a young guy planted his car right into a tree and walked away unharmed? Matt let him go without investigating closely because no one got hurt. He said he didn't entirely believe the story, but because he was already at the end of his shift, he just let it go. He told me he suspected the guy may have been driving recklessly or racing someone, but there was no way to prove it. And you know how I'm always curious when it comes to young people who risk their lives stupidly. So I asked for the report, and it turns out it's the same guy I dealt with at a break-in case that was involving drugs only half a year ago!"

James waited for Eli's reaction. Eli smiled ever so slightly. "And . . .?" he said, raising an eyebrow.

"Well, it just frustrates me beyond anything when somebody gets another chance and then throws it away as if it's nothing. Especially . . ." His voice trailed off. He was going to say "Especially when there are people like my brother, Ronnie, who didn't even get one chance," but he didn't want Eli to hear the bitterness in his voice.

Eli studied him for a moment. "So now you're wondering if you're making a difference at all." It was a statement, not a question.

James nodded slowly. "After all, if I give someone a break, I am at least to some degree risking my job. But I tell myself, if it changes a life, it's worth it. But if they turn around and drive into a tree, it makes me mad!" He was hoping for at least some affirmation from his friend. Instead, Eli leaned back in his chair and studied James silently. Then he reached into his bag and pulled out a book.

"Read this and call me when you have an answer. I sometimes read during my breaks, and I happened to pull this book off my shelf this morning. I've read it more than once, and although I don't agree with everything in the book, I think one part in it might help you with your question. I guess I didn't grab it for myself this morning."

James looked at him with surprise. A book was not the answer he had expected. As he looked down, expecting some self-help book, he was staring at a copy of *The Merchant of Venice*.

"Shakespeare? Seriously, Eli, I cannot figure you out for the life of me!" He shook his head, but his curiosity had already gotten the better of him. He walked back to his desk and kept the book out so he could bring it with him for his lunch break.

The following evening at 9:32 p.m., Eli Smith got a phone call. He smiled when he saw who it was. "Yes?" he asked, bemused.

"So I've been reading the book, and I never thought a British guy from four centuries ago would help me, but you know . . ." The voice on the other end of the line sounded happier than the day before.

Eli laughed. "I know, right? You want to read me the part you're talking about?"

James began to read quietly. His emotions made it challenging to get the words out.

"The quality of mercy is not strained.
It droppeth as the gentle rain from heaven
Upon the place beneath. It is twice blest:
It blesseth him that gives and him that takes."

James cleared his throat before he continued.

"Mercy . . . is enthroned in the hearts of kings;
It is an attribute of God Himself;
And earthly power doth then show likest God's
When mercy seasons justice."

"James, mercy is not a means to get somebody to do something. It is a way to live, and it changes you and the one who receives it on the inside, whether you will ever see it on the outside or not."

There was a long pause. "Thank you for the reminder, Eli. I really needed that."

Once more, Ronnie was the last image in James's mind before he fell asleep that night.

Chapter Seventeen

For years to come, Justin would grapple to explain what happened to him following the evening of his spiritual encounter. The outward changes were radical and immediate. He went to bed that night feeling completely at peace for the first time since he could remember. He woke up the next morning, got in the car to head to class, and routinely pulled out his pack of cigarettes. Oddly, instead of lighting one, he found himself crumpling the pack up and putting it in a trash bag in his car. His life had taken a full turn.

When telling his friends after class that day that he had become a Christian, he received a good-natured belly laugh in return. "Man, you are the biggest pothead I know," one of them said. "You get drunk all the time, and you're the last man standing at the end of a party. You can't be a Christian."

Justin was surprised by this response and shrugged. "I don't know about all of that. All I know is that Jesus is real, and I'm with him!"

Leaving his perplexed friends to their own thoughts, Justin called his dad, who lived in the same city. It was a Monday, the day after his experience. "Dad, I'm a Christian! I believe in Jesus!"

It was a profound event for Justin's dad, who had years of prayer answered in one night. They met for lunch, and as was always the case with Justin, once set on a path, he acted fast. Having lost the urge to get high and drunk, he flushed all his pot down the toilet and threw away his large collection of smoking paraphernalia. Never having stepped foot in a church in his life, he anxiously awaited his first chance on the upcoming Sunday.

A few days later, Justin got out of his car in the church parking lot, wearing the closest to what he had to a Sunday outfit. Under his arm was his brand-new Bible, a gift from his dad, which he'd picked out at the Christian bookstore the day before.

He walked onto the premises of the small charismatic church his dad attended regularly. His dad, having experienced a long spiritual journey with many mystical aspects over the course of his life, resonated strongly with the charismatic flavor of Christianity. He tried to describe what would await Justin inside, explaining that people might raise their hands or sing enthusiastically. Justin didn't care about the admonition. He was ready to experience whatever was going to happen.

While walking in, he was being hugged and smiled at by everyone he passed and, in general, felt like he was greeted like a celebrity. His dad explained how many people in the church had been praying for him, in some cases for years, and were overjoyed to see him here. But Justin noticed that other guests were welcomed the same way, as if the whole church was one huge family. Hugs, laughter, and chatter dominated the beginning of the meeting. Was he really at a church?

When the service started with loud, cheerful music, he didn't know where to direct his attention. For one thing, there were the excited, almost ecstatic expressions on the faces of both those in the band and the congregants. An almost tangible energy hung in the air, reminding him of the peace that filled his heart. Then there were the lyrics, giving expression to the joy and love for God that had consumed him for the past week and were so new to him. Justin soaked everything up and was almost disappointed when worship was over. His disappointment left, though, when the sermon started.

"Christianity is not a religion," the pastor said, introducing the topic. "It's a relationship with a real person. When you experience the grace and forgiveness Jesus offers you, you will never be the same!" He was a passionate man, his voice matching the excitement of his words, and it was easy for Justin to see that this was not just a job, but that this man loved what he was doing.

He didn't understand everything that was said and had several hushed side conversations with his dad as the sermon went on. The sermon resonated with his heart, and the atmosphere of freedom touched him, yet this world was so new to him, he had a thousand questions. His dad seemed not the least worried. "You have the rest of your life to get to know Jesus better and learn more about the Bible." So Justin relaxed and took in as much as he could.

Afterwards, dozens of people came up to him and hugged him like an old friend. He realized just how much they must love his dad to have been so concerned about his son's well-being. He wondered, not for the first time, why his dad had not mentioned the church more often. After his parents' divorce several years ago, his dad had moved out, and Justin would meet him for lunch every week. They talked about school and Justin's friends, about his dad's work and even politics. But religion never came up. Or had it? He wondered if his dad hadn't brought it up several times, only for Justin's sarcastic comments to stop him mid-sentence.

His musings were interrupted when the pastor's wife came to him after the end of the service and, without introducing herself, started talking to him. Except it wasn't *to* him as much as it was *over* him. "Young man, you are very special to God.

He has a unique plan for your life, and he is going to use you in a powerful way. All the things you've done in the past are washed away, and everything has been made new."

Justin was embarrassed, unsure of what she was doing and afraid he was going to say or do the wrong thing. But what happened next made him forget all self-conscious thoughts.

The pastor's wife reached out and put her hand over Justin's heart. His body started to feel strangely light, and he had an experience as if being outside of his body. Strange things had happened to his body before while on drugs, but this time he was completely drug free. Almost instinctively, Justin held his hands up to signify a surrender to this power and a desire for more.

"Do you want everything God has for you?" the pastor's wife asked, and Justin silently nodded, lost in the strange but beautiful sensations his body was feeling. He could almost watch himself sliding to the ground and felt an energy flowing up and down his body. He knew it was this presence he had encountered a week ago. This time it was more powerful, more overwhelming. He was laughing and rubbing his belly, oblivious to the people around him. He just laid on the floor in the presence of a peace, joy, and power far greater than he could understand.

This experience would give him a sense of fearlessness in the years to come, and as he now knew deep inside that God was with him, he also knew that Justin Friedman was never going to be the same again.

Chapter Eighteen

The months that followed felt like being on a new kind of high. Justin had never felt more alive. He moved in with his dad the week after his first church experience and dropped out of college in order to have more time to read the Bible. Although his dad was hesitant about Justin's decision, he was happy to have him at home and at any rate knew this move was not up for discussion, as Justin never did anything half-heartedly. He would work out in the morning, then sit in his little room in their apartment and read the Bible until his dad got back from work.

His former life had come to a standstill. Since drinking and partying had been the core activities of his old lifestyle, Justin now found it difficult to hang out with his friends. He still met with them at first, but since he had stopped drinking and smoking pot, his friends invited him less and less, bewildered and annoyed at the loss of the Justin they once knew. He, on the other hand, couldn't have cared less. He was living in another world, and nothing about his former life was of any importance anymore.

The change of lifestyle resulted in a physical change as well. He lost weight and became much stronger. His daily fitness routine was no longer disturbed by hangovers or lethargy. After six months of rigorously pouring over the Bible and working out, Justin went a step further. He decided that since Jesus had been a carpenter, so would he. Although he didn't really need the money since he still had plenty left from his drug-dealing days, he got a job at a small cabinet shop that did custom furniture for local clients. He saved the money he earned to prepare for the next, so far unknown step. He had never been afraid of the unknown and took it as just one more piece in the puzzle of his life that God was putting together.

Apart from reading the Bible, Justin was also introduced to a number of Christian preachers and teachers through his dad. Having been oblivious to the world of Christianity, Justin now thankfully read every book his dad shared with him.

He was specifically drawn to the teachings of a guy called Jonathan Parker. He had a ministry in Colorado and was experiencing things that, to Justin, sounded like they came right out of the Bible. He not only talked about people getting healed and becoming free from addictions but talked about a Christianity more powerful and exciting than what Justin had ever heard before. What got his attention the most was Jonathan's emphasis on God's grace given freely to all who receive Jesus, no matter their previous life. Justin was deeply aware of the sins of his past—not only toward a God who loved him, but also toward a large number of people, including high school kids whom he had negatively influenced. Getting away from that life over the past months had made Justin aware of its danger and destructiveness, so to realize that he had encouraged kids to take drugs burdened his heart. He soaked up the message of God's unconditional forgiveness like a desert flower soaks up rain.

He also liked Jonathan's personality—a man of extremes, like Justin, who gave his life fully to what he believed and didn't look back. This mirrored Justin's own desires. He got all the materials he could from the man's ministry, which consisted of several Bible colleges around the country as well as a TV show.

Immersing himself in Jonathan's teachings became part of his daily routine.

He had been working as a carpenter apprentice for just a few months when his Dad invited him for a lunch that would change the trajectory of his life in an unexpected way. It was a Tuesday in June, and they had ordered their usual sandwiches at a restaurant near his dad's office. Justin noticed his dad's excitement. They had shared almost everything in the past nine months, and he had gained a best friend in his dad. He had a few guesses as to where this was going.

"We've both been listening to Jonathan Parker for several months now, and I know you agree how much his teachings have changed our lives. I also know you want more than to be sitting at home and listening to podcasts." There was a dramatic pause, but Justin already knew what was coming, and his adrenaline kicked in like an old friend. He nodded his approval almost before his dad had uttered the words.

"I think it's time for you to pack your bags and move to Colorado to go to Bible college."

It took no longer than a day between that conversation and Justin's application being filled out and sent to Mountain Rock Bible College. Ten days later he received the confirmation of his slot at the school and information about housing and job opportunities in the small, bustling city of Colorado Springs. That same weekend, Justin and his dad flew out to see what was going to be Justin's home for the next year and to check out what Justin already endearingly called The Rock.

As the plane approached the Denver airport, Justin took time to marvel at the breathtaking scenery of the Rocky Mountains stretching to the west of the city as far as he could see. He closed his eyes for a moment to thank God for what he had brought him out of—and what he was bringing him into. He would give himself to the teachings, the truths, and the spirit of this college with the same zeal and devotion with which he had done everything else in life—only this time it wouldn't be for material gain.

They took a rental car and drove through an exhilarating scenery of wilderness between the cities of Denver and Colorado Springs. As they turned into the parking lot of their motel in the Springs, the evening sun set in beautiful colors behind the majestic Pikes Peak, only miles from the Rock's ministry building. The breathtaking view went hand in hand with Justin's conviction that his time at Bible college would turn out to be just as breathtaking and amazing.

Chapter Nineteen

The train rides to Bern had become a treasured routine for Sophie for the past year. Not only the beautiful scenery and relaxing atmosphere on the train, but also the anticipation of meeting with her friends, whom she considered family by now. She tried not to miss any of the weekly meetings, no matter her workload at the college.

It was now over a year since she had joined Thomas's group. Every Wednesday, she had traveled back and forth, feeling as if Bern was becoming more her home than her little village in the north. Now November had come again, and with it the usual cold, foggy, and cloudy weather characteristic of the Swiss winter. But that day, it was different. The bright sunshine brought out the beauty of the last fall foliage, and the air was crisp and fresh. The weather mirrored what was happening inside of Sophie. She felt alive in a new way. That evening, she tried to describe it to Thomas.

"I feel like my life is somehow more meaningful and more colorful. It almost feels like I'm getting younger!" She glanced over to see his reaction.

"You should invite me over sometime. I could use some of that!" he responded dryly, but then smiled. "Actually, I totally understand what you're saying. Being around people where you belong will make life fuller and more beautiful, and it will do the same to you personally. I feel honored that our group has become that kind of place for you."

He looked at her for a moment, considering something. Then she saw that spark come into his eyes again that reminded her of a child on Christmas morning. She had seen it before, and she knew he was up to something.

"You know, I've been thinking . . ." He purposely let his voice drift off until she could take it no longer.

"Ok! Spit it out already!" she nearly shouted.

He chuckled. "The way we meet on Wednesdays is wonderful, and I'm so glad you feel that way too. But being like family means that we want to experience each other in other settings as well. Getting to know some other sides of each other we haven't seen yet. Like figuring out how to tie those knots on starboard. . . ."

Sophie turned red at the reminder of an incident way back on the *Noordfries* where she had been unable to tie a simple knot while trying to dock the ship. She had to call for help before the vessel threatened to get loose and drift away. The memory made her laugh. She didn't know Thomas had noticed the incident since he had never brought it up before.

"Yes, getting to know each other in different ways. Got it! So what does that have to do with me?" she asked with a smile.

"Well, some of the group, mainly those of us who are lucky enough to take some time off work, will take a trip to the US national parks this coming spring. Two weeks with a big RV and tents for the men. Since we have teachers in our group, we chose spring break for our adventure. That means that technically, you should be able to join us as well . . . do you think you'd like that?"

Sophie's eyes grew bigger. "North American national parks? Next spring, with all of you? No, not really." Then she jumped up. "Would I like that? Would I *love* that more than anything?" She did a little happy dance right there in

Thomas's kitchen and almost knocked a chair over in his living room.

"Easy, my enthusiastic friend," he said with affection and then added, "but seriously, we would love to have you join us. We will fly from Zürich to Phoenix, Arizona, and rent an RV big enough for our group of eight people. Then it's off to the parks—Grand Canyon, Zion, Bryce Canyon, Arches, Rocky Mountain. And while we're in the Rockies . . . did you know that skiing season in Colorado doesn't end until almost May?"

Sophie was about to tear up. "I've wanted to ski in the Rocky Mountains since I was a little kid. This is almost too wonderful to be true!"

Sophie's next months were filled with preparations. The Swiss were big vacationers, many of them taking trips outside of Europe every year. She herself had been to many countries, the US included. She loved everything about traveling—the languages, the cultures, the scenery. But she had never been in the company she would be in this time. People whom she trusted, felt at ease around, and who were fun to be with. Also, traveling with RVs and tents meant very personal and close interactions. Although not a shy person, Sophie could not imagine going on a trip like that with any other group.

While preparing, she also thought of her aunt who lived in Butte, Montana, whom she had wanted to visit for a long time but had never gotten around to. This would be the perfect time if she could get some extra time off school after spring break.

A former colleague, who was now a stay-at-home mom, agreed to sub her classes for two weeks when she asked. Sophie's aunt said she was welcome to stay as long as she wished. Only a month after Thomas's invitation, she had worked out the last details and gotten her plane ticket.

One night shortly before Christmas, Sophie sat at her desk, looking at all the travel documentation, visa, travel guides, and maps she had collected. To be going to the US for a whole month was an exhilarating thought. She was especially looking forward to the highlight at the end of their trip together, skiing in the Rocky Mountains. Living almost at the foot of the Alps, Sophie had always loved the majesty and serenity of mountains. From what she learned, the Rockies were similar to the Alps but more spread out, vaster, and even wilder. Skiing those mountains must be as breathtaking as it was to fly down the slopes in Switzerland, something Sophie and her family had been doing since she was six years old.

Little did she know that skiing was going to be one of the least breathtaking events that waited for her across the ocean.

PART II

Spring 2018

Colorado

Chapter Twenty

"You can do nothing to make God love you more. And you can do nothing to make God love you less. God loves you because of who He is, and His love for you is free from any expectation." Jonathan Parker's voice was calm, yet persuasive, and Justin soaked up every word. He loved listening to this man of God preach.

So did the other roughly three hundred students who were attending the Rock. They sat in the large auditorium of the college grounds which also served as the headquarters of Jonathan Parker Ministries. Parker's teaching ministry reached millions across the nation and around the globe through a daily TV show, as well as his multimedia influence that included books, streaming materials, and online classes.

In the few months since starting classes at the Rock, Justin had heard numerous teachers and speakers, but no one had Jonathan's communication skills. He was funny, yet sincere. He was eloquent, yet down-to-earth. His boundless energy and enthusiastic approach to every subject belied the fact that he was sixty-six. But what impressed Justin the most was that Jonathan truly lived what he preached. He never prepared for sermons because he said what was inside of him was just waiting to get out. Although he quoted Scripture all throughout his lectures, he rarely opened his Bible, because he knew by heart every Scripture he expounded on. He was exactly what Justin needed—passionate, vision-oriented, and without compromise. Justin was one of his most ardent students.

His days were full. He attended classes all morning, spent the afternoons outdoors with his friends from the Rock, and then drove to his job as a server at an Italian restaurant where he waited tables all evening to earn money to pay for school. Although there had been money left from his drug-dealing days, ever since listening to Jonathan, Justin hadn't felt right about using it anymore. It was money earned in a sinful way, so he wasn't going to use it on himself but was waiting for an opportunity to give it away.

Justin had never felt better in his life than now, being a part of the Rock. He loved hearing amazing stories from fellow students, teachers, and guest speakers about the things they had experienced with God. Having an extreme personality himself, Justin was immediately drawn to other people with unusual lifestyles and pasts. He became close friends with Simon, an ex-convict from Denver, and Caleb, a logger from a small town in the Upper Peninsula. They took along other friends as well, but the three of them were the core of the group. They shared the dream to live life to its fullest and to spread the gospel around the world, as Jonathan taught them daily.

"Accepting God's love for us is the real challenge we face," Jonathan continued his lecture. "Christians often have a condition I call spiritual dyslexia, which means they see things backward when it comes to the love of God. They think that God will love them as a response to their good deeds or even their love for Him. But in reality, God loves us first, regardless of our behavior or even our response to Him. That's what I call Good News!"

There were numerous shouts of "Amen" in the room. The

students liked it when Jonathan started preaching, not just teaching.

"But you know what? God doesn't want us to stop there!" More people shouted as the energy in the room built with Jonathan's words. "This world is fallen, and there is an enemy whose goal is to kill, steal, and destroy. And he will if we let him! But God gave man authority over the devil. Jesus conquered the devil and then told us to use His name against anything that stands in God's way. This means He wants you to take this authority He's given you and go fight the devil. Where does this fight take place? I'm glad you asked!"

Chuckles ran through the auditorium. Justin was on the edge of his seat.

"It takes place right between your ears! It's what you're thinking that determines whether the truth of God or the lies of the devil are produced in your life." Jonathan closed his lecture with a Q&A, which ended pretty fast. His doctrine was tightly knit, thoroughly thought out, and hardly left room for questions.

Between classes, Justin hung out with some of the other younger students in the breakroom. Most of them came from the Bible Belt, but a few students were from the Northeast and overseas. One of them sparked Justin's interest early on. He was a blond-haired, tall young man from Norway. Justin heard him ask more questions in class than most others, and the nature of these questions at the same time fascinated and disturbed him. So one day, soon after the start of college, he went up to him and introduced himself.

"Hey, my name is Justin. I noticed you are quite the question man!"

The young man had a smile that seemed to spread across his whole face. "I'm Bjørn! It's a pleasure meeting you, Justin." His handshake was firm, and he had a pleasant way about him. "I have noticed you as well. You seem to come to class every morning ready to take on the world!"

"Well, I take on the world and you take on the teachers!"

They grinned at each other, and Justin knew right then they would be friends. "So . . .what made you come all the way to the US?"

"I wanted to see how other people believed and how they lived their faith," Bjørn answered. "And I have already realized that it is quite different from where I grew up."

At first, Justin was taken aback by this answer. He had expected something more spiritual like "God called me to the Rock, and here I am," which was the kind of answer he had gotten used to around the college. At the same time, Bjørn's answer fascinated him. He had never considered investigating how other Christians lived their faith. It seemed unnecessary since the place he had found was of such spiritual wealth and depth.

He wondered if Bjørn would see it the same way once he had listened to Jonathan as long as Justin had. Since his encounter with Jesus, Justin had adhered to the conviction that since he had found the Truth, he was going to stick with it and follow it no matter what. At least that was how he dealt with the questions his intellect had come up with sometimes while listening to a lecture at the Rock.

Sometimes Jonathan seemed to contradict himself, depending on what Scripture he was teaching. Even worse, sometimes the Bible seemed to contradict itself. In these moments, Justin was glad to have his friends around. Caleb would tell him, "Man, that's the devil trying to confuse you! The Bible doesn't contradict itself ever; it's the Word of God. It's just our doubts that give way to confusion. It's why I came here: to learn to shut out the voice of the devil and follow Jesus radically!" Words like these helped quiet Justin's occasional questions. He tried to single-mindedly follow the path set before him and do whatever it took to find God's perfect will for his life.

As Bjørn and he became friends and started hanging out, Justin realized that what made him uneasy about Bjørn's questions was that they often sounded dangerously close to the doubts Justin was trying to avoid. In the first couple of weeks, Justin just brushed this aside as the growing pains of somebody new to the teachings of the Rock, as most of the students were. But after a while he had to admit that Bjørn's questions were brilliant, not ignorant, and that the answers he got were often far from brilliant. One of the main lecturers even announced during their first session that he would not be listening to any student's comments, other than answering questions, until the end of the year because he didn't consider them mature enough to comment on spiritual matters. Bjørn had followed the rules and asked only questions, but some of his questions were as explosive as any comment.

"If it's God's will to heal everybody all the time," he once asked that same teacher not far into the school year, "then why did Jesus pass by so many sick people and only heal the one paralyzed man at the pool of Bethesda?"

The teacher had looked at Bjørn with the patient and slightly condescending look of a superior who takes on the arduous task of training an inferior.

"Son, this is the wrong question. We cannot find Truth by doubting. We find Truth by surrendering our doubts and building our faith. What we should ask is"—and there he locked eyes with Bjørn—"why did the other people in that pool not get healed? I think most of you in this room are beginning to sense the answer. It's because these people did not have enough faith in the healing power of Jesus. In that whole place, only one man had enough faith to receive his miracle from the Lord. He was the only one who didn't let his faith get clouded by doubts. And it was he who took up his mat and walked away. Hallelujah!"

The room filled with shouts of "Amen." Justin almost felt a physical relief, as if God's Word had been under attack and was now proven right once again. He had wondered that day how Bjørn felt after this reprimand. But glancing across the room, he didn't see shame or defeat on Bjørn's face. It was sadness written across his friend's troubled face.

While Justin admired the courage it took to ask that teacher a question, he also despised the lack of faith the question had revealed. He liked Bjørn but didn't like much of what he said. He was more used to encountering the opposite at the Rock: liking what somebody said but finding that sometimes he didn't particularly like the person themselves. This unsettled him. Was Bjørn just a worldly person with a winning personality who would influence him negatively? Would his questions lure Justin away from the Truth? But then, why did he like him so much?

One day not long after they first met, Bjørn approached him in the hallway. "Do you want to join me and some buddies on an adventure? We're going snowshoeing up by Mueller State Park this weekend. Real wilderness. You look like you could be up for it. What do you say?"

Justin might have his theological reservations about Bjørn, but he was also an adventurer and could easily recognize Bjørn as one as well. The prospect of experiencing the Colorado outdoors with a bunch of friends won over his reservations, and he agreed. Maybe their time together would give him a chance to talk more with Bjørn and help him get rid of some of the young Norwegian's doubts. "I'm in," he said.

Bjørn beamed. "I think you'll love it. Besides, it's good training for our real adventure. In April, when the snow has partially melted, our group will hike Pikes Peak. We'll go up and down in one day. It will be the ultimate adventure, and I'd love for you to join."

"Well, I'm not familiar with any of the outdoor stuff here, but if you're game, I am too!" It wasn't hard for Justin to talk tough. As a former drug dealer, he was used to establishing an image for himself right at the start, and in this crowd, he was rising to the top in no time.

"Awesome. We will train on several weekends before spring, and you're welcome to join us whenever you can. We plan on hiking it the first week of April. I'm super excited you're going to be part of it!"

Justin smiled at Bjørn's enthusiasm. Only after the Norwegian excused himself to talk to someone else did he take out his phone to look up the hike.

It was going to be twenty-six miles long and would cover an altitude change of nearly eight thousand feet.

Chapter Twenty-One

The already familiar sounds and smells of campground mornings were mixed into Sophie's dreams until they slowly woke her up. The atmosphere was similar every day: the noises of children playing and babies crying, early risers washing their breakfast dishes, and late risers like her group creating wonderful smells of fried bacon and steaming coffee. She took it all in for another moment before opening her eyes. She could hardly believe the trip she'd been anticipating for the last several months had turned into a reality, and she was actually on a campground in a US national park.

Her trip so far had been even more amazing than she'd expected. What a difference it made to be with people who enjoyed each other's company. Everything became easier in a group that was used to helping each other, so that even the difficult parts of travel—the waits, the uncomfortable flights, the paperwork to rent the RVs, and all the other minutiae—seemed like a walk in the park.

They had been on the road for almost a week now. Starting in Phoenix and driving north to the Grand Canyon, they had experienced their first taste of American roads and life on campgrounds. Sophie had loved it all. The best was their first day at the Grand Canyon. Rising well before dawn, they hiked to a perfect spot where they sat down with a packed breakfast of coffee and croissants. Together they watched the sun rising with a dramatic burst of light over the plateau and pouring into the countless valleys all the way down to the Colorado River. It was an unforgettable experience.

Next on their itinerary was Zion National Park. Many of the views in this park reminded Sophie of the Swiss Alps, although it lacked the mystery they experienced while hiking the valleys of the Grand Canyon the day before. After Zion they drove to Bryce Canyon. Sophie instantly fell in love with the hundreds of spires that looked like sugarcoated stalagmites. This breathtaking view stretched over miles and revealed rocks in all shapes and colors. They hiked down to the bottom of this canyon as well, and Sophie was for once glad her dad had taken her on countless hiking trips as a child and teenager. It certainly came in handy for this trip. She wondered how a man Thomas's age was able to keep up with such rigorous hiking.

Today was going to be their last day in the RV. After hiking Arches National Park, they would make the long drive to Colorado and exchange the RV for two cars. There, they would enjoy a night in real beds at a motel and then drive to Rocky Mountain National Park. They would end their trip by renting a cottage at Monarch, a ski area deep in the mountains, and spend two days experiencing the majesty of the Colorado wilderness.

They set out for Arches National Park right after breakfast. Delicately shaped natural bridges made of sandstone could be seen in any direction, each one different in size, shape, and color. They hiked among them for hours, taking pictures and marveling at their beauty. After returning, they packed the tents into the RV and started the journey to Colorado.

Over the next hours, the landscape changed. What had been a lonely, dry beauty in Utah slowly transformed in front of them. Pines started to dominate the view. The landscape was still wild, but a friendlier kind of wild, the one that makes you want to find a quiet place, take out a book, and stay there the whole day. When they stopped for a restroom break about a hundred miles into Colorado, she noticed something else. The air had changed as well. It had grown richer and sweeter. Although growing up in a country full of forests, Sophie had never smelled this kind of air before. It smelled of pinesap, sun-soaked meadows, and fresh mountain air.

Quite unexpectedly, Sophie teared up. It was as if her soul recognized this place, and the experience filled her with awe. At first, she was going to tell Thomas, as she usually did when something beautiful happened to her, but then she felt silly and decided against it.

Dusk had already set in when they arrived in Estes Park, a small town at the eastern border of the Rocky Mountain National Park. After returning their RV and eating a light dinner in one of the charming mountain cafés, Sophie said goodnight to the group. But a strange, unsettling feeling kept her from falling asleep, and she decided to go for a walk in the nearby park.

The air was crisp and surprisingly cool after the hot desert climate they had experienced the week before. Sophie sat down in the grass and looked over the small lake close to her motel. She had felt a tug at her heart when first experiencing this place with its smells and scenery. A tug that she had felt before when reading some of her favorite books, listening to classical music, or sitting in front of a sailing boat and looking out across the ocean while the salty breeze touched her face. She had also felt the tug when sitting by the fire with Nathan, watching the sparks fly off the logs and sensing an inexplicable happiness filling her heart. She sighed. There she went again, despite the fact that she'd thought she had gotten over Nathan.

But it wasn't just him. There were moments she wasn't thinking of him when she felt it too, like earlier today. As if her soul was aching for something when seeing beauty and goodness. As if all the good things in her life were still not enough.

As she walked back toward the motel, she started to wonder whether she would ever find true happiness anywhere.

Chapter Twenty-Two

Justin let out a shout both of satisfaction and exhaustion as he stood for a long time taking in the view and the realization that he had actually made it to the top of Pikes Peak. Stretched out as far as the eye could see to the east of them were the plains of Colorado, and the favorable weather conditions allowed for a view far into the neighboring state of Kansas. On the other side of their panorama were hundreds of miles of snow-covered peaks—the heart of the Rocky Mountains. Here, on top of the legendary mountain, towering majestically over the city of Colorado Springs, Justin felt like he was at the center of everything—literally and figuratively. It was an impressive spot to stand on, even if you hadn't spent the last eight hours climbing it as Justin, Bjørn, and some of their buddies had.

Hiking, snowboarding, and river rafting were just some of the outdoor activities Justin had found himself getting into after joining Bjørn and his group of friends in the winter. The air of adventure and wilderness started mere miles outside the city limits, and it was not by accident that Coloradans were some of the most healthy and active Americans. Justin loved it all from the beginning. He could see God in the breathtaking views while hiking, in the majestic peaks while snowboarding, and in the wild state parks where spotting a brown bear in the woods was not uncommon.

They had trained for months to prepare for climbing Pikes Peak, and during the strenuous weekends on trails and in the wilderness, something basic and previously dormant had stirred in him—a sense of wanting to be a real man. Somebody had given him a book called *Wild at Heart* shortly after starting Bible college, and it had awakened a longing to discover his own masculinity. Colorado seemed like the perfect place to live out this urge. The snowshoe trips throughout the winter were his favorites, and today he was really glad he had joined the others as many times as he did.

The hike had been everything he had hoped it to be. Bjørn and he had had several lengthy conversations that Justin loved, despite the fact that Bjørn still seemed to question far too many things. But Justin was smart enough to recognize the brilliant mind he was dealing with and to develop an appreciation for the depth and logic that was part of their discussions. And of course, Justin had his own questions too. Knowing the Bible as well as he did, he was only too aware of the things Bjørn brought up. The discrepancies. The parts nobody talked about. Sometimes also the tension between what Justin knew from the teachings to be true and what his heart wanted to be true. Talking to Bjørn was, although unsettling, like a fresh breeze. Bjørn sounded heretic at times, but to Justin's surprise, his words were actually far from ugly.

They took a long, well-deserved break at the top, devouring chocolate bars and energy drinks. Justin was proud of his accomplishment, although he had felt lightheaded at several points during their ascent and would have loved to take longer breaks. Also, near the top, he had developed a growing pain in his side. It started at a part of the mountain that was especially gruesome to hike at this time of year when the peak was still covered in a layer of snow. The pain was dull but growing, but Justin's pride would not allow him to ask his friends to slow down. After they had reached the top, it slowly subsided, and now it was going to be all downhill, so Justin decided to ignore it.

Starting the thirteen-mile hike back down, Justin walked in front of the group. He felt great knowing that he had been able to hold his pace with a Norwegian who grew up hiking in the mountains. Sure, many of the group had trained much harder than him, but Justin did not think of limits, only of challenges to be overcome.

By the time they entered the arboreous zone of the mountain, the pain had come back fully. The time of rest on the mountaintop didn't seem to have been sufficient. Ignoring his body's signals, Justin kept walking down the mountain at the exact same speed. Speaking to his body and commanding it to work according to Scripture was just one of the fascinating things they had learned early on at the Rock. As a Christian, he had the authority to command his body, and even things in nature, just as Jesus had commanded the storm and healed the sick. "You will do greater works than these," Jesus had encouraged his disciples, and Justin was ready to take on this promise.

"But he was wounded for our transgressions, he was bruised for our iniquities; the chastisement for our peace was upon him, and with his stripes we are healed." Justin quoted the prophet Isaiah aloud as he kept walking down the mountain with his friends.

He knew more Bible verses by heart than most students at the Rock, and he often quoted them from the original King James Version, which he believed to be the most inspired Bible translation. The pain had increased steadily, but Justin didn't care. He knew the importance of reminding his body and his soul about the truth—that he was healed by the stripes of Jesus, even if it didn't look or feel that way.

They were about three miles away from the end of the trail at the foot of Pikes Peak when he collapsed and fell to the ground with a silent groan. His friends gathered around him immediately and started to pray. Pain shot up and down all along one side of his body, so intense he couldn't speak. He just lay on the ground, trying to listen to the words of his friends. When he hadn't moved after several minutes, Bjørn suggested they call 911.

Hearing this brought back the fighting powers in Justin. "No way!" he almost shouted at Bjørn, who backed away with surprise. "We're not going to let the devil win. Help me get up. I'm going to walk down that mountain myself, because I'm healed by the stripes of Jesus!"

There was something heroic and grand in his statement, and nobody objected. They got Justin on his feet, and although he was still in too much pain to speak, he soon led the way again to the end of the trail.

When they finally got back to their cars, they had hiked twenty-six miles and climbed over seventy-eight hundred feet in altitude. It was a challenge that had brought all of them to their physical limits but also one they would remember for a lifetime. Justin had recovered enough to join the others for their victory treat at the Hungry Bear, a restaurant known for its all-day breakfast foods served in enormous sizes. They enjoyed massive amounts of pancakes, bacon and eggs, toast, and thick slices of country ham. Justin felt a pride that was hard to conceal. Not only had he climbed Pikes Peak, he had also put the devil in his place and commanded his body to function. He was making progress in his spiritual journey, and it made him feel good.

Bjørn was more silent than usual. Justin assumed he felt bad for displaying such unbelief on the mountain. Well, everything came with a price. *Maybe all those questions make it harder for you to take your authority or believe someone else could.* But at the same time, Justin had already forgiven him. Maybe he needed to tell Bjørn so he could move on. After they paid and the others left the restaurant, he pulled Bjørn aside. "Hey, man! Don't beat yourself up about what happened. We're all learning! Remember, God loves you not because you're perfect but because His love is perfect! We are all growing in our faith."

Bjørn looked at him for a long time, his face showing hurt as well as sadness. When he answered, his voice expressed not anger but disbelief. "Do you really think I feel bad about wanting to get help for someone on the verge of losing consciousness? Where is your common sense, Justin? I know you think I don't trust God enough, but God gave us a brain too. And He gave us each other. Sometimes I wonder if your concern is less for God's glory as it is for your own."

He shook his head sadly and disappeared into the dark parking lot.

Chapter Twenty-Three

Sophie set off slowly at first but soon picked up speed as she raced downhill, sending flurries of fresh snow flying everywhere. She shouted for joy, carving a rather impressive snake pattern in the deep powder snow she plowed through.

Going off the slopes into the untouched snow had always been her special pleasure. It was hard leg work and required more skill than one would think, but Sophie had been on skis all her life and found Colorado snow serving her just like its Swiss equivalent did. She ended her downhill dance with a graceful swoop that sprayed snow ten feet away from her and waited for Thomas to catch up.

It was a perfect day for skiing. The season nearing its end, only a small number of people shared the slopes with them. The coldest part of Colorado winter had passed, making it all the more enjoyable to be outside. Looking around her, Sophie could see nothing but snow-covered mountaintops stretching out over hundreds of miles. It had snowed the day before, so the slopes were soft, and the deep snow was beckoning her.

Thomas caught up with her, shaking his head and grinning. "I knew there was still lots to learn about you, but I didn't know we had a skiing master among us!"

Sophie laughed and gave him a thankful smile. It felt good to be admired by someone she also admired in so many ways.

The day before, they had hiked Rocky Mountain National Park with its rugged and wild beauty. Sophie could have stayed there forever. Pristine mountain lakes bordered on high-towering pines and delicate, beautiful aspens. Daniel, one of Thomas's friends who had been to Colorado before, told her about the stunning change of colors in this region. In the fall, the aspens would turn the mountains into balls of yellow and orange fire. Sophie made a mental note to come back here one day.

She set off once again, this time with Thomas on her heels. Sophie had realized right away that he was an amazing skier, although his age made him slow down a bit. Then it occurred to her that maybe it was not his age but his wisdom that made him decide to take it with more ease. She herself had experienced several near-accidents in the past and always attributed never getting hurt to her good luck. But being around Thomas in the past year had taught her how connected the decisions of her life were. In fact, she mused, just being with him had been slowly changing her in many ways, without him ever saying a word about it. She shook her head in amazement as she slowed down ever so slightly.

They skied all day, taking only the necessary bathroom and hot chocolate warm-up breaks. Sophie enjoyed hanging out with all her different friends in the group, but she felt herself hoping to catch a chair lift with Thomas more than with anybody else. Her affection toward him was unbroken, but it was now almost entirely healthy.

Now.

The thought reminded her of the fact that there was still a secret between them, and if there was one person in the world she didn't want to have secrets from, it was Thomas. The next time they sat alone on a lift, she asked, "Remember our last day on the *Noordfries*?"

"Of course I do!"

She gathered her courage and looked directly at him. "Although I didn't let on about it that day, when you told me there would never be a romantic relationship between us, it hurt deeply at first. Although my head had known all along the facts you were telling me, the rest of me was in a different place. My heart desperately searched for a way around our impossible age difference, right up to our last day."

Thomas didn't reply, but the fierce protectiveness and love in his eyes spoke louder than words.

"When you destroyed this unhealthy dream with your words, you at the same time liberated our friendship." Joy filled her as she realized she was now free enough to put this into words. "Since then, I've been able to freely express my love for you knowing you will keep our friendship on the right track. Now, instead of hiding part of who I am from you, you are my ally who helps me navigate the mysteries of my heart. That freedom means more to me than I can express."

They had reached the top of the lift, and after getting off, they stood next to each other without saying a word. Thomas had his arm wrapped tightly around her shoulders as they looked over the vast mountain range, and Sophie knew deep down he was God's gift of a father to her.

It was almost dark when they finally called it a day and started the descent to their cabin. After dinner, everybody decided to go play a few rounds of billiards and relax. Before Sophie could agree to join them, though, a strange heaviness swept over her. She couldn't get herself to go with them, although she wished to.

Something was wrong with her, and she couldn't figure out what. *Why on earth can't I just enjoy myself on this perfect trip?* Frustrated, she mumbled something about being tired from the day outside and excused herself. She went back to the cabin, threw herself onto her bed, and tried to sleep. She had found such freedom in her relationship with Thomas. Why couldn't she let go of Nathan in the same way? Was it even still him who made her feel so alone, or was it something else she couldn't understand? Confused and upset, she finally fell asleep exhausted, not knowing that in the cabin's adjacent room, Thomas had been sitting quietly in his chair for almost as long as she had been home. He had left the others shortly after her, and coming back and hearing quiet sobs from her room, had gone to his room and had a conversation with God about Sophie that lasted until long after she fell asleep.

Chapter Twenty-Four

Hiking Pikes Peak had a bigger impact on Justin than he could have imagined. For one, there were his physical problems. The pain in his side came back regularly in the days following their adventure, especially when Justin exerted himself in any way. Several times he was on the verge of calling a doctor, but before he could do so, he recalled Jonathan's words: *If you believe God can't heal you, He can't. If you believe He can, He will. Either way you'll be proven right!* Justin did not want to be in the way of God's power moving in his life, so he put down the phone and turned on worship music instead.

But something else nagged him, something that went deeper. It had to do with Bjørn. The day after the hike, Justin missed classes for the first time since joining the Rock. He found it impossible to face Bjørn after what had been the last words between them. The night of the hike, when he was finally alone in his room, Justin had tried to put the blame on his friend. *That's what happens when you doubt God's Word. You'll turn on your own friends!* He had sought peace through prayer and Bible reading, which kept him up halfway through the night. But the restlessness wouldn't go away. The truth was that Bjørn had been compassionate and helpful, while Justin had been proud and hurtful. He knew this intuitively, and it scared him to realize that Bjørn had shown more of Jesus's character than he had—and yet Justin had done exactly what he felt the Bible taught. Bjørn was critical and full of doubts, while Justin had offered up his life fully to God, without reservations or second thoughts. He was clearly following the way of the Lord. Yet why did he have this nagging thought that it was Bjørn who had acted like Jesus and not him?

Justin had never been one to avoid confrontation or choose the easy road. When he finally fell asleep way past midnight the following night, it was only after he had promised God he would be completely honest with his friend and listen to his side and get to the bottom of this tomorrow. Attack was the only way Justin Friedman knew how to deal with a problem.

When school was out the next day, he waited outside the front door for Bjørn. He came out with a few friends, but when he saw Justin, he immediately split from the group and walked toward him. His face showed genuine concern and relief at the same time. "Justin! Man, I'm glad to see you! I was super worried yesterday when you didn't show up for classes."

Justin didn't expect this at all. *How does he not even hold grudges about our conversation?*

"I misplaced my phone yesterday so I couldn't even text you . . . Are you feeling alright? Is the pain in the side gone?"

Justin had gotten so used to living in a world of spiritual answers and doctrine that he never considered Bjørn could worry about his physical well-being. The teachings at the Rock were about the principle, not the individual person. After all, these doctrines were true for everybody at all times, so the focus on a single person with their particular situation only distracted from understanding and applying a truth that was universal. That's what they had learned, and Justin had lived by it faithfully. Bjørn's concern caught him off guard.

His friend looked at him hard. "What is it?" he asked curiously. He seemed to be aware that something was bothering the usually cool American. For a moment, Justin battled the temptation to back away from the promise he had given God the night before. Then he pulled himself together and said, "Ehm . . . do you want to grab some lunch? I'd like to talk to you about the hike." He said it lightly, but his face betrayed his seriousness.

"Sure, I'd love to. You pick a place, it's on me!"

They hopped into Bjørn's old pickup truck and drove the short distance to Souper Salad, an inexpensive buffet always full of Bible school students. Justin picked a booth away from the crowds to give them more privacy. "I've been thinking a lot about your last words the night of the hike," he said and was surprised to see Bjørn turning red.

"Oh, I'm so sorry about what I said at the end. That was mean and unnecessary. Please forgive me."

It took Justin a moment to digest this. "Oh, it's ok . . . I actually like how honest you are. You think differently. And you have a lot of guts to speak up for what you think is right. I have always appreciated people like that. I guess I just don't see how you can trust God fully if you question so many things and handle situations the same way the world would."

Now it was Bjørn's turn to be surprised. "But I don't think I handled that situation the way the world would," he said without any defensiveness in his voice. "I believe it was God's protection that kept something more serious from happening to you on that mountain. And I believe He gave us reason so we could figure out what to do if we see signs in our bodies. And I believe our prayers on that mountain were answered, and God was helping you right then and there."

"But you don't believe Jesus gave us the authority to heal and speak to our bodies ourselves," Justin concluded with sadness in his voice. He had not realized how big the gap between their belief systems was.

Bjørn studied his face intensely. "I know what Jonathan is teaching, Justin. And I see the power of this kind of doctrine. It's positive and fascinating. And I believe that sometimes people do see healing through this kind of prayer. But I see other things that come with this belief system too." He looked at Justin to see if he was still listening. "There seems to be an awful lot of judging associated with it." He shook his head. "Shouldn't we be the ones who judge the least, as Jesus instructed us?"

Justin lowered his head but was still listening. Bjørn's voice was gentle, yet it revealed his hurt. "What are you afraid of, Justin? How is it possible that somebody's attempt at helping you would threaten you so much?"

"Because I believe there's no room for doubt if you want to change the world!" The words exploded out of Justin. "I have given up everything to follow Him. I don't care what the world thinks. I don't care what's sensible or logical. I have made a decision, and I will never go back on it. I thought you had done the same . . . but either way, I will follow my Savior no matter the costs or the ridicule or the persecution."

There, he had said it. Sometimes it was necessary for him to remind himself that his life was not ordinary and that he could not expect anybody to understand it, not even Bjørn. But his words didn't have the effect on Bjørn that he expected them to have. He ignored the dramatic parts and went right back to Justin's first sentence.

"There's no room for doubt if you want to change the world? Do you really believe that?" Bjørn looked incredulous. "Don't you think it was mostly people who doubted the status quo and the established rules of their time who changed the world?"

Justin didn't want to go there. He didn't understand why Bjørn would question something as basic as a commitment to faith. "Have you not listened to Jonathan? His testimonies of miracles and healings and salvations? Do you think he's lying?"

"No, Justin. As I said, I believe that God wants to help people, and I believe He is doing it all the time. What I don't believe is that our prayers or our faith control Him in any way."

"Well, of course not! That's not what Jonathan is saying!"

Justin was upset now. He felt as if Bjørn had turned into an enemy. "He just knows the danger of the enemy who wants our thoughts constantly distracted by doubts and reasonings, limited by our own understanding. What I want is the faith that goes beyond understanding. That's the faith that moves mountains!" Justin halfway expected somebody to say "Amen!" as so often happened when he spoke confidently to his fellow students. But Bjørn was unimpressed.

He replied in a quiet voice that marked a contrast to Justin's way of speaking. "I understand what Jonathan is trying to say. Once we find something of incredible value, we will try and protect it, no matter the cost. That's why you feel threatened by me right now. But please believe that Jesus is important to me too. More important than anything else. And I'm not trying to take anything from you or Jonathan. But I believe God does not need to be protected.

"Think of it, Justin. When we are protective, it's easy to get defensive. Sometimes we even get hostile toward people we perceive to be a threat. But these are not at all the traits of a Jesus follower, right? Jesus loved people and went toward them, embracing them with all their doubts. He was so secure that there were no barriers. That's how I want to live." He looked fully into Justin's eyes. "God is not fragile. He can handle any questioning you can come up with, and He can handle other people's doubts just as much. You might lose some beliefs, some traditions or assumptions, but you don't ever have to fear losing God or your faith over questions."

Chapter Twenty-Five

On their second day in Monarch, Sophie was unusually quiet. Daniel seemed to notice and tried to cheer her up during breakfast by telling funny stories, and Sophie appreciated the distraction.

She was again surprised at the beauty with which this group did life together. There was a gentleness and care, but it wasn't in a somber and heavy setting. It came wrapped in fun and lightheartedness. They were definitely the kind of people Sophie wanted to hang out with more. She joked around with Daniel and secretly hoped that it would be enough to at least mask the sadness if she couldn't overcome it.

Their second day was as sunny as the first, and they set out on the slopes while the day was still young. Being surrounded by this breathtaking beauty definitively helped lift Sophie's mood. Toward noon they crossed over to a new section of the resort with an extra-long chair lift that would bring them all the way to the very top of Monarch Mountain. Sophie actually tried to avoid sitting with Thomas this time, because she knew what was going to happen. But he knew too. And he made sure they got on the lift together.

"It's time to talk," he said simply when the bars had closed and their lift took off. His voice had the gentle urgency she had come to recognize. "I don't think I can bear seeing you carrying this load another minute. Please"—he looked into her eyes—"share it with me."

Sophie sighed. "I'm so confused. There are all these emotions, and I have no idea how to sort them out. Sometimes I still feel like I'm mourning for Nathan. But then I wonder if I'm just using him as an excuse for a sadness that I can't explain." She hesitated a moment and then decided to tell him. "When we drove into Colorado and got out of the car the first time, and I smelled the pines and felt the air and saw this incredible beauty . . . it made me tear up. It was all so good, but I felt sad at the same time. This has happened to me before—when I see or hear something too wonderful for words, I feel this incredible longing inside of me, brought out by the beauty I see. But I don't even get what I'm longing for."

Before answering, Thomas took his gloves off and gently wiped the tears from her cheek. It was a simple, beautiful gesture. They sat in silence for a while, then Thomas looked directly at her. "There are a few things I have not told you about my past yet, Sophie, and therefore it might be hard for you to believe what I'm going to say next. But I can tell you with confidence that I fully understand your grief about Nathan. I have experienced unspeakable loss myself, and I know that some people never overcome losing someone they loved deeply." He looked into the distance for a moment, but then addressed her again.

"But I'm confident that it will be different for you. In fact, I have already seen you moving beyond that point. You are choosing life, although the loss still hurts. You are young, beautiful, incredibly smart, and sensitive. There's no chance the right guy won't see that!" He smiled again, playfully. "I believe God will bring a wonderful man into your life one day. But I also think you're right in wondering whether Nathan wasn't the only reason for your sadness and your longing. There is something else. When you talked about the longing you feel while experiencing beauty in nature or music or, most of all, people, you're actually proving a spiritual principle."

Sophie raised her brows but waited for him to continue.

"You might agree there are experiences that seem too big for this world. Too beautiful, too moving, too captivating. It is expressed in sayings like 'There are just no words for this.' But it's more than a language problem. There is a longing in our soul that cannot be satisfied by anything or even anyone on this earth. Do you know what I mean?"

Sophie nodded.

"So, I assure you, there's nothing wrong with you; in fact, most people share this condition to some degree. Of course, many bury it because it can be confusing, and you can easily write it off as overboard emotions. But those who have learned to listen to their own hearts will recognize it."

He had Sophie's full attention now. "C.S. Lewis made a remarkable statement about this very condition. He said, 'If I find in myself desires which nothing in this world can satisfy, the only logical explanation is that I was made for another world.' That's pretty profound, don't you think?"

They sat in silence for a while. Sophie looked over the pines into the snow-capped mountaintops stretching far across any direction she was looking. She knew where he was going with this. She had recently read in the Bible about being in this world, but not of it. And she remembered the group talking about the Christian belief that a person's spirit was God-breathed and therefore didn't just belong to this earth. Could this be the reason she sometimes felt like she didn't belong either, even among friends? Why the beauty of Colorado made her cry? And why listening to Beethoven sent goosebumps down her spine?

Thomas confirmed her thoughts. "It's an experience shared by most humans but expressed most accurately by artists, poets, and writers. There is more to this world than meets the eye. More wonder, more beauty, more unexplainable things like compassion, grace, and love. We can try to measure our world, understand it, and explain it. And that's necessary for us to live productive and safe lives. But it's not enough. I love what Helen Keller said: 'The best and most beautiful things cannot be seen or even touched. They must be felt with the heart.' The same goes with truth. We can prove a great many things with our intellects, and we should, as it helps us understand the physical world around us, but at the end of the day we are faced with a longing in our heart that goes beyond all of it. It's a yearning essential to the human condition—a splendid, grand longing that seems to belong more to the whole universe than only to our earth. It is bursting with life, and its tears are those of someone overwhelmed by the realization of it. We are experiencing a glimpse of God's reality brushing our mortality. We are reminded that this physical life is more like a prequel than the real deal. An important, wonderful prequel, but one not even coming close to what's coming after it."

Sophie was silent. The only way Thomas was able to articulate something like this was because he was experiencing it. He was convinced about what he believed with a happy, quiet certainty. And she knew that all of it was true, because it spoke to the part of her that was most real and most important. When she had first befriended Thomas, she had felt it, although she would not have been able to put it into words then. He was connected to something that made him deeply happy, and he invited her to share that same happiness. In fact, she had been invited all her life. But today she chose to say yes.

They had reached the top of the mountain. Sophie couldn't talk. They got off the lift, and she moved to the side a little to be away from the other skiers. The view from up here was breathtaking. Sophie thought she was going to burst. Her heart opened, and she invited this life into her. She invited this world that was so much bigger than her, and this person who, she knew, was the only one able to satisfy the yearning of her soul.

A little while later, Sophie gave Thomas a long hug. She knew he understood without words and was able to share her joy. And she knew something fundamental had shifted in her life.

She was never going to be the same again.

Chapter Twenty-Six

Justin sipped on his Americano at the small table at Starbucks as he waited for Bjørn. The day before, he had excused himself after his friend had said that God didn't need to be protected. It had all been too much, and he'd asked if they could continue the conversation the next day before school.

Bjørn's way of speaking made more sense than he wanted to admit. And yet, he knew that the devil spoke eloquently and reasonably and could speak through nice and friendly people like Bjørn. The fact was that wide was the gate that led to destruction, but narrow the path that led to life. In this, the Bible was very clear. Justin sat at the coffee shop, anticipating the upcoming conversation as much as dreading it and wondering if it would mark the end of their friendship.

"I'm glad we get another chance to talk before spring break," Bjørn said after ordering his drink and joining Justin at their table. "I'm sorry if what I said yesterday upset you. I hope you know that wasn't my intention."

He had done so much thinking and battling with himself in the past days, Justin actually felt tired. So he decided to jump right into it. "I just want to know why you are still at the Rock if you don't believe half of what's taught there." For once, there wasn't any fire in his question, more a hint of resignation.

"Because there is a lot of good here, Justin. I'm actually not trying to paint a black-and-white picture. There are wonderful people at this school, you being one of them. There is devotion and a great love for God among the students and staff. And I'm not excluding Jonathan. He is one of the most generous people I have ever met. And he is not in this for himself. He doesn't seem to be trying to build his own empire like many preachers. I believe he truly and deeply loves God." Bjørn's voice turned somber. "But that doesn't mean that everything he preaches is life-giving. It doesn't keep him from becoming narrow, judgemental, and hurtful, even if he never intends to. I think it's an automatic by-product of religion. It's what happens if we, even subconsciously, become more focused on principles than on people."

He searched Justin's eyes. "I'm sorry this is so hard for you, Justin. I know how much of what I'm saying goes exactly against the things we hear every day. And honestly, it means a lot to me that you're even listening. But I believe the reason you *are* listening is that God has given you a hunger that goes deeper than any doctrine can. I think He has put in you the hunger to search for yourself and to become rooted in what God Himself teaches you. And I'd love to be your friend in the process."

Justin looked up, surprised. Had Bjørn felt his inclination to withdraw? To Justin, ending their friendship only seemed logical after hearing how differently they thought about things that mattered to both of them. But apparently, Bjørn saw it all in a different light. And regardless of their theological differences, Justin had to admit he liked Bjørn a lot, for all the right reasons. Yes, he felt threatened, just as Bjørn had said. Threatened that this nice, honest guy might have the power to take away Justin's faith. And at the same time, he wondered if another person *could* steal his faith. *Shouldn't I be secure enough in what I believe that nothing Bjørn says can shake it?*

He had to admit, there were moments he wished he had never met Bjørn. His faith had seemed easier before they met. The Rock was like a cocoon, a perfect environment shielded from the outside world of doubts, different opinions, and shades of gray. Most students seemed to follow an unwritten agreement not to burst that bubble. Not so with Bjørn. The problem was, had he done it in a rebellious, worldly fashion, it would have been easy to write him off as an unbeliever who was being controlled by the devil. But Justin had seen enough love and devotion for Jesus in Bjørn's life that he could not question his sincerity. He was at the same time one of them and yet questioning the very thing the Rock and its teachings stood for. It was all so confusing.

He changed the subject and was glad Bjørn didn't press further. They talked about the upcoming break that Bjørn was going to spend with his brother visiting from Norway, while Justin would join some friends on a snowboarding trip. When they finished their coffee and Bjørn left for class, Justin sat in his car for a long time, looking out the window at Pikes Peak in the distance and asking Jesus to sort out the tangled mess his heart and mind had gotten into.

The following week was a busy time at school. After the upcoming spring break, it was only one more month before graduation, a thought that filled Justin with excitement. As much as he loved school, he couldn't wait to go out there and bring the Good News to people. He wanted to become a missionary, as he couldn't think of a more adventurous, daring way to show his dedication to his faith. He was sure of neither where he was to go nor any of the details, but he trusted God to give him the answers he needed in time. Right now, he was ready for the break. Hopefully, snowboarding in the awesome Rocky Mountains would help alleviate the tension the conversations with Bjørn had produced in his heart.

It was a happy band of young men and women that hit the road that Saturday. First, Justin had protested against bringing girls on the trip. Of course they were going to rent two separate apartments, and of course they were not going to be alone with a girl overnight. Those were the rules everybody had agreed to when joining the Rock. It was more that Justin felt safer around guys. Girls could potentially bring out the worst in a guy trying to be godly. It was surely safer to keep a distance from them. On the other hand, Justin didn't want to be the bore of the group, so he agreed to letting some of the girls who hung out with his group join in. It was obvious that, had he said no, they would not be on the trip. Justin's personality made him the natural, unassigned leader almost everywhere he went.

It was only a three-hour drive to their favorite ski area, and since they had started early in the morning, they were on the slopes before noon. Justin wore his snowboarding gear and the bright blue scarf his dad had given him when he moved to Colorado.

Being surrounded by the beautiful scenery of the Rocky Mountains had an immediate, relaxing effect on Justin. He was laughing again and decided to leave theology behind for a few days and just have fun. Growing up in Atlanta, he was not an experienced snowboarder, but he was athletic and caught on quickly. He was soon trying out some tricks a friend showed him and was having the time of his life.

On his next ride on the lift, he noticed a woman with a red hat skiing below him. Justin first thought she had lost her balance and was about to fall, but then he watched with fascination how she turned herself on purpose so her skis were facing up the hill for a moment, then, using her arms as rotators, she flung her body around and completed a 360-degree turn on her skis. She had created an almost perfect circle in the snow and was repeating the pirouette several times in a row before coming to a halt. Justin had never seen anything like it. He stared at her intently, and right at that moment, she happened to glance up and notice him admiring her. They were quite a distance from each other, and he couldn't make out any facial expression. But before she took off down the hill, he saw her turn around and look at him again before disappearing in graceful swings behind a hill.

Justin had a wonderful day in the snow. He loved the feel of adventure and was definitely not a cautious snowboarder. He had always acquired new sports easily, and his year in Colorado had added to his fitness, as well as his confidence level. He flew down the powder-coated slopes and soon was happily distracted from disturbing thoughts about doubting friends.

It was past two o'clock when they decided it was time for a break. They found a nice-looking restaurant called the Lodge and filed in, looking forward to sitting close to the cozy fireplace that warmed the room. Justin threw his gear carelessly on the ledge between his booth and the next. His blue scarf fell back down, so he picked it up and placed it more carefully next to the gear already there from people in the adjacent booth.

That's when he noticed the red hat. It was unmistakable because of a big white cross that made it look like a medic's hat. The hat of the ski ballet girl! She sat with her back to him and was engaged in a conversation with an older man.

Justin hesitated. Before becoming a Christian, he had been quite confident around girls. But in the past year he had stayed away from them, and if he had found himself in a conversation with a girl, it had always been within the confines of Bible school. Striking up a conversation with the ballet girl was therefore not his first thought. But something in him really wanted to pay her a compliment. Was it because, even with her back to him, he could tell she was attractive? Suddenly, as if she had felt him staring at her back, she turned around. Justin turned his eyes away, but she was just getting something from her jacket behind her and didn't notice him.

But, oh, did he notice her! There was something about her face. It was almost aglow. Was it from the warmth of the fireplace? But it was in her eyes too. It looked like something wonderful had happened to her, and it had spread over her whole person. Justin was so intrigued that he found himself sitting in his booth trying to figure out how to say something to this girl amidst all these people. He studied the menu to distract himself when the people in her booth got up. Thankfully they were not leaving but just getting in line for food. Justin reacted immediately.

"Guys, I'm super hungry! Gonna get in line for some lunch." He jumped up from his booth and made his way over to where the girl stood at the dessert line. He could come up with an explanation should any of his friends ask why he decided to start his lunch with dessert. He got in line right behind her.

It took almost a minute for him to find enough courage to touch her shoulder.

Chapter Twenty-Seven

"Those were quite some tricks earlier."

Sophie spun around in surprise and looked into a pair of hazel eyes.

"Sorry to startle you. But I couldn't help but admire your ski ballet on the slope a while ago," the man behind her said.

Sophie turned red. She was not used to talking to strangers as the Swiss were a rather reserved culture. The friendliness of this young man helped overcome the initial unease a bit, but she was definitely guarded. "You're very observant! But playing around on skies is quite common where I'm from, so I don't think I deserve your compliment."

"I insist on my compliment!" He smiled, and Sophie noticed how intense his eyes were. "May I ask where that place is where everyone dances down the slopes?"

Sophie laughed. "I'm from Switzerland. And I guess not everyone skis, but they're very likely to be skilled at something to do with snow—even if it's just building snowmen."

He looked like he was about to reply when it was her turn at the counter. She picked a strawberry tart and a latte and paid while her drink was being prepared. What was that silly flutter in her stomach?

"Well, have fun on the slopes. It's a beautiful day," she said over her shoulder as she took her tray back to her booth. She noticed Thomas was not sitting there anymore and neither was Daniel. Somebody in the group told her they had gone outside to tighten a screw on Daniel's binding that had gotten loose.

Since the experience on the ski lift yesterday, Sophie felt like she was in a dream, and she couldn't wait for a good opportunity to tell the others what had happened to her. The night before, she had needed to be by herself and explore the new dimension her heart was experiencing, so she hadn't told anybody. Maybe later today would be the time.

She had just taken a bite of her dessert when she suddenly noticed the hazel-eyed man looking at her from across the booth next to hers. She turned red again. Only now did she realize that it was her red hat on the ledge between their booths that he had recognized her by, and that his bright blue scarf was now sitting right next to her hat.

"Enjoying that tart?" he asked.

She nodded and quickly surveyed the group he was with. Most of them were young men in snowboard outfits, but a couple of girls sat with them as well. She internally rolled her eyes at herself. *What does it matter who he's with*? In fact, what did it matter who he was? Trying to ignore him, she dedicated herself to her treat again. He started talking to the people in his group, but she couldn't help noticing that his eyes searched hers several times while they sat near each other. If she were being honest, the flutter in her stomach had not stopped either.

When she eventually got up and put her gear back on, she decided to look in his direction one more time before leaving her booth. He was looking straight at her, his eyes intense and deep. His posture and movements underlined what she saw in his eyes: He was . . . *fully present.* And it was this presence and intensity about the stranger that unsettled her. When she left a while later with her oblivious friends, his look followed her all the way out the restaurant.

Sophie joined Thomas and Daniel, who had been able to

fix his bindings, and headed back out to the slopes. She didn't mention the hazel-eyed guy to Thomas, as their conversations for the next hours were filled with the joy surrounding the decision Sophie had made in her heart the day before.

The shadows were beginning to stretch out longer when Thomas and a few others from their group called it a day. But Sophie wasn't done yet. She begged for them to go to the Lodge for a hot chocolate and wait there so she could use the last rays of sunshine and an almost empty slope for a few tricks she had taught herself as a teenager. She didn't want this day to stop. They agreed and set a time to meet back at the Lodge as Sophie set off alone, feeling a rush of adrenaline as she hit the almost-deserted slope. She practiced going downhill backward, a skill her dad had taught her as a child. The joy of her newfound love for God was so intense she had to let it out. "Whoo-hoo!" she shouted as the evening sun dipped the mountaintops in a golden light and as her heart thanked God for the peace and hope filling it.

She was so lost in thought that she didn't pay close attention to where she was going. She rounded a corner when she suddenly saw she was on the wrong slope. This one would bring her to a lift that was now closed. But keeping to her left would eventually get her back to the main slope for the Lodge if she just crossed the little wooded area that separated the two slopes. It included some off-slope skiing, but Sophie was used to that. Setting off into a little set of pines, curving gracefully around the trunks and avoiding the boulders sticking out among them, she already saw the main slope about a hundred feet ahead of her when she suddenly heard a loud crack, and a searing pain shot up her left leg. She landed in the soft snow and couldn't move.

After the initial shock, she tried to open her binding, but since this required a fair amount of pressure and weight, her seated position made this impossible. She tried until she was drenched with sweat and out of breath and had to lean back for a break. For some reason, she was neither able to free her foot from her shoe, nor her ski from the snow. Thankfully, the pain was decreasing slightly, reassuring her that the loud crack she'd heard hadn't been her leg breaking. However, something had definitely bruised it really badly and made the thought of getting back to the Lodge a daunting, if not impossible, task. Right now she wasn't even able to get up.

The sun was just setting behind one of the peaks. Although the snowplows would start to clean up every slope as soon as the lifts stopped, they wouldn't see her stuck in the little woods between two slopes. It might take several hours for a search-and-rescue team to find her here, and the temperatures in the Rockies easily dropped below zero at night.

The crisp, bright Colorado sky brimmed with thousands of stars. Despite her worry, she was in awe of the beauty above her. A Bible verse came to her mind: "He counts the stars and calls them all by name."

If God really knows each individual star, surely, He also knows I'm lying in the snow on a Colorado mountainside. She decided to try a prayer. "God, I'm pretty scared. I believe you can see me, and I think I just realized yesterday that you actually care about me. I could use some help right now."

Not knowing what to expect, she kept trying to free her leg. Her right leg was under her left, making it harder to free either of them. After many frustrating attempts, she suddenly heard the sound of someone yelling from a distance. Hope mobilizing her energy, she yelled as loud as she could. "Help! Over here! I'm stuck!"

She waited for an answer. *Did they not hear me? I shouldn't be imagining voices yet, should I?* That thought made her laugh despite the cold and the worry. "Can you hear me? I could really use some help!" she called again, and this time she didn't have to wait long.

"Where are you? I can't see you, but I hear you!" somebody shouted not far from her.

Sophie had an idea. She took her red hat off, stuck it on her pole, and held the pole up in the air as far as she could reach. A minute later, a person appeared over the edge of the little ravine where she sat. Sophie was so relieved, she dropped the pole and buried her head in her hands. It had gotten dark, and she couldn't see who had come to rescue her, but she didn't care. Her prayer had been answered! It was hard thinking about anything else.

Whoever it was snapped out of their skis or board below her and approached from behind. Then something warm was draped around her shoulders. She recognized it in the failing light, her heart skipping a beat.

It was a bright blue scarf.

Chapter Twenty-Eight

"Are you hurt?"

"I think I'm fine. My leg hurts, but it's not too bad. But I can't get up. My ski got stuck, and I can't get out of the binding." She looked up at her rescuer, and as he came closer, she wondered how it was possible.

He gently pulled the leg of her ski pants up and examined her shin. It was bruised but otherwise seemed unharmed. When his hand touched her leg, it sent goosebumps up her whole body. He then leaned all his weight onto the binding until it snapped open and her leg was free. She let out a sigh of relief, opened her boot, and rubbed her leg to get the circulation going. Meanwhile, the blue-scarved man tried to pull out the ski, digging away the snow around it until he found the problem.

"Your ski got caught under this root here and probably snapped in half when it got stopped. The root is what bruised your leg. You're lucky you didn't break it."

As Sophie's shock wore off, embarrassment kicked in. *He must be thinking I'm out of my mind to go off-slope after dark.* But she saw only relief in his eyes as he helped her get up and collect the gear that she had lost in the fall. They decided to leave the broken ski since it was beyond repair. It was going to be challenging enough to get back without extra gear to carry.

Walking back took longer than they liked. There was no cell phone reception for either of them, so they were anxious to get to the Lodge to avoid people starting to look for them.

"I think if I can hold on to you with my left arm for balance, I can ski with the right leg and hold the left up. Does that work with your snowboard?"

"We're about to find out!" He grinned and helped her get stable on her right ski.

Their descent from the mountain was far from graceful. Sophie had to lean heavily on him to keep her balance, and he in turn had to lean in so he wouldn't fall backward. They went slowly, but still with much more speed than if they had to walk through the soft snow. Although the lifts had closed about twenty minutes earlier, they had not seen any snowplows yet. After a while they sat down to catch their breath.

"Well, what an unlikely way to meet again!" he said, amused.

"Yes, you owe me the whole story—how on earth did you find me? And what were you doing out there anyway?"

She tried to sound scolding, but the relief in her voice betrayed her. When she looked at him, she had to laugh. She had definitely caught him off guard.

"Well, I was still out there enjoying the empty slopes like you, I guess. I saw you racing by and I . . . I happened to stay close."

"You were following me?" Sophie couldn't decide whether to be flattered or alarmed.

"Well, sort of, yeah. I loved watching you do your ballet and your acrobatics, and I thought I might learn something from you!" His face looked so innocent, the butterflies did their dance in her belly again.

"Well, I guess whatever your intentions, thank you for getting me out of here. By the way, my name is Sophie."

"I thought you'd never tell me. I'm Justin. Nice to meet you, Sophie."

When they reached the Lodge, it had turned completely dark. Cheers broke out when they walked in. Sandra threw herself around Sophie's neck, and several of Justin's friends showed their relief upon seeing him. A search team had been sent out only fifteen minutes earlier, and the manager of the Lodge was already contacting them to call it off.

"Where is Thomas?" Sophie asked Daniel.

"He insisted they let him join the search team. Normally they don't let guests go with them, but he wouldn't take no for an answer. He was going to find you, with or without a team."

Sophie and Justin sat down exhausted and started explaining to their friends what had happened. But Justin's group was also urging him to pack up his stuff. They had plans for a movie night and had already given up dinner to wait for him. Now that everyone was safe, they wanted to move on. Sophie could tell Justin was not particularly happy with their decision to leave. When he couldn't come up with an excuse to stay any longer, he searched through his stuff for a pen and paper.

"Looks like I gotta go. In case you ever need someone to help you get off a mountain again . . . let me know!" He grinned and gave her the piece of paper with his email and phone number on it.

"I appreciate it. No more mountain rescues for me, though, thank you!"

He smiled and they looked at each other. The blood pulsed in Sophie's temples, just as it had when she was leaning on him on the way down the mountain and feeling his breath next to hers. She felt it still as she watched him walk out with his friends into the freezing night.

A few minutes later, Thomas came into the Lodge, folded Sophie into an embrace, and held her tight for a long time, saying nothing. Then he put on a stern face. "Somebody should give you a little speech, my friend. I can't remember the last time I was that scared."

Sophie felt bad and put on her most remorseful face possible, but she couldn't help thinking that she wasn't particularly unhappy the incident had happened, especially considering the piece of paper in her pocket.

Chapter Twenty-Nine

Sophie's group stayed at the Lodge long after Justin and his friends had left. Thomas asked the manager for some blankets and hot tea, helped her to a chair next to the fire, and sat down beside her.

"Are you sure you're ok? Do you want me to bring you to the hospital?"

The concern in his voice only increased her guilt. "I'm so sorry I put you through all of this. I went down the wrong slope and was trying to find my way back by cutting through fresh snow when I got stuck under a root. It broke my ski, but it could have easily broken my leg as well. I'll definitely not repeat that ever again." She looked at him so contritely, she finally got him to laugh.

"Let's just say I'm happy you are back and unharmed. Now let's get you home!"

Back at the cabin, Sophie took a long, hot shower, and Daniel and Thomas cooked a very late dinner. The others were already busy packing, as everybody except Sophie was going to catch a plane back to Switzerland the next day.

"Are you sure you will be ok with your leg? The drive to

Montana is very long. Maybe we should look into some last-minute flights?" Thomas, always watching out for Sophie, asked during dinner.

"Don't worry. I'll be totally fine on the trip." After all that had happened in the past few days, she was actually looking forward to a couple of days all by herself to process everything. After saying goodnight to the others, she went to her room, pulled out her computer, and walked over to where she had rid herself of her ski gear to jump into the shower. Her hand searched through the pocket of her ski pants. She was just going to thank Justin. Nothing elaborate, no more than a few lines of small talk.

When she pulled the piece of paper out, her heart skipped a beat. Her pants were still soaked from the snow she'd been sitting in when she fell. She hadn't given it any thought when she put away Justin's note. But looking at it now, her heart sank. He had written with an ink roller, and the letters and numbers had bled hopelessly into each other. She could make out three of the ten phone numbers, and nothing but the very beginning of his email. It didn't help her, because *Justin* was the one part she knew anyway.

She was more upset than she wanted to admit. Not writing a word of thanks after Justin had rescued her would be just ungrateful. For a while, this worked as an excuse, but finally she admitted to herself that she had really looked forward to staying in touch with him. It seemed like an unfair irony that something as trivial as wet pants would keep her from ever seeing him again.

Should she stay a few extra days in Monarch and look for Justin on the slopes? But the dull pain radiating from her leg reminded her that she would definitely not be on a slope in the next couple of days. She would have to let it go.

When she turned back to her computer, her glance fell on an email that had just come in. It was from her aunt in Montana.

My Dear Sophie,

I'm so sorry to have to tell you this at such last-minute notice, but I don't think it will work out for you to come visit right now. Your uncle had a minor stroke yesterday. They're saying he'll be alright, but there will be tons of tests, doctors visits, and hours in the waiting room. I don't think it will be any fun for you, and frankly, it will be too much for me too. I need to concentrate fully on Sam's recovery now. I'm so sorry this happened right now. I sincerely hope you'll be able to visit us another time and that you will come up with a fun idea of how to spend the rest of your time here in the USA.

Love,
Aunt Sybille

An accident, losing Justin's number, and now my uncle. Is it enough for today? Crawling under her sheets, Sophie started to feel sorry for herself but then decided that prayer seemed like a good idea, mostly because no other ideas presented themselves. She asked God to help her decide whether or not to reschedule her flight and try to go home as soon as a flight became available.

After being quiet for a while, she realized that being in this country had, if anything, increased her desire for adventure and exploration. She decided she would find somewhere to go, something to see. It might not be as much fun to do it by herself instead of with friends, but she would make it work. Too wound up to sleep, she put her clothes back on and went down to the kitchen to see if anybody was still up. She found Daniel there, packing up his last few belongings. Sophie made herself some tea.

"How's your leg?" Daniel asked.

"It's alright. I'm glad this happened on our last day because I won't be doing any acrobatics for a while."

"Well, I'm sure glad that guy found you out there!" Daniel grinned. Then he added, "Seemed like a nice group he was with. We chatted while we were waiting for you two adventurers."

A new idea popped into Sophie's head. "Really? I wonder where they're from?"

"They were actually a group of Bible school students from Colorado Springs. Pretty cool, huh?"

Sophie's heart was beating so hard she was wondering if Daniel could hear it. Justin was a Christian! Learning that Justin believed the same thing that had become so important to her made her feel even more connected to him.

She thought for a moment on how to proceed. "Actually, I was going to thank him, but the note he gave me with his email was destroyed in my wet pants. If I could look him up online, I could still thank him . . . do you happen to know what the name of the Bible school was?"

"They didn't mention that, but one guy talked about the founder of their school who seems to be their hero. Let me think. Yes, Parker was the guy's name."

"Great, so I can probably find the school and send them a thank you note to pass on to him," she said as casually as she could manage. Back in her room, she googled "Parker Colorado Springs Bible college." The top search result brought her to the website of Mountain Rock Bible College.

Sophie was not prepared for what she read there. She expected a Bible college to be some form of theological seminary focusing on Greek and Hebrew, as well as studies of biblical history. What she read on the website of the Rock was nothing like it. The college was talking about experiencing the healing power of God, the moving of the Holy Spirit with supernatural manifestations, worship meetings, prayer events, and classes on your authority as a believer in Jesus. She had never heard of anything like that and was fascinated and bewildered at the same time. She sat at her computer way past midnight, reading about all of Jonathan Parker's events, the doctrine, and the impressive ministry headquarters in

Colorado Springs. By the time she closed her eyes, she had an idea. It was crazy, even for her, but she knew exactly what she was going to do with the two weeks that had freed up ahead of her.

Chapter Thirty

The sound of the clanging bars unraveled him every time, before he even made it to the mess hall or saw a single person. Not once in the past six months, since James McLeod had joined Eli's prison ministry team, had he been able to hear the sounds and smell the odors of prison without internally falling apart. Why he ever agreed to this program, God only knew.

The prisoners started filing in, their feet shuffling and most gazes on the ground. An air of defeat surrounded them, something he had noticed not only during his ministry time at Phillips State Prison but every time he visited Ronnie. It was as if the huge prison machinery was sucking the life out of the inmates like a relentless, cruel vacuum cleaner. Sometimes, the group's efforts in restoring some dignity, hope, and even joy into the prisoners' lives during their short visit felt like one drop of water in an endless desert.

Eli opened with a simple prayer, then took his time to look at each of the men. Finally, his eyes rested on James, who sat next to him. "Today, instead of going around and listening to and praying for each other, I'd like you to hear the story of my friend James, who has been coming with me for several months now."

James's body stiffened.

"Most of you don't know this, but James's brother is at Long State Prison, serving what turned into a six-year sentence for a silly prank that went south." Eli looked at James, and his eyes were gentle. "Every time he comes here with me is a terrible reminder of his brother's fate. And yet, he keeps coming. I think there's a reason for that." Eli now had the attention of most of the group. "But I will not tell you what it is. He will."

For a moment, anger rose in James. *How dare you put me on the spot like that?* But turning toward Eli, he saw such compassion in his friend's eyes, his anger dissipated immediately. Closing his eyes for a moment, he thought about what Eli had said. It was true, he seemed to be drawn back here every time by some inexplicable force. And in that moment, he knew the reason. He breathed out slowly and looked around the room.

"Eli is right—it isn't easy for me to come here and meet with you all. But the reminder of my brother's imprisonment is only one reason. The other is that although I've been trying to see differently, I'm still full of prejudices toward people with a criminal record. You see, I'm a police officer."

The statement was met with several murmurs and a few expletives. His heart beating faster, he continued. "I think my brother's imprisonment has helped me question the neat boxes I used to put people into. Knowing that my kid brother is now one of you, I realize how little I know of the stories that got all of you here. How, like my brother, many of you never intended to hurt people, never considered the consequences of your behavior. And how, like my brother"—here his voice caught for a moment—"the years behind bars have turned some of you into different people and have robbed you of so much more than your freedom."

His eyes met those of one inmate whose expletives had accelerated his heartbeat just moments ago. The anger in the man's eyes had given way to something gentler, as if a memory had stirred of a life almost forgotten. It lasted only a second, but it gave James the courage to continue.

"This is why I'm trying to make a small difference as an officer who wishes to look for humanity and redemption instead of just upholding the law. This is why I've been looking to keep men from experiencing what you all have gone through, and why I'm here to try and help you make the best of your time in here. Because I believe all of you have great potential, and I believe God's plans for you are far from over."

A smile played around Eli's lips when James bowed his head to lead the group in a prayer.

Chapter Thirty-One

Sunday morning, Sophie woke up with mixed feelings. Excited about driving to Colorado Springs, she was at the same time sad about saying goodbye to her friends whom she had become even closer to since traveling and experiencing so much together in the past weeks. On top of that, she felt a tinge of guilt for not telling Thomas the truth about her upcoming plans. He had a fatherly concern for her, and the idea of visiting somebody—a man, all the more—whom she didn't know, in a place that was foreign to her, would definitely result in him advising against her plans. So she decided to keep it to herself for now and apologize later for not telling him.

The moment the Swiss group had disappeared behind the security doors in the Denver airport, the feeling of sadness over the goodbyes turned into exhilaration. Sophie spent half an hour at the car rental booth and fueled up on Starbucks coffee and chocolate bars before getting in her car and heading south on I-25. It was Sunday afternoon, the air was clear and crisp, and Sophie felt like a true adventurer. She rolled down the window of her car and sang "On the Road Again" out loud. Something about the fact that she was all by herself made her feel strong and free. The fact that her plan was very vague and contained many unknown factors just made it all the more exciting.

She arrived in Colorado Springs at around four in the afternoon and checked into the Best Western right off the highway. After a shower, she decided to scout out the land and drive by the school. She followed her GPS and took exit 146 onto Garden of the Gods Road, a name that sparked her interest. She soon saw the buildings of Jonathan Parker Ministries slightly off the main road, nestled among pine trees, rocks, and a hill that rose behind the main building. Whoever designed the surroundings did a great job depicting Jonathan's obvious love for the west, for the mountains and for rustic settings, a theme Sophie had noticed immediately when going to his website the night before.

After driving around the area for a while, her leg started hurting, and she decided to stop at a fast-food chain for dinner and then head back to the hotel. She was looking forward to a special day tomorrow, although she still wouldn't admit to herself that her interest in the school and in Justin was more than just casual.

The next morning, Sophie was up early and had a quick breakfast. Back in her room, she spent a little longer than usual on her choice of clothes and shoes and definitely longer than usual on her makeup. She scolded herself about the fuss she was making but couldn't help it. It was nine a.m. when she was finally ready. She would probably get there right after classes started, which would give her the surprise effect she desired.

Pulling up to the ministry parking lot soon after, the first thing she noticed was the small number of cars. Maybe classes didn't start until ten a.m.? She entered through the main entrance and walked up to the school receptionist.

"Hi! I'm Sophie, and I'm here to see a student. Actually, it's supposed to be a surprise . . . I was wondering if you could tell me what classroom he's in and if I could visit him there?"

The receptionist smiled warmly. "Well, isn't that sweet of you! You're definitely welcome to visit our school anytime.

Unfortunately, this week, the students are on spring break. They won't be back until next Monday. Your friend must have forgotten to tell you!" Sophie's face fell. "I'm sorry, dear. I'm sure he'd love for you to come back next week. Are you staying in town?"

Sophie needed a moment to collect herself. She'd never considered that Justin's stay in Monarch might have been the beginning of a week-long vacation. She just assumed they were there for the weekend. She suddenly felt silly. Was she going to spend a week of her overseas vacation waiting for a guy who, for all she knew, might be embarrassed if she just walked into his classroom uninvited? Insecurity, her old acquaintance, crawled up inside her. Maybe she should go home after all.

"Is everything ok?" the lady behind the desk asked.

"Yes . . . I'm fine. Sorry to bother you." Sophie turned and almost fled the office. Outside, she sat on the stairs leading to the deserted parking lot and buried her head in her hands. Insecurity was joined by shame. She had acted like a stupid teenager, and now reality set in. Justin probably had a girlfriend, anyway, and if Sophie stayed for a whole week just to see him again, she would definitely look like a silly fifteen-year-old. She got back in her car and drove to the motel to call the airline and try and reschedule for the first available flight to Switzerland. Before anybody from the airline answered, however, she hung up, overcome by an unfamiliar feeling. Something inside of her was telling her to wait. In years to come, Sophie would learn to recognize this voice for what it was, but for now she had no idea other than she was not supposed to call the airline now.

She put the phone away, a little frustrated, and for lack of other things to do, decided on a little sightseeing tour. It revealed a charming city against the impressive backdrop of the Rocky Mountains. The modern downtown area wasn't too far from a funky, alternative part of town with little organic coffee shops and hookah dens, followed by beautiful parks with pines and aspens. The town definitely had a wild, beautiful, independent feel to it that Sophie liked immediately. At lunchtime she picked the first restaurant she saw, filled her plate with food carelessly, and sat down to eat. She had barely started when somebody walked up to her booth.

"Excuse me for interrupting, but I remember you from this morning!"

Sophie looked up in surprise to find the receptionist from the Bible college smiling at her.

"Wow, what a coincidence!" Sophie was happy to see the woman despite the embarrassing encounter she'd had with her earlier.

"Do you mind me sitting down with you?"

"Not at all, I'd love that!"

"My name's Cindy, and I'm sorry again for the disappointment I had to cause you earlier. I sure hope you'll come back and see us next Monday?"

Sophie didn't know how to respond.

"May I ask who it is you're going to surprise?" the woman, now seated across from her, asked. Her voice was warm and friendly.

Sophie was desperate to talk to somebody, so she decided to tell her story, with the risk of sounding completely ridiculous. While talking, she noticed her own effort to conceal any feelings that would portray an interest in Justin. Also, she decided to leave out the mention of flights for now, as the story was complicated enough as it was.

Cindy had an expression on her face that reminded Sophie of a person watching a romantic movie. *Oh, great, she thinks I have a crush on him.* Sophie groaned internally. But judging from the heat coming off her cheeks, even someone not particularly romantic could sense what was going on. *I just hope she's not going to make fun of me!*

"I tell you what we'll do," Cindy suddenly said, leaning over the booth as if sharing a secret. "I know Justin well. He's a wonderful young man, one who's always ready for anything.

How about we prepare a really good surprise for him next Monday? I've got an idea. . . ."

Over the next hour, the two women devised a plan. Sophie had immediately dismissed her idea of changing her plane ticket, as Cindy's exuberance and excitement had given her all the motivation she needed to see her initial plan in a positive light again. When the plan was forged, they considered themselves partners in crime. Sophie told her how she'd gotten here and where she was staying, but Cindy would not have it and convinced Sophie to come stay at her apartment for the week.

"Don't you worry about being bored until Monday. I only work mornings since the students are out of school this week, so we're going to have a lot of fun together!"

As she drove back to the hotel to get her stuff and move in with her new friend for a week, Sophie marveled at her luck. As before in her life, one person coming along at a crucial moment changed everything, even though at the moment all she could see ahead was a surprise for a guy she barely knew.

Chapter Thirty-Two

The days following his encounter with the Swiss girl, Justin pretended to enjoy skiing every different slope Monarch had to offer and went to the Lodge for more hot chocolate than he could possibly enjoy. He was looking for Sophie, searching the slopes for her red hat and the booths in the restaurant for her face. But she seemed to have disappeared. He knew her leg must hurt, but he hoped she'd ski anyway. Maybe not the next day, but surely after a few days?

When a day on the slopes was over without a sign of her, he shifted his focus. As soon as he got down the mountain and had cellphone reception, he looked for a text or an email from her. But after three days, there was still no sign from her. Justin was surprised at how deep his disappointment went. After all, they had only met for an hour or so. They had hardly talked on their walk down the mountain because of the physical strain it had put on both of them. So why was he desperate for a sign of life from her?

It had taken all his courage to give her his number in front of his friends, and of course they had teased him plenty about it in the following days. But he didn't care. If only she would show some little sign that this had been a special encounter for her as well, he would be happy.

His search ended abruptly on the fourth day. Soon after hitting the slope, the pain in his side, appearing on and off in the ten days since hiking Pikes Peak, came back with unexpected fury. He snowboarded down a black diamond when it hit him, this time all over his abdomen, causing him to double over and fall into the snow.

"Are you alright? Did you hurt yourself?" Simon asked when he caught up with him.

Justin wanted to say he was ok like he had on the mountain, but the pain was too overwhelming. It sucked every ounce of will out of his body, and he just shook his head in defeat. Simon and Caleb got him off the mountain and immediately drove him to the nearest hospital in Salida. When they got there, Justin nearly lost consciousness and was immediately rushed to the ER.

Six hours later, the doctors conducted an emergency appendectomy and moved Justin to the general hospital for recovery. Simon and Caleb spent the night at a motel in Salida and were allowed to see Justin the following morning. When they entered his room, Justin looked tired but also depressed.

"Way to end our trip with a bang!" Simon joked, hoping to lighten the mood. "How're you feeling?"

"I guess I'm fine. Hurts a lot, and they pumped me full of drugs, but the doc said I'll recover quickly. No, it's not the pain that's the problem."

"Then what is it?"

"The doc said my appendix had been partially ruptured for around ten days. He said had I come in immediately, the surgery could have been much easier."

"The hike! It started rupturing on that trip up Pikes Peak." Caleb sounded apologetic.

"Yes. And while I thought God had healed whatever this was, it was instead quietly simmering inside me and getting worse. Nothing got healed when we prayed that day!" Justin's words were so full of disappointment and confusion, none of his friends dared to respond. They were used to him telling them to have more faith, not questioning an issue of faith. They left soon after to wait at the motel until his release from the hospital the next morning.

The rest of the day was difficult for Justin. His faith had suffered its first real blow, his friends had to cut their vacation short because of him, and there was still no sign of life from Sophie. *God, what am I doing wrong? Is this a test?*

His recovery was even faster than anticipated, and when they hit the road back to Colorado Springs on Saturday, Justin felt well enough to crack jokes and appeared almost his old self. But it was a disguise. Sophie's silence as well as the doctor's words cast a shadow over him, and it was without his usual excitement that he showed up at the Rock for classes the following Monday.

His mood brightened considerably during the morning worship service. He loved the atmosphere of prayer, songs, and celebration that was part of it. Also, he needed to put his focus back on God. The past week had been really tough on him as he tried to shove Sophie out of his mind with her sneaking back in every time. Why she had become so important to him was still a mystery. He knew nothing about her, and from all he'd heard about Western Europe's spiritual climate, chances were very high she wasn't even a follower of Jesus. Of course he had noticed how attractive she was. But in the past year he had put the things of God ahead of girls with surprising ease. So why did he feel himself clinging to the hope of seeing her again?

Closing his eyes and listening to the words of the songs, he felt the same effect this music always had on him, especially the hymns. They were powerful declarations of faith and reminded him that he was part of an amazing plan God had that went well beyond his little world. Like many times before, he got emotional as he recalled what God had done in his life in the past year and a half. He would never forget, and he would never stop being thankful.

The worship hour ended with a few announcements from the dean of students, a young and energetic man. Justin kept his eyes closed to stay in the atmosphere of prayer. It was the most effective way to distract himself from unwanted thoughts, which at the moment involved unanswered prayers as well as a certain girl from across the Atlantic.

The dean came on stage and took the mic. "Good morning, Rock! You know we usually reserve the last minutes of worship hour for testimonies, and it's what we will do today as well. Normally, it is our own students giving testimony of what God has done in their lives. Today, we have the privilege of having someone from outside our school testify what God did for her through a student here."

A few "Amen" shouts rang out through the crowd. Justin gave up trying to stay in prayer and focused on the stage.

The dean continued, "Our guest today has a special story to tell, not least because this is her first trip to the US as an adult, and the student who helped her was the first American Christian she'd ever encountered!"

When, a second later, Sophie walked onto the stage, Justin was so shocked he was completely unable to move.

"Thank you so much for having me here!" Sophie said with her unmistakable Swiss accent. "This is quite the surprise for one student here, who had no idea I was going to be here. I met him in rather unfortunate circumstances, in the snow with a broken ski, a leg stuck under a root, and the ski lifts closing down one evening just a week ago in Monarch. I would have been in deep trouble without his help getting me down the slope in the darkness with only one ski left.

"Unfortunately, I lost the number he gave me, and I just couldn't leave the country without thanking him. Through some fortunate circumstances, I found out about the school, and your amazing receptionist Cindy has been my tour guide for the past week while I was waiting for school to be in session again. I'm very honored to be your guest today."

Sophie gave the mic back to the dean, while people started shouting, "Who is it? Get up on stage!" The whole place had gotten caught up in the unusual story.

Justin was still sitting, oblivious to the side cuffs of his friends and the looks in his direction. *She came all the way here for me. She waited a whole week to see me.* He felt terrible for having been disappointed with her when all this time she had had no way of communicating with him. Her presence produced feelings in his stomach that made it hard to decide if he was excited or just plain terrified.

"Well, we won't keep you guessing. Justin, it's time for you to come up here!"

Justin got out of his seat and walked on stage like in a dream, followed by the shouts and high-fives of his friends. When he reached Sophie, he realized he had no idea what to do now. But before he could start worrying, Sophie embraced him in an enthusiastic, joyful hug. The crowd cheered.

"How awesome is that," the dean said, energized by the excitement in the room. "Now tell us your side of the story, Justin!"

Justin realized that his side of the story was a bit more complicated to tell than Sophie's. He couldn't exactly say he was following Sophie because he had been fascinated by her eyes. Fortunately, he'd heard enough testimonies in the past year that he knew intuitively how to spin the story.

"A bunch of us went for a week of skiing at Monarch," he said. "On the first day I saw this skier with a red hat perform these awesome tricks on the slopes. And guess what? Out of all the thousands of people at Monarch, who happens to sit down in the booth next to ours later that day at lunch? It's the girl with the red hat. Do you know that there are no coincidences with God? Because later that day, I happen to still be out there with my board right before the lifts close—you know me, I always have to test the limits—when I suddenly hear a voice far off the slope, calling for help. I find Sophie sitting in the snow, her leg stuck and her ski broken. It was God's divine intervention that gave me the opportunity to help her."

"Praise God!" the dean exclaimed. "This is what happens when we are walking in obedience to God and listen to His voice—He will bring people across our path who need our help. So, Sophie, before we leave, tell us a bit about your spiritual journey. I heard Justin was the first American Christian you ever met?"

Sophie nodded. "Well, I myself have only just started following Jesus, so this is all new to me. I was so excited to hear that the person who helped me out was a Christian as well. Where I'm from, not many people follow Jesus. Visiting your school is a wonderful experience for me."

"Well, we definitely hope for you to stick around for a while and enjoy the fellowship of our student body here and the teachings you will hear. You're welcome to sit in on classes anytime during your visit. Sounds like Switzerland could use some of the Rock's messages!"

The students applauded again, and the dean dismissed the class. Several people surrounded both of them and started asking questions so that they had no chance of even talking to each other. When the bell rang for the next class, Cindy appeared, telling Justin that he had been excused for the next period.

"Go get yourselves some coffee at the cafeteria; you need it after all this excitement. The place should be nice and quiet now," she added with a smile as she walked back to the reception.

They got coffee and chose one of the cozy lounge areas in the back corner of the cafeteria. When they had settled in their chairs, Sophie had a teasing smile playing on her lips.

"How's that for a little surprise?"

Justin shook his head. He was never at a loss for words, but Sophie had pretty much blown him away this morning.

"You're something else!" he finally offered with a grin. In reality, he was deeply touched. Although he usually knew how to play it cool and force emotions to the back of his mind, the feelings Sophie now produced in him were quite overwhelming. "I must have looked like an idiot up there on stage. I was so blown away. How did you find the school? How long have you been here? Where are you staying?"

What he actually wanted to ask was, *Did you really drive all the way here and then wait a week just to see me?* But not only would that question put her in an awkward position, it would also reveal that he cared, and telling a beautiful girl he cared was way too risky. Had she been an overreacting teenager romanticizing over him, he would have thought it silly. But Sophie was not a teenager, and although she was definitely excited to be here, Justin could also tell she was in no way silly in her approach toward him. In fact, it was her sincerity that reached under his skin.

As Sophie answered his questions about her past week, Justin quietly marveled at this turn of events. She had burst back into his life with a blast, and while she was happily chatting across from him, she was tugging at his heart with surprising force.

Chapter Thirty-Three

The rest of the period went by fast as they recalled their mountain adventure and the events that took place since then. They decided to attend classes together for the rest of the morning, and they were treated like celebrities and were the topic of the day at the school.

Sophie loved everything about the school. She experienced none of the insecurity and awkwardness she usually felt in large groups of people. Instead, she felt part of a celebration that was not about her, but more like a party she got to join in. As she sat in class with Justin for the remaining lessons, she heard the teachers at the Rock talk about a bold, exciting, adventurous kind of faith. They talked about things she had never heard before. Some of it she didn't understand, but she could feel the bond of shared experience and values that united these people and could tell it was powerful. *I wonder what it will be like when Jonathan Parker comes back?* she thought, as Justin had told her he was out of town until Wednesday.

After school, Sophie joined Justin, Caleb, and Simon for lunch. The ease with which Justin's friends invited her into their circle astounded her. In Switzerland, friendships developed slowly and cautiously, often over long periods of time.

She would have felt like an outsider for sure in a similar situation at home. Here, though, she was part of the fun right away, and Justin's friends all made her feel welcome. There was a lot of laughter and a lot of teasing Justin about his heroic feat. They asked Sophie questions about Christians in Switzerland, and she had to admit that she knew very little about them.

The courtesy with which Justin and his friends treated her surprised her. In her culture, the urge for equal treatment of women had eliminated almost any chance for men to act as gentlemen toward them. Sophie realized how good it felt to have Caleb hold the door of the restaurant open for her. She also noticed that while there was plenty of teasing for Justin to take, nobody said anything but nice and complimentary things to her. As they left the restaurant and Simon told her they were looking forward to seeing her in class the next morning, Sophie knew she had already been adopted into this lively, enthusiastic community.

Justin drove Sophie back to the school's parking lot after lunch. It had been such an emotional first part of the day, she had no idea what was going to happen next, but she was ready for anything. After getting out of the car, they stood there for an awkward moment.

"Well . . . I had a great time at the Rock," Sophie offered, "and I'll definitely be back tomorrow. Unless . . ." she hoped he would say something or offer to spend more of the day together, but all that followed was silence. She suddenly felt too insecure to make any suggestions for spending more time together. After all, it had been her bursting into his life unannounced this morning. Maybe he had just been playing along so he wouldn't spoil her surprise?

"Ok, have a good rest of the day," she said at last and offered her hand to him, which he shook almost robotically.

"Ok, see you tomorrow," he said and turned around a little too quickly before getting back in his car and driving off.

Disappointment settled over Sophie as she drove back to Cindy's house. Whatever just happened was not what she had expected. She replayed the events of the day in her mind. Nothing had happened that could explain him suddenly becoming distant. On the other hand, what did she expect? She still didn't know anything about this man. Maybe he did have a girlfriend she didn't know about? Her expectations and hopes had little to do with reality, and she had just gotten caught up in the magic of it all—the rescue on the mountain, the fact that Justin was a passionate Christian, the TV-like surprise this morning. But no matter what she told herself, she couldn't shake her disappointment.

Fear of rejection had been part of her life for as long as she could remember. As a rather nerdy child, Sophie had always had a hard time making friends at school. When she got older, she carried the same insecurity when dating men. But Nathan . . . he had made her feel like the most special woman in the world. He gave her hope that there were people out there who could see her for more than the things she lacked. With some anguish, Sophie had to admit that she had hoped and convinced herself that Justin was such a person.

In her desire to sort out her tangled emotions, Thomas popped into her mind. But right now, the thought of her old friend carried guilt with it. It had been over a week since she had contacted him. He had written her the day after the group got back to Switzerland and wanted to make sure she had arrived safely at her aunt's. Sophie had answered elusively, saying everything was ok and that she would write more at a later time. *Or rather, when I figure out how to explain to you what I'm doing in Colorado,* she had thought to herself. She really didn't want to deal with Thomas's well-meant concerns right now.

Her glance fell on Cindy's piano in the corner of her room. She went over and played a simple tune Thomas had taught her soon after she'd started attending his group. It had immediately touched her, although at that time she wasn't sure she believed what it said. But the beautiful melody resonated with her soul, and she had been singing it to herself often recently. And on that day on the mountain, when her heart had opened up to Jesus in a new way, the song had become even more important to her. Now, Sophie sang the lines repeatedly like a chant: *Dans nos obscurités, allume le feu qui ne s'éteint jamais, qui ne s'éteint jamais . . .*

As she sang, she reminded herself that it wasn't her own wisdom, nor her relational skill, nor her attempts to control that brought light into the darkness of her life. As the song said, only God could illuminate a fire in mankind so bright that none of life's dark places were able to extinguish it. Thomas's words came back to her: "The most difficult thing you'll ever do is hand over control of your life to God. But if you do, it will result in a joy and freedom beyond comparison."

Her mood improved slightly. She changed tunes and started playing a more joyful song, one she had also learned from Thomas. She was concentrating so much on the music, she almost missed the hesitant knock on the front door.

Chapter Thirty-Four

"I'm such an idiot," Justin murmured to himself while waiting at Cindy's front door. He had been standing there for a whole five minutes, trying to gather the courage to ring the doorbell. He still couldn't believe what had happened just an hour ago. He was so embarrassed, it had taken him all of that hour to drum up enough guts to drive to Cindy's. Sophie probably didn't even want to see him now, but he had to explain what happened—as far as he could understand it himself.

When coming up to the house now and hearing worship music and Sophie singing in a happy voice, he was so relieved he almost rang the doorbell immediately. But then he realized he didn't know what to say to her. *Hi Sophie. Sorry about before, but I freaked out and when I do, I run. That's just me.* Not very impressive. Saying a heartfelt apology was not really in his repertoire. But backing out wasn't either. He was here, and he was going to man up. He rang the bell and heard the piano stop. A while later Sophie appeared at the door.

He coughed. "Hey! Uhm . . . do you think we could talk for a moment?"

"Sure, come on in."

They sat down on the couch, and Sophie's friendly tone

gave Justin the courage to talk. "I was quite an idiot earlier in the parking lot. I don't really know what happened to me."

In reality, Justin knew pretty well what had happened. All throughout the morning, all throughout last week actually, he had felt for Sophie what he had never felt for a girl before. Having her here now, embracing him on the stage, talking like old friends at the cafeteria, and sitting next to him at lunch had produced uncontrollable and scary feelings in him. There in the parking lot, he had felt the terror of losing control and becoming vulnerable. So he had run once again. Obviously he wasn't going to tell her this, although something inside him yearned to. Instead, he worked hard at getting everything back to where it was before the parking lot.

"Anyway, I wanted to ask if you were up for a little exploring of the town this afternoon," he said as casually as he could.

Sophie seemed to have the same desire to get back on safe ground. "I would love to do that," she replied. "Where should we go?"

"Well, the first thing any visitor needs to see is the Garden of the Gods," Justin suggested, "but you've got to hike it to really experience its full beauty. Are you ready to go?"

Justin was always ready, with his keys and phone in his pockets at all times and his jacket and water bottle in the car. Sophie took a little longer, but soon they were on the way to Colorado Springs' famous formations of red rocks beautifully shaped right in front of Pikes Peak. Justin chose a long but moderate hiking trail to give them plenty of time to talk while going easy on his still recovering abdomen. He started by asking about her trip and where she'd been before visiting Colorado. He was also inquisitive about the group she'd been with. Sophie told him about her experience with Thomas's Bible study and how it had prepared her for the decision she'd made a week ago.

Her enthusiasm for the group made Justin smile. On one side he felt happy for her, but his smile had a condescending edge to it. She was a new and inexperienced believer. After asking several questions about some of the topics Thomas's group had covered while she'd been with them, he was convinced they were neither spirit-filled nor particularly conservative. But Justin tried not to judge her because Sophie came from a very secular country and might have never heard about the power of God. Would the short time she had left here be enough for him to show her the Truth?

Chapter Thirty-Five

Sophie enjoyed every part of the breathtaking hike: the beautiful views of the snow-covered Pikes Peak around one bend, the rugged beauty of the red rock formations on the other. Her thrill that Justin was a Christian and shared her love for Jesus only added to her happiness. As they hiked, she expressed her interest in everything concerning the school and told Justin how the excitement and energy she felt at the Rock was a new experience to her. Although Thomas's meetings were warm and down-to-earth, they weren't nearly as exciting as this.

After an hour of hiking, they sat on a hill overlooking the park, and Sophie unpacked a few granola bars and water bottles from her backpack. "It's my turn to ask questions," she then declared in between bites. "Tell me how you found Jesus."

A beaming smile lit up Justin's face at the question. He told her of his crazy past, his brushes with death, and finally the supernatural encounter with Jesus. Sophie was impressed and told him that it had become obvious to her how passionate and radical the people at the Rock were. And in her opinion, Justin's own colorful, adventurous and crazy life made him fit in with the Rock perfectly. She also told him, a little apologetically almost, that the calm and commonsense mentality of Thomas seemed somewhat gray in comparison to today's classes.

Throughout the remainder of their hike, she asked question after question. She was astonished at how well-versed Justin was in Scripture, and how he had an answer or explanation to every one of her questions. Thomas had often told her to ask God herself, sometimes adding his little joke that she should let him know God's answer, as he himself was still looking for it. Justin, although so much younger, sounded way more confident. There was not one question she asked that Justin didn't answer with a scriptural reference backing it up. He definitely was lightyears ahead of her when it came to his knowledge and experience about spiritual things. But Sophie was so in love with Jesus, she felt nothing but gratitude and excitement about a person who was ahead of her in this journey.

They got back to the beginning of the trail when the sun was already setting.

"Watch this," Justin said and led her away from the parking lot. He kept looking up at a funny-shaped, huge rock formation with a big hole in it. Sophie only realized what they were looking at when the orange rays of the setting sun shone right through the hole in that rock. They both fell silent. For a minute, the rays burst in all directions, bathing the world around them in a sea of light and creating a Kodak moment just for the two of them. When the sun had moved past the hole and the magic was over, Sophie was almost afraid to turn her face to his because she was sure he would see right into her heart, and she would be found out.

By the time they were back at the car, it was completely dark. They were in high spirits and very hungry. Justin suggested they have dinner at the Marigold, a French restaurant, since Sophie was from Europe. When they ordered, Sophie pronounced her dish with a French accent.

"I didn't know you speak French as well!" Justin marveled.

"Well, it's one of our national languages, together with German, Italian, and a lesser-known language called Rhaeto-Romanic. I took Italian as well, but it's pretty rusty at this point." Speaking several languages wasn't a big deal to her. "Tell me more about Jonathan Parker," she continued when they had placed their orders. "Why did you choose his school over all the others?"

Justin seemed to have been waiting for this opportunity. When he talked about Jonathan, his cheeks got red from excitement. "Jonathan is the real deal. I have never met a godlier man in my life. He preaches from the Bible all day long, yet he hardly ever has to open it. Whatever he preaches comes from his heart. He had a supernatural encounter with God when he was a teenager and has been on fire ever since. He is the most inspiring person ever."

"Just like you!" Sophie turned a deep red as the thought, which had just crossed her mind, unintentionally slipped out of her mouth. But there really was a striking resemblance. Justin blushed almost as much as her.

"Wow, what a compliment! But our past was very different. Jonathan grew up religious. He always did what was right and grew self-righteous in it. He thought he *deserved* salvation, until the day God overwhelmed him with his grace. When Jonathan saw that it was the grace of God and not his own good works that brought him salvation, he broke down and completely surrendered his life. He says he was living in a bubble for a couple of months, just experiencing the unconditional love of God over and over until nothing else mattered. In a way, he says he's still living in this bubble, because ever since then, all he has lived for and accomplished served as a response to this encounter with God."

Sophie could tell Justin had the utmost respect and love for Jonathan, and she couldn't wait to meet him later in the week when he would be back at the college.

Chapter Thirty-Six

The next day, Sophie set her alarm to five a.m. She wanted to drive back to the Garden of the Gods park and watch the sun rise. There were so many things going on in her heart right now, she needed some time before getting even more input from the school and before seeing Justin again.

There was little doubt now that she was falling in love. Yesterday had probably been the most emotional day of her life. She had hardly slept that night, waking up with a mix of excitement and restless anticipation every couple of hours. She had felt it before, when Nathan and she first started dating and, to a much lesser degree, on some of the nights on the *Noordfries*. They were vibrations of hope, stirring the fabric of her heart and expanding it. She also felt it sometimes in books and songs, this invitation to experience life deeper and richer.

When she arrived at the park well before sunrise, she bundled up, took her Bible under her arm, and walked a short way up one of the paths until she found a secluded spot with a view of Pikes Peak. She sat still for a long time and prayed silently. But however hard she tried to focus, her thoughts kept wandering back to Justin. Finally, she gave up trying to pray about something else.

"Lord, you obviously know how I feel about Justin. I can definitely tell I'm falling in love with him, but I have no idea where he stands. And I haven't even asked you about the whole thing. What do you think?"

The sun was slowly rising, dipping the park and the gorgeous mountaintop in a sea of light. There was nothing to do or say. Sophie was experiencing the moment, witnessing this earth-old spectacle in silence. Sunrise and sunset always created emotions in her. *There is so much unseen beauty in this world.* An incident from her childhood came to her mind. She'd hiked with her parents to a secluded, small mountain lake in the Swiss Alps, and when rounding the bend that led to that lake, the view opened to lavish fields of alpine flowers. Thousands of them blanketed the lake shore in wild and bright beauty. The whole time her family was there, not a single other hiker showed up. They might have been the only people who saw this breathtaking display of creativity that day or even week. Had they not come, maybe nobody would have ever seen it like that—and yet it was there, painted with abundant colors and extravagant detail. Could this be just a random act of nature? Was this nothing but biology playing out its course? Even as a child she intuitively knew it was not so. Nature was too breathtakingly beautiful and intricate to be a product of chance or randomness.

On the way out of the park, she texted Justin. He was already at the Rock and met her in the auditorium right as worship started. Again, Sophie noticed the powerful atmosphere in the school and the infectious enthusiasm of the people. The worship was upbeat; most hands were raised and some students were dancing in the front of the auditorium. *This must be what a perfect party looks like,* she thought.

Once she had visited the church Thomas attended in Bern. She had liked the people and the message, but she had wished people were more expressive, more enthusiastic, more fun. Was it just the reserved way of the Swiss, or did it also have to do with what they believed? Sophie was aware that what Jonathan was teaching was vastly different from what she had heard from Thomas and others so far. The thought of Thomas once again got her feeling guilty. She made a mental note to email him tonight, no matter how late it was going to be.

Sophie thoroughly enjoyed the morning at the Rock. A great variety of subjects were taught from surveys of the Old and New Testament, to classes on missions, to studies on faith principles. All of it was new to her and added to her fascination with this entirely new world. When school was out, Justin pulled her away from the breakroom and toward the exit. "Let's not go out with the whole gang today. We could get some sandwiches on the way if you like. I have a surprise for you that will take all afternoon."

The butterflies in Sophie's stomach did their dance again. Justin's powerful and positive presence swept her off her feet. And then there was the way he approached their time together. She was used to planning things, calculating time and guarding it carefully. In her circle of friends back home, things were hardly done spontaneously. People needed time to decide whether the activity was worth their time or not. Even seeing her girlfriends was considered a meeting. They would agree on a date and time and note it in the calendar. Because of the many different kinds of friends she had, meetings were scheduled well ahead, often two weeks or more. The thought of just showing up on someone's doorstep or asking someone to spend that very afternoon together was considered rather unrealistic. When it did happen, people would mention how cool that was and how they really wanted to live that way, and then it would not happen again for months. People didn't just join others for random activities, mostly because time was considered such a precious thing. Control was another. If you couldn't control the outcome of time spent together, it was safer just not to do it and instead follow the well-planned routine of meetings with friends. *Thomas calls this another price for compartmentalizing our life.* It created a life so fragmented that it robbed people of their peace and ability to relax and welcome life as it happened.

Justin, on the other hand, naturally seemed to expect that she'd come on this surprise trip with him, without knowing where they were going, how long it would take, and what they would do. As they walked to his car, she realized that this might be why it was so much more fun than all her meetings and controlled events. Justin liked to be with her, so he invited her to join him in whatever he was doing that day. It was as simple and beautiful as that.

Twenty minutes later, armed with sandwiches and coffee, they drove toward the mountains. Nestled into the very eastern end of the Rocky Mountains, Colorado Springs required only a short drive from the city to reveal a beautiful, wild mountain scenery.

"I'm glad you're wearing sneakers," Justin mentioned with a side glance at her shoes. "I'm going to show you one of the most beautiful sceneries around here. But you have to earn it!" He smiled warmly when their eyes met. Sophie tried to stay calm. To be in the car with this intriguing man, so physically close, half a world away from home, was not on the scale of emotions she had learned to control.

They drove further up and into the mountains, passing little towns with charming names like Green Mountain Falls or Woodland Park. The aspens in their young, light green foliage contrasted beautifully with the dark green pines along their route. Every bend in the road was a possible surprise of a view into a gorgeous valley or another range of snow-covered mountaintops.

After a long drive, Justin suddenly pulled off the main road. Sophie caught the sign and saw they were entering a state park. They gathered their gear out of the car and set off on a trail westward.

"This is one of my favorite places around town. We might not meet another person here all day. Instead, we might spot a bear if we're lucky," Justin said, cheeks red from what looked like excitement.

Sophie jerked back instantly. "Tell me you have not seen a bear here yourself," she demanded in a reproachful tone.

"Oh, I have! But don't worry. They're not aggressive, especially this time of year. They stay out of people's way. Mostly anyway." He laughed when Sophie gave him a look of terror. "Seriously. You're fine. And besides, he would have to eat me before he could get to you."

Although still undecided if she was mad at Justin for bringing her into some bear-infested wilderness or if she should treat the whole thing as a joke, Sophie could tell that his statement touched her. She could not remember anybody ever implying they'd risk their life for her, even if it was partially a joke. His statement made her feel cherished and protected, and she was not used to being treated that way—her emancipated Swiss upbringing would have taught her to either stay out of the bear's way or fight it herself. A man telling her that he would fight for her was an old-fashioned but surprisingly moving thought.

They hiked along ridges overlooking vast hills covered with woods. The views were majestic, and the solitude of the place deepened its impression on Sophie. She loved that Justin didn't take her downtown or to a tourist place, but instead to a deserted place wild with beauty. When they got hungry, they sat on a rock, shared their food, and both drank from the little thermos of coffee they had filled up earlier. Being so close to him, she noticed the difference in emotions Justin produced in her than what Nathan had. Her first love had been security and joy. Justin was adventure. She loved his excitement, his drive, but was definitely also touched by the gentler side she saw. And then there was the God part. She still felt on the outside of the kind of faith Justin was talking about, but it sounded adventurous and powerful and had a strong draw on her.

They hiked all afternoon, taking in the views, the silence and the closeness of each other. His feelings for her remained a mystery. He definitely must be enjoying her company, or he wouldn't spend all this time with her. And from the way he was looking at her, she was pretty sure he liked what he saw too. Was he just holding out on her? She was sure by now that he didn't have a girlfriend, but maybe there had been somebody whom he was still getting over?

They watched the sun set over the vast mountain vista before returning to their car. On the long ride home, Sophie started wondering where this was going. She was leaving in a few days, and she felt no freedom to steer the conversation in any direction that would address a time afterwards. *Is he not interested, or is he afraid?*

She'd been so happy to do whatever in the past two days, maybe she was too easy a catch. Maybe Justin Friedman needed to feel like he had to conquer her? Although she hated the idea of being pretentious, she also knew that playing hard to get had worked for many of her girlfriends. Maybe she needed to back off for a bit and see if he could be forced out of the comfortable position she'd put him in. She hated the idea, but it seemed better than leaving in a couple of days and never seeing Justin again.

When they had gotten back to the city and Justin suggested they eat dinner somewhere, she reacted fast, before her heart would have a chance to catch up. "I think I'll have an early night tonight. I've been up since five a.m., you know. Thank you so much for the wonderful afternoon, though, I really enjoyed myself. See you tomorrow."

Her eyes met his long enough to see the shadow that came over his sunny face. Then she turned around and headed for her car. The awful feeling in her stomach reminded her painfully that this was not who she was. As she drove off without looking back, she got angry at herself and angry at him. After all, throughout the last two days she had signaled her excitement and her interest in him countless times, and his reaction had been, although friendly, clearly reluctant. What else was she supposed to do?

As soon as she got home, she wrote to Thomas, telling him

how her trip to her aunt's house hadn't worked out and how she had decided instead to visit the school attended by the group from the Lodge. She made a point in showing her interest in the school and was careful to mention the group as opposed to Justin individually.

Thomas would figure it out sooner or later anyway, but she'd rather it be later. She talked about Cindy and Jonathan and the wonderful people she'd met and how she was having a great time. *I'm at least halfway honest,* she thought to herself. She wasn't making anything up; there were just things she wasn't telling. Her friendship to Justin was too confusing for her to describe right now. And maybe there wouldn't be anything left to describe in a few days.

Chapter Thirty-Seven

The next morning, Justin woke up with a start. The first conscious thought made him jump out of bed: *I might lose her.*

He got up, fixed himself coffee, and paced around the room. He didn't know what had happened yesterday, but the effect it had on him spoke volumes. He wasn't just crushed—he felt guilty. He knew why she'd decided to leave, as his inability to fully open up was all the more obvious when contrasted with her trusting and vulnerable attitude toward him. Other girls had danced the dance with him. Give a little, take a little, stay in control, and ultimately trust only yourself. Justin knew how to dance like that, and because of his winning personality he was an excellent dancer. He fooled his parents, his teachers, his exes, and his friends.

But Sophie was different. She held her heart out to him. She extended trust toward him he hadn't earned. And yet, she wasn't just naïve. He could feel that what she did was intentional and that she knew the risk. And yet she did it anyway. He felt so safe with her—and that feeling was the very thing that frightened him the most. His skillfully crafted guard was in danger, and he'd rather run than find himself in a position of vulnerability in front of a woman.

Sophie forced him to leave known territory. Although several girls had been interested in him during his time at the Rock, he had no problem politely declining. He was here to study the Bible and to prepare himself for ministry, not to find a girlfriend. It was probably this single-mindedness that most attracted these girls to him. He had had no intention of changing anything about this until at least the end of school. Sophie had turned all of this upside down. There was no chance he could keep up his cool-headed not-interested attitude toward her. He was extremely interested—and very afraid it would be found out. Sophie had shown that she wanted to continue the friendship beyond the couple of days they had left and maybe was hoping for it to grow into more than a friendship. He knew it was the same for him, knew it passionately. But there was no telling what would happen if Sophie cracked the walls around his heart and discovered that boy who still wondered if he had what it took—what would happen if she saw he was lacking.

And then there was his desire to follow God wherever He led. Would she, with her more liberal approach and her spiritual inexperience, rob him of his ability to listen to God? He had made up his mind about who was to be first for the rest of his life. He would do whatever it took to honor God, even if it would break his heart.

He fell to his knees right there on his kitchen floor. That battle raged in him again, the battle between his selfish desires and his desire to live for God. But was it really meant to be such a battle? It seemed that some people lived their spiritual life with much more peace than what he was feeling right now. As he was quiet, trying to listen to God, he suddenly felt like God was asking him a question too.

What do you *want, Justin?*

It was an unexpected thought, although he realized that it shouldn't surprise him that much. If God was really a loving

Father, why wouldn't He be interested in Justin's longings? But then again, that could be a trick of his own mind to justify his selfishness. And yet, a thought had just been planted in Justin. He might not know exactly what he wanted, or what God wanted from him, but he knew very well what he didn't want.

I don't want to lose Sophie.

She had told him her flight back to Switzerland was on Friday, and it was Wednesday. He had exactly two days not to mess this up and hopefully turn their budding friendship into a lasting relationship.

First of all, he had to try and talk to her before classes started. He sent her a text, asking to get some Starbucks before heading to class. The noncommittal atmosphere of a coffee place might help at the moment. To his relief, he got an answer within minutes. Encouraged by her response, he practically flew the short distance between his apartment and Starbucks. He got there before her and ordered drinks for both of them, remembering what she had ordered the day before.

He felt all silly, being so giddy about seeing her again when it was he who was the hesitant one. He had never before felt for anyone what he felt for her, and he didn't seem to be handling this new reality very well. He clutched his drink nervously when Sophie walked into the place. Seeing her smile made him choke up. When their eyes met, she held his gaze only briefly.

"Good morning, Justin!"

She noticed the drink he had ordered her and a light blush spread across her face. She must've been the most beautiful woman he had ever seen. His heart ached, and he wanted to get up and embrace her and not let go. Instead, he stayed glued to his seat and watched her take her jacket off.

"So what's going to be in store for us at the school today?" Her tone was reserved, and it made his insides knot up.

"Jonathan's back today. Don't know what he'll be talking about, but I know it will be good!" he said, avoiding her eyes as well now.

"I think I believe you. It's impressive how well he knows the Bible, and how he has thought through every possible question one could have regarding it. And yet, he seems like a totally humble guy."

He knew she meant what she said, and although she was clearly hurting, she did not take this opportunity to hurt him back. For him, one thing that would have ended any thought of their being together would have been her criticizing or even ridiculing Jonathan, because in Justin's mind, ridiculing Jonathan was pretty close to ridiculing Jesus.

"Oh yeah! He's such an awesome person. He's not worried about himself, his reputation, his fame, or anything else. This is why God can achieve so much through him. He doesn't let his own desires get in the way of doing God's will."

He felt as if his own words had just voiced an accusation against himself, and his face darkened. Sophie must have noticed, because immediately, her reservation disappeared and she looked at him with this warm, caring look that caused such cracks in his walls.

"What just happened?" Her question sounded shy.

Justin threw up his hands inwardly. There was no point trying to change the topic with this woman once she set her mind to talk about something that mattered. "I guess I just wish I could be so single-minded, so radical in my commitment to God, that I could hear His voice beyond any doubt. I'm afraid my own self gets in the way of that quite frequently."

Sophie thought about this for a while. "It seems to me that you are as committed and radical as anybody could be. I think you are an incredible role model of somebody giving his life to Jesus."

Justin looked to the floor. Here she was doing it again, breaking right through his barriers and saying things nobody had ever said to him, and all with a sincerity he could not brush off. She was not merely flirting with him either. She meant exactly what she said, and it had all the more weight because of it. When he looked up again, Sophie's eyes were moist. She wiped them with a little Starbucks napkin.

"Justin . . . I think Jonathan isn't teaching until later in the morning. How about we skip the first lesson and go for a little walk? I'd like to talk to you about something."

They drove the short drive to the Garden of the Gods and started out on what they had already dubbed *their* path. It was astounding how quickly things with Sophie could turn into cherished, personalized memories. He had walked this trail so many times, and it had been just a trail. Since Monday, it was *their* trail.

Nobody else was out on that Wednesday morning. They walked silently. "I want to apologize for yesterday," Sophie finally offered. "I'm afraid I wasn't entirely truthful when I said I was tired. Or at least it wasn't the only reason I decided against dinner."

Justin's insides tightened. He looked at her and saw the confusion and hurt in her eyes. It felt terrible to know he had caused it, and yet he didn't know how to change it even now. Instead, he intuitively did something that took himself by surprise. He took her hand and held it tightly. It sent an electric shock through him, as if he were coming alive in a new way. His heart had momentarily overridden his brain and taken over and done what he had wanted to do all along. If he was honest, it was only part of what he'd wanted to do all along. He looked over, but she had turned her head. Her hand was holding his tightly and they were walking side by side.

When she spoke, her voice was raw. "I don't know what to think, Justin. I don't know how you feel about me. So I guess I tried to play hard to get yesterday . . . and I hated it. It's so not me. You know, I really have no idea where all of this will lead, but I will not play games any longer. I don't want to pretend like you don't mean anything to me. But I also don't want you to feel pressured. I just want to be honest with you. I want us both to be ourselves." She looked over to him and then added with a shy smile, "God can handle that, right?"

Justin didn't let go of her hand. Two voices were arguing in his head. He had come to Bible college to learn about God and to prepare for ministry. And unless Sophie could embrace the way he had learned to believe, there was no way they could ever be together, this much he was sure of. And who could guarantee him she would ever follow Jesus the way he did? Was he willing to risk his faith for a woman he'd only met two weeks ago?

He wanted to take her in his arms and kiss her.

Instead he said, "Yes, I believe He can handle it. Those who trust Him will always find His will." It wasn't what he wanted to say. He pushed himself. "Thank you for being so honest with me. I think you are the best friend I have ever had." He looked at her only briefly, fearing that the conflict in his heart would betray him instantly. Because his concern about God was only one side of the story. The other was that Sophie offered him her love, and she did it unconditionally. It reminded him of how he experienced the love of God—regardless of all his shortcomings, without reservations, and with no strings attached. But it was one thing to feel loved by God in that way and an entirely different thing when it came to a woman. Sophie's love scared him. Accepting it meant opening himself up and becoming vulnerable like her. He'd be forced to face his own insecurity instead of running from himself. He wasn't sure he could do it.

He forced his voice to sound casual as he turned toward the parking lot. "Maybe we should head back so we don't miss Jonathan's teaching. His lesson will start any minute."

Chapter Thirty-Eight

"What I'm about to teach makes the world mad, but it makes Christians glad!" Jonathan said with his strong southern accent. The class was laughing and stirring in anticipation. Controversial subjects were well loved at the Rock, as students were always looking for ways to explain their faith to the people around them.

Justin and Sophie sat toward the back of the classroom. They had returned from their walk in silence, and Justin noticed that Sophie was avoiding his eyes for the first time. He felt terrible. He knew he had hurt her again, but he didn't know how he could have prevented it. How could he make her understand that God came first in his life, as he was barely able to understand all of it himself?

As Jonathan went on, Justin glanced over at her from time to time. Maybe if Sophie could understand faith the way he had experienced it, she would understand him as well. *Lord, please touch Sophie's heart. Let her experience the power of a life surrendered to you.* Then his face brightened a little. If anyone was going to help make that prayer a reality, it was Jonathan.

"Our society is getting weaker, more selfish, and more arrogant day by day," Jonathan continued. "People want all their needs met, but without committing or even surrendering to a higher power. But you have to understand that everything comes with a price. Our nation with its media, educational system, and complacency of lazy citizens is heading straight toward hell. And we"—he paused and locked eyes with several students—"we are given the privilege and task to show them a better way!" There were nods and words of agreement. But Jonathan was only warming up.

"We are in a war, folks. It's not a war against people, but against the devil, who puts lies in people's heads. Lies telling them they are self-sufficient, that they can have it their own way. The lies of secular humanism that try to eliminate the need for God. The lies of modern science that try to disprove the Bible. And the lies of politicians and culture that call godly morals outdated and discriminating. Brothers and sisters, this is a real war, and we don't have the luxury of sparing ourselves or our loved ones the Truth."

Jonathan's voice was calm, yet intense. Justin nodded with enthusiasm and glanced over at Sophie again but couldn't decipher her facial expression. Well, she probably hadn't heard anything like it before. She clearly was hungry, but as a European she was probably more skeptical toward the moving of the Holy Spirit than Americans—at least that's what Jonathan had told them from his ministry trips to Europe.

"There's one thing you learn in the army whether you want to or not." Jonathan's eyes met Justin's and a proud smile entered his expression. "There is no place there for the weak. I could tell you many stories about my time in Vietnam, but one thing's for sure—when faced with the enemy, those boys had to pull their thumbs out of their mouths and grow up!"

Laughter filled the room, mainly from the men. Justin realized that Sophie was actually hanging her head by now. He knew this was no longer about this morning's conversation, but a reaction to what she was hearing right now. *There we go*, he thought to himself. *She's confronted with the truth.* It was a tough truth, but Jesus never said it was going to be easy.

"We are living in the most prosperous nation on the planet. We are the leaders, and the world is looking to us for answers. God has given us a unique calling to bring people into a deeper revelation of Him and His power. For this to happen, we need to give ourselves fully to Him. Our flesh hates this thought. It wants you to focus on yourself, your emotions, and your perceived needs. But God's army needs strong soldiers who have died to their own self. Or, in other words, all of us need to learn what the soldiers in Vietnam had to do. We need to pull our thumbs out of our mouths and grow up!"

For the rest of the class, Justin observed Sophie intently. Her body language had definitely changed. She was no longer leaning forward in anticipation but leaning back in her chair, hands clasped and face expressionless. Maybe she was not ready for this. After all, she had just gotten saved a couple of weeks ago. These messages were the *meat* the Apostle Paul talked about. Maybe Sophie needed milk first.

After class, an unusual amount of chatter filled the breakroom. Jonathan's comments had stirred much passion, especially in the many veterans that attended the school. Although raised in a different generation, Justin felt he could relate to what they were saying. It was about fighting an important battle. Like most boys, he had loved stories about war and good vs. bad. Now though, they were fighting for the souls of people. It was a spiritual fight, more important than any physical war had ever been. To be at the forefront of this spiritual warfare gave Justin goosebumps. It was what he was made for.

After leaving class, Sophie had excused herself and disappeared in the restroom. When he looked over again after a while, he saw Sophie standing with a few older students who were vividly discussing Jonathan's lesson. Her face showed concentration, as if she was trying hard to understand, but also bewilderment and hurt. He went over to her and lightly touched her shoulder.

"What stories are they trying to sell you?" he said, trying to sound lighthearted.

"Well, your friend here has asked us about the connection between war and the message of Jesus," one older gentleman replied before Sophie could answer. "And we explained to her that as the world's leading superpower and a nation chosen by God, we have the responsibility to save, restore, and protect those in need, both physically and spiritually—like Jesus did in his time."

"Are you saying that Jesus was commanding wars in the Bible?" Sophie asked the older man. Her voice showed interest as well as skepticism.

"Well, not directly, I suppose. But look at the Old Testament. There are countless incidents where God told Israel to go to war. And God doesn't change between the Old and New Testament." The older man looked around for confirmation from his friends and got several Amens as a result.

"I guess that's true," Sophie admitted. But Justin noticed that her sentence sounded more like a resignation than a revelation.

When the bell rang for the next class, he quickly pulled her aside. "How about we call it a day? It's been an intense morning. Maybe we could go for an early lunch?"

"That's a good idea. I think I need some time." Her voice was as apologetic as his.

At least she doesn't seem mad. "Since it's only eleven a.m., how about we get some brunch? I know the place with the best breakfast food in town, if you don't mind driving a bit."

They drove toward the mountains, and Sophie mentioned once again the spectacular views and how she had fallen in love with the wild landscape around the city. The similarity of her words and his own experience when first moving to Colorado Springs was remarkable. When they arrived at the Hungry Bear in the little town of Woodland Park, Justin assured her that the portions matched the name of the restaurant.

"I guess I'm just getting immersed in the American

culture," Sophie responded with a smile. Justin was so relieved over her brightening mood that he didn't mind her teasing his culture.

"I have to admit that Jonathan's teaching threw me off quite a bit," Sophie opened the conversation after they had ordered. There was no challenge in her voice, only confusion. "I have never thought of God as somebody who would talk to his people like an impatient dad to his four-year-old. Does God really tell *you* to pull your thumb out of your mouth?"

Jonathan is just bringing a point across. Maybe her sensitivity had to do with her liberal upbringing. "I think Jonathan has seen many lazy, complacent, spoiled Christians in his time, and this is his way of trying to wake them up and show them the great plan God has for their lives. Scripture tells us we can do greater things than even Jesus did. But we can't do those things if we have doubts and listen to our feelings and don't want to step on people's toes. That's why Jonathan uses strong words."

A long silence followed his words. Justin could tell Sophie was uncomfortable but didn't want to be confrontational. "It just sounds so insensitive and uncaring," she finally offered. "Isn't God interested in people on an individual basis? Surely this cannot be the way one should talk to everybody . . . at least I can't imagine saying something like this to my friends or a family member."

The innocence of her questions pierced Justin's heart. He knew Sophie was really trying to understand. And he wanted her to see the importance of this topic. "When you have really given your life to Jesus, you no longer care what people think about you. People will misunderstand you, ridicule you, and even persecute you. It's a promise in the Bible. You can't be a follower of Jesus if you love your own life or your reputation among your friends."

Again, there was a long silence before Sophie spoke. "I guess you must be right. It makes sense what you're saying, although I feel like I wished it wasn't so. Has this happened to you often since you became a Christian—coming across a truth you wished wasn't so?"

"Of course! The Bible says our flesh, or our worldly, unredeemed nature, is seeking only its own. It wants comfort, compromise, and selfish things. The message of the cross goes in the opposite direction. That's why we need to die to ourselves and live for Christ." He liked the fact that he was able to speak as eloquently as many of the teachers at the Rock by now. Since Sophie didn't say anything, he continued right on. "Our feelings, our heart, will often tell us things that are contrary to the Bible if we haven't learned to fine-tune ourselves with the leading of the Holy Spirit. The Scriptures are always above our own feelings. We cannot always trust our heart, but we can always trust the Bible." He could tell he had out-argued her, but his victory felt stale. He suddenly realized that with her, he wanted more than to just win the argument.

"Well, you know much more about this than me, obviously," she offered at last with a voice that told him she was trying to end the conversation. "Right now, I can't imagine following God if I have to go against my own heart to do so. It might be wishful thinking, but I'm trying to find a faith where my feelings, my heart, and God's will aren't at war."

She looked at him apologetically and with that innocence that got right under his skin. A part of him was disappointed by her words, but another part was falling more wildly in love with her every hour they spent together. It might rip him apart in the end.

"Justin, I think I need the rest of the day to myself. I need to process all I've heard today and sort things out a bit. I'm sorry if I've been weird this morning. I think God and I need to talk about a few things. I'd love to come back to school with you tomorrow, though."

Justin nodded silently. A terrible feeling crept up inside of him. This was not going the way he had hoped at all. She was leaving soon, and it didn't sound as if he would have many chances left to influence her. Even if she believed the way he did, a committed relationship would have been challenge enough for him. Adding in her liberal, watered-down Christianity, there were just too many unknowns. It wasn't worth the risk. No one was worth that risk.

Not even the most fascinating, charming, and beautiful woman he had ever met.

Chapter Thirty-Nine

Sophie drove down the Garden of the Gods road so lost in thought, she almost hit the car in front of her at the stop-light. She slammed on the brakes at the last second, and a cuss word almost escaped her mouth. This day had turned into quite a mess.

Justin had dropped her off where she'd left her car, and she was now driving around aimlessly. She was not in the mood for sightseeing. She felt hurt, confused, and a little panicky. Was this going to be the end of it? Would Justin and she become acquaintances across the ocean, dropping a note every once in a while and assuring each other they'd stay in touch? She choked up just thinking about this. She had never met anybody like Justin, and she feared she never might again. But right now, she saw no way forward.

Feeling a headache coming on, she decided to drive home and take a nap. But laying in her bed, the events of the day came back to her in a ceaseless stream of images and sentences. Jonathan's sermon. The words of the veterans. And Justin's side glances in class, which hadn't gone unnoticed by her. It had made her feel like a child whose teacher feverishly waits for the coin to drop. Was she really missing the point?

Was the Christianity Thomas had introduced her to timid and powerless? She had to admit that the Rock was much more exciting than Thomas's group. The people around Jonathan sounded like they were dynamic, significant, and on the forefront of the Christian movement. And there was an atmosphere of belonging and victory at the Rock. Why then was it hard for her to just join in? She loved all of it—except for the parts she didn't love, like Jonathan's sermon from this morning. She loved the students—except that she didn't like how they had laughed at Jonathan's remark about toughening up. Was she trying to cling to a version of Christianity that suited her personality, rather than the real truth? But then why was this quiet voice inside her saying otherwise? How much she missed talking through all this with Thomas.

Thomas! She shot out of bed. She had totally forgotten her email to him the night before. Surely he had replied by now, as he was a very faithful communicator. She ran to her computer and opened her mail. There it was.

My dearest Sophie,

I'm so glad to hear you are doing well. I was beginning to worry about you after not having heard from you for a whole week. This old heart is connected very tightly to yours, you know.

What a wonderful coincidence that you found a different place to visit after your aunt was unavailable. I read that Colorado Springs must be a city of breathtaking beauty. And that Bible college . . . I can't wait to hear all about it! Jonathan Parker must be quite a dynamic personality (yes, I did look up the college on the internet).

I'm very happy for you, Sophie. To experience how other people express their faith will always enhance our lives and help us define and shape our own. Keep your heart and mind open and remember that God has as many expressions of faith as He has children!

I'm so thankful that your friend Cindy is hosting you. I'm sure you've met many wonderful people at the school and are enjoying yourself. Please give a very big hug to the wonderful man who rescued you off the mountain—I feel like you might have met him a time or two as well during this week.

I would love to pick you up from the airport when you get back early Saturday if I may. Please email me the details and I will be there.

Love, Thomas

Sophie's cheeks turned red when she got to the sentence about Justin. Had it been *that* apparent at the Lodge? It hadn't even been apparent to herself at that time—nobody else had made any comment, and Thomas hadn't met Justin. But it wasn't the first time her old friend surprised her in this way, showing her how deep his affection and how keen his observation was. Oh, she missed him, and she actually *wanted* him to know what was going on. She needed somebody to process this through with, and there was no question he was the one. She decided to call him right away. To save herself from international call charges, she tried Skype. No answer. FaceTime. Nothing. WhatsApp. Again, she had to eventually hang up. Getting upset, she forgot about the charges and dialed his phone number. When his voicemail came on, she nearly started swearing. Too upset now to leave a message, she hung up and threw herself back on the bed.

It was past dinnertime when Cindy stuck her head into Sophie's bedroom. All she could see was her new friend's head sticking out of the sheets, deep asleep.

I sure hope that boy Justin's treating her right, Cindy thought to herself. She had seen the signs of love all over Sophie from the start, and she felt protective of her new friend with her innocent faith and beautiful spirit. Unfortunately, love stories didn't always end well. She was really hoping Sophie and Justin's story could be different.

Chapter Forty

The next morning, Sophie texted Justin as soon as she got out of bed.

> Good morning, Justin! I'm feeling a lot better today. I think I just needed to recharge. See you in class soon.

She made herself a nice, hot breakfast. Cindy had already left, but maybe it was better not to discuss things with anybody at the moment. Instead, she planned to enjoy the last day she had at the Rock and with Justin. Beyond that, she didn't know anything, and for right now, it was surprisingly ok.

The morning at school went by quickly. The lessons were less controversial than yesterday's, since it was mainly on topics like Old Testament survey or Pauline Epistles. The day had again started with worship, which Sophie loved dearly. Music always helped her look inside herself and get to a place of peace. After the last lesson of the day, Sophie said goodbye to the many students she had gotten to know this week. It was hard to believe it had actually only been four days, as it felt like such a long time to her. The Rock was definitely a place with a sense of belonging, joy, and exuberance, and despite the difficult parts, she was very glad she had experienced it.

"I'd say it's time for one last hike," Justin suggested on the way out the door. They drove toward the mountains and were already a ways outside of Colorado Springs when Justin got a call. From his irritated expression, Sophie could tell something was not going as planned.

"Caleb just called. His car broke down on the side of the road, and he needs me to bring him home while they tow his car. Simon is at work, and he can't get a hold of anyone else. I'm so sorry! We should definitely go for that walk later in the afternoon, though. Do you want me to drop you back at the school?"

She thought for a moment. "Actually, aren't we right by that lovely town where we ate brunch the other day? There were all these cute shops, and I know I saw a Starbucks with a view of Pikes Peak there too. Why don't you just drop me off there, and I'll stroll around and have some coffee, and you pick me back up when you're done?"

After Justin left, Sophie enjoyed the many artsy mountain stores in the little town of Woodland Park. After some strolling around, she decided to treat herself to her last mocha Frappuccino and that beautiful view of Pikes Peak. She settled with her drink at a free table outside the coffee shop and was about to get her book out when she overheard a conversation a few tables behind her. She couldn't see them, but she knew immediately that the people talking were part of the Rock.

"Well, you might not understand this, coming from a different country. But here in America, there really is no choice in what side you're on when you're a Christian, as I'm sure you've heard Jonathan say many times!" a deep voice said.

There was a pause. Then a young man spoke, and from his accent Sophie knew he was from Europe. "In my country, we have nine different parties making up our parliament. Christians are found in most, if not all, of these parties. Because there are so many political and social issues that are of importance to a Christian and so many different views that derive themselves from the Bible, I cannot imagine all Christians being in the same party. And here, you only really have two parties, which seems to make this even more impossible!"

His remark was met with so many different voices talking at the same time that Sophie couldn't really understand what was being said. But she could tell that some of those who reacted were quite upset. In the end, one voice carried louder than the others.

"Real Christians cannot have differing views on important political topics," the deep voice from before stated. "How are we going to change the world if we fight among ourselves? The Bible is our only standard, and it is proclaiming only one Truth. And I can assure you, there is only one party in the US that is adhering to this Truth."

"So you're saying that one cannot be a Christian and a member of the other party then?" The young man's voice was heard again. Sophie was completely absorbed in the conversation by now.

"I guess you can be a misguided Christian. I don't think you'd be a Spirit-filled Christian, because the Spirit of God will lead you to the Truth. But of course there are tons of Christians who have not yet understood the full Gospel, and many of them are liberals. We need to pray for them, because Satan is trying to sow confusion and division through them and others whose hearts are full of worldly thoughts and who doubt the inerrant Word of God."

At this, Sophie heard a chair being pushed back and a person walk out the coffee shop quickly. She still had her back to the group and was afraid of turning around because she already felt guilty of eavesdropping. Involuntarily, she found herself rallying for the young European and hoped it wasn't him that just left.

"Sorry for Nick's behavior. We know you're not trying to sow division. He's just very protective of his faith, and he actually just wants to help you see. But he didn't need to be rude.

He's quite the hothead at times. Hey, how about we head back to town and get ready for Bible study tonight?"

"Okay. I'll be there tonight. I think I'll sit here for a while and read. Just go ahead. I'll see you in a bit." There was rustling of chairs and people leaving, and then it got quiet. Sophie was excited, because from what she understood, the young man was by himself now. She finally turned around and did see only one person left at the table. She gathered her stuff, as well as her courage, and walked over to him.

"Excuse me . . . I overheard you talking about Jonathan Parker. Are you a student at the Rock?"

"I am. And I'm sorry we were loud enough to entertain the whole place! Sit down, please. I remember you from Monday on the stage." He held out his hand to her with a big smile and Sophie shook it. "My name is Bjørn. And I'm afraid I forgot yours, although they mentioned it on stage," he said with an apologetic smile. Sophie introduced herself and sat down across from him.

"I do remember that you're visiting from Switzerland and that you met our friend Justin under special circumstances." Here he winked at her, and she almost turned red again.

"That's right. And from what I hear, you're also from Europe. Somewhere in Scandinavia?" she suggested.

"Yes, Norway. I came here last fall to attend the Rock."

"And you're friends with Justin?" Sophie made sure her voice was as nonchalant as possible.

"Well, at least I thought we were. There was an incident a couple of weeks ago, and we haven't really talked since then, but I'm hoping we still are friends."

Quite a mysterious answer. But there was something else on her mind. "I overheard some of your conversation with your friends before. I wasn't trying to eavesdrop, but I have to admit the conversation caught my attention."

Bjørn smiled, then got serious. "Well, I don't know where you stand on all this, but coming from a European country with political diversity, you might understand my position a bit better. It saddens me every time my questions are interpreted as doubt in God's word or even as an attempt to sow discord. I just have a hard time with the way politics and religion are married here."

"Well, all of this is new to me, as I've only been a Christian for a very short time. But I have to admit that some things I've heard at the Rock have confused me. I've just assumed it is because I have not read the Bible much. So it's interesting to hear you, who's been studying the Bible much longer, having similar questions."

Bjørn's face lit up. She could tell he was delighted to have someone to share these thoughts with. "Sometimes it is very valuable to hear things from the perspective of someone who is new to Christianity. We can get blind inside our own little circles." He looked at Sophie with warmth. "I'd be interested in what things have caught your attention, if you'd like to share."

"I guess the most difficult was Jonathan's class yesterday about soldiers and America being the most prosperous nation in the world—considering that the US is only number nine in terms of GPD per capita, behind both our countries for that matter. But more than that, I think the comment about adults pulling their thumbs out of their mouths was just insensitive and arrogant." Until saying this, she hadn't really realized how much Jonathan's words had bothered her.

To her surprise, Bjørn burst out laughing. "Oh, Sophie! Can you imagine me hearing this kind of language for a whole year? I came here because of Jonathan's teaching on the unconditional love of God for us. Little did I know when I enrolled that his school was going to be so . . . so patriotic! Most students here have never been outside of their country. Many actually believe that most countries overseas are developing nations, or at least way behind the US. When I tried to explain to some of them the social and economic system of Norway and other northern European countries, they were at the same time baffled and offended. They had heard about it, yes. But surely their country was the greatest. It reminds me of kids on the playground, bragging about who's the biggest and strongest. It really seems that the school supports this notion when it comes to patriotism, although they are quick to condemn it in other parts of the human experience. I have heard Jonathan say many times that as the greatest nation in the world America has a mandate from God to lead the world in spiritual matters as well."

Sophie frowned. It was scary to think of grown men bragging about their country's superiority over all the others. She knew it all too well from the history of her continent. Of course, as a citizen of an incredibly small country, this idea hadn't really presented itself to her. The Swiss thought of their country more with endearing fondness and taught in school that every country should celebrate their uniqueness and culture. What she had heard in the past week was different.

"But you're still here," she said, more to herself than to him.

It took a while before Bjørn replied. "This school has given me incredibly much. I have experienced wonderful friendships and met awesome people. There is an atmosphere of enthusiasm and energy, and the people who are a part of it are very sincere.

"At first, I was able to concentrate on Jonathan's original message of God's unconditional love, an incredibly powerful truth. But as time went on, other voices in the school have gotten louder as well. And those voices didn't carry much love or compassion. Rather, they were voices of people so sure of their own truths, they called everything else doubt. I have seen it affect people I love dearly. It feels like a movement away from celebrating the foundations we share, and instead arguing about the peripherals we disagree about. Only that now to some at the Rock, the peripherals have become the foundation."

Sophie could see how something like that might happen, especially in a group as dynamic and high-spirited as the Rock.

She wholeheartedly agreed with what Bjørn said—except that she didn't know what to do with it when it came to a specific person she cared very much about. Was Justin like the people Bjørn described? Admittedly, he was quite a hardliner. But she also somehow knew a different side to Justin, and what she saw at the moment was shaped heavily by the influence of the people he currently listened to. What would Justin be like outside of the Rock? And was she ever going to experience it?

Her phone interrupted her musings. Justin would be back to pick her up at Starbucks in fifteen minutes. She looked at Bjørn. "Well, it was really good getting to know you. I'm happy to have heard a different side of this whole experience as well. I think I feel similar to you about the school. In the past week, I have met wonderful people and felt the connection and community at the Rock. It is a powerful experience, but I have also had moments where my heart cringed at what was being taught. I don't really understand yet how the heart plays into all of this and how I can reconcile some things in the Bible with it. Since I'm so new to this, I feel like I have to take it with me, let it sit for a while, and see what it will do to me."

Bjørn smiled. "That sounds like a wise plan. Receiving thoughts, even though they might be unsettling at the moment, and giving them room inside of you is one of the surest ways to grow. Don't ever be afraid that this mindset will destroy your faith, as some at the Rock say. Our faith is not based on blind loyalty or on shutting out the rest of the world. Our faith rests on a Person. And He is well able to deal with our questions, doubts, and crazy ideas, because none of them change Him. You cannot miss Him if you are truly looking for Him."

Sophie nodded. She glanced at her phone. Should she wait for Justin outside? She wasn't sure if he was going to be happy seeing her with Bjørn. He seemed to read her mind. "Is Justin picking you up? You might want to meet him outside since he and I are not on the best terms right now. You will be able to imagine what our disagreements were about now that I have told you my view of things. But I highly respect Justin, and I know he has a big heart, even if it's sometimes hidden under some religious stuff. He's a born leader with a real passion for God. And besides, he's one of the most fun people to hang out with. But I feel like you might have found that out yourself already!"

He winked and gave her a warm smile. Sophie didn't even turn red, so safe did her new friend make her feel. She got up and gave him a hug. She was surely going to stay in touch with this man whose experience of the Rock was so similar to hers. Then she left and braced herself for what she knew was going to be the last few hours together with Justin.

Chapter Forty-One

When Justin pulled up to Starbucks, Sophie was already waiting for him, her blonde hair playing in the wind and her face still animated from the conversation she'd just left.

"Ready for a hike?" Justin asked, and she got in the car. "How about we go to that state park again . . . you know, the one with the bears who have to go through me to get to you?" He winked and made her laugh.

They chose a shorter trail since it was already later in the day. It was a perfectly beautiful Colorado day, and Sophie once more thought that this part of the US must be the best-kept secret since they didn't encounter another person on their hike. After an hour's hike, they rested on a fallen log overlooking the vast landscape around them. Sophie closed her eyes and took in the sounds and smells of this place she had already grown to love. When she opened them again, she saw his dark eyes resting on her. His face was soft.

"We've come quite far," he said quietly, seemingly lost in thought. She knew he wasn't talking about the hike. Her eyes locked with his, and her thoughts were so strong she was sure he must be able to read them.

I'm ready to go further.

For a moment, time stood still, and she thought he would take her into his arms. Then the spell broke.

"Tell me more about you," he said, his voice catching a little. "What do you want to do in life?"

She willed herself back to reality and thought about what he had asked. "That's a good question. I wouldn't say I have ever thought that far into the future. I love my job at the college . . . but of course that doesn't mean I necessarily want to do this for the rest of my life. I don't really know." Even to herself, the response seemed pretty lame. She had never before been ashamed for not having a more cut-out plan for her life, but being asked by Justin made her wish she had thought of a better answer. Something that sounded more spiritual, more exciting. "What about you?"

"Well, I'm going to go out and change the world."

This was a boastful statement, but Sophie could tell she was buying it. He talked about it as a matter of fact, without any excuse for how outlandish it sounded. Sophie would never have said anything like it in a million years. The Swiss had a reputation for underestimating their own abilities and influence. Showing your wealth was considered just as arrogant as boasting about your abilities or successes. When thinking about the future, the Swiss would talk about taking things step-by-step and, at best, talk about a mid-term goal.

Apparently, at the Rock it was different. In a matter of only a few days, she had heard several teachers talk about planting churches, healing people, bringing the gospel to the ends of the earth and, in general, changing the world. It was the kind of generalized hyperbole talk that Sophie usually couldn't stand. But in Justin's case, it hardly seemed like exaggeration. She could almost feel herself wishing for it to be true.

"Where are you going to start?" she asked while still digesting his statement.

"India."

"Wow, that's a surprise!"

"Why? What surprises you about this?" His question was

innocent, as if India was the most obvious answer he could have given.

"Well, I just didn't know you had any interest in the Indian culture or had any relationship with it."

Justin shrugged. "Well, I don't. But there are one point three billion people there, and ninety-seven percent of them are not Christians. Seems like a good place to start."

Sophie shook her head. She could tell he was serious, and she didn't doubt he would do what he was implying. But to her, making a decision with as far-reaching consequences as moving around the world couldn't just be explained in one sentence.

I want to understand you. Again, she felt that thought so strongly she thought he must have heard it. Instead she said, "Have you ever been to India?"

"No. But my dad went there last summer with a friend of his. It was like a private mission trip, just the two of them. His friend had some contacts in India, and he said it was life changing. They visited people in villages who came out of their homes when they saw them and said, 'What did these white people come all the way out here for?' It was the perfect setup to tell them the gospel. They saw people saved after just a few hours of teaching."

Considering Justin's powerfully convincing personality, coupled with his honest enthusiasm, Sophie didn't doubt he was going to be successful. Still, the way he told the story made her somewhat uneasy. "When will you leave?"

"My ticket is booked for two days after graduation. It will be in, let's see . . . not even a month from now."

"You are pretty wild. Do you know that?" When she said it, Sophie hoped Justin wouldn't look too deeply into her eyes.

"Well, this is just what makes sense to me. I can't think of doing anything else more exciting than this."

For a moment, their eyes met fully. It was a challenge—and an invitation for her to join him.

But could she? And if she could, did she actually want to? Something in her wanted to put the nagging questions aside and shout out, *I'm coming with you!* She knew he would accept, but it would be on his terms. There would not be room for doubts or ways of thinking outside of Jonathan's doctrine. She got up quickly, walked a few steps, and looked over the mountain range for a long time.

She couldn't do it.

During the mostly quiet rest of their walk, Sophie made up her mind. She would enjoy this last evening and say goodbye to this wonderful, fascinating, stubborn man. It wouldn't be goodbye forever. Maybe she'd visit him in India one day, or maybe he'd travel to Switzerland. Everything was possible. But for now, she was telling her heart to let him go.

Chapter Forty-Two

They decided to have dinner at a place called Wines of Colorado on the way back to town. After finishing their meal, they sat across from each other, avoiding long eye contact that could lead to things getting out of control. Justin knew Sophie had been trying to make the best of the situation, but he also sensed her melancholy mood.

He knew what he wanted. He wanted Sophie to be as radical as him, to let go of all her what-ifs, her reservations, and her humanistic baggage. He wanted her to come with him to India and join him on an adventure of knowing nothing but the grace and provision of God. But if he was entirely honest, he just wanted her. Beyond her faith, and beyond even his own calling, he wanted to be with her, to walk through life with her, to experience God and adventure and beauty with her.

But he was scared. He had heard stories of people with great callings stuck in mundane lives and blaming their spouses for it. People destined for great works for God reduced to living a sorry, average life because they weren't willing to sacrifice their romantic desires for the Kingdom of God. He was not going to be one of them, because not even Sophie was worth that.

He had to admit that, at least on a heart level, it did look like Sophie really loved God and had a desire to live for Him. She was a Christian, yes. But she wasn't spirit-filled, and she obviously didn't believe in many parts of the worldview Justin had embraced. And as much as he tried, there was nothing he could do about it.

"So . . . what will you do when you get back home?" he finally asked to break the uncomfortable silence that had developed since they'd finished eating.

"Well, the final quarter of college starts Monday, so I'll be back to teaching full time for a couple of months. In Switzerland, school won't be over until the end of June. Final exams are around the corner, and grading all these papers will keep me very busy until the end of the semester. I haven't thought of what to do during summer yet since I've been having quite an extravagant spring break this year." A little smile came back to her eyes. "So I guess your summer is bound to be more exciting than mine."

"I think it's definitely going to be an adventure—especially because my plan is pretty vague at this point."

"What do you mean? Won't you be with any mission organization?"

"Nope."

"But you must have some sort of lodging arranged?"

"I don't have anything arranged. I have one contact, a local pastor who drove my dad and his friend to villages to preach, but I'm not too sure yet how anything is going to play out. It's all in God's hands."

People at the Rock had been encouraging him, telling him that God would provide and that Justin was an example of a twenty-first century apostle. Sophie on the other hand seemed to work on hiding her surprise and maybe even disapproval.

"How are you going to support yourself?" Her question wasn't accusing, which helped Justin ease back from the defensive position he had felt himself slipping into.

"I'm going to send out a newsletter each month, telling my

friends about what's happening in India and how they can be a part of it. My dad helped me set up a 501(c)3 already." When he saw the question mark on Sophie's face, he added, "That's the nonprofit status that will allow me to receive tax-deductible donations. I already have around eighty people signed up to be on the list. Even Jonathan asked to be on it when I told him about my plans. Besides, living in India will be dirt cheap."

Sophie seemed to try and piece all of this together. "So what activities will you start out with when you get there?"

"I'll go out to villages and preach the gospel—with a pack on my back and a Bible in my hands. I don't want to stay in big cities since most people there have already heard about Jesus. I want to do what Paul said in Romans 15 and go 'Preach the Good News where the name of Christ has never been heard.'"

Justin looked off into the distance as he repeated those words he had said to himself so many times in the past months. It was the noblest of all missions as far as he was concerned. He secretly looked down on missionaries working in well-established centers and big cities. Where was the danger in that? It was reaching the unreached, the indigenous tribes in remote villages, that interested him. If the choice was between the easy and the hard task, he chose the hardest.

Even Sophie seemed to have caught a bit of the fire that came out of him. She kept asking question after question, and with each answer he gave, she became a bit less skeptical and a bit more excited. He could also tell she wanted to end this on a good note and did her best to sound supportive.

Suddenly, a shy smile appeared on her face. "You know, I just had an idea! Of course it's totally up to you . . . but I remember you saying that you're not into design and graphics. If you want to send out a newsletter to ask for support, it should look appealing and have lots of pictures and all that. I've been doing the newsletter for our college for the past two years and have gotten quite good at it . . ." Her voice trailed off, her hands clasped together nervously, and she looked away as if preparing for a rejection.

The sudden realization that she doubted he'd want her help struck Justin with full force. It was so obvious how much she cared and how open she was. Why couldn't he respond with the same openness? Guilt seared itself into him as he realized that his internal judgement of her spiritual inferiority had made its way straight to her heart. What was he doing to this wonderful, innocent person, who constantly made herself so vulnerable in front of him? He reeled. There it was again, his instinct to flee from situations too personal, too terrifying. His eyes actually went to the door of the restaurant. He wanted to run.

But not from Sophie. She was too safe, too genuine.

Without thinking, he allowed his heart to speak. "Sophie, that is a wonderful offer. And I'm really sorry if things I've said or the way I've acted has made you feel insecure. You have no idea how much your help would mean to me. I would totally love to work with you, and I know the newsletter will turn out way better with your help."

Sophie blushed but stayed silent.

The words came out of Justin now as if he had wanted to say nothing else for the past days. "Sophie, I was so afraid you would disappear out of my life after tonight. Not that I would blame you. Life is confusing at the moment, and I know the last few days have been wonderful but also challenging for both of us. I'm so sorry if I've hurt you."

He stopped when tears welled up in Sophie's eyes, but then decided to continue anyway. "I want you to know that I have never known anyone like you. I know how much you care about me; you have shown it over and over. And I care about you too. . . ." Here his voice broke, and he had to look away. When his voice was firm again, he simply said, "I truly hope this is only the beginning."

Sophie nodded, then wiped her eyes and smiled. "I'm sorry I'm such a mess. It's been quite a week for sure. Well, I'm excited to help you with your fundraising and stay in the loop with what's going on in your life." She looked at him. "I've had the most amazing time, Justin. Thank you so much for showing me your world and for all the wonderful conversations. I will never forget them." She picked up her purse. "By the way, I will leave for the airport early tomorrow morning, so this will probably be goodbye."

"Oh, please allow me to come to the airport with you and see you off. I'd really love to."

"But I will leave at seven a.m., and it's a Friday. There'll be traffic."

Justin put on his most indignant face possible. "Traffic? I'll be at Cindy's at six forty-five with two extra hot lattes, thank you very much!"

Sophie laughed out loud at his facial expression, and the sting shot through Justin once more, leaving him to wonder if he was making the single most stupid decision in his life by not kissing her at that very moment.

Chapter Forty-Three

It was 6:40 a.m. when Sophie answered her door the next morning. Not only did Justin bring Starbucks, he had also gone to the French bakery and gotten some croissants for their breakfast in the car.

They left after a heartfelt goodbye to Cindy. Sophie first dropped off her rental car and then joined Justin in his truck. The drive to Denver was cheerful. It was the feeling of relief after a decision is made, and they both enjoyed the relaxed atmosphere it created. They discussed ideas about the newsletters, talked about the Rock, Colorado, and Switzerland.

Check-in was taken care of quickly, giving them time for one last coffee. As they sat across from each other, Sophie shook her head. "I just can't believe it's only been five days. I feel like I've known you half my life and as if Colorado has become a part of me."

"It feels the same way for me. It's hard to believe that if I hadn't glanced down at that red hat dancing in the snow, we might never have met. Ha! If that isn't God, I don't know what is."

They both smiled at each other as they enjoyed the lightheartedness of their last moments.

When the time came for Sophie to go through security, they got in line and fell silent. Before they approached the security officer who was going to separate them, Justin pulled Sophie to the side and told the people behind them to pass. He took her hands, and they looked into each other's eyes for a long time without saying a word.

Sophie knew what she saw in Justin's eyes was love. She still didn't understand what it was exactly that stood in their way, but seeing his eyes speak so clearly was all she needed. He pulled her into an embrace and held her so close she could feel his heart beating wildly. There were no words, but his strong arms held her tightly as if he was trying to keep her here. When at last he released his grip, Sophie touched his face lightly with her hands. Justin closed his eyes.

"Goodbye, Justin," she whispered and spun around to walk through security without looking back.

As she tried to find her way down the hall through tear-blurred eyes, she knew she was leaving with hope in her heart. This would not be the last time they would see each other. It wasn't what she had wished for, but it was enough to get through right now. She didn't care anymore that this plane was going to take her thousands of miles away from Justin. It was his eyes, the way he looked at her just then. She had recognized the love, and it was all she needed to know.

PART III

Summer 2018

Chennai, India
Rasa, Switzerland

Chapter Forty-Four

The honks of cars and rickshaws blended with the yelling of street vendors, the sounds of police sirens, and the mooing of cows, creating a chaotic, beautiful symphony. Smells of fried samosas and tea lingered in the air, rivaled by the fruity scent of the marigold flowers worn around the neck of sari-clad ladies. It was one of those days in late May when the thermometer had long passed a hundred degrees, and the vendors selling coconut water right out of the fruit did excellent business. Traffic was slow, testing the patience of drivers like it did every day.

A young man stood out from the crowd. He was white, but more than that, he clearly did not know how to navigate the traffic. He was on foot and tried to cross a busy street with no markings. Standing at the curb for several minutes, he darted his head left to right and back again, as he would do in his home country, trying to find a chance to slip through. But traffic was so heavy, there never seemed a safe moment to do so. Finally, he just took his chances and plunged himself into traffic. He had mostly watched for cars and rickshaws, and therefore didn't anticipate the motorcycle coming out from behind a truck and nearly hitting him. The man swerved and yelled at him, but the man had no time to listen. He was now in the middle of the road, avoiding a bus here and a rickshaw there, until he finally made the dart over the second half. He landed on the curb only to find himself face-to-face with an emaciated cow eating its way through the trash pile next to his feet.

For a while, the young man stood by the side of the street, regaining his composure. He was carrying a little backpack with some groceries he had purchased on the other side of the road. It had been a long process since he could not read the signs on the little storefronts and had to enter several shops until he found one that actually sold food. Then came the task of finding items he could recognize and was willing to eat. Finally, he had stuffed a loaf of bread, four bananas, six eggs, and a plastic bag filled with milk in his backpack. He hoped that the woman at the cash register would give him the right amount of change, and once out of the store, he tackled the way back to the other side of the street. Several pairs of eyes followed him as he disappeared into a run-down apartment complex right off one of the busiest streets in Chennai.

Chapter Forty-Five

The wind played in Sophie's hair as she stood at the pier looking across Lake Lucerne. She had anticipated spending this day with Thomas, and taking a round trip on a passenger ship on this lake would take several hours—enough time for her to finally tell him about Justin.

He had picked her up from the airport almost a month ago, but they had only a short time to talk as Thomas had to leave for an international trip only days after her return to Switzerland. So Sophie had been on her own trying to work through all that had happened to her in the US. She confided in Laura, and her girlfriend was excited for her to have finally fallen in love again and at the same time worried about Justin's religious zeal. Her parents were skeptical as well, mentioning their different cultures and all the challenges that would pose for a serious relationship. Sophie had to admit they were right, and yet it didn't change anything about her feelings for the fascinating, stubborn American who had captivated her heart.

Thomas arrived on the pier just in time for boarding. They chose outside seats on the top deck that would give them the best views of the rugged, wild landscape that characterized this part of central Switzerland.

"Now, tell me all about your week at the Bible school," Thomas said after they got settled.

She couldn't get herself to begin with Justin right away, so she first started off telling him about Jonathan's charisma, his incredible stories, the energy surrounding the school. Thomas listened with great interest. When she mentioned the questions she had concerning some of the doctrine, Thomas smiled slightly and gave her the look she wished her own dad had given her more often. She knew he understood the place she was in, torn between the fascination of something exciting and powerful and the caution she had learned to use when things sounded too good to be true.

"And what do you think about all of this now, a month later?"

"Getting back into my Swiss routine was harder than I thought it'd be. While grading papers, my mind has been wandering back to the Rock and all its excitement, and I think it created a sort of discontentment about my job I didn't expect. Things that were just a part of my life until now suddenly seemed boring and shortsighted. Life at the Rock was just so exuberant and colorful that I felt like I had changed back from a sparkly evening dress into sweatpants."

Thomas chuckled, but then added in a more serious tone, "I know exactly what you're talking about. It's called reverse culture shock, and it's quite normal. The question is what you'll do with these inputs now."

"Yes, that's exactly the question." Sophie looked over the water. She had always loved teaching, but since having met Justin and hearing the teachings at the Rock, she wondered if she was wasting her time here. Was she doing "the Lord's work here," as they called it at the Rock? Creating Justin's first newsletter last week had been a work of art as well as one of love. She had put her heart into it, amazed at his gift of painting a vision and believing in it so strongly himself. Some of the statements had been a bit exaggerated and definitely idealistic. But maybe the Swiss cut-and-dry, factual approach was too boring for anyone to catch on to a bold vision. She had even sat down one evening and sought out several missions organizations who offered short-term mission trips around the world. She wasn't ready to do something like Justin was doing, but maybe she could go on a short trip and get a feel for this kind of work? She had asked God for wisdom about what to do while the advertisements had started piling up on her desk. But despite the inviting, encouraging words of the organizations, something in her had kept her hesitating.

So yes, Thomas's question definitely rang true. But if she was honest, the biggest part of her excitement about the Rock was the presence of a particular man. She decided to finally tackle the subject. "I actually spent quite some time with Justin—you know, the guy from the mountain." She looked up to see his reaction.

Thomas lifted an eyebrow. "Is that so?" he asked, and she knew he'd found her out the moment he saw her at the airport.

"I can see that you suspected something. Well, Justin and I hung out all week. We went hiking a lot, and we talked all the time. He is a very special person . . . and I'm pretty sure I've fallen in love."

Thomas studied her face, love and concern written all over his own. She knew his desire to see her happy was battling his urge to protect her.

"Your eyes talk strongly about your feelings for this man, and that is a good thing. Our hearts are made to love, even though it's not always safe and certainly not always easy." He leaned back and looked at her. "Please go on. I want to hear everything you care to tell me about him."

Running the risk of sounding naïve and romantic at times, she told him everything about her time at the Rock. She left nothing out, as she knew he was as far from judging her than anyone she knew. She told him about Justin's past, his character, his visionary personality, and his all-or-nothing approach. She told him about the long walks, the intimacy of sitting so close and of sharing things like the special sunset at the Garden of the Gods. And she told him how they had held each other on that last day.

"The funny thing is," she said at last, "that we are really very unlike each other. Many of the things he says or plans are crazy in my eyes. Awesome, but crazy. For us to have such a connection, such ease of conversation, and such a desire to be around each other was blowing my mind."

Thomas nodded in agreement, but he still didn't say anything, waiting for her to continue. The hard part of the story didn't come so easily. She told him how sometimes Justin's clear-cut faith had made her feel insecure and inferior. How some of the stuff that was said at the Rock, or maybe even more *how* it was said, constricted her heart. And how she was quite certain that for Justin, a future with her would be possible only if she saw faith the exact way he did. When she was finished, there was a long silence.

Finally, Thomas spoke, and his voice was as emotional as she had ever heard it. "The fact that you can analyze your relationship with Justin to this degree makes me so happy and proud. You are learning early on in your faith that things are hardly ever black and white, and that those who paint life without color miss out on an awful lot."

He paused a moment before continuing. "It is never wise to judge an organization or person whom you have never talked to and know only from their website. Therefore, I want to be careful and open in how I think about Jonathan and the school.

"What caught my attention, though, was you noticing the constriction of your heart. Whenever that happens, it's time to pause. That's when we need to stand back and look at the doctrine, the method, the person, or the event more carefully. Because your heart is the most powerful tool God uses to guide you through life."

Sophie nodded. She knew it was the right decision to be mindful of those signals that came from within, even if it sometimes resulted in a hard decision. That reminded her of another topic she was currently wrestling with.

"By the way, I've been helping Justin with his newsletter, and reading about all the thoughts and dreams of a missionary, I've recently been wondering if maybe I should be taking a step in this direction just to see if anything comes from it. I haven't made any plans for the summer, so maybe I could go on a short-term mission trip? I've been looking at all kinds of brochures in the past week." She realized she was hoping to sell this idea to him—and maybe to herself too. Maybe that's why she didn't mention the hesitations that went with those thoughts.

Thomas again studied her and finally said, "What would be your goal in going on a trip like this?"

"Well . . . I guess it has to do with finding God's will for my life. I don't know if I want to stay a teacher all my life. Maybe I'm supposed to do something more impactful for the body of Christ. It seems that missionary work is as impactful a work as you could ever do."

"You're not trying to prove yourself to anyone, are you?" His question stung, and she looked away.

"Sophie, I'm not judging you. I hope you know me well enough by now to be sure of that. But I do want to make sure the motivation for your actions is what you want it to be."

"Well, I hope my motivation would be to share Jesus with people who have not met him." She knew her answer was a bit short, although Thomas acted as if he hadn't noticed.

"That is a wonderful motivation. Have you noticed, though, that a person is the best witness for Jesus when they try the least? When your everyday life reminds others of Jesus, then you are a true witness. I'm not totally sure a mission trip is the best place to learn this as you are very focused on trying to be a witness, and there is at times a whole lot of pressure to perform."

Sophie brushed the hair out of her face and looked at Thomas across the little table on the top deck of the ship. What he said made sense, and he was again bringing up a point of view she hadn't thought of before. Not a very exciting one, but one that made her feel grounded, like when she got off the *Noordfries* for the first time and realized how shaky the ship had been all that time at sea.

"I'm glad you brought up your summer plans, Sophie," he continued after a while. "I actually might have an alternative to a mission trip that could end up being just as life-changing. Do you want to hear about it?"

"Of course I do."

"Well, there is a place in the Centovalli—you might have heard of this valley in the Ticino?"

Sophie nodded. The Ticino was the southernmost canton of Switzerland, with several valleys and mountain ranges bordering Italy. She had visited the canton many times but had never been to that specific valley yet.

"Well, there is a small village on top of one of the mountain ranges. It is totally secluded. No roads lead up there, there is no store, just a number of century-old brick houses and cobblestone walking paths."

Sophie's interest was sparked. "How do you get up there?"

"A cable car goes up from the valley every so often during the day. After eight p.m. it can only be used for emergencies."

"Sounds peaceful. So what's up there that I might be interested in?"

"There is a Christian retreat center run by a variety of people from different denominations and backgrounds. Most of them work with university students, helping them to tie together their intellect and their faith. But the little community is much more than a gathering of academics. I have found it to be a place of deep spirituality and peace. Nothing helps your contemplative side come out better than a place without anywhere to go, with no luxury and no distractions."

"Sounds a bit like a modern monastery," Sophie said, only half joking.

Thomas smiled. "Actually, you are quite right. Many aspects of the monastic lifestyle are observed. Not so much the outside aspects like fasting or getting up at four a.m. to pray"—

he chuckled at Sophie's mock sigh of relief—"but some inward aspects that have to do with giving our soul space for community with God. The way I have gotten to know you, I feel like you could enjoy yourself greatly up there."

"What kind of programs do they offer? Retreats normally only go for a couple of days, right? I'm looking more for something to fill my whole summer break." *Since I'm not exactly on my way to India like other people.*

"You're right. There are several short retreats, but most of them are week-long programs. You might want to check out their website. But what I was actually thinking of was not the programs the community offers. It's the community itself. Campo Rasa, which is what the place is called, is run by a small team of staff and volunteers. The volunteers spend anything between two months to a whole season up there, while a couple of employees actually work and live there year-round. I was thinking you might be a perfect fit for a two-month summer volunteer."

The way he said it gave her an idea. "Let me guess . . . you have volunteered there yourself, haven't you?"

"I spent, let's see . . . six different seasons up there over a period of about thirty years. I guess you could call me a frequent visitor." He chuckled.

Thomas never ceased to amaze her. "When was the last time you were there?"

"Well, I go up there at least three to four times a year, mostly to either attend or co-lead a retreat. I haven't spent a whole summer there for several years, but I still know most of the people who frequent there. I can definitely recommend it highly."

Their lake cruise had come to an end, and Sophie told Thomas she'd check Rasa out when she got home. When her train left the station in Lucerne and Thomas was out of sight, she sat quietly for a while. There was one thing she hadn't done all day for the first time in a while. She hadn't looked for a text or email from Justin. It had been a welcomed break, because thinking of what adventures he might be experiencing this minute was too painful and too distracting. And yet, as the neat, pretty villages flew past her on the train ride home, she again wondered what sights were meeting Justin's eyes right now.

Chapter Forty-Six

Justin fell onto his bed utterly exhausted. An hour in the sweltering, humid heat of Chennai was enough to drain all the energy from his body. It took several minutes of laying still and letting the air conditioner cool his body and head until he could think again. Panic was always just below the surface of his conscience. If his life in India was going to look anything like the first two weeks he had experienced here, he did not know if he was going to survive.

He took out his groceries from his backpack, boiled the eggs, and fixed himself a sorry little sandwich. Just as he thought he'd finally tackle the impossible task of trying to get the internet working in his little room, the noise of the street right outside his window became much louder. It took a moment for him to realize that the power had gone out and the constant white noise of the little A/C unit above his head was missing, amplifying the rest of the unceasing stream of louder noise outside.

Justin grimaced. Power outages were no fun. In the past two weeks he had experienced six power cuts. The first time he had been unfazed, convinced that it would come right back on. Only when he had to go to sleep fighting off merciless mosquitos while drenched in sweat did he realize that this could be a serious problem, and he started wondering how long power outages lasted in Chennai. It had come back on toward the morning, but only to leave him covered in bites and feeling miserable from heat and humidity. *Well, here we go again*, he thought and got up to arm himself with mosquito spray and prepare for the next hours.

One thing was for sure: life in India was not as easy as he had imagined. Gone was the glory of constant encouragement from admiring friends. What he saw now was the curious and often quite amused faces of the Indians he met while trying to navigate this city. Every simple task was a nightmare to accomplish. What took minutes back home easily turned into an hour-long trip, often unsuccessful and always exhausting. Going to the ATM. Getting groceries. Buying a cell phone. This one actually took nearly a full day, and Justin was sure he got ripped off good. Finally having a way to call home, he wasted no time after getting back to the apartment and first called his mom, who didn't answer. He then tried his dad and was luckier.

"Oh my God, Dad, it's so good to hear your voice. This is totally crazy." Justin broke into a somewhat hysterical laugh. "I have been here for three days, and all I accomplished is getting a cell phone, finding some food, and crossing the street without getting killed. It is unbelievably hot here. The A/C in my apartment went out yesterday afternoon and only came back on this morning. I think I counted sixty-six mosquito bites, but it might as well have been six hundred and sixty-six! It's completely insane."

His dad sounded worried about Justin's situation despite his son's efforts to make light of it. He started asking questions, but Justin was concerned about the costs of the call and therefore kept it short. After hanging up, he sat in his noisy apartment with the even noisier traffic, trying to keep the memory of the familiar voice with him for as long as possible.

After a lonely lunch he curled up on his bed and wondered

what to do with the rest of the day with the power gone. Even more than his dad's, he longed to hear Sophie's voice. They had been in email contact since she left Colorado but had not talked on the phone. Maybe both of them thought it would be too emotional, too risky. Their emails had been matter-of-fact, letting each other know what was going on in their lives and talking about Justin's newsletters. The first one had gone out earlier in May, right before he left. He had drafted a text and had sent her a couple of pictures of himself, the school in Colorado, and of course a picture of him and Jonathan. Sophie had created a stunning newsletter, modern and inviting, from the little he had given her. He was amazed. She hadn't edited any of his text. He knew that some of it probably sounded too glorious, too flashy for her, but if it did, she hadn't said anything. She had treated his adventure with the same graciousness she seemed to treat most things in life.

Laying there in his run-down apartment with nothing to do, he finally allowed himself to reminisce about the past weeks since their time together in April. It had been a roller coaster ride, emotionally as well as circumstantially. After Sophie had disappeared through the security doors at the airport on that Friday, a numbness had descended on Justin's heart. The following weeks, a sensation grew in him that something was wrong, although he tried hard to convince himself otherwise. Something with him, or rather, in him, was off. He was still the happy, positive, soon-to-be missionary who inspired his classmates to live radically for Jesus. But at the same time there was a sadness in him he couldn't get rid of. A gnawing feeling that the outcome of his time with Sophie was not just God's will but had a lot to do with his own decisions, which he became more and more unsure of.

Meanwhile, he had heard the opposite at school every day. Very few of the other soon-to-be graduates had the guts to do what he was doing. In fact, he knew of nobody who moved around the globe two days after graduation to live in a country they had never visited and where they didn't know anybody. As a result of that, he had gained quite a status among the school before he even left for India. Jonathan mentioned him several times during the last month as an example of a life fully dedicated to God. He had to admit that it felt good to be recognized and called a spiritual example by the man he admired more than anyone in the world. It had helped Justin shove those uncomfortable thoughts about Sophie to the back of his mind.

But since his arrival in India, a lot had changed. For the first time, Justin had absolutely no control over his life. He had nobody he loved, trusted, or even knew around him. He was constantly tired because of the difficult living conditions. The romantic ideas of his radical missionary life were being drowned out by traffic, melted away by heat, and overpowered by exhaustion.

And yet, Justin did not feel hopeless. His faith was an anchor so strong in his heart that losing all outward security and comfort also doubled his zeal. He had a mission to accomplish. Tomorrow morning, he was going to visit Pastor Ashish, the contact he had from his dad's trip to India. He knew his address and was going to try and find a rickshaw to bring him there. So far, he had not dared tackling this feat, as his days had been full of trying to meet his basic needs. But with the first moment of relaxation, the fervor had come back as well. Going out into the villages and preaching the gospel was what he had come here for, so why let a lack of internet or groceries keep him from doing exactly this? He was living the adventure! And even though it was more challenging than what he had anticipated, he knew he was going to be able to live through it.

Before going to bed, he packed his backpack with the few things he needed in life—his Bible, a few clothes, toothbrush and shaver, passport, money. He added a few granola bars he still had from the US and a bottle of water. Now he was ready for whatever life and India had in store for him. That night, even the most ferocious mosquitos could not keep him from falling asleep with a determined smile on his face.

Chapter Forty-Seven

James didn't know the last time his heart had been filled with as much hope and joy, but also fearful anticipation. After years of back-and-forth with lawyers, judges, and review panels, Ronnie was finally being released. And now, finally, James was allowed to pick his brother up from prison and bring him to the apartment they were going to share for the near future.

Their first stop was Levino's, Ronnie's favorite Italian restaurant, where they enjoyed pizza and beer. But despite the laughter and happy chatter between them, James could tell his brother was distracted. His happiness about his release seemed strangely faked. After the meal, James felt an almost physical despair creep up on him.

"Come on, talk to me, man!" He tried to break the awkward silence.

"Don't push me now, not you! I've had enough of that crap in there. Gimme some space."

When they had settled Ronnie into his new home, he excused himself and said he needed some air. He didn't return to the apartment until after midnight.

The days following the release, Ronnie's restlessness nearly drove James mad. He tried to talk to him about finding a job, talking to a counselor, playing soccer with him and his buddies. The stuff free people do. But he had half of Ronnie's attention at best. And after a short time, his brother would excuse himself and restlessly pace up and down the living room. James knew things had happened to Ronnie in jail that had changed him. He had become part of a different world. And not even Eli, James's source for every sort of help needed, seemed to know what could be done, not without Ronnie's consent.

"Until your brother regains his will to live, you can only try and keep him out of harm's way. He needs to *want* to get his life back together on his own terms."

Then, one day, Ronnie was gone.

He had come home late for a couple of nights in a row now, but no matter what time it was, James was still up, waiting. He couldn't sleep until he knew Ronnie was safe. But that night, his brother didn't come home at all. James finally fell asleep exhausted in the early morning hours. A day of painful waiting, praying, and making phone calls ensued. James couldn't eat, he couldn't work, and he broke out in cold sweats every time his phone rang.

Finally, late the next evening, James heard the apartment door. One look at his brother, and all hope drained from James. His eyes filled with tears.

Ronnie sat down and looked at him, and James saw a trace of guilt in his brother's eyes. "Look, man, I'm sorry. I got . . . carried away a bit. But it won't happen again, ok? I promise!"

"No, Ronnie, you won't promise. Because it will happen again. I'm a *cop*, don't you understand? I have seen people on dope more times than I care to remember." He wiped his eyes. "You're going to tell me everything. Now. Please, Ronnie."

Ronnie stared at the floor. "You don't know what it's like in there, James. I was just trying to survive, and once I had a taste, I went completely numb, and then I couldn't stop." His voice broke. "When I got out, I thought I could kick it. But you don't understand the power of that stuff. And then, yesterday, I met a guy at a bar who knows a guy. . . "

The last sentence had an air of such defeat that James thought his heart would break. But he didn't give up yet. "I do understand, Ronnie. And we're going to get you help. Tomorrow morning, I'm taking you to one of Atlanta's best rehab center. I have connections, and I know they can help you." He looked Ronnie in the eyes. "And I will help you too. I will be there for you every step of the way. I promise."

He pulled Ronnie into a hug, hoping his positive words would mask the panic inside him.

When he woke up the next morning, Ronnie was gone.

James sat in his apartment, praying, pleading with God. After the first day, his begging turned to cursing.

He thought he'd go mad.

The call from the morgue came the third night after Ronnie had run away. Someone had found him in an overlooked alley of a run-down part of town. Paramedics administered Naloxone as soon as they got there, but any help came too late.

A slow, steady rain had settled over the mourning congregation, but James didn't even notice when his face, clothes, and shoes got soaking wet. The last ounce of feeling had left him when they had lowered Ronnie's casket into the soggy dirt. He stood motionless in the downpour, enduring the eulogy his pastor gave. Normally, his pastor and friend knew how to catch James's interest and even passion. But since Ronnie's death, James had been completely unapproachable to anyone from his church, his family, or his friends.

James remained stock-still in front of the casket, long after the funeral party had dispersed. His grief had no measure, and there was only one passion left in him. He was going to do whatever it took to make sure no other teenager had to go through what had destroyed Ronnie's, and with it, to some degree, his own life—and he didn't care what price he was going to pay for it.

Chapter Forty-Eight

The motorcycle weaved in and out of traffic skillfully, and Justin shouted loudly enough to be heard even above Chennai traffic. Whether it was more from the thrill of fear or excitement, he didn't know. He was certainly feeling both at this moment.

Justin had so much fun on the ride, he almost forgot that he was actually on his way to his first pastors meeting. After meeting with Ashish only days ago, the pastor had managed to set up an event in his church in a village called Avadi on the outskirts of Chennai for that same Saturday. When Justin had told him he would love to preach to local pastors and mentioned his diploma from an American Bible school, Ashish assured him that people would show up.

"We will need to feed these pastors at the end of the conference; that's the tradition here. I can arrange food to be delivered to the venue," Ashish offered. Relieved to hear that the cost to feed the pastors would be less than a dollar per person, Justin asked if Ashish had an estimation of how many people might show up at a random first meeting like this.

"We will have twenty people for sure, maybe many more!" The answer was accompanied by a characteristic side-to-side head movement, which Justin had misinterpreted as a shaking of the head the first time he'd seen it. Only when he heard several people say, "Ok, sir. Not a problem," while bobbing their head, did he realize how little he knew about Indian body language and customs.

He had liked Ashish from the start. During their first meeting he found out that the father of two young children was a hustler like him. He had several jobs to provide for his family, but his position as pastor of the church in Avadi was his true calling. Ashish was also part of the Bible League, an interdenominational organization that worked with foreigners, which helped explain his ease around Justin and his knowledge of English. He was street smart, witty, and Justin could sense a loyalty in him, which for the moment was the most important character trait he was looking for. Too many things were unknown to him in this culture, and having someone by his side that had his best interest at heart was more than he could have hoped for. His dad had talked very positively about Ashish after his recent trip to India, and Justin was relieved to find his dad's words confirmed.

If Ashish's predictions were right, it would be quite a turnout for a first preaching event, considering that Justin didn't know anyone here and had no record other than having been in Bible school. He had spent the day before preparing and praying. Traditional institutions would have had him spend weeks and months in advance to study the Indian culture and the religious background his sermons would fall onto. But Justin thought this to be a waste of time. God was going to help him, and He would tell him everything he needed to know about the Indian culture. Instead, he focused on praying and asking God to open the hearts of the pastors who would attend his meeting the next day.

Just then, they nearly collided with an oncoming bike. It was not uncommon, especially in busy intersections, to have opposite traffic in your lane. Ashish swung to the right and let out a string of Tamil expressions Justin, although he didn't understand them, was not sure were supposed to be in the vocabulary of a pastor.

After driving for nearly an hour, the scenery started changing into more rural patterns of fields and clusters of houses here and there when Ashish finally left the main street and swung down a dirt path that ran along some jackfruit trees. They stopped in front of a low building with a tin roof. The paint had chipped off in more places than not, but the entrance was swept meticulously clean. A sign on top of the building read Praise the Lord! Justin noticed there was no parking lot. A bicycle was parked there already, and out of the door came a young woman in a beautiful, bright green sari.

"Mister Justin, this is my wife Suri!"

Justin got off and was about to shake the woman's hand but then decided to do what she was doing—pressing his palms together in front of his chest.

"She has been getting the church ready. We meet here every Sunday and Wednesday with our congregation of around forty people."

Justin heard the pride in Ashish's words. He tried to sound genuine as he congratulated him for the building and church attendance, although he was still getting over the shock of how run-down everything looked. The meeting wasn't going to start for another hour, but the first pastors were already on their way. Justin soon realized why there was no parking lot—nobody owned a car. They came by bicycle, motorcycle, or on foot. Some were dropped off by rickshaw. Everybody wore long dress shirts and dress pants despite the heat. Justin wished he had worn something that matched the crowd. Instead, he was wearing what he always wore everywhere: a polo shirt and shorts.

But the pastors didn't seem to care. They nodded toward him with a smile, settling into their plastic chairs and chatting with each other. When two o'clock came around and Justin got ready to start, Ashish touched his arm. "We can't start. Many people are not here yet. We need to wait at least another thirty minutes so they won't be offended."

Justin didn't like the idea but realized it might be a good thing to do what a local was suggesting. While they waited, Ashish introduced him to several of his pastor friends. Each one told him the size of his congregation and invited him to come speak at their church before they had even heard him preach. It simultaneously created excitement and hesitation in Justin. This could keep him busy for weeks or even months. And yet, his dream was to go out there and preach where the name of Christ had not been heard as instructed in the book of Romans. He didn't just want to travel around and visit churches. On the other hand, he had to start somewhere, and getting so many invitations on his first day in ministry was certainly encouraging.

When Ashish finally gave him the signal to start, Justin counted forty-three people in the little church. Ashish and Suri had been bringing in more chairs, and some pastors sat on the floor. Nobody seemed in a hurry, nor did they seem to mind waiting.

Once started, Justin wasted no time. He told the pastors that God had a bigger plan for their lives, no matter where they were with their churches right now. God wanted them to be successful, prosperous, and walking in health. The audience was attentive, and although Justin had to talk through an interpreter, his convincing personality and Jonathan's powerful messages did not fail to impress them. There were affirmations of "Praise the Lord" and "Amen" throughout his sermon, and on several occasions, the pastors gave Justin spontaneous applause. When, in the end, he told people he would pray for anyone who needed something from God, the line included almost the entire audience. Justin was in his element. It was only after being presented the first child to pray for that he even noticed people from the village having arrived at the meeting. He got slightly nervous, wondering how they would feed all these people after the service, but at the same time got goosebumps realizing that this was exactly what had happened in the days of Jesus's ministry. The positive response from the people also strengthened his confidence. Almost every question he asked was answered with a confirmation.

"Is the pain gone?"

"Do you believe what God is saying to you?"

"Can you see yourself successful?"

"Do you agree with God that you are healed?"

People would beam at him, some even touching him, and many brought their whole families for Justin to pray over.

He was still praying with people long after the food had come and the others had started eating. They sat in circles on the floor, chatting in Tamil and skillfully forming little balls of rice with their hands from their banana leaves filled with biriyani. When Justin was finally done with the prayer line, he felt dizzy. He hadn't drunk a sip of water since the service had started, and the sweat had been dripping down his back and forehead the entire day. There was no air conditioning in the building, and the two ceiling fans were only strong enough to keep the mosquitos off his body.

He walked over to a big water container, poured himself a cup, and then joined Ashish, who sat in a circle with his wife and the interpreter. He noticed the banana leaf prepared for him had much more meat on it than everybody else's.

Eating the rice with his hand while balancing the leaf on his lap was no small feat for Justin. Ashish showed him how to gather a bit of rice into a ball, mush it together to make it stick, and then flick it into the mouth with a quick motion of your thumb. Justin's rice went all over his shirt, earning him a good-natured laugh from the people around him. Ashish repeated his instructions and put his hand over Justin's to show the correct movements. In a moment of embarrassment, Justin realized Ashish was graciously teaching him to eat—something that is usually taught to a child—and he again wished he had prepared better for his move around the world. He resisted the urge to ask for a fork and instead forced himself to try the ball technique until at least half of it went into his mouth. It took a long time for him to finish his plate. The food was delicious, but his mouth was on fire afterward.

Cookies and steaming tea with milk and sugar were passed around. Even though the place was so hot, the tea still felt refreshing. Justin's body was not used to this heat, nor the breathtaking bike ride he had experienced this morning. He longed to go home and take a long, cool shower and a nap.

But Ashish had other plans. "Please do me the honor of visiting my house."

Justin moaned on the inside but went along as he didn't want to be rude. They went back on the bike and drove a short while before stopping at a simple, colorful brick building. The rooms were comprised of a tiny kitchen, a bedroom with a twin-sized bed and mats on the floor, and a living room with another mattress and a TV.

Justin noticed there were only two plastic chairs in the house. Suri proudly showed him around. When he had to use the restroom, Suri took him behind the house to a little wooden box that obviously held a latrine. Flies swarmed around it, and the smell made Justin understand its location. Once back inside, Suri made Justin sit down on one of the chairs. Then she disappeared into the kitchen. Justin panicked, as there was no way he could possibly eat more, nor did he think he could bear to sit in this heat for much longer. Ashish started talking about a plan to hold pastors meetings like this in the churches of some of the other pastors who had already invited him to preach. This vision revived Justin, and they spent another hour discussing a strategy to reach even more people. When Suri returned after a while with hot chai and sweets, Justin learned another lesson in how unprepared he was regarding the customs of the Indian culture. Not wanting to offend Suri, he forced himself to eat the treats placed on his plate and drink his tea. He was terrified when Suri refilled everything almost instantly. There was no chance he was going to be able to eat another bite.

Ashish must have noticed his dilemma. "Forgive me, Justin! I should have explained. In our culture, a good host will refill your plate until you insist you are full. If you don't say anything, they will keep filling it!" They both laughed and Justin was once more grateful his first friend in India was both patient and gracious toward him.

Justin never dreamed that his ministry in India would take off so easily. Now all he needed to do was to be patient until an opportunity would arise to go further into the villages and find the people who had never heard of Jesus before. His backpack was ready, and so was he.

It was beginning to get dark when Ashish finally dropped him back at his apartment. Justin had never been more exhausted in his life. He silently thanked God that the A/C was working, plopped on his bed, and fell asleep in an instant. That night, he dreamed of buying his own motorcycle and riding it through the bush in rural India, bringing the gospel to all those who hadn't heard.

Chapter Forty-Nine

The soft rattling of the train had a lulling effect on Sophie. She watched the landscape starting to change as they approached the Alps. Soon it would all disappear as the train entered the Gotthard-Basistunnel and ran under the massive mountain for over thirty-five miles. When she came out on the other side of the Alps, she would be in the Ticino, greeted by a different landscape and even a different language than when she entered the tunnel.

She had made the journey through the old tunnel countless times. It was ten miles long, and for a tunnel built over 130 years ago, it was an impressive feat. But the new one, opened only two years ago, was the longest tunnel in the world and one of the great prides of her country.

It had been only two weeks since her conversation with Thomas on Lake Lucerne. His description of Rasa had so impacted her that she decided to take a scouting trip the next available weekend. Not only was she curious, she also really hoped this could be an option for her summer plans. Thinking of an unplanned summer was more stressful for Sophie right now than it would have been in other years.

Just before entering the tunnel, her phone showed an

incoming message from Justin. She had not heard from him in a while—the last time they communicated, he had just returned from his first pastors conference and had told her all about it. Sophie couldn't help but feel proud of him, proud with a strangely aching pain about it.

So far, none of their short, informative emails had contained any mention of what had gone on between them. It was as if neither of them dared going there—not now when the physical distance added to the vulnerability of their relationship anyway. Both seemed happy to keep things going as well as they had been. And yet, every time Sophie thought of him or was reminded of him, she was right back there in Colorado, where her hands had held his face and their eyes had locked into each other's.

The email contained Justin's rough draft of his second newsletter. In it was a skillful and upbeat description of his first conference, complete with pictures that seemed to come right out of a missionary handbook. There was Justin preaching with a Tamil interpreter next to him. Another picture showed Justin praying and laying hands on a woman. And there was Justin with his Bible open, discussing something with a pastor. And lastly, Justin sitting with a banana leaf full of delicious-looking food and eating with his hands.

Sophie had to admit she was jealous. That little voice inside came back at the sight of these pictures. *What are you doing? Going to some little retreat with a bunch of old Christians. How's that changing any lives? Whom are you bringing the gospel to?* She shook her head angrily, as if she was able to get these thoughts out of her mind by physical force. Not everybody's life could be like Justin Friedman's, and surely that was ok with God. *It's just not ok with me*, she admitted to herself, as she sped through the dark, long tunnel.

In the town of Locarno she changed to a local train that would run all the way through the wild and rugged Centovalli and then on into Italy. As the ride progressed, she found herself glued to the window, watching tree-covered mountain ranges followed by deep gorges and ferocious streams swollen from recent rainfalls. The valleys looked so pristine and lonely, it was hard to imagine people lived there. When the train stopped at the little station called Verdasio, Sophie was the only person getting off. She quickly walked to the cable car station that was situated below the train station. She secretly hoped to find another passenger there but soon realized she'd be boarding the cable car alone that would bring her across the valley up to her destination.

The cable car was operated from the top, and a security camera ensured every passenger was inside at the bottom before the car took off. Nobody else had joined her by the time the bell rang for the cable car to start. When the car soared into the air, Sophie saw the Melezza River far, far below that formed the gorge of this particular valley. The water was a beautiful deep blue, and Sophie imagined how it must feel to dive into one of the naturally formed pools in the gorge, miles and miles from all of civilization.

Five minutes later, the car reached its destination. When Sophie saw the little cluster of Rasa for the first time, she felt a strong impression of coming home. She paused for a moment and tried to make sense of it. Yes, Thomas had talked about it endearingly. And yes, she had spent time checking it out online, anticipating the upcoming retreat. Yet it still felt as if she had known this place before. Not with her mind, but with her heart.

She climbed the little hill up to the first buildings and soon found herself in a small atrium surrounded by several stone houses. Everything looked old. Not in a run-down way, but in an ancient way. It somehow looked wise, simple, and solemn.

A lady came out of one of the houses. "Welcome to Rasa," she said, beaming at Sophie and holding out her hand. "I'm Rachel, the welcoming committee." She smiled warmly. "We're so happy to have you here. You look like it's your first time here."

After Sophie introduced herself, Rachel showed her around

the buildings. It was obvious that she loved every last corner of them, and Sophie noticed how most rooms and buildings were given names in the local Italian dialect. She was given a room in a building called Ca dal Soo. Its name was apparent once Rachel led Sophie onto the adjacent patio. A sun-flooded terrace overlooked the whole valley and was surrounded by wild bushes and alpine flowers. Sophie could see herself reading a book and forgetting the world in this spot.

After the tour, she went to her room to freshen up and then walked around the village by herself. In half an hour, she was going to meet the group of people who had chosen the same weekend retreat as her. Walking on the unpaved paths along the old buildings, she could almost *hear* how utterly still it was in this town. There was no car within miles of this place and no other noise of civilization either. No wonder Thomas loved the place so much!

Twenty minutes later, their small group had gathered and was enjoying some hors-d'oeuvre before dinner. A white-haired man that reminded her strongly of Thomas welcomed them.

"Thank you all for finding your way to this special place for the weekend. Many of you are regulars, but I also see a few new faces. Welcome to Rasa. I find it safe to say it might be your first but not your last time here." He looked around, his friendly eyes sparkling. "This weekend, we will enjoy some exercises in contemplation together. Contemplation, as many of you know, is the art of listening to and looking for God. This includes looking inside of us and listening to our own hearts, but for many people it also means looking at creation and the many ways in which God reveals Himself through it.

"Many of us have found that the stillness and solitude of this place greatly help our souls to experience God's unique voice inside of us." His eyes rested on some of the group, and he smiled kindly when Sophie's eyes met his. "We will have times of fellowship and worship but also times alone with room to meditate, read, or go for a hike. Mealtimes are at eight thirty a.m., noon, and six p.m. in the Casa Fontina. As part of the monastic tradition of starting the day looking inward, we will enjoy a silent breakfast every morning."

Sophie chuckled. This sounded like it was going to be different for sure. The group was very diverse in background as well as age. Benny, the leader of the retreat, then led them to a cozy room in one of the buildings that had a fireplace and several rows of chairs stacked at the sides. Cushions were arranged on the floor in the shape of a circle, and they sat down. Sitting on the floor made Sophie's perception of the group and the experience less formal and herself more curious. What followed, though, was completely unexpected. Without any introduction or explanation, the group started singing. Sophie recognized the song as one of the Taizé songs, music from an ecumenical, monastic community in France, and knew now why Thomas's group sang these songs so often. He must have gotten the idea here.

The voices, undistracted by instruments or other noise, found themselves in simple harmonies, effortlessly flowing together and apart again. This seemed to be the place these songs had been written for. Songs of worship and songs of peace, as Thomas called them. They sang some in Latin, some in German, some in French, and a few in English. There were no books, no one to lead the group. When one chant ended, somebody would begin a new one. Others would join and create their own harmonies. Lyrics were picked up along the way by those unfamiliar with Taizé. The whole experience was so overwhelmingly beautiful, Sophie sometimes stopped singing to let the emotions sweep over her. They ended with "Adoramus Te, Domine," and Sophie could not think of a more suitable way to express adoration for God than singing this song to Him right here.

They left their circle in time to freshen up before dinner, which was served in the vine-covered atrium outside the main building. Sophie loved the family-style atmosphere, the big bowls of steaming food that were passed around, and the relaxed conversations that buzzed around her. That night, she crawled into bed after a short sermon on the church fathers given by Benny in an eloquence that marked a stark contrast to the sermons she still had in her ear from the Rock. Before drifting off to sleep, she pondered her luck to have found a place like this. It was a coming home on more levels than she could name. How much she wished to be able to show this treasure to Justin! Not that that was likely to ever happen. But this seemed as good a place as any she'd ever been in to believe in miracles.

Chapter Fifty

Sweat ran down Justin's back in small, continuous streams. It was unbearably hot under the tin roof of the tiny church in rural Tamil Nadu. Ashish had taken Justin's pleas seriously and brought him further outside the city than ever before. They had been holding several conferences in the past two weeks, and each had been a bigger success than the one before. News seemed to spread quickly among pastors in Chennai when it came to American evangelists.

He was nearing the end of his sermon and was dreading what came next, although he would have never admitted it. His conferences always started off with some worship music, played usually by members of whatever church he was preaching in. Then he would teach, talking about how God wanted them to be healed, prosperous, successful, and happy.

His sermon was received with enthusiasm in almost all places he went. He would take up an offering for the church at the end, and the band would close with a song. Up until that part, he loved every minute. And then he would ask those who wanted to accept Jesus into their lives or needed prayer for anything to line up in the middle aisle. The first couple of conferences, he was thrilled to see half the people get in line. It was confirmation not only that they were receiving what he was teaching, but also of people's need for his ministry. Ashish would snap pictures while he was praying for people.

Most of them asked that he lay hands on them. Many came with their whole families, asking for general blessings or specific healing from certain illnesses. While Justin prayed, the church members would set up lunch and eventually start eating. Justin was concentrating hard and hardly realized how time flew by. He prayed over people for healing, for increased finances, for favor with employers, teachers, congregations, family members. He would bless people, stand for pictures with them, even touch their infants because it was seen as a way to keep sickness away from the child.

By the time the last person had gone through the line, Justin was close to fainting. He would sink down in a chair but sometimes hardly touch the food they set before him. The heat, the intense concentration, the back and forth with the translator, drained every bit of energy from his body. It was often late afternoon when Ashish drove him back to his little apartment.

This day, as he got ready to start the prayer line, he could feel the exhaustion coming over him even at the onset of his ministry time. There were just so many people! And he sometimes wasn't sure they understood exactly what he was praying over them. Many of them just kept touching him and trying to pull his hand forward to touch all their family members. Of course there was the language barrier. He had noticed that the interpreter's English was not exactly impressive. But he trusted God to speak to the hearts of the people anyway.

The first person in line was a woman surrounded by her large family with several small children. The interpreter told him she had a malignant brain tumor. Justin went right into work mode. He had long memorized the Scriptures to use with cases that were medically hopeless. He prayed with conviction and authority.

"I shall not die, but live, and declare the works of the LORD." Psalm 118 was one of his favorites. "He was wounded for our transgressions, he was bruised for our iniquities. The chastisement of our peace was upon Him, and with His stripes we are healed." That one from Isaiah was his absolute favorite.

As he prayed, the lady nodded approvingly. The eyes of her family members were on Justin, and as he continued to urge her to believe in her healing, he could feel the burden again. It was the realization that all these people looked to him for answers, for help, healing, and encouragement. Of course it was understood that the healing ultimately came from God. But Justin was the one standing here right now, and fearful children's eyes were fixed on him.

Not for the first time, the thought flashed through his mind that he was glad most of the sicknesses that he encountered while preaching were such that no physical symptoms of healing could be detected on the outside. Not that he didn't believe the healings actually happened, but it sure relieved a lot of the pressure to not require physical proof right away.

When he was done praying for her, the woman thanked Justin, they took pictures, and then she and her family left him to the rest of the people in line. As he kept praying, his glance fell to where she was eating lunch. Something about the way she was behaving irritated him. There she was, eating, chatting, laughing with her family. He couldn't help the feeling that this experience was an everyday activity for her.

When the line was finally done and Justin fell in his chair exhaustedly, he couldn't relax like he usually did. The whole thing suddenly bothered him. It had not only been that one woman. Most of the people who had him pray for them went immediately on to eating, chatting, and he even saw one man engage in what clearly looked like a business deal with another pastor right after he had left the prayer line. He could no longer hide his irritation and decided to bring it up with Ashish.

"How often do these pastors attend conferences similar to this?"

"Oh, whenever there's an evangelist around. Chennai is well loved by western preachers. Normally there are at least two meetings a month." Ashish's face turned slightly red as he added with an apologetic smile, "They also love the food. Some of them hardly ever eat meat except at the conferences held by foreign evangelists. It's a special treat for them. So they try to be a part of it every time. Some go to three conferences a month."

Justin frowned. There was something so wrong, so . . . secular about going to a pastor's conference because of food. And he had a feeling that was not all there was to it. "What about the prayer line? Do they go to receive prayer every time?"

"Yes, definitely! It's considered good luck to have a preacher lay hands on you, especially if he's white." This time, Ashish's face showed no sign of embarrassment. While admitting that some pastors might come primarily for the food embarrassed him a little, the mention of a racial bias did not do so in the slightest.

It was quite different for Justin. "Are you saying they believe westerners have more spiritual authority?" As the words left Justin's mouth, he had to admit that he himself was maybe not so far from believing this.

Ashish thought for only a moment. "Definitely. Americans have more money, more influence, more power. It seems obvious to most of them that God is blessing white people in a special way. Many believe that by touching you, they will receive the same blessing from God."

Justin put his half-eaten banana leaf plate away. His appetite had left him. His pastor friend was talking about superstition as if it were the most natural Christian practice in the world. Ashish watched Justin shake his head and seemed surprised by Justin's disapproval.

He was quiet for a while, and when he spoke, Justin could

see his desire to not be offensive. "Many things we see on American Christian TV are foreign to us, but we try to see it as a different way God reveals Himself in other cultures. And it often seems that Americans connect being blessed with being wealthy and successful. This is a message we cannot easily preach here, as most of our pastors will never be wealthy, nor do they have enough resources or education to become successful in the way Americans talk about. I believe this has led many pastors to try and connect themselves to Western preachers because it's the only way they feel they can tap into this kind of blessing from God that would otherwise be denied them."

There was no accusation in Ashish's voice, but Justin's ears turned red. Was American Christianity really so shallow that in the eyes of the world it portrayed spiritual success mainly in terms of money? The idea of America's spiritual leadership sounded a lot better back home than it did here in Avadi. But there was more that bothered Justin about Ashish's initial statement.

"You said they believe touching me will give them God's blessings. Are they really that superstitious?" The moment he said it, Justin regretted the judgemental tone it was said in.

This time, however, Ashish was quick to reply. "But you Americans do the same! I watch TBN sometimes, and I have watched American TV preachers selling prayer cloths and other things that were touched by them. They say the items have healing power and bring blessings."

This was more solid ground for Justin. "People who do this aren't real Christians. At our school, we never approve of prayer cloths or other superstitious actions. Jonathan is a strong critic of religious acts that are not based on scripture."

Ashish seemed surprised but did not object. As they started to clean up, Justin argued within himself, defending Jonathan but also feeling a new, uneasy sense of responsibility when hearing about how influential American Christians were to these pastors and how naturally they saw Justin as a representation of all this assumed spiritual authority. Was he really able to give them what they trusted him for?

When most of the pastors had left the church, Ashish introduced Justin to a man who had just arrived. Unlike the pastors he had met earlier in the day, this man's clothes fit neatly, and his shiny shoes suggested he had come here by car rather than by bicycle.

"Pastor Justin, please meet Reverend Ravi. He's the associate pastor of Victory Church Chennai, and he was so kind to come meet you here and offer an invitation!"

Justin quickly pushed away any distracting thoughts and concentrated on Reverend Ravi. The tall man's body language was different from that of most pastors he had met. This was a man who was used to giving orders and enjoying respect. Justin felt a certain pride that somebody like this, who was obviously an important man, had come to seek him out. After they exchanged a few pleasantries, Ravi came straight to the point.

"Pastor Justin, we want you to come and speak to our congregation. Pastor Moses has heard of you and sent me to invite you personally. You will speak in the main service two weeks from now. Your message will be one hour long, and you will pray for people afterwards alongside Pastor Moses."

The way the words were spoken, it was clear that this was already decided, and that Justin was very lucky to be able to minister together with Moses, who, he assumed, was the senior pastor. Justin also had the feeling that he was supposed to have heard of Victory Church and felt too embarrassed to ask about it. Instead, he allowed himself to imagine what this would do for his ministry. He would be exposed to hundreds, possibly thousands of people. If an important pastor endorsed him like that, surely he would not have any problems getting people to come to his meetings in a larger style. His excitement grew as Ravi pulled out a high-gloss brochure of Victory Church and handed it to him. Compared to what he had seen so far, this had to be one of the wealthier churches in Chennai. He silently thanked God for bringing somebody so influential across his path as he shook hands with Ravi and discussed the details of his upcoming visit. As the excitement of it all started to set in, the memories of his uneasy feelings about people's behavior during his conferences were pushed far back, and by the next day he had forgotten about them altogether.

Chapter Fifty-One

Sophie had been sitting in the cozy café in downtown Bern, waiting to meet with Thomas and tell him all about her trip to Rasa, when she saw an incoming message on her phone.

Justin had often shot her a short line or two, telling her about a conference or a funny thing that happened to him, as there was apparently never a shortage of strange things happening to someone who wasn't used to the Indian culture. *TII,* Justin would call it, *This Is India—in other words, I have given up trying to understand it all.* But as Sophie read the email she had just received, she noticed that this time it was different. Justin mentioned a pastor he had just met who had invited him to a big church in Chennai, and that he was supposed to preach there Sunday a week from now. Sophie could almost hear the excitement coming off her screen, and that little tinge of jealousy returned. Justin's ministry was no doubt growing, and he was doing just fine without her. She was thankful that he kept communicating with her, and yet . . . *Who's to say he sees me as more than his little fan club organizer by now?* Sophie frowned as she closed her laptop in the café and took another sip of her coffee.

"Looking at you, I'm really curious what you were just thinking about." Thomas's voice pulled her out of her musings.

"It's so good to see you, too, Thomas!" She laughed. Although they hadn't met since their boat ride on Lake Lucerne almost a month ago, they always picked it right back up, and she knew no small talk, no warm-up was needed when they were together.

"I need to tell you all about Rasa. But first . . . I get these little updates from Justin every once in a while and got one right now, and I can't stop that ugly jealousy sometimes. He is really successful, and I'm so happy for him. But it also makes me daydream about what my life would look like if we had gotten together." She blushed.

"I understand that, Sophie. And as long as it doesn't consume you, I don't think there's anything wrong with a bit of conscious dreaming. But remember, even if you were there with him, it would not automatically mean that you were doing something that would make you happy."

"You're right. I guess I couldn't exactly preach what he's preaching anyway. It just sounds so adventurous. And a little scary."

Thomas lifted his eyebrows. "What's Justin up to?"

"Well, he just told me today that he will be preaching at a big church called Victory Church Chennai. I looked them up a moment ago, and they have over a thousand members in their church. That would be a bit scary, at least for me!"

Thomas had looked up quickly at her mention of Chennai. "You never told me Justin is in Chennai."

"Oh, I guess not. . . Well, that's where he is, at least right now. And I imagine he will stay there for a while if the speaking engagement works out with that church. But why does it matter which city he's in?"

"I visit Chennai often for the work I do and know the city quite well."

"What a coincidence. But I guess it would still be a miracle for you to ever walk into him there—I looked it up and saw that over five million people live within the city limits!"

"That's right. And honestly, I wouldn't want to meet him at

the moment anyway, not while your relationship with him is in the place it is right now. My experience is that this only complicates things. But concerning those emails, I think you need to give yourself some grace. It's very natural to have conflicting thoughts about difficult relationships. Just remember to include God in your thoughts about it. Which brings me to my burning question—your first experience of Rasa. You can be very honest with me. Even though it actually would get to me if you didn't like Rasa, I'd make a big effort in trying not to show it." He made a face as if ready to receive a blow.

Sophie laughed. "Well, it would really be hard to find something negative to say about Rasa. I think you can imagine how much I loved it there. In fact, I loved it so much, I decided I will need a lot more of it in the next months. . . "

"You signed up for the internship during the summer!" he exclaimed, clapping his hands.

"Yes. I will start my summer there in exactly"—she looked on the calendar in her phone for a moment—"twelve days, the day after I finish teaching. I knew I wanted to come back after the first day of being there. I can't even tell you how much I love the whole village, the views, but mostly the people."

This made her think of something. "You know, the guy who led the retreat somehow reminded me of you. His name is Benny. Do you know him?"

A grin spread across Thomas's face. "Yeah, you could say so. We met, let's see . . . thirty-six years ago. We even studied theology together for a semester, and yet we managed to stay friends throughout all this time, amazing as that sounds! But what about him reminded you of me?"

Sophie blushed. "Well, you both have this wise look and demeanor, you know, and the gray hair. . . "

Thomas's laughter interrupted her. "I will have to report this to Benny. I'll tell him you said I look wise and he looks old."

"I think it's also your relationship with God," Sophie added, smiling. "Benny told us about the contemplative lifestyle, being aware of God in everything from nature to the people around you to the little things in your everyday life. This is something you might have said and are practicing as well."

"That means a lot to me, Sophie. I'm so excited for you. It will be a wonderful experience, and you will not regret the time and effort you're putting into it. And of course I will come visit you! How long will your internship last?"

"I committed for six weeks, so most of July and August. It'll get me back home just in time to start the fall semester of teaching."

"That's wonderful. Summer in Rasa is beautiful. I'll only be able to visit you toward the end of your stay, probably middle of August. And I'm pretty sure Benny will be there then, so you can compare our wisdom . . . and the gray hair!" he said with a smile.

Chapter Fifty-Two

Justin had never felt more special or important in his life than this day, sitting across from Pastor Moses in one of the finest restaurants in Chennai. It was Sunday, and they had just finished ministering to hundreds of people who came forward to be touched and receive a word of blessing from both Pastor Moses and Justin after hearing Justin preach. The air-conditioned church made the hours of standing less taxing, and as they arrived at the restaurant for what was to be more dinner than lunch, Justin felt more relaxed than usual.

Moses had treated him like a celebrity—and so had the twelve hundred members of the church. He had received more invitations from visiting pastors, small group leaders, and missionaries than he could keep track of. Ravi had taken care of all the logistics. While Justin was ministering to and greeting people in line, he had taken their emails and phone numbers. It all felt like such a well-orchestrated event that Justin wondered how often Moses had people like him visit.

He also started wondering if Moses was doing all of this just to try and help Justin, or if there was some additional motive that he had not figured out. He wanted to believe that the pastor simply wanted to help him, but he couldn't fully convince himself of this idea.

Victory Church was definitely impressive. Some aspects were foreign to Justin, but he had figured out by now that the Indian Christian culture was far different from what he had gotten used to around American Christians. For one, Moses wore a white robe and flower garments throughout the service. He sat on a velvety chair, not unlike a throne, toward the middle of the stage. He had what Justin assumed to be deacons sit to the left and right of him during Justin's sermon. Before Justin was asked to preach, there was a lengthy worship session in which Moses not only sang, but gave words of prophecy, as Ravi explained to him after the service. He prophesied that God had chosen Victory Church to be His light in Chennai and that people from all across the world would find their way to it.

"Our guest speaker for today has come all the way from America," he had said after the worship ended, "and we want to show him the generosity of this church. At the time of the offering, I want every one of you to match your usual church offering with one to Pastor Justin. Let's show him and his American friends that we at Victory Church believe in generosity as much as we believe in prosperity, healing, and the supernatural gifts of the Holy Spirit!"

Justin had sat there on the platform, waiting for his turn to preach, and couldn't help starting to think how much money he would get today. At the same time, he felt a certain discomfort at the thought of these people, many of whom were clearly not wealthy, giving him money.

Fortunately, Jonathan had taught them how to deal with this question while they prepared for missions. "Think of people's tithes and offerings not as money they give you, but seeds they sow for themselves. The Bible promises that when you give out of faith, you will receive back more."

By accepting their offerings, Justin was only helping them receive the financial miracles many of them clearly had need for. And he couldn't help but be impressed by the generosity of Moses to take up an offering for him in a church that had so many attendants.

The waiter pulled him out of his thoughts, ready to take the order.

"Please, order anything you like, anything!" Moses encouraged him.

"I . . . I don't know most of these dishes. I've only eaten out a couple of times since I got here." Justin suddenly wished he had at least paid some attention to the names of the dishes the few times he had gone out to eat. Searching for whatever sounded closest to a western dish had been his only concern so far. *What else have I missed out on?*

Moses smiled patronizingly. "Ah, don't worry! We will take care of you. The Indian cuisine is among the world's finest. I will order for you and make sure you get a taste worthy of its claims." He turned to the waiter and ordered a range of dishes in Tamil. Then he turned his attention back to Justin. "So, what do you think of our church?" he asked proudly.

Justin was honest when he told Moses how very impressed he was. The pastor looked at him with an intense, almost hungry expression. He asked him about the Rock, about Jonathan, and about other big Christian ministers Jonathan had connections to.

The food arrived on more plates than Justin had ever seen in one meal. There was biriyani, the famous rice dish cooked for a whole day and saturated with spices, and chicken tikka masala—a creamy, spicy tomato curry with big chunks of chicken. It was accompanied by several vegetable curries with names Justin couldn't figure out, Indian naan, and several dips and sauces that were at times so hot they brought tears to Justin's eyes. He loved all of it and scolded himself for not having tried these dishes before and instead making himself sorry egg sandwiches at home. Moses seemed to approve of his guest's appetite. When Justin finally surrendered and told his host that he could not possibly eat anything more, Moses ordered tea and Gulab Jamun, a hot, fried dough ball dipped in syrup, for dessert. Then he leaned back and looked at Justin.

"I'm going to tell you something, Pastor Justin. I've been feeling the Holy Spirit talking to me all day, from when I heard you preach and then while ministering together. I believe God has big plans. Do you believe in big plans?"

Justin had started to feel drowsy from all the food, but Moses's words woke him back up, and he nodded with conviction.

"Well, I believe God might have brought you here for such a time like this. I believe we are called to work together for the glory of His kingdom. God has raised me up here in Chennai, and I can see he has raised up Jonathan and you in the US for the same purpose. We both need to fast and pray about this, but I believe we are meant to start an international ministry together."

The dizziness increased. Did he just get an offer from a successful pastor to create an international ministry? Justin was tempted to shout yes but remembered Moses had said that they needed to pray about it. The pastor didn't seem to be waiting for a response anyway but continued explaining his plans.

"Pastor Jonathan has not been to India, right? There are over a billion people who need to hear the gospel here. I can help your friend expand his ministry to a country of three times the amount of people than the US." He looked at Justin, and the words clearly had the desired effect.

Justin couldn't believe his luck. He had wondered why Moses treated him so royally, and now he knew. Moses had the same message as Jonathan, and he wanted to spread it across India through a teamwork with implications Justin couldn't even fathom yet. He was instantly sold. He knew that Jonathan was going to be interested in expanding his reach into India, as he had often told them he was looking for ways to bring this message to the people outside the US. And here he was, holding the key in the form of an influential Indian pastor.

The rest of the evening was spent making plans. They

included, first of all, a better living situation for Justin. Moses offered to organize a nice apartment close to the church, which he would get for a good rent because the owner was a member of the church. Second, it was unthinkable for a pastor, a title he used for Justin all the time, to ride rickshaws and walk on foot. Moses's personal driver was going to take him to a dealer and help him buy a small car.

"You are receiving donations from the US, right?"

Justin nodded, although he was secretly thinking that the donations might not yet have added up to the price of a car. But he would deal with that later.

Throughout the following week, Justin's life changed dramatically. He moved into a small, but in comparison, luxurious apartment in a much better part of town. Moses's driver had managed to get an incredible deal for a small Tata, India's favorite car. Justin didn't understand any of the bargaining that went on, but from the face of the dealer he could easily see that Moses's driver had more, if not all, of the bargaining power.

A thought suddenly flashed across his mind, and he asked the driver if the car dealer was a church member as well. When he nodded, an unwelcome red flag appeared in Justin's mind, but a moment later he heard the price for the car—which was well inside his donation budget—and he pushed aside any thoughts that might endanger a solution to his logistical challenges.

As the following Sunday rolled around and Justin took his seat in the front row next to Pastor Moses, he mused over how God was shining his favor on him so much. Then he remembered a concept Jonathan had talked about often: those who give their whole lives to God and hold nothing back will be rewarded greatly with favor and blessings, in this life as well as in the one coming. He felt confident that he was experiencing some of this blessing now, as he was living a life of obedience as a missionary to India. And as Moses got in the pulpit and told his congregation about how Victory Church would team up with Justin and the successful American minister Jonathan Parker, Justin could almost feel his chest sticking out as he stood and basked in the admiration of the sea of faces looking up at him.

Chapter Fifty-Three

The train left the small tunnel and kept tugging along the side of the Melezza River in one of the tributary valleys of the Centovalli. It had been going in and out of little tunnels for a while, and each turn might reveal Sophie's new home for the next weeks.

When she arrived in Verdasio, she got off the train and entered the tiny cable car. After it had taken off, Sophie could see the river way below her, the woods to her side and the hills and mountains in the distance. She could feel the peace moving in.

In the village, Rachel greeted her warmly and showed her to her living quarters. The interns lived in a small house a little to the side of the guest quarters. It was a simple dwelling with several bedrooms, a cozy living room, a small kitchen, and one bathroom. Five girls would live there together for whatever length of time they chose to join the team.

After she had unpacked her stuff, Rachel introduced her to Michael, the head chef. Sophie was mainly going to work in the kitchens for the first week. She was impressed that in such a small kitchen the chefs could provide healthy, local food from scratch for the number of guests and staff that lived on campus any given week.

The interns' workday didn't end until almost eight at night. When the last dishes were put away and the food preparations for the next breakfast were complete, everybody gathered in the little living room of the girls' house for a devotion to end the day. Most of the interns were Sophie's age, or even a bit younger. Many of them had gotten to know Rasa through college student ministry and had been visiting on and off for years until they could carve out the time to spend a whole summer here.

On Sophie's first evening, they were reading through a devotional put together from different texts by C.S. Lewis. Sophie had heard Thomas mention him several times and noticed that most Christians seemed to know the British author from the middle of the last century.

That night, they were reading a passage from his autobiography. When Sophie heard his description of experiencing a joy that existed beyond the common forms of enjoyment, fun, or pleasure, it resonated deeply with her. A joy that made you cry and want to become a better person. A joy that reminded you of home, but not the physical home you grew up in, and a joy that showed the author the way to Jesus.

"Growing up a strong atheist, it was not intellectual arguments or religious sentiments but a personal, powerful experience that changed everything for Lewis," one of the interns explained to her.

I need to check out that guy's work, Sophie immediately decided.

They closed their time with a prayer and a simple, beautiful song. Although none of the others had known each other for more than a month or so, Sophie could tell there was a strong bond between them that showed in the way they sang. Singing together, especially without instruments, was an intimate experience to Sophie. And although so new to the group, she felt like she fit right in as they sang in beautiful harmony. After the devotion, the male interns went over to their housing quarters, and the girls had some tea before going to bed. The day's physical work had exhausted Sophie so much that she was glad she got to sink into her bed soon after.

By the end of the week, Sophie thought she couldn't remember feeling as happy as she did right now. The work was hard, but she enjoyed every minute. The people made her feel like family, and she found herself looking forward to all the different parts of the day—preparing meals for the guests in the main kitchen, helping the other interns when she had a free minute, and doing chores in and around the guest houses.

One of her favorite things was the daily team meal that was always preceded by some Taizé song and followed by happy chatter. She marveled at how effortlessly she got along with everyone and how uplifting their short time together was. In the afternoon, the kitchen crew had an almost three-hour-long siesta. They either took naps, read, or communicated with family and friends on their computers. If the weather was nice, they hiked in the woods and hills surrounding the village.

Sophie went on her first long hike one week after she got to Rasa. Armed with a hiker's map, water, and a granola bar, she took off by herself on a foggy afternoon. Nobody else felt like braving the weather, as it had been raining all morning, but to Sophie, the fog made the hike more mysterious and beautiful. For over an hour, she hiked upwards along a little footpath through big chestnut trees. The fog was so thick, it immersed everything she saw in a mysterious, silent blanket. Sophie felt encapsulated in an otherworldly peace and beauty. Walking in this surreal world, her soul opened up wide, as if she could feel her connection with the trees, the smell of the steaming ground, the dripping of the leaves from the recent rain. Everything around her was alive, and so was she. She prayed out loud, telling Jesus about Justin, the dreams that involved him, and her difficulty letting him go. Then she went quiet, as if to let her invisible hiking partner speak. After a long time, her heart felt lighter, and she realized that although she had no answer, the questions seemed further away. In their stead, a palpable peace permeated her. She felt like nature was joining with the Creator in a dance of confirmation. *All will be well.*

Chapter Fifty-Four

Justin was unnerved, and it made his headaches worse. The past two weeks had been immensely stressful for sure, but the headaches were caused not by stress but by a growing unease he wasn't able to shake.

Moses had wasted no time after announcing the collaboration between his church and Jonathan's ministry. He had asked Justin to get written permission from Jonathan to use some of his teaching material in Moses's church and to translate it. Justin, a natural salesperson, had written his request with great conviction. He told Jonathan how Moses had taken him under his wing and helped with everything Justin needed. He assured him that he trusted Moses and what great potential this connection would have for the expansion of Jonathan's ministry. Such was the visionary zeal and craft with which the letter was written that he got permission from Parker personally within three days.

They got to work immediately. Moses's church had a graphic design team, a PR person, and many volunteers who were eager to be part of a project involving an American ministry. Jonathan's discipleship materials were translated into

Tamil, and a weekly discipleship study, held by Justin and Ravi, was set up. In addition, a pastors conference was birthed through what felt like a well-oiled machinery of flyers, social media announcements, and registration forms. Justin noticed that the conference flyer sounded like Moses and Jonathan were best friends. A collage of both of their faces underscored this, somewhat implying that Jonathan was going to be at the conference in person. Justin also couldn't help but notice how they had changed the name of the material they were going to preach, which now included the word *Victory*, further insinuating the material had originated within Moses's church.

The growing feeling of being used had surfaced before in the past two weeks. He tried to push it away by justifying that he just didn't know the culture yet. Clearly, thousands of people trusted Moses, and every Sunday many people got baptized. And then, of course, all those people coming forward to receive salvation and healing! "You will know them by their fruits," Jesus had said. Moses's fruits were clearly visible. Maybe Justin just needed to focus on the goal of leading people to Christ. He could not let any doubts cloud his decisions.

Just one week later, he sat in his now-familiar seat in the first row and was awestruck by the amount of people who showed up for the first Victory Discipleship Conference. Moses's church had an even bigger draw than Justin had realized. Hundreds of pastors, worship leaders, and other men and women in ministry filed into the spacious sanctuary. By the looks on the faces of many, they might have never been to a building as impressive as this.

Although still an hour before the start of the conference, Moses was already standing on the platform. A great number of pastors were lined up in front of him, wanting to talk to him and put in a word about their congregation. Justin stood to the side, talking to Ashish, whom he had invited to join. Moses had frowned at this, but Justin insisted. He felt strangely small and lost in Moses's church despite the attention he was getting. In the past weeks, he had felt more like a prize that was shown around than a human being. Having Ashish with him eased a lot of the tension that came right along with the excitement he felt around Moses and his people.

"How come they all want to talk to Moses?" he asked Ashish in a hushed voice as they watched the line.

His friend looked at him for a moment, and Justin thought he detected a trace of resignation in Ashish's voice. "They're looking for *influence*. Moses is one of the most influential pastors in Chennai, and if he remembers your name, your church attendance is likely to double overnight. You might have noticed that he sometimes mentions names from the pulpit. It's not by accident. It mostly means the pastor will provide a service or favor for Moses, and in return, Moses will mention the pastor's name during the sermon. It will boost attendance in that congregation and raise the status of the pastor."

An explanation of worldly politics if ever I have heard one. The thought disturbed Justin, but the sudden sound of his name from the pulpit jerked him out of his thoughts.

"Pastor Justin will join me now with a word from the Most Reverend Pastor Jonathan Parker from America. He was unfortunately not able to join us in person, but we have with us his assistant, who will share the vision of this great servant of God. Welcome with me Pastor Justin!"

Amid roaring applause, Justin stepped on the platform. Moses had not told him what he wanted him to preach on or say during the conference, but Justin was used to improvising. It was part of Jonathan's world to be spontaneous or, the term Justin preferred, to let the Spirit lead. When he started talking, the excitement of the crowd led him straight to his comfort zone. For the next half an hour, his nagging questions were gone and he did what he did best—painting a picture of

Jonathan's vision to cover the world with the gospel. He made sure to mention also what a crucial role Pastor Moses and his church were going to have in this work of God.

For the rest of the day, Moses and he took turns preaching, presenting the newly christened Victory discipleship program and advertising the materials for sale in Tamil in a few short weeks. Then they prayed. The lines accumulated beyond the door, and Justin knew it was going to be a long afternoon. After a while, he noticed an usher talking to each person in line and then sending them either to Moses's or Justin's side. He wondered what factors determined the decision and felt slightly irritated by the way things were decided without his consent, even though this was a conference set up as a collaboration and funded to a large part by Jonathan's ministry. When his translator had to step out for a moment, Justin was relieved for an opportunity to have Ashish at his side. He asked him, whispering in between prayer requests, "How are they selecting who's going to pray for whom?" He tried to hide it, but his voice betrayed his insecurity.

Ashish shrugged. "He wants to deal with the difficult cases himself. You know, cancers and such. Also, some pastors know him and want his blessings, while others want to be blessed and prayed over by an American. That's why the lines are a similar length."

This time, Justin thought he could detect a hint of frustration in Ashish's voice, and he suddenly saw the situation through his friend's eyes. There was certainly not a lot of space for a pastor of his scope in a system like this. And surely someone's nationality should not matter when it came to prayer anyway. He felt his annoyance grow at the pastors in line, which made praying for them all the more challenging. He also started feeling dizzy and realized he hadn't had any water all day. He decided to take a break.

"Ashish, could you take over my line for a bit? I need to use the restroom. I'll be back shortly." He turned and walked toward the exit when he heard a sharp voice call his name.

"Pastor Justin! Please come here for a moment." Moses's voice was friendly, but only on the surface. When he got over to his line, Moses took him aside. "Where are you going?"

Was he imagining things, or did Moses's voice sound slightly threatening?

"I just need a break for a moment. I'm feeling a bit dizzy. Ashish is taking over my line for a while and I'll be back shortly."

Moses looked at him strangely. "Pastor Justin, these people have come from far away to hear us teach and let us pray for them. Do you think they came to be prayed for by your friend? What do you think they will tell their congregation about Victory Church if we let a nameless person pray over them? Do you think they will come back? Are you aware of what honor you have been given to be allowed to preach and pray from this pulpit?"

His face suddenly changed and took on a rather fatherly expression. "My dear son, there's a lot for you to learn. Don't worry, you will catch on in time. I have taught many inexperienced young men. Now go back to your line and give these pastors what they came for."

Although spoken good-naturedly, there was no question that Moses's instructions were to be followed. Justin asked Ashish for a cup of water and went back to pray for people but found it almost impossible to concentrate. His face burned with humiliation, and although nobody else had heard what Moses said, Justin felt as if everybody was staring at him. Moses certainly had the ability to reduce any man to nothing in an instant.

When the line was finally gone, Justin avoided Moses's eyes as they packed up. He was still fuming inside and knew it would show. But Moses seemed used to these situations.

"Gentlemen, thank you all for your wonderful work and helping us minister to all these pastors. Pastor Justin and I will retreat to my private office now for a debriefing."

And with that, he turned around and started walking

upstairs. He was so used to his orders being followed that he didn't even turn around. For a moment, Justin thought of walking out the door just to prove his independence. But he could only imagine how Moses would receive such an action. He silently followed him into a large office filled with oversized furniture and countless pictures of Moses standing next to what Justin assumed to be important leaders and politicians. After the door was shut, Moses looked at him with a mix of fatherly patience and disappointment.

"I never want to let things like this ruin a friendship. Tell me your thoughts, Justin."

Surprised and relieved to hear such an invitation to honesty, Justin said, "I . . . I just don't see why it was such a big deal who was praying for them. After all, they are supposed to look to Jesus and not to the minister, right?" When Moses didn't answer, Justin continued with another thought that had occurred to him following the incident. "You said you didn't want a nameless person to pray for them. My friend's name is Ashish."

It was a simple comment, but apparently Moses could see behind it. His eyes narrowed. "I have nothing against your little friend, Justin. But this church is not accustomed to letting just anybody who calls themselves a Christian pray from the pulpit. You are apparently too young to understand this, but the Christian office is one of honor, of calling, and of well-earned reputation. Pastor Parker is well known for all of these virtues, and since you are his representative, I am willing to extend my trust to you as well." His voice left no doubt about what honor he was extending to Justin. "In regard to your friend, however, I know nothing of him, and that's why he will not stand in the office of a servant of the Lord in my church."

The sentence came much like a closing statement, and Justin almost intuitively felt himself get up. The meeting was over. As he turned toward the door, lost for words, the voice came again. This time it was as cold as ice. "One more thing, Justin. I am your elder. You will never question my judgement again, whether in front of others or just between you and me. Instead, you will show me the respect I deserve. Have I made myself clear?"

Justin left the room silently, and although it was comfortably warm in the building, he was shivering violently.

Chapter Fifty-Five

During the course of her internship, Sophie made new discoveries every day. When one day she mentioned to Rachel how happy she was here despite the hard work and lack of luxury, her friend, who had spent many years in Rasa, smiled broadly.

"It's the same reason money or a leisurely lifestyle or an absence of hardships won't make you happy. We are not created to avoid work. We're created to find the work we're made for. And do you know how you can tell you have found it? When you'd do it without pay, without a thank you or any other form of reward. It will bring a happiness you won't ever get cured of."

A conversation with Thomas came to Sophie's mind. *No compartmentalization*. Living a life in which the different parts all played together into a beautiful harmony. Life as she had known it so far was too fragmented. Now, for the first time, she knew what Thomas meant when he talked about work, friends, play, and worship coming together, creating a unique tapestry. Right now, it seemed ridiculous to her to think of fighting for more money or less work hours in hopes for more happiness. It made much more sense that peace had to do with purpose rather than with money or time.

Before going to bed that night, she decided to write to Justin. After all, what he was doing was exactly this—giving up money and comfort to be able to work and live for something worthwhile. She missed talking to him and hearing his thoughts. She had never thought it was going to be this hard. And even now, she wondered in certain moments whether, had she decided differently, she would now be experiencing this fulfillment next to a man and for maybe a lifetime instead of an internship that would end in a couple of weeks.

She started the email by writing about her experiences here. About the peace. The songs. The beauty that seemed to lay in the simplicity of everything. But when she wrote about the mist that surrounded the trees and bathed everything in an unearthly beauty, she hesitated. How was he going to react to this kind of poetic language? He was probably sweating under an Indian tin roof, trying to focus on his mission. He might not appreciate her musings.

She sat at her computer for a long time, battling with herself. Then she deleted the email and went to bed.

Chapter Fifty-Six

As Ashish drove in silence, Justin's arms clutched the passenger seat almost violently. He had left Moses's office pale as a ghost and had not said a word while packing up his stuff. They left without saying goodbye to anybody at Victory.

It was impossible for Justin to speak. Hurt and confusion consumed him, and he felt utterly alone. To his surprise, the usually quiet Ashish broke the silence.

"Justin, my friend. I don't usually say much, but I feel led to share some things with you." He looked Justin in the eyes. "Today my heart is aching for you. There's a lot I don't understand about you, but I've felt from the start a kind of kindred spirit in you—a passion for God and a heart that wants to do the right thing."

Justin suddenly realized he had hardly paid attention to his friend before. He was just a tool for him to get what he needed, a helper, a "little guy." Shame welled up in him as Ashish continued.

"I want to apologize for not warning you about Victory Church earlier. My own fear of possible retaliation from Moses has kept me from speaking out against Victory Church for too long. But seeing you so shaken and hurt . . . I wonder if the time has come." He stopped the car on the side of the road and turned so he fully faced Justin.

"I won't tell you what to do, or who's right or wrong. But I believe you have already realized that not everything that shines is gold at Victory. I will not speak negatively of a fellow pastor, but I encourage you to listen to your heart. Do not build your ministry here on anything but what your conscience can fully support. And remember that, like everywhere else, the body of Jesus has many different expressions in this country. Don't judge us on one experience."

Justin was too preoccupied to answer but nodded to show he had heard Ashish's words. When they arrived at Justin's apartment, he quickly said goodbye and fled inside his apartment.

Justin stood in the shower for what seemed like hours. He felt dirty, but it was the kind of dirt that would not wash off. Although Ashish's words had soothed his anguish a little, they had not been able to lift the despair he felt. Nobody had ever treated him like this. When he was a drug dealer, people showed him respect because of his influence and his generosity. In Bible school, people liked him because of his friendly way and his knowledge of the Bible. He had never in his life experienced this kind of open hostility. Moses had made him feel like a boy who could not live up to an adult's expectations.

What a fool he had been to think Moses shared his vision! When he finally got out of the shower, his apartment felt like a prison and Justin like a miserable prisoner in it. The worst thing was that he knew there was nothing he could do about it. The apartment lease was in Moses's name, as well as his car title. All was done with the assumption that they were men of God and needed no worldly contracts like people who don't trust each other.

His drug-dealing days had supplied Justin with plenty of suspicion toward people, but all this had changed when he met Jesus. He simply couldn't imagine one follower of Jesus taking advantage of another. Besides, his status as a tourist in India made it impossible for him to buy a car, so he was not left with much of an option other than trusting people, and in his case, he had been trusting Moses.

And now? He could walk away from the apartment, since all he would lose was the rest of the month's rent. But his car—if he walked away, he would also lose it, and although it had not been expensive in American terms, he still could not get another one. He would be back to using rickshaws and bargaining with the drivers for each little trip.

The alternative was to try and work things out with Moses. This idea, practical as it was, made his stomach turn. Moses had shown his true colors this morning, and Justin had no intention of experiencing more of it. Besides, Ashish's words still rung in his ears. *Don't build your ministry on something your conscience can't support.*

For the first time since becoming a Christian, Justin just wanted to go get a beer and smoke a cigarette.

The next day, for lack of a better idea, Justin decided to give himself a break for a while and see how things would work out. He would relax, maybe see some tourist attractions in Chennai and put some time between him and this negative experience. Then he remembered the discipleship training that was set up for him and Ravi to teach on Wednesday. He would see how he was feeling by Tuesday and then either just not show up or go and hope Moses would not be around.

His few days of playing tourist turned out to be much more enjoyable than he expected. Ashish had told him about a beach about forty minutes south of Chennai, where many westerners went to relax. Inside the city with its traffic, pollution, and noise, Justin never even thought about the fact that Chennai was on the Bay of Bengal. Now he was thankful for the prospect of a break. He spent Monday at the Chennai zoo and visited some historic and religious sites. Then on Tuesday, he took his beach towel, bathing suit, and a good book and paid a driver to take him to Mahabalipuram Beach. Since he had his own car, he could have driven himself there, but deciphering traffic signs and understanding the unwritten rules of driving in this city made that task rather daunting.

When they got there, Justin felt like he had entered another world. Half of the people on the beach weren't Indians. He had not seen so many white people in one place since he had arrived in Chennai. Ashish had told him that many westerners came from America and Europe as specialists sent from western companies that have their factories in India. Justin wondered if among all these people were any missionaries like him.

He dove into the waves for a refreshing swim, then spread out his towel in the shade of a coconut tree and settled down for a nap. He realized how tiring it was to live in this high-energy city with its crazy traffic and its constant noise. Sitting there under the palm tree and looking out over the ocean was exactly what he needed.

As he relaxed, a face appeared before his inner eye, a face he had tried to push out of his memory—and yet there she was again, as if she naturally belonged to any beautiful, peaceful, and happy moments in his life. Justin smiled with his eyes closed and drifted off to sleep with the memory of the beautiful Swiss woman who seemed to still be very much alive in his heart.

He awoke to the annoying ring of his cell phone. For a moment, he felt disoriented, as people do when they sleep in unfamiliar places and at unusual times of the day. He finally looked at his screen. It was Ravi. He picked up the phone, somewhat irritated. "Hello?"

"Pastor Justin? It's Ravi. Listen, Pastor Moses wants us to meet this afternoon to discuss tomorrow's training. Can you be at the church in half an hour? Sorry for the late notice."

Justin was still waking up. "What? Today? No, I can't. . . . I'm actually at the beach right now."

There was a pause.

"You're at the beach?" Ravi's voice sounded shocked, almost embarrassed. "Justin, I thought you are doing missionary work! What are you doing at the beach?"

Justin didn't really know what to reply and remained silent.

"Anyway . . . how long will it take you to get back? Maybe I can ask Pastor Moses to schedule an appointment in between so we can meet an hour from now. Can you be there in an hour?" Ravi sounded as if he had just given Justin an extra dose of grace.

Justin's pulse accelerated. Moses was doing it again! Commanding him around as if Justin's life belonged to him. "Actually . . . I really can't come this afternoon. I have time tonight or tomorrow morning for a meeting. If Moses is busy, you and I can just meet and go through the curriculum. I know it inside out and have taught it several times and can answer any questions you might have about it."

There was a long silence at the other end. Surely, the prospect of doing something without the direct supervision of the senior pastor must sound exciting to Ravi. But maybe having been part of the church for quite a while, it was also an idea quite outside of the realm of possibility for him, Justin suddenly realized.

"Very well," Ravi said finally. "I'll tell pastor Moses what you said and will get back to you. Have a good day." As he hung up, Justin noticed that Ravi's voice had become noticeably cooler than at the beginning of the conversation.

Justin couldn't go back to sleep. This was getting out of hand. Sophie came to his mind again. It struck him now that he had intuitively known Sophie would have frowned at Moses even at their first encounter. That's why he had not mentioned him in his last short update to her. What bad judgement he had had! What would Sophie think if he told her about the mess he had gotten himself into? He decided to read a bit to get his mind off the conversation with Ravi, but he had not gotten further than a few pages when his phone rang again. It was Ravi once more.

His insides tightened.

"Justin? Pastor Moses was quite upset at your response, for which I do not blame him. He is telling you to be at his office in an hour. Don't be late, Justin. Oh, and one more thing . . . he will tell you himself, but I thought I'd let you know beforehand. He has assigned Pastor Kumar to teach the discipleship program with me tomorrow. I think he feels unsure of your commitment at this point. So just be there and be sure to show him the respect he deserves. You have done enough damage already. Good luck."

Justin was close to throwing his cell phone into the ocean. He was furious. Who on earth did this guy think he was? He made his decision then and there. He would not go. Not today, not the next day, and not any day. He didn't care about his car anymore. Moses could come and take it if he wanted. He could throw him out of the apartment. After all, he had been living in his shaggy room and been using rickshaws before. He could do it again.

The thoughts produced in him a wild, rebellious feeling of freedom. In a sudden inspiration, he walked over to the concession stand and asked if they sold beer. He had not drunk a sip of alcohol since that day he met Jesus. And even now, he didn't do it as an act of rebellion toward Jesus. It was defiance against people like Moses, who would surely be outraged at the sight of a missionary drinking beer. The thought of him lying on the beach and sipping a beer while Moses was waiting for him in his oversized office full of pictures with important people put the first smile on Justin's face in at least a week.

He couldn't remember anything tasting better than his beach beer. He turned off his phone and stayed on the beach the whole afternoon, reading, staring over the water, and thinking of Sophie. He didn't know what the coming weeks would hold but felt more free right now than he had in a long time. He ate a sandwich and watched a beautiful sunset before walking out to the parking lot. He wasn't going to turn his phone back on until tomorrow. He was going to have a peaceful evening, maybe watch a movie, and then call his old landlord about getting his room back. He was sure it wouldn't take too long before Moses kicked him out of the apartment.

Back home, Justin settled in his bedroom with a few snacks and his favorite *Star Wars* movie. His cell phone was still turned off. The sun and ocean breeze had made him tired, and he had just dozed off peacefully when an urgent, repeated knock woke him up.

"What the . . .?" Justin murmured to himself as he shot out of bed and put a shirt on. Did Moses have the nerve to harass him at his apartment at night? He looked through the security hole and saw an older white man standing outside. Relieved that it seemed nobody related to Victory Church, he opened the door.

"Justin?" the man asked. He was visibly worried and seemed in a hurry. "Listen, you don't know me, but I need you to trust me. Grab your passport and computer and let's get out of here if you prefer not to spend time in a Chennai prison, because I know for a fact that the police are on their way to your apartment right now."

Chapter Fifty-Seven

Justin rushed down the stairs as if in a dream. Laptop and important documents clutched under his arm, he tried to keep up with the older man, whose agility surprised him. The man shoved him into his car that was parked right outside the apartment complex. Curious eyes followed them as they sped away and soon were immersed in Chennai traffic. They had only just turned the corner into a side street when police sirens blared in the distance. Justin was immediately in drug-dealing mode, ready to jump out of the car and run for it if the police were to pursue them. But then he heard the sirens stop. They must have gotten to the building and not yet known the apartment was going to be empty.

Justin's mysterious friend was now weaving in and out of side streets until Justin was sure nobody would find them anymore. Finally, they came to a gated community, and after the man had punched in some numbers, the gates opened. Justin felt an odd relief when they closed behind them, as if the police would not be able to find him in here. They parked behind the building, and the man led Justin into a small, modern apartment. When the doors were locked and the blinds were down, the man pulled out a kitchen chair for

Justin, got a pot of coffee and two mugs, and finally let himself fall into a chair with a sigh of relief.

"That was close," he said, cheeks flushed and his worried expression giving way to hardly disguised excitement. It made him look almost like a boy who had just done something delightfully adventurous.

Justin was still in shock. Had he really just escaped the police by mere seconds? And who was his rescuer? He tried to calm his nerves enough to speak, but the man beat him to it. "Alright. Since we've got through the difficult part of the evening, let me be a good host and introduce myself. By the way, would you like some coffee?"

Justin held out his cup as if in a trance.

"My name is Luke. Among other things, I work with an NGO here in Chennai. We're a team of volunteers from all over the world who help victims of human trafficking. But more about me later. Because of the nature of our NGO, I have good connections to the local police and have acquired a number of friends there over the years. I have an agreement with an officer friend of mine who lets me know when unusual police activities are taking place in the area. Since only few white men get in trouble here, your planned arrest was pointed out to me, and here we are."

Justin looked at Luke as if he had just landed from a different planet. Finally, he asked the most urgent question at hand. "But what did they want to arrest me for?"

Luke gave him a long, searching look. It was friendly, but Justin felt like he shouldn't try to lie to this man.

"Do *you* have any idea what they could have been after?" Luke asked.

"No. That is, unless . . . I had quite a disagreement today with a pastor I started working with recently. But I can't imagine he would try and send the police after me just because I didn't want to work with him anymore."

Justin looked so innocently surprised that Luke laughed. "You would be surprised at what happens here among pastors,

Justin. But he couldn't have had you arrested over a disagreement. Are there any legal issues he could have brought against you?"

Justin decided he could trust this man. "I guess so, yes. First of all, there's my car. I paid for it myself, but since I'm on a tourist visa, I'm not able to buy a car in my own name, so it's the pastor's name on the title." He paused and looked at Luke. "Do you think it's possible that he told the police I stole the car?"

Luke didn't seem to agree. "Were you there when the car was bought? He would risk being questioned himself if people at the car shop witnessed the two of you there together."

"Maybe. But the car dealer was a member of his church and would probably cover for the pastor." Anger welled up in Justin at the injustice of the situation.

But Luke seemed to be thinking about something else. "What kind of tourist activities have you been doing here, Justin?"

Suddenly it dawned on Justin. "Wow. I know what he might have used against me. I'm on a tourist visa, but I'm holding Christian meetings and I'm preaching at churches." He had to pause as the truth of the situation sank in. "*Proselytizing*! This pastor was going to hand me over to the police for doing the exact work he himself believes every Christian in the world is called to do!"

Although he hadn't known Moses well, the fact that he was a preacher along the lines of Jonathan's teachings had made it impossible for Justin to think the man could ever go against him. To him, one Christian betraying another was possibly worse than betraying a family member. The hurt went deeper than even his friend breaking into his apartment. Justin slumped in his chair and almost forgot Luke was there until the old man spoke. His voice was extremely tender now, and when Justin looked into his eyes, he saw compassion in them.

"My friend, I know learning those lessons sometimes costs us dearly. Man's pride will take him where he never wanted to go, and when pride is coupled with power, he will get there even quicker, and it will cost him even dearer. Victory Church's leadership has had a reputation for years for ruthlessness, arrogance, and a lack of love. I'm very sorry you had to experience this in such a hurtful way. And I agree that what Moses did was maybe one of the most despicable things a pastor could do. I'm glad we got you out of there in time. And let me tell you also that there are many wonderful pastors and churches here in Chennai. You just happened to have gotten in with the wrong crowd, as they say."

Justin sat in his chair, hardly hearing what Luke said. He had lost all of his belongings, his car, and his place to stay. His name was now on a police search list. He had no friends apart from Ashish and no ministry. He didn't even want to think about what kind of trouble Jonathan would get into because of the consent Justin had persuaded him to sign.

Before he could try and pull himself together, he suddenly felt strong arms pulling him into an embrace. He was pretty sure Luke was praying, although no words came out of his mouth.

When he felt in control of himself again, Justin said, "I can't thank you enough for what you've done for me, Luke. I have no clue what I'm going to do now."

"First of all, we both need to get a good night's sleep. You'll sleep in my guest room. I'm getting you a toothbrush, and you can wear some of my pajamas. Don't worry, they're freshly washed," he said with a grin. Not letting Justin protest his hospitality, he continued, "Tomorrow morning, we will figure out how to try and get some of your stuff back and see if we can solve the car situation. Good night, Justin. And welcome to my humble abode."

Justin thankfully accepted what Luke offered. He fell asleep the moment his head touched the pillow, and he dreamed of Moses dressed up as a policeman, chasing him up to the altar and scolding him in front of his congregation.

Chapter Fifty-Eight

Of all the interesting courses offered during her time in Rasa, Sophie knew this one was one she couldn't miss.

Occasionally, the interns were allowed to sit in and follow a program of their choice during their long afternoon break. Her first few weeks had been too busy for Sophie to do that, but this week's course was led by Benny, and she went at once and asked Rachel if it was ok to sit in on the course called *Among Friends*.

Over the next days, she joined the group in the afternoons. Benny encouraged the participants, most of them students of theology, to ask whatever questions they liked about God and the world. From creation to the role of the Bible to the existence of hell, no topic seemed taboo, and the ensuing discussions among the students proved even more interesting than the questions.

Their conversations reminded Sophie of something she had read just the other day in the little library: Christianity was not a religion for which you had to check your intellect at the door. Listening to these students using their common sense and sharp thinking to question religious concepts encouraged her to do the same as she was growing in her faith. After all, these people with their rich faith had loads of unanswered questions and seemed to be ok with it. They were people with deep questions alongside a deep faith and a robust sense of humor. It was a most attractive thing to experience, and she again wondered how Justin would experience this same group if he were here.

Chapter Fifty-Nine

When Justin woke up the next morning, the wonderful smell of pancakes and scrambled eggs wafted into the bedroom. *Where did Luke find pancakes here in India?* He felt refreshed, and his mood was definitely better than it had been for days. He walked into the kitchen and received a cup of steaming coffee from Luke, who apparently had been up and about for a while. Justin had a feeling he might not be the first person who had spent the night here after Luke had gotten them out of a bad situation. He devoured his breakfast and tried to ask questions in between bites.

"So, you work for a nonprofit organization, you said. Does that mean you live here?"

Luke smiled. "In a way, you could say so. I spend quite a number of weeks here every year, and I have a growing network of friends and colleagues. Also, I'm getting to know the city better and better, and I truly love the people here. From that point of view, you could say I live here."

Suddenly, Justin realized how strangely familiar Luke's accent sounded to him. "Are you from Europe?"

"Yes, I'm from Switzerland and still live there the better part of each year."

At the mention of the country's name, Justin felt an instant connection to this man, as if by mere sharing of nationality, Luke could bring him closer to Sophie.

But before Justin could ask more questions, Luke had one of his own. "Tell me how you got involved with Moses. The more I know, the easier it will be for me to help you get your car and your belongings back and clear your name with the police. Because right now"—he looked at Justin with a serious expression—"you are not leaving this country in any normal fashion."

Justin hadn't even thought of the fact that if he tried to fly back to the US, the immigration at Chennai airport was likely to notify the police, and he might be arrested right at the airport. He was not free to go back home—a thought that immediately produced severe homesickness in him.

His emotions didn't escape Luke's attention. "Don't worry, Justin. I have dealt with situations like this before. They are more interested in putting on an intimidating face than actually getting into a dispute with the US embassy about a US citizen being arrested for expressing his faith. And sadly, or fortunately in your case, a little money always helps to make your case look more innocent—which, in many ways, it actually is. Let's just get the facts first."

Justin was relieved and started to tell his story about coming here straight from Bible school in Colorado, his endeavors with Ashish and, finally, his short-lived tenure with Moses. Luke listened, but Justin couldn't tell what he was thinking. Was Luke a Christian himself? What did he think about hot-blooded missionaries who had no clue what they were doing and almost got themselves locked up?

When he finished his story, he felt rather foolish. Some representative of Jesus he was! To get the attention off himself, he asked, "What kind of organization do you work for?"

"One that helps vulnerable kids get off the streets here in Chennai. We connect them with shelters if they're younger and help them find work if they're older. We try to reconnect them with their families too, but that is often a process unlikely to succeed. Some of our kids are . . . stigmatized and unfortunately will be rejected by their families. When they come to our shelters, they often don't have a single friend in the world." Luke's eyes were full of compassion, and although his face showed grief, his voice was gentle. "We try and help the older ones build an independent future by assisting them in acquiring work skills. We also work with some wonderful organizations that help the younger ones find new families and a chance to go to school."

"That's great," Justin replied somewhat mechanically. He realized he knew nothing of the plight of the countless kids that had followed him around in the streets or came right up to his car and put their dirt-stained little hands on the window, begging for some rupees or food. If he was being honest, he hadn't really been interested in them either. They were not his target group.

His next question came out of habit. "Is it a Christian organization?"

"Some of the people in the organization are deeply religious, others are not. But a specific faith is not our group's focus. We try to rally around our common goal to save the lives of as many kids as we can and try to ease some of the pain life has dealt them at such a young age."

Luke's voice was soft, but Justin could tell the passion that lay behind his words. He was unsure how to react. The missionary part in him wanted to tell Luke that without saving their souls, they missed the most important aspect of helping these kids. The shaken, vulnerable part of him on the other hand, the part that had accepted Luke's help yesterday, was not sure it made sense to discredit the practical help he brought to these children. He decided to ask the question, the one he always needed to have answered, in a more direct way.

"So . . . are you one of the religious people in the group?"

To his surprise, Luke started laughing. "They really taught

you not to waste time, didn't they? But to set your mind at ease —yes, Justin, I am a Christian."

"Then why do you work in an organization that is not centered around the Christian faith?" The question had escaped Justin before he was even aware of it.

"Because I believe God has given all of us the command to help those who cannot help themselves. There is definitely enough work to do for anybody who is willing to join in, no matter what they believe."

"But don't you think that if you just help them get off the streets and don't tell them about Jesus, they might never have another chance to hear of him and get saved?" Justin spoke with a certain indignation. *How can this guy take the chance to bring Jesus to other people so lightly?*

"Justin, has it ever occurred to you that you might be underestimating God drastically? Just because we don't stuff Christianity down the throats of these traumatized, exhausted children doesn't mean we don't care whether they will ever get to know Jesus or not." His voice was calm, but Justin detected a trace of hurt in it. "Before you judge the extremely difficult and often dangerous work these people do every day just by the religion they do or do not follow, you might want to look at the fruit of their work, to use a biblical term. It seems to me they *serve the widows and orphans* well, even if no pamphlets are being given out."

Justin looked at his feet. Before he could think of anything to say, Luke spoke again, quietly this time. "Forgive me, Justin. I am in no position to criticize your views. And believe me, I do understand the place you're coming from. I was there myself for many years. But as I got older, I started wondering if we might not be doing the Christian faith a huge disfavor by judging the majority of the world unworthy of doing their part in helping to build the Kingdom of God. Personally, I believe every word of love spoken, every act of mercy committed, every helping hand extended is building a piece of Heaven on earth, even if the people committing those acts do not call themselves Christians."

There was a long pause as Justin struggled with what he heard. He felt nothing but gratefulness and admiration for Luke, but for him to say that non-Christians could help to build the Kingdom of God seemed quite heretic. Too fresh in his mind were the teachings he had heard with such authority, dividing the world neatly into friends and enemies of God, and Justin's conviction to know exactly who belonged in which category was still deeply instilled.

Luke's expression was tender, and his voice revealed the weight of what he was saying. "Justin, those arms that bore the nails . . . they were stretched out to the whole world. Only when we understand how deeply God loves every person on this earth—the Christian, the Muslim, the Jew, the atheist and everybody else—only then can we really start working with Him. As long as we put people in categories of value or worthiness, we are actually hindering the work of the Holy Spirit, who is moving in this world, sparking acts of kindness, of forgiveness, and reconciliation in people of all persuasions. He is weaving a tapestry of healing in this broken world right now. And you can be assured that He not only accepts but encourages works of love from every person, regardless of their religious beliefs."

Justin didn't reply and turned away slightly from Luke's gaze. His heart reacted in an unexpected and unwanted fashion to the words he had just heard. Only weeks ago, he would have wasted no time and countered Luke's words with well-chosen Scripture references and dogmatic certitude. But at this moment, Justin realized with a slight tinge of panic, that despite all the convincing arguments he knew in his head, his heart had just taken Luke's side.

Chapter Sixty

"It's time we had a little chat, McLeod. Privately."

The chief's office door closed quietly behind James, whose heart beat wildly in his chest.

"You know I like you, James. I really do. You have a stellar reputation and strong work ethic. Which is exactly why I waited so long to have this conversation."

Chief Miller's eyebrow lifted. "But I feel your behavior is getting out of control. It's stirring up trouble."

James's insides started to boil, and his voice was harsher than intended. "Since when is reminding your peers of the humanity of these kids on the streets called *stirring up trouble*? I'm only asking them to show a bit of compassion."

The chief looked away. "We all know how hard your brother's death has been on you, and we understand. But I just cannot have you talk this way to your colleagues." He now looked fully at James. "We all gave an oath to serve this city. We cannot fulfill this oath if we get soft on every young kid because he reminds us of someone we know. In order to protect this city, we need to be tough."

He put a hand on James's shoulder as if to emphasize his next words. "James, we need to think like soldiers. This is a war we're fighting every day. And in war, you can't think of the enemy's humanity, or they will get the first shot in. You shoot or you get shot, you know that. Your talk of compassion is upsetting many at the station. They're starting to see you as a weak link, McLeod. Don't make them lose trust in you. Show them you know what's at stake and whose side you're on."

James thought he heard an edge of threat in the chief's voice, but he could have cared less as he stepped out of the office. *I know exactly whose side I'm on, and you have only confirmed my choice.*

Chapter Sixty-One

Justin and Luke spent the rest of the morning talking on a lighter note. Justin discovered his rescuer was a wonderful person to be with—funny, practical, and with a wisdom that seemed to shine through the simplest of topics.

After lunch, Luke asked for Justin's car keys, which he had thankfully grabbed while fleeing last night. Luke left the house with the promise to try and get the rest of Justin's belongings and to work on a solution for his car. Even if he was unsuccessful, Justin would never forget this stranger's willingness to help.

After Luke left, Justin lay down on the couch and was asleep within seconds. When he woke up, it took him a full minute to recall the events of the last day and convince himself that all of it had actually happened. He got up, made himself a sandwich from things he found in Luke's fridge, and walked around the apartment erratically. Finally, he decided to email his dad and tell him what had happened. When he opened the computer, he saw a message from Sophie in his inbox. They hadn't heard from each other in a while, as if there was an unspoken barrier between them. He was nervous when he opened the letter.

Dear Justin,

How are you doing? I assume you are getting quite busy with your pastors meetings. In your last newsletter it sounded as if doors are opening to you left and right. I'm very happy for you. Please keep me updated on your adventures.

Over here in Switzerland things are much quieter, but I'm loving the work I'm doing right now. I'm meeting a lot of interesting people and have been part of some very fascinating conversations about faith, God, and life. In fact, I believe you would have enjoyed them a lot too. Or at least I hope you would have.

I'm going to stay here in the mountains for another few weeks before heading back to Wettingen for the start of the new semester. Looking at the beauty that surrounds me here, I am often reminded of Colorado and of the sunrises we experienced together. I will certainly never forget them.

Please say hi to Ashish, although he does not know me. I'm praying that you can accomplish all you are setting out to do in India.

Yours, Sophie

He looked up from the computer and stared at the wall. A strange sense of loss overcame him. *Or at least I hope you would have enjoyed it.* She even used caution in proposing he'd have enjoyed a conversation she enjoyed. Why was she feeling so insecure about him now?

On top of his confusion came shame about the fact that there were not likely to be any conferences or anything of that sort for him in the future, at least not in India. Sophie, as well as all his supporters in the US, were still under the impression that he was preaching to pastors at this very moment, maybe healing somebody, maybe leading someone to Christ. What was he going to tell them? What was his ministry going to look like now that his name was registered with the authorities and he could not preach openly anymore?

Thankfully, Luke returned with good news that distracted Justin from his dark thoughts. "It really never hurts to have friends in all kinds of places," he said happily as he plopped down in a chair. "I visited a few people, and I'm happy to tell you that they will put in a request with the police to drop the warrant. I explained your situation, and since Pastor Moses does not own the best reputation in town, I believe that the authorities will conclude you are much more innocent than what Moses is making you out to be. After all, it is no crime, even in this country, to be a tourist who visits a church and shares in that church. As for your other activities, I doubt Moses wants to go through the trouble of trying to prove you really held conferences. I suspect he acted in rage, not with calculation. He is not exactly a friend of the police either. Therefore, I think we are allowed a bit of hope. We should get word from my friend about your status in less than a week."

Justin relaxed. The prospect of not being able to leave the country had been looming over him more than he realized. He was wondering again what kind of man Luke was to have such connections.

"As far as your apartment is concerned, another friend of mine went there and found everything untouched. He packed your belongings for you, and they are all safely stowed away in the trunk of my car right now." He smiled at the elated expression on Justin's face, but then turned serious. "The car is a bigger problem. Since your visa does not allow you to own a car, there is no way of transferring the title to you. I do have a friend, though, whose brother works at the place where you bought your car. We might be able to convince the original seller to buy the car back. This way, it would be hard for Moses to make a case for being the owner since these people witnessed you paying for it. I can't make any guarantees, but I will try my best."

Justin had no words to express the gratitude he felt toward

Luke. He had no idea what would have happened had God not sent this man to his doorstep last night. He wanted to find out more about Luke and become his friend. And unlike most of his acquaintances since joining the Rock, he suddenly realized he was interested in Luke the person, not just Luke the Christian.

The next few days, Luke introduced Justin to some of his friends and coworkers and showed him several of the shelters and workshops they operated in. The volunteers were from all over the world and had the most unique stories to tell. What united them was a hunger for justice and an unending compassion for the suffering children on the streets.

Justin was deeply impressed. What he marveled at most was the fact that these people had moved away from their families and culture to endure hardship and danger and to work long hours without pay—and all of it without the glory many missionaries associated with their calling. Many of these people did not believe that God was impressed with their work or that they were necessarily changing the world, as Jonathan had imprinted on them so often. These people were simply here because their hearts cried out in compassion for the suffering of innocent children. Justin had never considered this before.

After three days of following Luke around, listening to him encourage people, counsel them, or just listen to their problems, Justin knew he had to bring up the question which, despite the new thoughts added to his mind, still burned too hot inside of him to ignore.

When they got home that night and plopped on the couch, he burst out, "There's something I still can't wrap my mind around. I've been watching you interact with people around you, particularly with those who are not Christians. It's easy to see that you care deeply for all of them. But I still don't get why you refuse to give them what they need most—the gospel!"

Instead of replying, Luke nodded for Justin to continue.

"I mean, I heard you talk with that coworker whose husband got into an accident yesterday. You took so much time to try and help her, and you even prayed with her. But I did not hear you say the name of Jesus once or tell her to turn to the Bible for encouragement or to join a church where people could help her through this hard time!" Although he tried hard to make it sound just like a question, he feared Luke could hear the accusation just below the surface of his words.

"Justin, what do you think this woman needs most right now, a day after that terrible accident that leaves her family without income for possibly months and might leave her husband handicapped for life?"

Justin looked down at his feet. He wanted to say, "She needs Jesus!" just as he'd been taught. But he could not bring himself to say the words. They seemed hollow, careless, and unloving. His own thoughts scared him, and his eyes met Luke's. He knew the older man was waiting for an answer. Finally, he said simply, "I guess she needs somebody who cares." It almost felt like admitting defeat. Luke seemed to know what he was thinking.

"You're right, Justin. She needs somebody who loves her through the pain, who helps her in practical ways, and who gives her a reason to hope. And do you know what she does not need, what she cannot handle right now? Somebody who abuses her vulnerable situation to try and change her religious beliefs. The name *Jesus* to this Hindu woman is associated with political tensions, religious hatred, and fear. Because of that, Christianity cannot yet mean to her what it means to us. And let me assure you, God can handle that. He is interested in her, not her confession."

He looked intently at Justin, who wondered if his internal struggles were visible on his face. "What am I saying then, Justin? I know your fear. Am I saying it doesn't matter what she believes or who she believes in?" He let his words hang in the air while Justin resisted an urge to get up from the couch and leave the apartment.

"Have you read *The Shack*?" Luke asked gently after a pause.

Justin shook his head.

"It is a powerful tale of a man who spends a weekend with the Father, Son, and Holy Spirit at the place of the man's greatest hurt. At one point, after a similar discussion as ours, he asks Jesus, 'Does this mean that all roads lead to you?'"

Luke looked at Justin, his eyes filled with urge as well as empathy. "Do you know what Jesus replies in this story? 'Not at all! Most roads don't lead anywhere. What it does mean is that *I will travel any road to find you.*'"

Justin stayed silent. The battle raging in him during the past weeks was overwhelming. Why did God keep putting people across his path whose version of faith destroyed all the carefully built certitudes around him? Bjørn. Sophie. And now Luke. He had no problem having to fight for his faith. He just never thought he would have to fight the most wonderful people he knew.

Chapter Sixty-Two

The sun warmed her tanned skin, and the sound of splashing water and laughing voices carried up to the rock on which Sophie lay. The carefree hours of the interns' free afternoons led to many excursions, and today, they had climbed all the way down the ravine that formed the Melezza Valley below Rasa. It was a strenuous hike but well worth it. The whole valley stretched out wild and beautiful ahead of them, and nobody else was going to come here, as there was no road access.

She had just dozed off when an incoming email on her phone woke her up.

> Dear Sophie,
>
> I'm so glad to hear you're enjoying your mountain retreat. I can definitely imagine you happy in such an environment.
>
> I wonder what the discussions are about that you love so much? Knowing you, I imagine you making deep and meaningful contributions to them. And yes, I believe I would enjoy them as well. Thinking about the things of God has always made me the happiest.

My past week has been quite eventful. I think I mentioned the big church I was invited to preach at last month. Well, things were really amazing at first, but then they turned quite crazy. I don't want to say too much because I'm a bit concerned about my visa status and internet connections are not always safe. But I was quite close to getting thrown out of the country, or worse, if God hadn't sent me an angel at just the right time. He helped me out of the situation and has become a really good friend.

His name is Luke, and guess where he's from? Switzerland! He's been taking me to a social organization he works with. I can't figure him out. He's a Christian, but he sees things differently than anybody else I know. Actually, I think you would like him. Anyway, because of what happened at the other church, I don't think I can continue what I'm doing here in India right now. I have no idea what that means for me, but I'm trying to trust God and leave the outcome to Him. Not an easy task for me, as you might imagine. I think you would be much better at it. Like at most things, actually.

Well, gotta go and see what India has for me today!

Take care,
Justin

The butterflies in Sophie's stomach danced wildly as she stared at the email. Despite the noncommittal ending, the message showed that Sophie was still very much on Justin's mind. His cautious report of whatever happened to him the past week concerned her immediately. She knew Justin was downplaying it, and she could only imagine how he must be feeling all by himself in a foreign culture.

A different thought stole itself into her heart as well. Did he sound as if he wished for her to be there? But it was doubtful that her presence would make things easier for him in India, and the thought was probably little more than wishful thinking.

The best way she could support him, she decided, was to pray for him and to trust that God had more cards in His hands than what either of them knew.

Chapter Sixty-Three

The ceaseless sounds of Chennai traffic penetrated Justin's closed bedroom window like bizarre background music. He slowly opened his eyes and savored the fact that it was Sunday morning, and he was not in church. He couldn't remember this happening since he had met Jesus on that couch almost two years ago. Most of all, he would never have thought that he would enjoy staying away from church. The past weeks had brought so many changes that he was experiencing a range of emotions entirely new to him.

When he went down and joined Luke for breakfast, he was in high spirits. The events of the past week had, next to turmoil and uncertainty, also brought a feeling of undeniable relief. Although it was hard to swallow, Justin had to admit that the kind of ministry he had been doing in India had started to weigh on him. He had found himself questioning the prayer lines, the stardom of Western preachers, and the sales tactics used on spiritual issues such as conversion or healing. The unforeseeable events that now made it unlikely for him to continue his ministry here seemed to open up a window to breathe, to reconsider.

And Luke was the best person to have around for a time

like this. Not that the old man didn't come with challenges. Yesterday's conversation about the Hindu woman was still fresh in Justin's mind, and a good night's rest had not taken away his confusion. But, almost in spite of himself, he had to admit he trusted Luke on a different level than he had trusted people like Jonathan.

He helped himself to some toast and coffee. "Please, Luke, tell me more about yourself. We've been preoccupied with me this whole time, but I really want to learn more about you. And I'll try not to be judgemental anymore, although I can't make any guarantees, I fear." An apologetic smile accompanied his statement.

"Me? I don't know that I'm a very interesting subject for a conversation," Luke said with a wink.

Justin didn't accept this answer. "How do you earn a living? Surely working for a nonprofit in India is not very lucrative."

"Oh, you're flattering me, but I think I look like a retired man, don't I?"

It occurred to Justin that Luke actually came across more like a very young man trapped in an old man's body. He adjusted his question. "Ok, what did you do before you retired?"

This time Luke took a bit longer to answer. "I have done many things in my life. From a financial standpoint, I was a rather successful businessman for part of my career, and the sale of my company has enabled me to lead a nice and comfortable life as a retiree."

I wouldn't call living and working in India very comfortable. He wanted to learn more, but he could tell he would have to draw it out of Luke. "Are you a part of a church in Switzerland?"

"It's not a church in the traditional sense. We are a group of followers of Jesus who meet regularly to bounce ideas off each other, encourage one another, and live life together. We are friends, first of all, and companions on the road through life. In that way, we are maybe the truest form of a church. I'm highly fortunate to have these people around me."

A longing stirred in Justin's heart. He had many friends from the Rock, but a description of his friendship with them would have sounded entirely different. They were fellow soldiers in a fight where, in the end, everybody fought alone. Though they supported each other financially and with encouraging words, Justin was suddenly aware that most of them, himself included, would try to grow their own ministry before helping others. He told Luke what he had just thought.

Luke nodded. "That is quite an insight you're having there. Do you know why everyone will inevitably look to themselves in this system?"

Justin shook his head.

"Because our current religious system is performance based. If you believe God's idea for your life is to make converts or gather an assembly or create a following, then you will see others as a distraction. Either they will follow your exact goal in life, in which case you will be partners, or you will leave them at the fringes of your life so you can fulfill the great mission you think God has for you."

Justin waited, wondering what Luke's point was.

"If, on the other hand, you see your life as a gift meant to enjoy, you can invite others in as expressions of that gift. You will be able to meet them without wondering how they can benefit you or whether they will team up with you on some great endeavor. You can just be companions and friends. And often those friendships prove to be the ones which are longest-lasting and most beautiful."

Suddenly, a face flashed in front of Justin. Hadn't he hoped Sophie would team up with him? Come to India and help him establish his ministry, fulfill the job he believed God had given him? Had he ever considered her outside of this context? Would there have been a future for them if he hadn't insisted on his own plans? A terrible emptiness washed over him. Had he given Sophie up for a dream that had crashed around him within only two months?

"You can experience these kinds of friendships as well,

Justin," Luke continued. "I can see the longing for it in your eyes. If you let go of seeing God as an oversized CEO who keeps you at the job day and night, you will allow people to enter"—here he looked up with an expression Justin didn't understand—"or maybe reenter your life and become your true friends."

After breakfast, they packed their swimsuits, towels, and some good books and set out to Mahabalipuram Beach. When they had settled in their chairs under a palm tree, Justin told Luke about the phone call he had received under the same tree only six days ago, and how his phone had almost landed in the Bay of Bengal. Luke laughed, and they lay lazily in the sun.

And just when Justin thought it was the perfect day, Luke ruined it all.

"I'm going to leave Chennai next week," he said, completely unexpected.

Justin shot up and looked at him incredulously. He knew his disappointment was visible, but he couldn't help it.

Luke continued with a firm, but gentle, voice, "I have things to take care of in several places, mainly in Switzerland, in the coming weeks. I'm not sure yet when I will return here. You are, of course, welcome to stay at my apartment and use my car while I'm gone."

Justin looked away. He couldn't bring himself to say the obvious, the polite "Oh, no problem. And thank you for all you've done for me." His feeling of abandonment was ridiculous, but it was as real and strong as anything.

"I'm sorry, Justin." Luke's voice had a tone that reminded Justin of his own dad's in times of closeness. "I'm aware this is a very bad time to leave you on your own. I wish I had a choice, and I did try and rearrange my business in Switzerland, but it seems like I really need to go there. I will get you together with some other friends of mine who will check in with you while I'm gone and whom you can call anytime if you need help."

"I'll be fine," Justin answered hurriedly. "Don't worry

about me." His old defenses had sprung up surprisingly fast. Of course he knew how to play that game, and his expression of indifference had appeared almost automatically.

But Luke wouldn't play along. "No, you're not ok. You're going through a hell of a time, Justin. And I hate to leave you alone right now. I know that you have no idea what your future looks like—where you're going to live, what you'll do next, who's going to be by your side. And that, together with what you have experienced in the past weeks, is more than most men have to deal with at your age. Please accept my invitation to have friends by your side here in Chennai while I'm gone. And until I'm back, I expect to get emails from you on a regular basis."

And before Justin knew what was happening, Luke had pulled him into a strong embrace. Justin was not used to hugs but found himself returning Luke's.

"Thank you." He felt better already, so he added, "Can I turn your stereo on as loud as I want to?"

They spent the whole day at the beach, surfing the waves and reading.

"Where in Switzerland will you be spending the next weeks?" Justin asked after returning with some sandwiches and chips from a snack stand.

"I first have to attend to some business matters that require some travel but will get to Switzerland in a week or so. At that time, I will take a group of students to a Christian retreat in the South of the country."

Justin thought of Sophie, and he suddenly realized all he knew about her retreat was that it was in the mountains. But wasn't a large part of Switzerland mountainous?

"What kind of place is it?" he asked casually.

"It's like a piece of Heaven on earth. A place where students can take a break for a while, enjoy nature, and have fellowship with each other and God. Many students have a hard time with their faith as they go through high school and college. The secular viewpoint of European culture can be intimidating, especially if you're new to faith and in an academic setting where Christianity is pretty much ridiculed. We try and help them get grounded in their own faith and become comfortable discussing it and wrestling with it among people of other convictions. We're not trying to tell them what to think, though, as some groups do. They are smart enough, as is every human being, to find the truth themselves if they want it badly enough. I would say those at our retreats do. As a result, some really interesting conversations happen at that place."

Again, Justin remembered something Sophie had said. *I have been part of some very fascinating conversations about faith and God and the world here.* Was it possible that Luke was talking about the same place Sophie was at? But then again, surely there were many Christian retreats in the mountains that were described as a piece of Heaven by those visiting.

It was dark when they packed up their stuff and headed home. Justin took a shower and went straight to bed. While lying there, his thoughts ran wildly around in his head. He was glad for the remaining few days he had with Luke but also intimidated by the prospect of being here by himself. His mission and calling had definitely gotten some bruises in the past week. And without the calling, he wasn't sure he had the confidence for staying in this foreign place.

Chapter Sixty-Four

Although she had never heard of the guy who was going to lead the retreat, what Sophie read about him on the bulletin board was enough for her to ask Rachel for a work break so she could attend part of this upcoming course. The flyer introducing the guest speaker read: Deconstruction—Letting go of unhealthy notions and practices in our faith. A week with Ryan W., former pastor of a charismatic megachurch in Wichita, KS.

Not only was Sophie interested in what Ryan had to say, she also hoped it might help her understand a bit better what strong bonds still tied Justin to the charismatic movement and its deep connection to the American culture. Although fascinated by the things she had heard and experienced at the Rock, there had always been warning signs inside her regarding this kind of teaching. Maybe it was her Swiss upbringing. Maybe it was just the fact that she had gotten to know Jesus in a different context. But she wondered if understanding this form of Christianity would provide a way for her to reconnect with Justin.

The next morning, she got her chores done extra fast and got to the meeting room early. A middle-aged man was there, apparently preparing for the meeting. He looked up when he saw Sophie, gave her a welcoming smile, and started walking toward her.

"Oh, I don't want to interrupt you," Sophie said quickly and in English, assuming him to be the guest speaker.

But the man only waved his hand. "No problem! Most of the time I end up saying something else than what's on the script anyway." His eyes were kind, and Sophie felt comfortable around him at once.

"My name's Ryan. It's a pleasure to meet you."

Sophie introduced herself, and since Ryan asked what brought her here, she mentioned her brief encounter with fundamentalist Christianity and how it had brought up many questions in her.

Ryan nodded. "It's always an honor for me to meet people outside the US who share their experiences of American fundamentalism with me. Americans so easily forget that their way of living the Christian faith is very unique and not at all the measuring stick for the experience of other believers around the world."

Sophie's smile had a sad touch as she thought of Justin. "How did you start to question things?" she asked and wondered if he could hear the longing in her voice.

He smiled. "This will be the topic of this week—recognizing the things we believe but cannot reconcile with our hearts or our conscience. I do believe that Europe in general has a little less trouble with this than me and my fellow citizens. Some of my friends from European countries believe the emphasis your cultures put on moderation might have something to do with it. Americans are sometimes so passionate that their passion drives out compassion. But we will get into that more this week. We still have a few minutes—tell me about your experiences, if you would."

Sophie described her time at the Rock, the doctrine, the sense of community, but also the many things she didn't understand. Then she remembered something. "One thing that's very hard for me as a Swiss is to understand how American Christians connect patriotism, and even militarism, with faith. Maybe it's because our country is too small for us to ever assume we're some especially select people. But it seems silly even for a big country to think that God plays favorites according to size or strength. That seems such an arrogant assumption!" As soon as she said it, Sophie blushed. The last thing she wanted to do was insult this kind man.

But he seemed to share her thoughts. "Yes, this is one of the most tragic assumptions countries and empires can make, and have made for millennia, about the nature of God. That He would look at borders and petty political issues and take sides. You know, in my country, the majority of believers are absolutely convinced that God is on one side of the political spectrum. They go so far as to be convinced that you cannot be a follower of Jesus if you are in the other party. Pretty crazy, isn't it?"

This was in fact hard for Sophie to imagine, although she remembered the conversation between Bjørn and others from the Rock at the café in the Colorado mountains. Switzerland had numerous parties whose representatives made up the Federal Council, which in turn consisted of seven members. There was no single president in charge. Decisions were made by the majority of the council, which meant there had to always be some kind of teamwork between several parties to get anything done. This made it harder for anyone to believe that God was part of a particular party or to assume the others were all ungodly.

She was about to ask another question when the other participants started coming in. Ryan told her to find him after the meeting as he turned to greet the others. Sophie sat down, memories flooding her mind. The voice of that older student at the Rock came back to her as he had replied to her questions about Jesus and war. *As the world's leading superpower and a nation chosen by God, we have the responsibility to save, restore, and protect those in need*, he had told her and with it, had justified any war the

US had fought in the last centuries. The thought of it repulsed her. A nation chosen by God . . . what did that make the other nations? She shook off the disturbing thoughts and focused her attention on Ryan.

"I used to be a pastor of a megachurch. And I would tell everybody all about it. In fact, I knew the current number of members on any given day for twenty-six years. We were charismatic. We spoke in tongues. We preached the full gospel. We were patriotic, conservative, and we believed in the literal interpretation of every word in the Bible."

Ryan paused to look what effect his words had on the twenty people in the room. Then he smiled. "It always gives me great pleasure to see that many of you have no clue what I'm even talking about. Let me tell you what a blessing it is that you don't! On the other side, with the world getting more and more connected, I see little chance that Switzerland will be forever safe from the influence of American fundamentalism.

"But even if it were, you would face a similar challenge from your own culture. Because every nation, every denomination in any given culture, has certain ideas that are, if observed carefully, inconsistent with the life and teachings of Jesus Christ and should therefore be *deconstructed.*" He said the last word slowly, as if he was spelling it out.

"What an odd word, you might think. Sounds a little like destruction, right? And that's exactly what we need to do with some of the ideas that have crept into our faith. This week, we will look at some of these ideas as they have sprung up in our faith cultures. They are cancers, and I will call them as such, because they destroy the Christian faith from within. But don't worry. We will not only deconstruct. We will look at tools to help reconstruct as well. We could call the whole process a renovation." He smiled and looked into the eyes of the people gathered. "And now, let's gather some thoughts on what you feel could be an idea that needs renovation in the Christian culture in your context."

An attractive woman in her forties raised her hand. Her

eyes were kind, but there was a fire in them. "How about the notion that Jesus had to die on the cross to appease the wrath of a God who is supposed to be nothing but love?" she asked. Some of the people sitting around Sophie turned around, surprised by her suggestion.

Ryan, however, nodded empathetically. "Ah, we're not wasting time. An excellent example, and I'm looking forward to us examining this further in our time together. For now, let's keep collecting ideas!"

Another hand came up, and a rather timid man, barely out of his teens, said, "I'd love to hear everybody's thoughts on the idea that people who don't confess the name of Jesus before they die will burn in hell for eternity." The man sounded as if it took an effort to even utter those words.

Again, Ryan nodded. "Another notion that is definitely in need of renovation, and one we will also get into this week. Keep going!"

Sophie was listening breathlessly, but she was not prepared for what happened next.

"How about the tendency to see the world in compartments of 'us' and 'them' when clearly God sees nothing but 'us' when He looks at any person He created?"

It wasn't what the person said, but his voice that made her jump. She whipped around in her chair and for the first time saw the people who had entered the room after her. When she met the man's eyes, she realized he hadn't recognized her from behind either until now. Both of them stood up at the same time, momentarily putting an end to the conversation in the room, and they both spoke at the same time too.

"Sophie!"

"Bjørn!"

Chapter Sixty-Five

Everybody's eyes were on the two, and for a second, Sophie thought she was imagining things. How was it possible that her Norwegian friend, whom she had not had contact with since leaving Colorado, would end up at the same little tiny Swiss village as her? Apparently, Ryan had the same question.

"It looks like we're having the pleasure of experiencing a little reunion here. Now, before I bore you with American fundamentalism, why don't you two tell us the story behind this? I'd rather hear this story than my own voice," he said with a smile.

Sophie couldn't speak. There was the surprise, yes. But seeing Bjørn here so unexpectedly also brought back memories of Justin. And those memories washed over her with such force that she stood there like in a trance. Bjørn must have guessed what was going on, because after giving her a warm smile, he turned and addressed the group.

"Well, I don't know who is more surprised to see the other one here, Sophie or I, and it's definitely an unusual set of circumstances that has brought us back to the same place."

Now that's an understatement, Sophie thought, still regaining her composure.

"The two of us met this spring in Colorado at a Bible school that teaches pretty similarly to what my friend Ryan used to teach. I had come all the way from Norway to sit under the teaching of its leader, Jonathan Parker. Sophie was visiting a friend there, and during her visit, we had the pleasure to chat for a while.

"I think what's interesting is that some of the questions we will be addressing this week had already formed in my head during my time at the school, as I think they had in Sophie's. When I graduated this May, I still had two months left on my visa. I had more questions than when I started school." When Bjørn said this, several people nodded in agreement.

"Then one day, at a Christian bookstore, I stumbled upon a book that addressed many of those questions. It was written by a former megachurch pastor named Ryan. . . . And since it was not that far of a drive from Colorado Springs to Wichita, that's what I did the following week. I met this amazing man here"—he pointed to Ryan with a smile—"and decided I needed to stick around for a while."

Ryan grinned. "His sticking around has been a real pleasure, by the way. I've hardly met a more brilliant young man, and together we've been exploring some religious wildernesses, so to speak, in the past two months. So when, a month or so ago, I was invited to lead this group here, I knew exactly whom to bring with me."

The people applauded, moved by the surprise, and then continued talking about religious beliefs that were hurting the relationship between God and people. Even though this topic was of burning interest to Sophie, she was too distracted to pay attention anymore. Listening to Bjørn almost felt like having Justin here in person. And she was not prepared for the physical longing this thought produced. Memories resurfaced with overwhelming intensity. The smell of Justin's hair. His skin that electrified her when she touched it. The dimples when he smiled and those eyes she could not forget.

When Ryan dismissed them for lunch, Bjørn walked over to her seat and embraced her in a big hug. Sophie wanted to ask a million questions, but to her own horror her eyes started to fill with tears. She just stood there, wishing everybody would disappear. Apparently, Ryan had anticipated this wish, because when she looked around a few moments later, there was nobody else in the room.

"Bjørn, I'm so excited to see you. I'm sorry I'm crying, but some memories just seem to turn me into a mess."

Bjørn didn't seem to mind, and they sat down outside the cottage. "I'd like to ask you a lot of questions later, but I feel like I need to get the big one out of the way first," he said a little shyly. "Justin and you . . . how are you two doing?"

Sophie didn't answer.

"I guess then I know how to interpret your reaction. I'm sorry, Sophie. And I don't need to bother you with talking about him if you don't want to."

Sophie smiled ruefully. "It's ok. We're not mad at each other or anything. It's just . . . not what it might have been. We're keeping up contact, though."

They filled each other in on the events of their lives in the past months, and Sophie told Bjørn what little she had heard from Justin through his emails and newsletters. Bjørn was silent for a moment. "It doesn't sound like he has started to question any of Jonathan's doctrines yet, does it?" he said quietly.

Sophie shook her head. "It's partially why I was excited to hear Ryan teach. I still have a hard time understanding what's going on in Justin's head, and I feel like hearing from a fellow American who's been there would be a great help."

"Oh, you will love Ryan! He has helped me so much in the last months. You know"—and Bjørn's voice became distant for a moment—"by the end of Bible school I was seriously doubting my salvation. I could no longer find a way to adhere to Jonathan's teachings. And you know how the school comes quite close to saying that if you don't agree with Jonathan's teachings, you cannot be a real Christian. But I still loved God very much. I loved the Bible, and I loved my fellow students. And I still wanted nothing more than to follow Jesus. And this, by definition, made me a Christian. But I had started to detest the direction the school was taking. I was very confused by the time I stumbled upon that book."

A smile crept onto his face. "At first, I was suspicious, as I was taught to be. Was Ryan going to undermine my faith, as Jonathan warned us concerning people like him? But I could tell that Ryan wrote from a position of honesty and humility. And humility never undermines anything worth keeping. So I kept reading, and I haven't stopped since. There's a lot of baggage one picks up from a group that thinks they know the entire truth. I'm working on dropping the baggage now."

Sophie nodded. She still had Justin's face in front of her.

"The thing I probably love most about Ryan is that he surrounds himself with people so different from him. He preaches at places across the entire Christian spectrum, from Orthodox to Pentecostal congregations, from monasteries to classic Evangelical events. He has Muslim friends, Jewish friends, and friends with almost any other conviction you can think of. And in all that, he is one of the most deeply devoted followers of Jesus I have ever met."

The two friends joined the others for lunch. Sophie was thrilled to hear that Ryan was scheduled to teach another course the week after this and that Bjørn was going to stay in Rasa with him for the whole time. She would have plenty of time to ask questions and learn from both of them.

When she and Bjørn went for a walk among the chestnut trees surrounding the village after lunch, Sophie was deep in thought. What her Norwegian friend had said about Ryan's way of following Jesus reminded her of how Thomas and others like him were living their faith—free of fear toward people with different views and full of love for all of them. They possessed a beautiful theology. *This is the kind of Christianity I fell in love with.*

Chapter Sixty-Six

The last days before Luke's departure, Justin and his friend made the most of their time together and visited tourist sites in Chennai, went to the zoo, and spent an entire day at the beach. Their conversations were deep and challenging. They talked about doctrine, about personal convictions, about the fear of change, and the great lengths people go to in order to avoid having to face their own insecurities. Justin was not ready to give up the beliefs he had found in the past years, but he was slowly starting to consider that the Christian faith might be bigger and wider than what Jonathan had introduced them to.

They didn't only talk about faith, though. Justin shared things from his past with Luke, from his childhood to his drug-dealing days. Whatever topic came up, he could tell the old man's wisdom and empathy not only touched him, it was starting to change him. Luke's gentleness and compassion, his love for those unlike him, and the personal sacrifice he was willing to pay to help other people—it all stood in stark contrast to the world Justin had lived in before meeting Jesus but, sadly, also to a lot of what he learned at Bible school.

Two days before Luke's departure, they were sitting on

Luke's couch sipping coffee when Justin finally decided he had to talk about the one thing he had been hiding from his friend.

"You know that friend from Switzerland I told you I met at the Rock . . . well, it's a girl. And she"—it took him a second to muster the courage to actually say it out loud—"might be a bit more than a friend to me."

If Luke was surprised that Justin hadn't told him until now, he didn't show it. His face was calm but concentrated, and Justin knew he had Luke's undivided attention. He told him about meeting Sophie in Monarch and how something about her captivated him from the start. How he searched the slopes for days for a woman he'd met for only one hour, and how deep his disappointment went when he didn't hear back from her. When he came to the part where Sophie showed up at the school, Justin's face lit up in such a way that it gave away where the story was heading, even to someone who didn't pay as much attention as Luke did.

"We spent all of our time together attending classes, hiking, talking, laughing . . .," he trailed off. Looking over at Luke, he was surprised at just how deeply Luke seemed to be touched by what he said. The old man hadn't said a word, but Justin could feel that it wasn't lack of interest that kept him from talking. "She went back to Switzerland, and I finished the last weeks of school before heading straight out to India."

"What happened?" Luke finally broke his silence.

"I think I scared her away. I had all these amazing dreams about starting a successful ministry in India. And I could have seen her coming with me. Except that . . ." He looked up, and his face reflected the shame he felt. "Sophie had quite different ideas about what following God looks like than me. I don't think she would have wanted to do what I set out to do. She would have had to change too much, since I was unfortunately not going to change. Looking back, I truly wish I had considered her views more openly instead of being so arrogant." He stopped again, lost in thought. "I just couldn't see it work. At least I couldn't at the time," he added quietly.

To his surprise, Justin thought he saw a brief moment of joy sweep over Luke's face. "Well, it looks like you've learned a lesson, Justin," he said with warmth. But it sounded more like a question than a statement.

"Do you think I should try and talk to her, tell her how I see things now?"

Luke smiled at him. "Maybe you should spend some time talking with God about *her*. Try to walk in her shoes for a while. It's amazing how much wiser we tend to become when our thoughts stop circling around ourselves."

His statement was kind, and Justin knew he was right. This had all been about him. It was time to shift the focus if he truly hoped for a future for him and that woman who had captivated his heart.

Chapter Sixty-Seven

James's hands trembled only lightly as he moved the pills around in his palms. It wouldn't even take that many, he realized. It always sounded so dramatic, so colorful on TV. In reality, he was going to die quietly and probably without anyone noticing for a few days. Maybe Eli would call and wonder where his friend was. They had gotten very close in the past months. But Eli had a family. He wouldn't bother driving over and checking on James until quite a few days from now. *Eli has a family*, he repeated in his mind, while a new wave of despair overwhelmed him, *like I did*. The realization of what he had lost threatened to choke him.

He had lost Ronnie.

And then, when all he had left in his life was the passion to keep others from suffering like his little brother, he had gotten careless. He had let a young guy go one too many times. An internal investigation had found James guilty of failing to do his duty as an officer on several accounts. He was let go within the week. But his nightmares had only started. James's long-time girlfriend Jenny was devastated. She accused him of self-ishness and told him she couldn't imagine starting a family with a guy who put the needs of strangers ahead of those of his family. She moved out only days later, which was just as well since James didn't know where he was going to come up with the money for the next rent payment.

He looked at the pills again. All those people had been wrong. All the stuff Eli had given him to read. There was no redemption, no grace in the end. There was only suffering, and if you were lucky like him and knew the right people in a pharmacy, you could find an easy and sure way out of the misery called life. He clutched the glass of water in one hand and the pills to end it all in the other.

Out of habit, his glance fell on his open computer next to the pill bottle as he heard the ping of an incoming message. The subject line of the received email caught his attention. *Inquiry regarding a break-in case in 2016*, it said. Slowly, his curiosity won over, and James opened the mail, setting the pills aside for a moment.

James,

I don't know how this finds you, and I'm certainly sorry for the way things have worked out for you. We all miss you a lot here at the station. It's just not the same without you. Hope all is well and you're adjusting to a different routine. Have you found a new job yet?

Just wanted to let you know that we got a curious email inquiry yesterday. It concerns a break-in case you were working on a couple of years ago that involved a kid named Justin Friedman. The guy who wrote the email said he believed whoever was on duty that day would remember the situation. I replied saying I'd try and find out who it was, and my records show you were on duty that day. I'm forwarding his email so you can contact him if you'd like.

Give my wishes to Jenny,
Jack

James sat on his couch, a flood of emotions washing over him. The kid from the break-in! The one whom Matt had let go again only six months later. Were they going to tell him they found him lying in a gutter as well? James almost gave up the thought of contacting the guy. But then his curiosity got the better of him. He had never been able to find out anything about the boy. Apparently, he was neither on Facebook nor any other social media. The prospect of finding out what had happened to him drove James to open his mail and write a short reply.

Sir,

You were inquiring about an incident that involved a young man named Justin Friedman. I was the officer on duty that morning, although I'm no longer a member of the police force. I would appreciate any updates you have on Justin. Let me know when we can talk.

James McLeod

He sent the mail and then sat restlessly on the couch. It was the oddest thing for him to get distracted from ending his life by a meaningless inquiry from a stranger about another stranger. Except, for some inexplainable reason, James did not feel like Justin Friedman was a stranger to him. Something was connecting their lives, and James couldn't escape the draw of that connection.

He must have fallen asleep when another ping from his computer startled him almost two hours later.

Dear Mr. McLeod,

You cannot know what joy you give me in replying to my inquiry. There is so much to tell you about Justin Friedman and so much to thank you for. I will be visiting Atlanta briefly next week and would love to meet you in person. We have a lot to talk about. Let me know where and when we can meet.

Sincerely,
Thomas Wenger

James sat up straight and typed a reply with a time and place that very minute. Life seemed to have come back into his body, and the unused pills fell onto the floor and under the couch unnoticed.

Chapter Sixty-Eight

The afternoon before his departure, Luke introduced Justin to some of his longtime friends who promised to look out for him, visit him every now and then, and help in any way they could. Afterwards, they went to dinner, and Justin asked Luke more about his upcoming retreat.

"I certainly love this retreat and have been there countless times," Luke said. "You know, there are places in the world that become home to you no matter where they are."

Justin nodded. To him, every place where Sophie and he had been together now felt like it could be home. If she would be there, that was. Before retreating to his room that night, Justin walked past Luke's open laptop and happened to glance at it. On the screen was a travel itinerary, showing the train connection for his upcoming retreat in Switzerland. He didn't know if it was just the fact that it was Sophie's country that made everything related to it important to him, but he quickly glanced at the name of the end destination and made a mental note before getting ready for bed.

When the airport security doors shut behind Luke, and Justin turned away slowly to leave, it wasn't without a feeling of sadness. It was harder than he'd thought to say goodbye to a man he, after all, had only known for ten days.

He got back to the apartment and walked around aimlessly like a tiger in a cage. His ambitions of preaching to pastors seemed to have disappeared completely. He tried reading the Bible but was so distracted he gave up. He started writing his overdue newsletter only to find himself wondering what Sophie would think of each sentence. Besides, writing about Justin's poor judgement of Moses's character was still a bit too humbling. Finally, he called Ashish and asked him out for lunch. He needed to talk to somebody with an undistracted view. When they had finished their biriyani, Justin asked his friend what he should do.

"Has your name been cleared yet?" Ashish asked.

"Yes. The papers came in the mail yesterday, and I'm again allowed to travel freely inside India and abroad as well." Relieving as this was, Justin wasn't really happy about it. He was free, but free to do what?

Ashish seemed to read his mind. "It will not be a good idea to try and preach openly anymore. You are cleared, but if your name gets mentioned again concerning proselytizing, I think you can no longer count on them turning a blind eye."

Justin knew he was right. Besides, he was not sure he had it in him anymore to preach, at least not at the moment. When he said goodbye to Ashish and went back to the apartment, he felt incredibly discouraged. Maybe he needed to just go home. Weighing this option, he could almost hear his friends encouraging him to go back or go to a different country to do the same thing there. *Don't let the devil push you around, Justin.* They would repeat Jonathan's words. *You have to resist him. Show him you're victorious! Keep up the good fight!*

He suddenly felt very tired. *Jesus, is it really that hard to be a Christian?*

He was still sitting on his couch when the phone rang. "Hey, Justin, it's Paul from the shelter. If you've got time, we'd love to put you into the volunteer roster for a couple of times this week. We're quite short-staffed at the moment. You'd be serving lunch at the shelter and helping at the studio where the women craft jewelry in the afternoon. We'd love to have you come."

Justin agreed with relief. He suspected that it wasn't just the lack of helpers that had prompted them to call him, but a certain old friend from Switzerland as well.

The next morning, Justin woke up with much more energy than the day before. He got dressed and was out the door in no time. He realized the prospect of being able to help people, practically and without trying to sell them any ideas, was like a breath of fresh air.

The work was unlike anything Justin had ever done. He saw for the first time the reality of something he had only, if ever, read about before. The girls in the shelter were shockingly young. Justin knew they had gotten rescued mainly out of brothels, and the thought of these children being forced to have sex with grown men made his stomach turn. He felt so sorry for them that he decided to pray for each girl that came through the lunch line as he put food on their plates.

After helping with lunch clean up, he followed another volunteer upstairs to the jewelry studio. His guide, a beautiful woman named Saraya, showed him around and explained the idea behind the studio. "The worst danger these girls face is not over once they are rescued. Because of what happened to them, they are now social outcasts. Their families often reject them, and since they had to work instead of going to school, they have no education and no means of independence. We are teaching them a trade that will allow them to stand on their own."

She showed Justin around the spacious studio flooded with sunlight where maybe twenty teenage girls were working. Happy chatter and occasional laughter filled the room. Justin was impressed by the beautiful jewelry these young artists were creating. As he stood there, a girl of maybe sixteen years came toward him. She limped heavily but had a broad grin on her face. She started talking to him, obvious pride in her voice, as she held out a pair of earrings to him. Justin looked over to Saraya to translate.

"She finished her first pair of earrings just today. She's very happy you're here to see them," Saraya said proudly.

Justin looked at the girl limping back to her workplace. "What happened to her?"

Saraya's voice showed no emotion when she replied. "Some of the pimps beat the girls to scare them so they won't try and run. Sometimes they beat them if a customer complains about the service he received. Ananya here got beaten so hard her leg broke. Her pimp made her continue to see customers, so her bones grew back in a crooked way. She will limp forever."

Justin closed his eyes and felt sick. He could not believe girls who had endured horrors like these would be smiling and singing like they were. But above all, he felt utterly sorry—sorry for being a man, sorry for what had happened to her, sorry for life's injustices. He felt like he needed to tell her. He asked Saraya if she would translate for him. She agreed and they went over to Ananya's bench. But when Justin was through apologizing for the way men had treated her and was expressing his regret about the girls' fate, Saraya stopped translating and turned to him.

"We don't want you to feel sorry for us," she told him in a friendly but firm voice. "We don't need pity. Instead, Ananya needs encouragement and people who believe in her future. If you see her only as a victim, you will feel sorry. But if you see her as a woman who has her life ahead of her, you will help to bring that potential out of her."

Ananya was looking back and forth between the two English-speaking people, still holding her jewelry in her hand. There was a long silence. Then Justin said simply, "Please tell her that these are the most beautiful earrings I have ever seen, and that I cannot wait to bring some of them to America to show people there what an amazing artist I met in Chennai."

The following days went by fast. Justin could not wait to get out of bed in the morning and get to the shelter. He became friends with the English-speaking staff in no time and spent hours asking them questions about the work of the different anti-human trafficking organizations in Chennai. He wanted to know about the girls, about what kind of life lay ahead of them, and how he could help. He wanted to know how the other volunteers had come here, and he found a similar story to what Luke had told him. It was several days until he realized that he had completely forgotten that they were not all Christians. It was the first time since his conversion that he had not thought about a person's religious convictions ahead of anything else.

After the first week of working at the shelter, Justin was bursting with energy and new impressions. He was given the weekend off and spent Saturday relaxing in Luke's apartment, playing music, and thinking about life. He admitted to himself now that he had been the biggest fool ever to let Sophie go. And he was quite aware of the fact that it was going to be his turn if he wanted her back. He could not expect Sophie to make another first move, not with the way he had left for India all smug and convinced of his fundamentalist ways. He thought of what a possible first step from his side could be. Write her emails and tell her of his change of heart? Somehow it seemed like too lame a way to try and win back a woman like Sophie. Justin's adventurous nature was seeking for something more romantic. He needed to see her face-to-face. And he would love to talk to Luke, even before that. If only . . .

He turned on the computer and went online to his bank statement. There was no way it was going to happen. But once Justin had actually thought of a plan, it was very hard for him to give it up. There was no reason for anybody to give him a $1,000 right now, he knew, especially since he had not sent out a newsletter this month and was really not doing any kind of Christian ministry he could talk about. And yet . . .

He shut the computer and closed his eyes. His prayers had started to be shorter and more personal in the past months. But if anything, they had only increased in intensity. After asking God for help, he spent the rest of the day sleeping, exhausted from a week of physical work. When he woke up, he opened the computer back up to read some American news. A couple of emails had come in during his nap. He glanced over them and found that one was from his dad.

Dear Justin,

I hope everything is going well with you. I understand that you are very busy and might not have the energy to write or call. I am, naturally, always wondering how you're doing, especially since I haven't heard from you in quite a while, and I'm praying that you are fine.

This morning, as I was praying for you, I had a very unusual impression. I had the very strong feeling that I should send you some money. This does not normally happen to me, as you might know. Of course, I hope you'd have told me if you were in some financial need. But maybe it is not so much to meet a physical need, but the money can help meet an emotional or even spiritual need you might have right now. As I said, I don't know. But I trust you will know what to do with it.

I love you always.
Dad.

With a dry throat, Justin refreshed the still open tab with the bank statement. It now read a balance of $1352.

Justin let out a shout, and his feet had barely touched the ground before he had his passport and suitcase thrown onto his bed.

Chapter Sixty-Nine

Sophie stood at the cable car station, shifting from one leg to the other and waiting for the little glass-encased cable car to come into view. In the almost two weeks since Ryan's arrival in Rasa, Sophie had made it a habit to sit and listen to him speak every morning after the end of her chores, but not today. Today, she would celebrate.

Just then, the car appeared from behind the trees beneath the village. She strained to see inside, and although the reflection on the windows made it hard for her to recognize anything, she could make out a hand waving energetically. As soon as the car stopped and the doors opened, she found herself in Thomas's embrace.

"It sure looks like you're enjoying yourself here," he said happily after giving her a long hug and a kiss on the forehead.

"Thomas, I can't even begin to tell you. I feel like a world of things have happened to me since I last saw you."

"I've had quite the time myself, actually." He smiled mysteriously. "But as far as your experience goes, it doesn't surprise me as much as you might think. First of all, this place has a peculiar tendency to change people. In that quiet, hidden place called your soul, that is. I'm happy to hear from your emails that this is what seems to be happening to you as well. Secondly, knowing who was leading the retreats the past two weeks makes me think you might have had an interesting time, am I right?"

"You know Ryan?"

"Yes. We have been close friends for many years." When he saw the incredulity on Sophie's face, he added, "And, guess what? We met here in Rasa. It looks like an unassuming place, but you'd be surprised by how many people from around the world find their way here."

Sophie laughed. "Well, I guess you've stolen one of my surprises, then," she admitted, "but I don't think you can beat me to the second part of it."

"I'm at a loss."

"Guess who Ryan's friend is who accompanies him?"

"If I remember correctly, it's a bright young man from Norway."

Sophie clapped her hands, but now Thomas was just as surprised as her. "Do *you* know him too?"

"Yes, he was at the Rock when I visited. We talked on several occasions, and he was friends with Justin."

"How about that! Ryan had mentioned his Norwegian friend coming from a Word of Faith background, but I never asked which one. Well, some might call this a coincidence, but not me."

"I have learned from you that far fewer things are coincidences than what I used to think," Sophie remarked with a smile. "Let's get you settled in and . . . well, I guess I don't need to introduce you to anyone since you basically live here, but humor me anyway and come for a little tour."

They both laughed and set off chatting. They had not even reached Thomas's room when they walked into Ryan. The two men embraced in a way that reminded Sophie of how long Thomas had lived before her and how rich his friendships and his whole life were. Ryan was excited to hear that Thomas and Sophie knew each other.

"This man's friendship has blessed me over the course of many years, and I don't know where I would be today without him," Ryan told Sophie. "It's interesting that this place has earned a special spot in your heart as well, Sophie. It's no coincidence."

Thomas and Sophie chuckled.

Since Sophie had to get back to her duties for most of that day, she didn't see Thomas again until after dinner in the little library over the sitting room. Curling up comfortably in an armchair, Sophie asked, "So how was your past month?" She couldn't keep the curiosity out of her voice.

"I'll report about my travels soon. What I'm dying to know is what have Ryan's thoughts done to *you* over the past weeks?"

Her face lit up. "It was fascinating. And challenging, for sure. But maybe hopeful and inspiring are the best words. It reminded me of what, or who, I have fallen in love with in the past year. Ryan brought a simplicity and a beauty back to my relationship with Jesus, and I'm very grateful for that. Of course, I have had way less exposure to some of the stuff the group was discussing than others, but even during my short trip to Colorado, I got to know many doctrines whose appeal and danger I can now clearly see."

Thomas looked at her and seemed to wait for her to say something else. Her thoughts had gone directly back to Justin at the mentioning of Colorado, and she wondered if he knew. Giving him a playfully scolding look, she admitted, "Ok, ok. I'm thinking of Justin. And yes, I feel like I can at the same time understand him being drawn to some of the doctrines like healing and prosperity and victory . . . and on the other hand, I can't understand it at all."

Thomas nodded.

"You know, I felt the pull myself," she added thoughtfully. "It feels good to think you're doing something for God—preaching, evangelizing, praying in this convincing, triumphant way. It sounds good and it looks good. And yet, it comes with a price. Humility and honesty seem to leave. Compassion, gentleness, and brokenness go into hiding in a person who lives like that. And I can't help but mourn for Justin because I *know* this has happened in his own life, and I even think he can tell himself. But I don't know if he can imagine a way out of where he is, stuck in his self-righteous, black-and-white religion!"

She didn't intend for her assessment to come out with such passion. Thomas looked at her intently, and she couldn't make sense of the joy she saw in his eyes.

He simply said, "I understand what you are saying, Sophie, maybe better than you can imagine. It hurts like crazy to see someone you love violate their own heart in order to be something they were never meant to be. But never forget who you're dealing with, Sophie Schmid! The Creator of Heaven and earth and Justin's best friend. There is more God can do in the heart of a person than any of us can ever imagine. Do not give up hope—not for him and not for anyone else."

They sat in silence for a while. "I don't want to give up on him," Sophie finally said quietly. "But I don't see what would have to happen to him to give up this doctrine that is giving him so much security and belonging and importance. It would have to be quite an event to shake his life like that."

Again, Thomas smiled at her, and Sophie couldn't help but feel as if he knew something she didn't.

"So what do you suggest I do?"

"You could tell him what you just told me, for a start. Be honest and humble, modeling the qualities you think have left his life. And yes, I know that will make you vulnerable," he added when she was about to protest, "but if there's one thing that will keep you from ever having real relationships and joy and peace, it's keeping yourself from the possibility of getting hurt."

"So you think I should just tell him everything I believe, even the points where we differ so much?" Sophie asked.

"Maybe. Some of that might find its way into that conversation. But no, that's not really what I meant." He looked into her eyes. "I'd say you don't need to tell him what you know or believe. You need to tell him what you *feel.* What you *hope.* Especially when it comes to him. And you."

A cool late-summer breeze whirled around Sophie's blonde hair as she walked to the deserted precipice outside the village. It was her favorite place to sit and think. In the evening light just after sunset, the whole valley was immersed in soft light, distant mountaintops forming a backdrop that added to the wild, lonely beauty that echoed so well in her own soul.

"Lord, I'm scared. I don't know if I can go through another loss of someone I love. Maybe that's why I settled for being friends. But now it feels like you're asking me to risk it all and to let him go like I had to let Nathan go." Only this time, the decision was hers.

She sat for a long time in silent conversation. Her eyes were turned inward, and the beauty around her seemed to reach her soul. There was no sound or movement, and somebody passing by might have wondered if she was asleep. But Sophie was communing with the One who had made her, in a mysterious, beautiful, deep place within her.

Trust me.

After a long time, she smiled and looked up into the sky where the first stars had appeared. "Ok, I will do it. It's not like you haven't shown me by example." Her face had a gentle glow as she walked back to her room, to her computer, and to the email that was going to change everything, one way or another.

Chapter Seventy

The sight of rolling hills and meadows alternated with villages below him, and the impressive horizon of the Alps behind them gave Justin a feeling of otherworldliness. The US and India were the only countries he had ever been to before, and the beauty of the Swiss landscape below made him think he was flying over an oversized TV set. Rivers made their way lazily through the countryside, and patches of woods bordered those of small family farms. Even the cities looked small from the air. He couldn't believe how close up the mountains were until he remembered Sophie telling him you could cross Switzerland in less than four hours.

After landing at the Zürich airport and getting through immigration, he collected his small suitcase and headed toward the underground train station. The excitement gave way to nervousness. He hadn't exactly planned this trip for weeks, and he was planning on surprising the only two people who could have given him insider tips. Thankfully, a friendly man approached him at the ticket machine and asked if he needed help.

"Yes, I need a one-way ticket to Wettingen, please."

He was not prepared for the amount. No wonder Sophie had never been fazed by any of the prices she had encountered in Colorado.

Once on the train, Justin thought back on the past two crazy days. The night he had received the money from his dad, he had gone online to find the cheapest possible last-minute ticket to Switzerland. When he had seen that it was doable, he had tackled the next step of his plan—he needed to see Luke and talk to him about Sophie. The surprise part was not least because he feared if he told him ahead of time, Luke would disagree with his plan to fly all the way just to see him.

After booking the plane ticket, he had also put in his search engine the name of the town he had noticed on the train itinerary on Luke's computer. When he typed in Verdasio, Switzerland, a couple of tourist attractions came up but nothing that would help him locate Luke. He had tried again and added Christian retreat to the search. Still nothing. Then, remembering Sophie's mother tongue to be German, he had pulled up an online translation service and tried the same search with the equivalent German words. Still nothing. Finally, he remembered Luke saying something about it being a retreat for students. He added that word to the search as well. Suddenly, in between other links, one had caught his attention. He clicked on it and hit the translation button. Campo Rasa—Christian student retreat came up. He scrolled through the sentences, and then he saw it: The Campo is accessible only by cable car. The cable car station is located next to the Verdasio train station.

"Yes!" Justin had shouted into the empty apartment. He was going to see Luke, and he would help him find the courage to win Sophie back.

He got ready for a long night. First, he looked up train schedules for the day of his arrival in Switzerland and was disappointed when he realized that he would not be able to reach Rasa the day he flew in. It was at the other end of the country, and the cable cars stopped running in the early evening. While trying to find out what to do in Zürich for a day, his eyes suddenly fell on an article about Wettingen. It was the town of Sophie's college, he remembered. Of course she wasn't there, as her internship in the mountains would last another two weeks. But Wettingen was only twenty-five minutes by train from the airport, and he would be able to see where she worked.

Justin's last day in India was filled with feverish preparations to make sure his surprises for both Luke and Sophie would work out.

The train loudspeaker jerked him out of his memories as it announced "Nächster Halt Wettingen." He jumped up and was the first person to exit the train. He didn't need to look hard to see the beautiful monastery buildings about half a mile down the road. Before heading there, he deposited his suitcase at the hostel near the college where he would spend the night. He checked in, took a quick shower, and then set out on foot. As he approached the college grounds, he realized Sophie must have walked this path a hundred times. A strong sensation of longing washed over him.

It took him a while to find the right offices, as everything was written in German. Approaching an older lady who looked like she might be the school secretary, he said, "Excuse me," and realized he had the eyes of all three people in the office on him. They must not hear American English every day here. "Ehm, I'm a friend of Sophie Schmid's. And . . . I know she's not here right now, but she told me about her workplace and how beautiful it is, and I thought maybe I could check it out? It's my first time visiting Switzerland," he added with a winning smile.

It had the effect he intended. Apparently, the lady took

fondly to his accent, and maybe she wasn't too busy that day. Before he knew it, Justin was invited to a little tour around the monastery. Amanda, the secretary, was very proud of the grounds and their long history. She chatted happily as she walked Justin around the buildings.

"Do you happen to know where Soph—I mean, Ms. Schmid's classroom is?" he asked nonchalantly.

"Of course I do! We will be there in a minute. Isn't it so nice of you to show interest in Ms. Schmid's work," Amanda added in a friendly tone.

When they got to Sophie's room, Amanda unlocked it and showed him around. She was very talkative, and Justin wished he was alone. Everything here was Sophie. He felt like he was intruding her private space, entering her life uninvited. A moment later, Amanda's phone rang, and she excused herself and stepped out of the room for a moment.

Justin looked around the room. His curiosity got the better of him, and after making sure Amanda was still engaged on the phone, he picked up Sophie's teacher workbook. It was well worn, filled with notes, dates, and lesson plans from the past year. She must have used it every day. He flipped through it randomly, feeling strangely close to her.

When he came to the inner back cover, a single photograph was attached to the back, and underneath it, Sophie had written out Jeremiah 29:11.

The picture showed Sophie and him in selfie-pose in front of the Garden of the Gods.

Justin was glad when the tour was over. If he interpreted his discovery correctly, his whole life might be about to turn upside down. He thanked Amanda for the tour and almost fled the college grounds. Back at the hostel, he fell on his bed and thought about the day ahead—how he was going to attempt to find Luke across a country he didn't know and a language he didn't speak. A smile stole itself across his face. It didn't matter. He would find him because he needed him. He needed him to help find the courage to confess to another person he needed even more.

Chapter Seventy-One

The next morning, Justin woke up well before his alarm went off. After two cups of excellent coffee, he brought his few belongings down the stairs, paid, and walked toward the train station. He was looking forward to what the internet had described as a scenic ride through some of the country's most beautiful parts.

He had brought a book and a map to follow his journey, but after a short while on the train he knew he was not going to use either. His mind and his heart were far too preoccupied. Something had happened yesterday when he discovered that picture in Sophie's book. Yes, his heart had leapt with joy, but he also felt guilty. He had given Sophie no reason to hope and lots of reasons to be hurt and offended. And yet, it was him and her in her workbook, as if to show that what she felt for him was not going to be determined by his carelessness.

Sophie's care for him stirred up a memory from the day of his conversion. He had discovered the selfless act of sacrifice with which Jesus had shown his love for him that day. It had made him want to run to Jesus and abandon everything for him. In a much lesser way, and yet very powerfully, he now realized that Sophie had loved him from the first day, had accepted his extreme views she didn't share, had not judged him as much as he had judged her, and had never given up on him. It was more than what he deserved. Again, he was getting what he did not deserve.

That was if it wasn't too late now.

Emotions welled up in Justin as the breathtaking Swiss landscape passed by unnoticed. He knew now what he had to do. And being Justin Friedman, he wasn't going to waste another day. He took out the computer from his backpack and opened his mail. Only then did he realize he had no connection on the train. Well, it would send whenever he got to his destination, but he was going to write to her, now or never.

It was over an hour later when Justin looked up from his computer again. He had a smile on his face that was more genuine and a joy in his heart that made him feel more alive than he had felt in months, maybe years. Maybe ever.

By the time the small local train stopped at the tiny station of Verdasio, Justin was one big grin. A few more minutes and he would embrace Luke—but instead of trying to get him to help make the most important decision of his life, he was going to let him know how he had just made that decision himself.

When the cable car arrived in Rasa, Justin got out and looked around. It was definitely unlike anything he'd ever seen. Nothing but a small stone path leading upward past some tiny cottages that looked more than a hundred years old. Was this really a retreat? He doubted anyone could seriously be living up here. Slightly insecure, he took his bag and walked up the path until he came to what looked like a main building. He hadn't seen a single person on his walk.

He opened the wooden door of the building, peeked his head in, and finally called, "Hello?" After a moment, a man who was clearly in the middle of cooking stepped out from a side door. From behind him escaped a waft of a delicious-smelling stew.

"Oh, you speak English? Sorry, the Campo is a bit empty right now as many of the team have a day off. But I'm here to make sure there's some lunch served in a minute." He beamed, wiped his hands on his apron, and held out a hand to Justin. "My name's Michael. It's a pleasure meeting you!"

Justin shook his hand, surprised by the fluent English spoken by a man in the middle of nowhere in an ancient Swiss village without road access.

"I hear you're from America," Michael continued. "I say, it's quite the international week! We already have a guest here from America this and last week. And his friend is from Norway, if I'm not mistaken. But come with me, I'll bring you to the office where they'll help you get settled."

Justin followed Michael out of one house, down another small footpath, and into a similar stone-built cottage. He wondered what Norwegian would find their way to Rasa, let alone another American. When they entered the small, cozy office, Michael introduced him to the receptionist and excused himself to go back to the kitchen.

"How can I help you?" the woman asked.

"Well, I'm here to visit a friend."

"How nice! Who is it?"

"Actually, it's a surprise visit, so he doesn't even know I'm here. His name is Luke." He smiled expectantly at the lady, whose helpful smile faded a little.

"I'm sorry, but I'm pretty sure we don't have anyone with that name visiting right now. But let me double-check the guest list."

Justin's face fell for a moment, but then he had an idea. "Of course! He probably told me his name in English and you're saying it differently in German, right?"

She nodded. "Yes, we use the name Lukas. But I'm afraid there is also nobody with that name on the list this week."

Justin began to feel like a fool. He had just traveled across

Switzerland with no other plan than to surprise somebody whose exact travel plans or whereabouts he didn't even know and who might be in a different part of the country right now. He was wasting precious time. He decided to head back immediately, contact Luke, and try to get to him before the end of the day.

The young woman saw his facial expression and tried to cheer him up. "I'm so sorry about this, sir. But may I suggest you take this turn of events and treat yourself to a day in what we tend to call a piece of paradise? We have rooms free for tonight, and I'm pretty confident you wouldn't regret spending a day at our retreat. You're welcome to sit in on today's retreat meetings as well."

Justin considered this for a minute, but what he was about to do was too important for him to just sit at a nice retreat and relax. "Thank you so much, but I think I'll try and find my friend. If you don't mind, could I use a phone here for a local call? I'll just give him a call and see where he is."

"Oh, no problem at all! You can use the phone here in the living room next to the library. I hope things work out!" She led him into a living room with an old-fashioned fireplace. Justin dialed the number Luke had given him "Just in case you need to reach me urgently about the apartment or anything." After a few rings, Luke's recorded voice came on. Justin hung up, irritated at the turn of events.

Just then, the receptionist poked her head in the room. "Whatever you've planned, you cannot possibly leave before joining us for lunch. You already met Michael, our cook. He's the best chef in town." She laughed and added, "Of course for a town of twenty-two people that's not that reassuring, but I promise you you'll love his stew!"

Her words reminded him of the fact that he hadn't eaten anything all day, and the smell coming from the kitchen made him decide he could delay his departure for just an hour. He followed the receptionist out the building and back into the main house. Tables were set on a beautiful outside patio, shaded by vines and enclosed by ancient-looking brick walls. Justin sat down at one of the end tables and watched as a group of young people started filing in and sitting down. Big pots of stew and bowls of salad were put on the community tables, and Justin filled his plate. After a beautiful-sounding song and a short prayer, Justin was about to take his first bite of stew when he heard a voice on the other side of the patio he would have recognized out of a thousand others.

His fork fell back on his plate, and he shot out of his seat. His eyes fell on the last person he ever expected to see in Rasa sitting just a few tables down from him. But before he had time to call out to Bjørn, the man whose voice Justin had recognized a moment earlier ran across the patio and pulled Justin into an enormous hug.

Chapter Seventy-Two

The turmoil that ensued was quite unusual for the retreat community in this picturesque village. The retreat leaders were trying to figure out who knew who in all the commotion, and in the end, it was Justin who spoke first.

"Luke! They told me you weren't here! And Bjørn . . . how in the world did you get here? Do you know each other? But why . . . ?"

He couldn't go on, because Bjørn had now turned to the old man with an equally confused look. "Why is he calling you Luke?"

The retreat members looked between the three men with anticipation. Clearly, something out of the ordinary was happening here. Then Thomas spoke, his voice trembling slightly.

"The confusion is my doing, and I promise you we will all tell you quite a story later today. But right now, you will need to excuse us for a moment." Then he pulled Bjørn aside and whispered in his ear for a moment. Bjørn's eyes got wide, but then his face erupted into a wide grin. He walked over to Justin and embraced him.

"Man, it's so good to see you. We need to talk. But first, I think you and . . . Luke need to chat." Justin returned the embrace but was too confused to say anything.

The old man pulled him away from the dining area and out to the patio where they were alone. "Well, congratulations, Justin. I don't think too many things can surprise me anymore, but you've definitely managed to be the exception today." He shook his head and smiled. "I'm not sure who was more baffled—you, Bjørn, or I!"

Bjørn's name reminded Justin of the many questions he had. "How do you know Bjørn?"

"Actually, I hardly do. He came with a good friend of mine, a pastor from Wichita, Kansas, who led a group here last week. But I could return the question—how do *you* know him?"

"He went to Bible school with me! Can you believe it? Who would have ever thought I'd meet him here."

Luke smiled and shook his head. "Coincidence, they say . . . but I think the real question is how you ended up at the exact same place as me, when I was under the impression that you'd be sitting in my apartment in Chennai?"

Justin thought of many things to say but finally simply said, "I needed to see you so you could help me figure out what to do regarding Sophie. But then . . ." He took a breath and told Luke about his visit to Sophie's college, the picture in her workbook, and his realization on the train that he had, in fact, known the truth in his heart all along.

"I was such a fool, Luke. I really thought I needed to put some doctrine over what my heart had seen all along—that Sophie is the best thing that has ever happened to me. You know, I have no idea if she'll want me still, but at least I finally know what *I* want. And I'm planning on being quite persistent in pursuing the girl who didn't give up on me when I was being such a hypocrite."

Luke laughed, and his smile lingered. There was something on his mind. "So what are you going to do now?" he asked inquiringly.

"Well, seeing that I found you here, I will definitely stay the night and email Sophie tomorrow to ask her where exactly her internship is taking place. And then I plan on taking the first train available that will take me to her."

Luke seemed to take a moment to get what Justin was saying. "Ah . . . so she just told you she's doing an internship somewhere?" he asked slowly.

"Yes. I don't really know where in Switzerland she is, she said something about mountains. But it doesn't matter, I'll find her soon."

"I see, I see." Luke was definitely distracted and seemed to think hard for a while. Then, a sparkle came into his eyes, but he stayed silent. *I swear I will never figure him out,* Justin thought to himself.

"One more thing," Luke said with an apologetic tone, "you might wonder when we get back to the others why nobody is calling me Luke."

Justin looked up in surprise. "Yes, I was already wondering about it earlier with the receptionist."

"Yes, she would not have known a Luke. It's because Luke is not my real name."

"What?"

"I hope you know it has nothing to do with not trusting you, Justin. But the kind of work I do in India requires a certain level of anonymity, and it is too hard for me to be more than one person in a specific place. That's why I'm Luke to all of my friends in India. It protects the organization I'm working with there, as well as my friends here in Switzerland, should anything ever happen. I've been Luke in India for many years now, and it feels like my real name. But in Switzerland, I go by my given name. People here call me Thomas."

Thomas. The various conversations in which Sophie had mentioned that name all came back to Justin. What a weird coincidence that her best friend, whom she talked about so endearingly, and Luke actually shared the same name and were probably even around the same age.

Thomas was looking at him intently. Then he said, "When

we head back to the group, could you do one thing for me? Don't tell the group about where you're from, about you and me, or about your friendship with Sophie. Can you hold off telling them until tomorrow?"

"Sure, but why?"

"Do you trust me, Justin?"

Justin's face softened. "I do."

They sat down on a bench outside the village, catching up, and enjoying each other's company. At some point, Thomas told him that he would have to get back to lead the retreat he was in charge of this week. Justin decided he'd find Bjørn and catch up with him while Thomas was busy. Thinking of his friend with his Swiss name was still weird to him.

He found Bjørn back on the patio drinking espresso. As they embraced, Justin realized how much he had missed the Norwegian.

"I've been an arrogant fool, Bjørn," he started off right away, because memories of his own judgement toward his friend started popping into his head. "I hope you can forgive me. There's been quite a change in me in the past months. I feel like I'd love to start our friendship over if you're still interested."

Bjørn smiled at him. "I'd love that, Justin. I think we've got quite some catching up to do."

They spent the next hour reminiscing on their time at the Rock and their experiences afterwards. Justin was fascinated with what Bjørn told him about Ryan, and he thought once more about how small his own Christianity had been. "Why did you even want to hang out with me at the Rock?" he asked Bjørn.

"Come on, Justin! I've always admired the passion and heart I saw in you, and without the legalistic muzzle weighing you down now, there's no telling what you're going to do in the future. Don't beat yourself up about the past. You have your whole life ahead of you."

His words reminded Justin of Sophie. He had avoided

mentioning her to Bjørn because he needed to talk to her first. He suddenly remembered he had not sent the email written on the train yet. He excused himself and went to the reception, told them he'd stay the night, and asked for the internet password. In his room, he connected his computer and phone. As his mails were sent and new ones downloaded, there was a knock on the door.

Thomas stood outside. "I've got to show you something. Come with me!" Justin grabbed his phone and followed him. Thomas lead him back through the village and then beyond the bench they had sat on earlier.

"Where are we going?" Justin inquired.

"Patience, my friend! We'll be there in a minute."

They walked out of the village on a narrowing path that turned into a ridge. At the end, he saw countless little valleys below them carved into the hills and a blue river making its way down the valley.

"It's magnificent," Justin whispered.

Thomas smiled. "I thought you might like it. I come here every day when I'm in Rasa. The beauty of the valleys and hills and gorges reminds me of just how small I am. That sometimes helps," he added with a wink. Then he looked at an incoming text on his phone. His expression was unreadable, but Justin knew something important had happened.

"I gotta go back to the village for a moment, but I want you to stay here," he said and then added a little mysteriously, "I'm working on something I want to show you. Can you hang out here for about thirty minutes or so?"

Justin didn't mind playing along with whatever surprise Thomas had lined up. "Ok, I'll stay here since dinner isn't for an hour or so anyway."

"I'll see you very soon," Thomas said and walked, or rather bounced, back toward the village. Justin smiled as he watched him leave.

Thinking of his friendship with Thomas brought his mind

back to Sophie immediately, and he realized he never actually checked to see if his emails had sent. He took out his phone and opened his email. His heart was beating wildly in his chest, as it had done every time he had seen Sophie's name in a message. Had she already replied within the last ten minutes? He looked closer and saw that she had sent *her* email the day before—he just hadn't been online all day today.

Their messages had crossed. For a moment, he panicked. What if she was letting him know she was ending their friendship, and then she'd get *his* email?

For a moment, he looked over the distant mountains and the soft evening sun in the valleys before beginning to read.

Dear Justin,

I don't know how this finds you. The last I heard, you were having some real struggles with that pastor, and it sounded like you could use some help. I really hope this has been resolved, and I would love an update on it when you find the time. How is Luke? I'm so glad to know you have found a friend in Chennai, and I'm very grateful for his help and friendship to you.

This is going to be a difficult letter to write, but I also feel that it's overdue. Our friendship has been the most special one of my life. But we're both aware that there are quite some topics we disagree about.

She was going to end it, he knew it. He was hardly breathing as he continued reading.

I think it's safe to say that for both of us, spirituality has become the most important part of our lives. So up until now, I had convinced myself that there is no future for us as long as we don't see eye to eye on some of these issues.

At the words *up until now,* Justin perked up. His heart was beating hard and something gentle, yet powerful, stirred in his soul. It was as if God was wrapping His arms around him, whispering, *it's time to let me show you what I can do when my children choose love.*

When he read on, it was to him as if even the birds around him stopped their song in anticipation of Sophie's next words.

> But I have come to understand something important. I found that from the very beginning, I saw something in you maybe even you didn't see. I saw a love for God and others that was not limited to the way Jonathan's ministry expressed it. And although your personality caused you to become quite an extreme follower of a certain way of seeing faith, I always knew there was more in you. More depth. More width. I saw compassion and tenderness and vulnerability just beneath the surface of the successful student and zealous missionary.
>
> The reason I saw all that, I now understand, is because from the very first day I met you, I fell completely in love with you. With your strength, your wit, your personality that swept me off my feet. But also with that beauty I saw in you, that light that is hard to describe but that I believe you know about. As far as our differing views are concerned, I can see your love for God, and ultimately, that is what matters to me, not how you express that love or interpret the words. I strongly disagree with some of the things Jonathan teaches, as you know. But God has shown me that I need to judge neither Jonathan nor you for your way of living your faith. I found hope in my heart when I stopped judging—a hope that we could find our love for each other among the various ways we express our love for God. And the hope that you find in your heart some of the same things I have just described.

I have no idea where this leaves us. I'm aware of the awkwardness I might have put myself and you in. Maybe you're even upset about the way I described you above. If so, I'm truly sorry. But I have decided that I can no longer just be friends with you because I have always wanted it to be more than that. I love you more than I have ever loved another person, and I cannot show myself any more real to you than as this woman deeply in love.

Yours always,
Sophie

Chapter Seventy-Three

Sophie settled into her seat on the Centovalli train. The others were still in the tourist town of Locarno, enjoying their day off and eating ice cream at the lake. But Sophie had to get back. More than that, she had to be alone. It was almost a full day since she had sent that email. It was possible that she'd get a reply any minute, and she had to be alone when that happened. She had therefore decided to return to Rasa a bit earlier than the others and spend the rest of the afternoon in her room. She sat back on her seat on the train and tried to relax. Since writing the email yesterday, she'd checked her inbox at least a hundred times. She didn't know if not hearing back was a good or a bad sign. Of course, she had no idea where exactly Justin was right now—he might be in a place without internet access. But she remembered him saying that he wouldn't be doing any ministry in the near future and was staying in Luke's flat, which surely had internet access. He must have seen it by now.

She checked her phone again almost automatically.

There it was.

She closed her eyes for a moment. The next minutes would

change everything—or then again, nothing at all. She started reading while the valleys outside flew by her.

> Dear Sophie,
>
> Sorry for my long silence between the last email and now. You must be in your last week or so of your internship if I remember correctly? How is it going?

Sophie's brows furrowed in confusion. This didn't sound like a possible reply to her email. Had he missed her message among other emails? She kept reading.

> I've been going through quite some changes in India. I'm hoping to tell you more in person soon, but more on that later. We haven't emailed in a while, so this might come as a surprise.

For whatever reason, he had not seen her email before writing this letter. Which meant that whatever he was about to write—and, from glancing at the email, it was a lot—it was independent of what she'd just told him. A tiny glimmer of hope rekindled in her, the hope that through this strange circumstance it could still be *him* making that first move she'd longed for him to make for such a long time. She kept reading.

> Right now, I need to tell you what I should have told you long ago, had I not been so preoccupied with saving the world and correcting everybody who didn't quote Scriptures the way I did.
>
> I've not listened to my heart for quite a while, Sophie. But recently I started to, and I found feelings there that made me want to run—it's a weakness of mine, and I think you might have felt it around me before.
>
> Those feelings scared me because I knew they revealed the actual me—a vulnerable man, scared of being rejected, and one who yearns to be loved without conditions.

> And do you know why these feelings came up lately? I think you might. It's because I met this amazing woman in Colorado who didn't fall for the game I was playing and yet wouldn't turn away from me either. She saw the guy I tried to be and knew there was somebody else in there. She didn't try and force that other guy out—and I'm so glad she didn't because it wouldn't have worked. Instead, she just loved the one she knew was in there. And over time, with the help of some good friends, he found that guy inside himself. And with it, he might have found a way back to her—if it's not too late.

Sophie closed her eyes. The joy that flooded her was so overwhelming she felt lightheaded. Her heart was pounding wildly as she continued reading.

> Sophie, I have no right to ask for this, but God has shown me that we are so often given what we don't deserve. Therefore, I dare to ask you to forgive me for being the judgemental hypocrite I was to you. My time in India has taught me many things, but above all, it showed me that loving people has to do with humility and vulnerability, not with righteousness and power. You knew that intuitively, and yet I believe you loved me through all my ignorance of it. It blows my mind.

How much she had longed to hear these words. The phone in her hands trembled, and hope rose like the sun in her heart.

Sophie, I'm asking you not only to forgive me, but to give me another chance. The chance to show you that there is that guy you saw all along, the guy on the inside who is hopelessly and crazily in love with you. The one who is definitely done with fundamentalist religion, but who's in love with Jesus more than ever before. The one who wants to live faith in a new way with you, who wants to laugh with you, share thoughts and stories and dreams—and breakfast and lunch and dinner, and all that the future holds.

There's so much more to tell. And as I mentioned, I hope to be able to do it in person much sooner than I thought. But for now, I'm going to see if I find the strength to hit the send button before the part of me that fears rejection gets the better of me.

I love you like I didn't think I could ever love. You have brought out the best in me in more ways than you know. Whatever your reply is, thank you for being your wonderful, smart, caring, sensitive, and sweeping-me-off-my-feet beautiful you.

Justin

Sophie sat in her seat, eyes closed and unable to move. A tear found its way out of her eye and ran down her cheek silently. The world had stopped turning, and for a while it was just her and God and the peace flooding her expanded heart. Then she opened her eyes. She looked around and found her train compartment empty.

Had anyone stood near the train tracks for the next minutes, they might have heard her shouts of unbridled joy even over the noise of the train rattling by.

Chapter Seventy-Four

Verdasio station was already in view when Sophie finally calmed down enough to think clearly. She had been dancing, praying, laughing, and crying for the past ten minutes in her empty train compartment. And she knew she would never make this train ride again without remembering this day, hour, and minute. But right now, she just needed to see Thomas before anyone else when she arrived. She sent a text asking him to meet her alone at the cable car station in five minutes as she entered the car at the bottom. The ride up seemed like a sacred moment given the fact that it marked the beginning of the rest of her life.

When the top station came in view, she saw Thomas standing there, grinning. She hadn't told him why she wanted him to meet her and was wondering about his good mood. She stepped out of the car and gave him a big hug.

"I take it from your radiating face that he has replied to your email and that those tears are tears of joy?" Thomas said tenderly, his voice so happy it shook slightly. She nodded.

"Well, my dear Sophie, I cannot tell you how happy this makes me, on more levels than you know. Thank you for including me in those priceless first moments." He hugged her again and then let go so he could look into her eyes. "Sophie, you deserve the absolute best man. And believe me, if I didn't think Justin was that man for you, I'd not be talking this way now."

You've never even met Justin, yet you seem so sure, she thought but was too happy to be thinking about anything beyond that email.

"I want you to read it right now," she said and gave him her phone. He read silently, and when he handed her the phone back, there were tears in his eyes too.

"Thomas, I need to pack! I need to tell Rachel to let me leave early so I can go to Chennai. I have no idea what I'm going to do there or how any of this is going to work, but I will leave as soon as possible. I think people have done crazier things than that, haven't they?" She looked at him a little self-consciously, but her face was set.

"Yes, I think there have been crazier plans than that. But you might be surprised, Sophie. More times than we think, God has planned ahead in our lives. You might find things working out differently than you thought because of his foreseeing."

Sophie wasn't sure what he was talking about, but she wanted to go at once to talk to the camp leaders and ask permission to leave. She felt a tinge of pain at the thought of leaving this place that had given her so much joy and peace, but there was only one thing on her mind now—to get to Justin in as little time as possible.

"What do you think—is it possible to get a last-minute flight to Chennai within days? How expensive would that be?"

Thomas seemed to almost enjoy her turmoil. "My friend, may I suggest you relax for a moment? I would like for you to take a walk right now."

Sophie looked at him in bewilderment. *A walk? Right now?* In all her excitement and her eyes puffy from crying and her heart longing to be halfway around the world? When Thomas continued, his voice was gentle, and in his eyes was love. "I need you to take a walk to your favorite lookout past the village. I have a surprise there for you. Can you trust me this one more time?"

In spite of her turmoil and anxiety to get to Justin, there was nothing this man could ask her she wouldn't do. She simply said, "I can," and walked off toward the end of the village.

When she approached the end of the path, she saw a figure from behind, sitting and watching the sun paint beautiful colors into the late-afternoon sky. Something seemed familiar about the posture of the person. It must be the surprise Thomas had talked about. But how did he know somebody was sitting here? And who did Thomas think she would want to see right now, right after she'd told him about Justin? She wiped the tears off her face and got ready to talk to a stranger. She was only a few feet away when the sound of her footsteps made the person in front of her turn around.

The next moment, the world stopped moving for two young people, or at least they would have never noticed if it did. Neither of them heard or saw anything in the world except each other as they looked at one another silently. It was impossible. And then again, they had both experienced enough in the past months to know this word was not in God's vocabulary. They took a step toward each other, timidly, as if still unsure if it might be a dream. A moment later he picked her up and swung her around, and then no words were spoken for a good while. Their first kiss was a physical expression of the tender, intimate, and breathtaking wonder that was true love. They held each other close, laughing, crying, and kissing more. To them, the whole world had turned to sheer beauty and joy as they lost themselves in the sacredness of the moment.

Chapter Seventy-Five

They had still not uttered many intelligible words when they finally heard the sound of footsteps behind them. There was a rather unusual, almost bashful look on Thomas's face.

"I really tried to be good and stay back there and let you two enjoy each other for a longer time. But I have to admit I can be quite selfish at times, and I just couldn't bear missing out on the most wonderful moments of your lives." His voice sounded so apologetic that both Sophie and Justin laughed and pulled him into an enthusiastic hug.

"Thomas! You knew all the time! How did you . . . when . . . but why?" Sophie stumbled over her own words. But Justin looked like somebody had turned a huge lightbulb on in his head.

"All the time—but why did you not tell us?" There was no accusation in his voice, just happiness. Thomas looked at both of them, beaming with joy.

"I just felt that you two needed to figure this out yourselves. I didn't want to get in the middle of it. Not because I didn't care, but because I've learned that God can manage these things quite well without my help."

"Well, I wouldn't underestimate your part in this miracle," Sophie said with tenderness in her voice. "You might not have written these two emails, but I'm quite sure neither of us would have without your friendship and wisdom either."

Justin nodded but still seemed too overwhelmed to say anything. Thomas looked at him.

"There was definitely a lot of divine intervention all along the way. The fact, for example, that Moses happened to report you to the police station my friend was working at so that I learned about your whereabouts. Or the fact that you, Justin, figured out where to find us here. I had planned this trip before I met you. And of course, I had no way of hoping you'd follow me and therefore meet Sophie. But I can't say I hadn't prayed a little in that direction. I didn't know how much each of you knew of the other's whereabouts. But as I said, I felt like God was quite able to orchestrate this.

"At times it was a challenge not to tell either of you that I knew about the other. I prayed about it often as the last thing I wanted to do was be untruthful toward you. But each time I prayed, I felt strongly that God wanted to bring you together without my help. So I trusted that our friendship would not get hurt by my temporary secrecy."

"God has definitely managed that," Sophie said with wonder in her voice. "Thank you for following His lead so we could figure this out ourselves. I would say it was worth it," she added as she pulled Justin into a hug.

"Tell you what," Thomas said happily, "I'll leave you two lovebirds alone and will go find out if the chef has anything in the kitchen for a late snack to match the occasion. And if you're not eating anything at all tonight, I won't be surprised either. I've been in love myself, so I know," he said with a wink and turned back toward the village.

Justin held Sophie close. His eyes were moist, and there was such a tenderness and love in them that Sophie thought her knees might fail her. He placed a kiss on her lips, hungry yet incredibly gentle. She closed her eyes.

"I can't believe I finally found you," Justin whispered. "Your letter . . . I thought my heart was going to explode when I read it earlier. I am the happiest man alive. And I will spend the rest of my life making you the happiest woman on earth, Sophie."

The sun was about to set over the valley below them, bathing them in a last ray of golden light.

"Well, then I am happy to report," she said as she caressingly traced the outlines of his face with her fingers, "that you have already reached your life's goal."

Epilogue

The soft autumn sun immersed the small village with a gentle light, and the brightly colored leaves created a perfect backdrop for the occasion. Every room was occupied in the guest quarters, and the little cable car had been packed with travelers from Switzerland and abroad since morning. The Campo was presenting itself from its best side. The lawn a little way up from the precipice was mown, the leaves blown, and chairs for the guests had been set, facing the valleys and mountains in the backdrop. Stunning flowers from surrounding meadows adorned the venue. But what captured people's attention the most were the faces of the bride and groom. They radiated with love, and a light seemed to shine from them. They held hands, and the woman's blonde hair fell beautifully over the back of her silk dress. Silence fell when a white-haired man addressed the wedding party.

"My dear friends from near and far. Although I'm not exactly a pastor, I have officiated many weddings in my life," he said, and an observant guest might have noticed his voice shaking a little, "but I can truthfully say that none has filled me with more joy and sheer jubilation than the wedding I am honored to officiate today."

His eyes met the bride's and groom's. "You will have to excuse an old man's emotions today. But to marry two people who have, completely apart from each other, become such dear friends of mine will happen only once in a lifetime, and mine has been quite a long one already."

He took a moment to regain his composure. "We have gathered here in this beautiful village that has been part of my own story for more than half my life. It has now become part of the bride's and groom's lives by what some might call coincidence, but I'm just not sure about that." He looked over to Justin and Sophie.

"It is certainly no accident," he continued, "that we have guests from all over the world here today to celebrate the life and the stories of Sophie and Justin. All of you here have played a part in their story. You have helped them, challenged them, and loved them through the ups and downs of their lives."

His eyes found Bjørn's and remained there. "You might never know exactly what your part is in the tapestry God is weaving in someone's life." Now his eyes moved on to Justin's and Sophie's parents in the front row. "But rest assured that God has never created anything but a beautiful piece of art out of the pieces of love we offer others."

As the ceremony went on, more and more people had tears in their eyes. The love and care that Thomas showed in his comments, encouragements, and anecdotes reminded many guests of that quiet part inside themselves where joy and peace and longing and awe and beauty met. And when bride and groom finally kissed and were pronounced husband and wife, there were few dry eyes left under the brilliant Rasa sky.

An hour later, Justin and Sophie stole away from the well-wishers for a few minutes and found Thomas alone on a bench outside the village. When he turned toward them, his face showed traces of tears.

"Forgive me, Sophie," he said when seeing her expression. "And let me assure you that these are tears of joy. I seem to get more emotional as I get older. But then again, I have just married two people who mean more to me than I can possibly express." He shook himself as if waking from a dream. "But what are you doing wasting time talking to an old man on your most important day! Go mingle with your guests!"

Instead, Sophie sat down on the bench. She had heard a small twinge of sadness in Thomas's voice. When she spoke, her face showed a fierce and deep love. "Thomas, you have so many wonderful attributes I wouldn't know where to start, but there's one thing I feel you are lacking somewhat." He looked up quickly and their eyes met. "I think you have no idea at all how much we love you."

At this moment, Sophie saw in his eyes that same vulnerability she knew from her own life but quite forgot was part of Thomas's as well. He didn't say anything.

A new boldness was ringing in her voice now. "God has used you to prepare us for each other, and then to bring us together. But he has also used you to teach us about ourselves. It is through your wisdom and your love that we have both become who we are today. You mean more to both of us than we could ever express."

Justin looked at Thomas. "Maybe you're wondering if now that we're married and off to all kinds of adventures, we just might slip out of your life a little bit over time. Well, do you know what our future plans are?"

Thomas smiled. "If I remember correctly, you will start your honeymoon tomorrow and, as of now, do not know which country you will end up living in, although you've had some quite adventurous ideas."

"That's right, we're still working it out. But wherever we end up, we plan on living only in a place that has a guest room ready for you, and if you don't spend at least several weeks a year visiting us, we will just find you and come live with you. If I could find you in a remote mountain village in Switzerland, I'll find you anywhere! Besides, we have already marked two weeks in our calendar for next summer that we plan on spending on the *Noordfries* in a cabin right next to yours."

When Thomas found his voice again, he smiled quietly and wiped a tear off his face. "I don't know what to say. I am beyond grateful, and I think you both know that. I have not felt a loneliness like today since my wife died almost twelve years ago. You cannot know what it means to me to receive your kindness. I know there are somewhat secretive parts to my life, which might just be a price I pay for the kind of work I have chosen to do. But I want you to know how deeply thankful I am to you for acknowledging this complicated part of me and responding with such kindness. As a mentor, there is no greater gift to receive than this, and as a friend, it connects me with both of you on an even deeper level than before."

He smiled at them, and the twinkle came back to his eyes. "But now you really need to get back to your guests. I know for a fact there are some surprises still waiting for you tonight."

The reception happened in the early evening on the same spot as the ceremony had, on a lawn that allowed a view of spectacular mountain ranges glowing in the soft evening light. It had been a day nobody would forget anytime soon. After a delicious wedding meal, everybody leaned back to hear Thomas, who had once more taken the microphone.

"I trust this evening will not end soon, but before we move on to kicking off our shoes and dancing on the lawn, I wanted to introduce you to a very special guest. I know not everybody has had a chance to get to know each other today, but even those who have talked to my friend here have not heard more than elusive answers from him. He has even refrained from saying his well wishes to the groom and bride so far for the sake of the surprise you are about to experience. Please." He nodded to a young man who had been sitting in the very back and now walked toward Thomas. Justin felt vaguely as if he'd seen the man before. He leaned over to see if Sophie knew him, but her face showed no sign of recognition at all.

"Thank you, Thomas. This is a most special day for me as you will see in a minute, and I first of all want to thank Thomas for his generous offer to fly me all the way out here." The man's eyes found Justin's, and Justin now was sure he had met him before. Even his voice sounded familiar, but he still couldn't place him anywhere.

"I met this man"—the man pointed to Thomas—"at a crucial turning point of my life only a few months ago, and I can say that he literally saved my life. Six years ago, my brother was arrested for a petty crime and entered a prison system that literally destroyed his life. It broke my heart to watch helplessly, and I decided to do what I could to keep others from experiencing the same fate. I joined the police force and tried to help young people who got in trouble, rather than punish them. I was just hoping it would make a difference in some of their lives."

Suddenly, Justin let go of Sophie's hand and almost shot up out of his seat. Thomas put his arm around him and whispered something in his ear. Justin was shaking but remained seated.

The man continued, "I'd like to think that I helped people. But sometimes it's hard to know. And then a year ago, I lost my job because I let one too many of those kids go without punishment. Along with my job I lost my girlfriend. I was at the end of myself. It was the night I tried to end my life when I heard about a man who was looking for me."

He looked at Thomas, and his voice trembled slightly.

"Thomas didn't know me yet. He was doing some investigating on behalf of a young friend of his called Justin. You see, several years ago, Justin was involved in some stuff he shouldn't have been, and my job as officer on duty that morning was to see that he was going to pay for it."

Now, the man's eyes met Justin's. "Instead, I let him go, because I have learned through many hard lessons that nobody is beyond redemption.

"I didn't know what had become of Justin, but that night, when I was at my lowest point, I heard that someone had inquired about him. My interest was sparked, and I could feel a glimmer of hope returning. I agreed to meet with Thomas, who told me how my actions that day had helped Justin to change his life. He told me of Justin's decision to follow Jesus, his Bible school attendance and missionary work, and of course the fact that he had met this beautiful Swiss woman and was about to marry her. Thomas and I spent several days together, and he not only restored in me a hope for my own future, but a new confidence that there is a God who can take our little offerings of love and create out of it something beyond our wildest dreams—and that our imperfect lives are in fact a symphony of broken but beautiful hallelujahs."

He looked over to Justin again, who now could no longer contain himself. He got up and engulfed James in an enormous hug amidst the cheers and shouts of the moved guests. Sophie joined him, and then Thomas. When they all turned to look at their guests again, the whole congregation was standing and offering an ovation to James, to Thomas, but maybe to more than them. As the sun was slowly setting over the tops of the Swiss mountains, everyone present felt a holiness linger in the air. And as the cheers, laughter, and celebrations moved on to dancing, many a guest felt a deep stirring in their heart. It was the awareness that in their moments of greatest joy, mankind was, even though only fleetingly aware of it, joining the Great Heavenly Dance that had been surrounding them since the dawn of time.

Acknowledgments

Writing a novel was a dream I've carried with me since childhood—but like many other writers, I couldn't see myself ever actually turning that dream into reality until I met someone who fully believed in me. I'm deeply grateful to my husband, David, whose encouragement and vision birthed this novel and whose love for me carried it to publication. On every level this book would have never been written without you. While parts of this novel are pure fiction, other parts happened almost word for word. Unearthing these stories forged us together on an even deeper level.

I'm also grateful for my children, Hannah, Joy, and Noah, who have shared their mom with this project for years and encouraged me over and over in their own wonderful ways. You're the greatest kids anyone could wish for.

A special thank you to the many beta readers who gave their inputs early on and helped shape the focus of the novel and the Atlanta Writer's Club for giving me so many tools for the trade.

Claudia Zimmermann and Erika Schibli-Suter, you took it to another level and believed in my dream in so many ways —*herzlichen Dank!*

Many thanks also to my editor Tiffany White who gave this story the professional touch it deserves, Michelle Fairbanks for the beautiful cover art, and Grace Wynter for helping with all the million details necessary to put a book into a reader's hands. It truly takes a team to write a book!

And to the real Campo Rasa . . . the kind of community and faith family you have been to me is one of the greatest gifts of my life. I wish every reader will find their own piece of "Heaven on Earth" as I've found mine in Rasa.

And last but not least—thank you, dear reader, for coming along on the journey. If this story has spoken to you, I'd love to hear from you. You can contact me through my website at www.judithforgoston.com, where you can also subscribe to my monthly blog on topics about faith and freedom.

About the Author

Judith Forgoston is a Swiss native and a former missionary, Bible school teacher, and passionate world traveler who's called four different continents her home. She has sailed a tjalk in the Dutch Seas, ridden bareback along the rugged Connemara coast, eaten buñuelos in rural Colombia and luwombo in Uganda, and taught Bible stories under tin roofs in India. Her mission work birthed in her a desire to help other followers of Jesus to lead authentic and compassionate lives free from religious burdens. She currently lives in Atlanta with her husband and three children and blogs at www.judithforgoston.com.

This is her first novel.